SIX CRIMSON CRANES

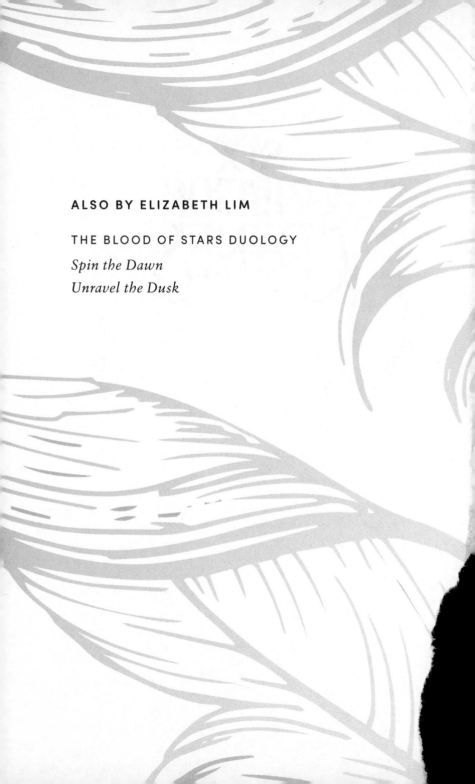

ALSO BY ELIZABETH LIM

THE BLOOD OF STARS DUOLOGY

Spin the Dawn
Unravel the Dusk

SIX CRIMSON CRANES

ELIZABETH LIM

Alfred A. Knopf
New York

THIS IS A BORZOI BOOK PUBLISHED BY ALFRED A. KNOPF

Text copyright © 2021 by Elizabeth Lim
Jacket art copyright © 2021 by Tran Nguyen
Map art copyright © 2021 by Virginia Allyn

All rights reserved. Published in the United States by Alfred A. Knopf,
an imprint of Random House Children's Books,
a division of Penguin Random House LLC, New York.

Knopf, Borzoi Books, and the colophon are registered trademarks of
Penguin Random House LLC.

Visit us on the Web! GetUnderlined.com

Educators and librarians, for a variety of teaching tools, visit us at
RHTeachersLibrarians.com

Library of Congress Cataloging-in-Publication Data
Names: Lim, Elizabeth, author.
Title: Six crimson cranes / Elizabeth Lim.
Description: First edition. | New York : Alfred A. Knopf, [2021] |
Audience: Ages 12 & up. | Audience: Grades 7–9. | Summary: The exiled Princess
Shiori must unravel the curse that turned her six brothers into cranes, and she is
assisted by her spurned betrothed, a capricious dragon, and a paper bird brought to
life by her own magic.
Identifiers: LCCN 2020043183 (print) | LCCN 2020043184 (ebook) |
ISBN 978-0-593-30091-6 (hardcover) | ISBN 978-0-593-30092-3 (library binding) |
ISBN 978-0-593-30093-0 (ebook)
Subjects: CYAC: Princesses—Fiction. | Brothers and sisters—Fiction. |
Blessing and cursing—Fiction. | Cranes (Birds)—Fiction. | Betrothal—Fiction. |
Magic—Fiction. | Fantasy.
Classification: LCC PZ7.1.L5523 Si 2021 (print) | LCC PZ7.1.L5523 (ebook) |
DDC [Fic]—dc23

The text of this book is set in 11.25-point Sabon MT Pro.
Interior design by Andrea Lau
Jacket lettering by Alix Northrup

Printed in the United States of America
July 2021
10 9 8 7 6 5 4 3 2

First Edition

To Charlotte and Olivia, for being my greatest adventure.
You are my joys, my wonders, and my loves.

CHAPTER ONE

The bottom of the lake tasted like mud, salt, and regret. The water was so thick it was agony keeping my eyes open, but thank the great gods I did. Otherwise, I would have missed the dragon.

He was smaller than I'd imagined one to be. About the size of a rowboat, with glittering ruby eyes and scales green as the purest jade. Not at all like the village-sized beasts the legends claimed dragons to be, large enough to swallow entire warships.

He swam nearer until his round red eyes were so close they reflected my own.

He was watching me drown.

Help, I pleaded. I was out of air, and I had barely a second of life left before my world folded into itself.

The dragon regarded me, lifting a feathery eyebrow. For an instant, I dared hope he might help. But his tail wrapped around my neck, squeezing out the last of my breath.

And all went dark.

In hindsight, I probably shouldn't have told my maids I was going to jump into the Sacred Lake. I only said it because the heat this morning was insufferable. Even the chrysanthemum bushes outside had wilted, and the kitebirds soaring above the citrus trees were too parched to sing. Not to mention, diving into the lake seemed like a perfectly sensible alternative to attending my betrothal ceremony—or as I liked to call it, the dismal end of my future.

Unfortunately, my maids believed me, and word traveled faster than demonfire to Father. Within minutes, he sent one of my brothers—along with a retinue of stern-faced guards—to fetch me.

So here I was, being shepherded through the palace's catacomb of corridors, on the hottest day of the year. To the dismal end of my future.

As I followed my brother down yet another sun-soaked hall, I fidgeted with my sleeve, pretending to cover a yawn as I peeked inside.

"Stop yawning," Hasho chided.

I dropped my arm and yawned again. "If I let them all out now, I won't have to do it in front of Father."

"Shiori . . ."

"You try being woken up at dawn to have your hair brushed a thousand times," I countered. "You try walking in a god's ransom of silk." I lifted my arms, but my sleeves were so heavy I could barely keep them raised. "Look at all

2

these layers. I could outfit a ship with enough sails to cross the sea!"

The trace of a smile touched Hasho's mouth. "The gods are listening, dear sister. You keep complaining like that, and your betrothed will have a pockmark for each time you dishonor them."

My betrothed. Any mention of him went in one ear and out the other, as my mind drifted to more pleasant thoughts, like cajoling the palace chef for his red bean paste recipe—or better yet, stowing away on a ship and voyaging across the Taijin Sea.

Being the emperor's only daughter, I'd never been allowed to go anywhere, let alone journey outside of Gindara, the capital. In a year, I'd be too old for such an escapade. And too married.

The indignity of it all made me sigh aloud. "Then I'm doomed. He'll be hideous."

My brother chuckled and nudged me forward. "Come on, no more complaining. We're nearly there."

I rolled my eyes. Hasho was starting to sound like he was seventy, not seventeen. Of my six brothers, I liked him most—he was the only one with wits as quick as mine. But ever since he started taking being a prince so seriously and wasting those wits on chess games instead of mischief, there were certain things I couldn't tell him anymore.

Like what I was keeping inside my sleeve.

A tickle crawled up my arm, and I scratched my elbow.

Just to be safe, I pinched the wide opening of my sleeve

shut. If Hasho knew what I was hiding under its folds, I'd never hear the end of it.

From him, or from Father.

"Shiori," Hasho whispered. "What's the matter with your dress?"

"I thought I smudged the silk," I lied, pretending to rub at a spot on my sleeve. "It's so hot today." I made a show of looking out at the mountains and the lake. "Don't you wish we were outside swimming instead of going to some boring ceremony?"

Hasho eyed me suspiciously. "Shiori, don't change the topic."

I bowed my head, doing my best to look remorseful—and covertly adjusted my sleeve. "You're right, Brother. It's time I grew up. Thank you for . . . for . . ."

Another tickle brushed my arm, and I clapped my elbow to muffle the sound. My secret was growing restless, making the fabric of my robes ripple.

"For escorting me to meet my betrothed," I finished quickly.

I hastened toward the audience chamber, but Hasho caught my sleeve, raised it high, and gave it a good shake.

Out darted a paper bird as small as a dragonfly, and just as fast. From afar, she looked like a little sparrow, with an inky red dot on her head, and she flitted from my arm to my brother's head, wildly beating her slender wings as she hovered in front of his face.

Hasho's jaw dropped, his eyes widening with shock.

"Kiki!" I whispered urgently, opening my sleeve. "Come back inside!"

Kiki didn't obey. She perched on Hasho's nose and stroked it with a wing to show affection. My shoulders relaxed; animals always liked Hasho, and I was certain she would charm him the way she'd charmed me.

Then my brother swooped his hands over his face to catch her.

"Don't hurt her!" I cried.

Up Kiki flew, narrowly avoiding his clutches. She bounced against the wooden shutters on the windows, seeking one that was open as she darted farther and farther down the hall.

I started after her, but Hasho grabbed me, holding fast until my slippers skidded against the whispery wood.

"Let it go," he said into my ear. "We'll talk about this later."

The guards flung open the doors, and one of Father's ministers announced me: "Princess Shiori'anma, the youngest child, the only daughter of Emperor Hanriyu and the late empress—"

Inside, my father and his consort, my stepmother, sat at the head of the cavernous chamber. The air hummed with impatience, courtiers folding and refolding their damp handkerchiefs to wipe their perspiring temples. I saw the backs of Lord Bushian and his son—my betrothed—kneeling before the emperor. Only my stepmother noticed me, frozen at the threshold. She tilted her head, her pale eyes locking onto mine.

A chill shivered down my spine. I had a sudden fear that if I went through with the ceremony, I'd become like her: cold and sad and lonely. Worse, if I didn't find Kiki, someone else might, and my secret would get back to Father . . .

My secret: that I'd conjured a paper bird to life with magic.

Forbidden magic.

I spun away from the doors and pushed past Hasho, who was too startled to stop me.

"Princess Shiori!" the guards yelled. "Princess!"

I shed my ceremonial jacket as I ran after Kiki. The embroidery alone weighed as much as a sentinel's armor, and freeing my shoulders and arms of its heft was like growing wings. I left the pool of silk in the middle of the hall and jumped out a window into the garden.

The sun's glare was strong, and I squinted to keep my eyes on Kiki. She wove through the orchard of cherry trees, then past the citrus ones, where her frenzied flight caused the kite-birds to explode from the branches.

I'd intended to leave Kiki in my room, tucked away in a jewelry box, but she had flapped her wings and knocked against her prison so vigorously I was afraid a servant might find her while I was at the ceremony.

Best to keep her with me, I thought.

"Promise to be good?" I'd said.

Kiki bobbed her head, which I'd taken as a yes.

Wrong.

Demons take me, I had to be the biggest idiot in Kiata!

But I wouldn't blame myself for having a heart, even for a paper bird.

Kiki was *my* paper bird. With my brothers growing older and always occupied with princely duties, I had been lonely. But Kiki listened to me and kept my secrets, and she made me laugh. Every day, she became more alive. She was my friend.

I had to get her back.

My paper bird landed in the middle of the Sacred Lake, floating on its still waters with unflappable calm—as if she hadn't just upended my entire morning.

I was panting by the time I reached her. Even without the outer layer, my dress was so heavy I could hardly catch my breath.

"Kiki!" I tossed a pebble into the water to get her attention, but she merely floated farther away. "This isn't the time to play."

What was I going to do? If it was discovered I had a talent for magic, no matter how small, I'd be sent away from Kiata forever—a fate far worse than having to marry some faceless lord of the third rank.

Hurrying, I kicked off my slippers, not even bothering to shed my robes.

I jumped into the lake.

For a girl forced to stay indoors practicing calligraphy and playing the zither, I was a strong swimmer. I had my brothers to thank for that; before they all grew up, we used to sneak to this very lake for summer-evening dips. I knew these waters.

I kicked toward Kiki, the sun's heat prickling against my

back, but she was sinking deeper into the water. The folds of my dress wrapped around me tight, and my skirts clung to my legs every time I kicked. I began to tire, and the sky vanished as the lake pulled me down.

Choking, I flailed for the surface. The more I struggled, the faster I sank. Whorls of my long black hair floated around me like a storm. Terror rioted in my gut, and my throat burned, my pulse thudding madly in my ears.

I undid the gold sash over my robes and yanked at my skirts, but their weight brought me down and down, until the sun was but a faint pearl of light glimmering far above me.

Finally I ripped my skirts free and propelled myself up, but I was too deep. There was no way I would make it back to the surface before I ran out of breath.

I was going to die.

Kicking furiously, I fought for air, but it was no use. I tried not to panic. Panicking would only make me sink faster.

Lord Sharima'en, the god of death, was coming for me. He'd numb the burning soreness in my muscles, and the pain swelling in my throat. My blood began to chill, my eyelids began to close—

That was when I saw the dragon.

I thought him a snake at first. No one had seen a dragon in centuries, and from afar, he looked like one of my stepmother's pets. At least until I saw the claws.

He glided toward me, coming so close that I could have touched his whiskers, long and thin like strokes of silver.

His hand was extended, and above his palm, pinched between two talons, was Kiki.

For an instant, I bubbled to life. I kicked, trying to reach out. But I had no strength left. No breath. My world was shrinking, all color washed away.

With a mischievous glint in his eye, the dragon closed his hand. His tail swept over me from behind and encircled my neck.

And my heart gave one final thud.

CHAPTER TWO

"A . . . a snake," I heard Hasho stammer. He wasn't a very good liar. "She saw a snake."

"So she ran all the way to the lake? That doesn't make sense."

"Well—" Hasho faltered. "You know how much she hates snakes. She thought it might bite her."

My head hurt like a thunderstorm, but I blinked an eye half-open, spying my two eldest brothers, Andahai and Benkai, at my bedside. Hasho hung in the back, chewing on his lip.

I closed my eye. Maybe if they thought I was still asleep, they'd all go away.

But, curse him, Hasho noticed. "Look, she's stirring."

"Shiori," Andahai said sternly, his long face looming over me. He shook my shoulders. "We know you're awake. Shiori!"

I coughed, my body scrunching up with pain.

"Enough, Andahai," said Benkai. "Enough!"

My lungs still burned, greedy for air, and my mouth tasted

of dirt and salt. I gulped the water Hasho offered, then forced a smile at my brothers.

None smiled back.

"You missed your betrothal ceremony," Andahai chided. "We found you on the banks, half-drowned."

Only my oldest brother would scold me for almost dying.

Almost dying, I repeated to myself, my fingers flying to my neck. The dragon had wrapped his tail around it, as if to choke me. But I felt no bruises, no bandages, either. Had he saved me? The last thing I remembered was seeing two ruby eyes and a crooked grin. I didn't remember coming up to the surface, and I couldn't have floated up on my own. . . .

Wings fluttered against my thumb, and I became suddenly aware of my other hand, hidden under my blankets.

Kiki. Thank the Eternal Courts! She was a little soggy, like me. But alive.

"What happened, Shiori?" Andahai prodded.

"Give her a moment," said Benkai. He crouched beside my bed, patting my back as I drank. Ever gentle and patient, he would have been my favorite brother if only I didn't see so little of him. Father was training him to be the commander of Kiata's army, while Andahai was the heir to the throne.

"You worried us, Sister. Come, tell old Benben what you remember."

I leaned my head back, resting against my bed's rosewood frame. Hasho had already told them I'd run off because I saw a snake. Should I endorse such an atrocious lie?

No, Andahai and Benkai will only ask more questions

if I lie, I quickly reasoned. *Then again, I can't tell them the truth—they can't find out about Kiki.*

The answer was simple. When a lie wouldn't work, a diversion would.

"A dragon saved me," I replied.

The corners of Andahai's lips slid into a frown. "A dragon. Really."

"He was small for a dragon," I went on, "but I'm guessing that's because he's young. He had clever eyes, though. They were even sharper than Hasho's."

I grinned playfully, hoping to lighten everyone's mood, but my brothers' frowns only deepened.

"I don't have time for tall tales, Shiori," Andahai said crisply. He was the least imaginative of my brothers, and he crossed his arms, his long sleeves as stiff as his waxed black hair. "Of all the days to run off to the lake . . . you missed your ceremony with Lord Bushian's son!"

I'd completely forgotten my betrothed. Guilt bubbled to my chest, my grin quickly fading. *Father must be furious with me.*

"Father is on his way to see you now," Andahai continued. "I wouldn't count on your being his favorite to get you out of this one."

"Stop being so hard on her," said Benkai. He lowered his voice. "For all we know, it might have been an attack."

Now I frowned, too. "An attack?"

"There's word of uprisings," explained my second-eldest brother. "Many of the lords oppose your marriage to

Lord Bushian's son. They fear his family will become too powerful."

"I wasn't attacked," I assured them. "I saw a dragon, and he saved me."

Andahai's face reddened with exasperation. "Enough lying, Shiori. Because of you, Lord Bushian and his son have left Gindara, utterly shamed."

For once, I wasn't lying. "It's the truth," I swore. "I saw a dragon."

"Is that what you're going to tell Father?"

"Tell Father what?" boomed a voice, resonating around the room.

I hadn't heard my doors slide open, but they rattled now as my father and my stepmother strode into my chambers. My brothers bowed deeply, and I lowered my head until it almost touched my knees.

Andahai was the first to rise. "Father, Shiori is—"

Father silenced him with a gesture. I'd never seen him look so angry. Usually, a smile from me was all it took to melt the sternness in his eyes, but not today.

"Your nurse has informed us that you are unharmed," he said. "That, I am relieved to hear. But what you have done today is utterly inexcusable."

His voice, so low the wooden frame of my bed hummed, shook with fury—and disappointment. I kept my head bowed. "I'm sorry. I didn't mean to—"

"You will prepare a proper apology to Lord Bushian and his son," he interrupted. "Your stepmother has proposed that you embroider a tapestry to reverse the shame you have brought to his family."

Now I looked up. "But, Father! That could take weeks."

"Have you somewhere else to be?"

"What about my lessons?" I asked, desperate. "My duties, my afternoon prayers at the temple—"

Father was unmoved. "You have never once given a care about your duties before. They will be suspended until you have finished the tapestry. You will begin work on it immediately, under your stepmother's supervision, and you will not leave the palace until it is complete."

"But—" I saw Hasho shaking his head. I hesitated, knowing he was right. I shouldn't argue, shouldn't protest. . . . Unwisely the words spilled from my lips anyway: "But the Summer Festival is in two weeks—"

One of my brothers nudged me from behind. This time, the warning worked. I clamped my mouth shut.

For an instant, Father's eyes softened, but when he spoke, his voice was hard. "The Summer Festival comes every year, Shiori. It would do you good to learn the consequences of your behavior."

"Yes, Father," I whispered through the ache in my chest.

It was true that the Summer Festival came every year, but this would be the last with my brothers before I turned seventeen and was married—no, *cast off* to live with my future husband.

And I'd ruined it.

Father observed my silence, waiting for me to beg for leniency, to make excuses and do my best to change his mind. But Kiki's fluttering wings under my palm compelled me to stay silent. I knew what the consequences would be if she were found out, and they were far worse than missing the festival.

"I have been too soft on you, Shiori," Father said quietly. "Because you are the youngest of my children, I have given you many liberties and let you run wild among your brothers. But you are no longer a child. You are the Princess of Kiata, the *only* princess of the realm. It is time you behaved like a lady worthy of your title. Your stepmother has agreed to help you."

Dread curdled in my stomach as my eyes flew to my stepmother, who hadn't moved from her position in front of the windows. I'd forgotten she was there, which seemed impossible once I looked at her.

Her beauty was extraordinary, the kind that poets immortalized into legend. My own mother had been acknowledged the most beautiful woman in Kiata, and from the paintings that I'd seen of her, that was no exaggeration. But my stepmother was quite possibly the most beautiful woman in the world.

Striking opalescent eyes, a rosebud mouth, and ebony hair so lustrous it fell in a long satin sheet against her back. But what made her truly memorable was the diagonal scar across her face. On anyone else, it might have looked alarming, and anyone else might have tried to hide it. Not my stepmother, and somehow that added to her allure. She did not even powder her face, as was the fashion, or put wax in her hair to make it shine. Though her maids grumbled that she never wore cosmetics, no one could disagree that my stepmother's natural beauty was radiant.

Raikama, everyone called her behind her back. *The Nameless Queen*. She'd had a name once, back in her home south of Kiata, but only Father and a handful of his most trusted officials knew it. She never spoke of it or of the life she'd led before becoming the emperor's consort.

I avoided her gaze and stared at my hands. "I am truly sorry if I have shamed you, Father. And you, Stepmother. It was not my intent."

Father touched my shoulder. "I don't want you going near the lake again. The physician says you nearly drowned. What were you thinking, running off outside the palace in the first place?"

"I . . ." My mouth went dry. Kiki fluttered under my palm, as if warning me not to tell the truth. "Yes, I . . . thought I saw a sna—"

"She said she saw a dragon inside," Andahai said in a tone that made it clear he didn't believe me.

"Not inside the palace," I cried. "In the Sacred Lake."

My stepmother, who had been so still and silent until now, suddenly stiffened. "You saw a dragon?"

I blinked, startled by her curiosity. "I . . . yes, yes I did."

"What did it look like?"

Something about her pale, stony eyes made it hard for me, a natural liar, to lie. "He was small," I began, "with emerald scales and eyes like the red sun." The next words were hard for me to utter: "I'm sure I imagined it."

Ever so slightly, Raikama's shoulders dropped, then a careful composure settled over her face again, like a mask that she'd inadvertently taken off for an instant.

She offered me a pinched smile. "Your father is right, Shiori. You'd do well to spend more time indoors, and not to confuse fantasy and reality."

"Yes, Stepmother," I mumbled.

My response was enough to satisfy Father, who murmured something to her and then left. But my stepmother remained.

She was the one person I could not read. Flecks of gold rimmed her eyes, eyes that ensnared me with their coldness. I couldn't tell whether their depths were hollow or brimming with an untold story.

When my brothers teased me for being afraid of her, I would say, "Only of her snake eyes." But deep down, I knew it was more than that.

Though she never said it or showed it, I knew Raikama hated me.

I didn't know why. I used to think it was because I reminded Father of my mother—the light that made his lantern shine, he would say, the empress of his heart. When she died, he had a temple erected in her name, and he went there every morning to pray. It would make sense that my stepmother resented me for reminding him of her, a rival beyond her grasp.

Yet I didn't think that was the reason. Never once did she complain when my father paid homage to my mother; never once had she asked to be named empress instead of consort. She seemed to prefer being left alone, and often I wondered if she would have favored being called the Nameless Queen to her official form of address, Her Radiance, a nod to her beauty and title.

"What is that under your hand?" my stepmother asked. My bird had crawled almost to the edge of my bed, and I only now realized how awkward I looked still trying to cover her.

"Nothing," I said quickly.

"Then put your hands on your lap, as is proper for a princess of Kiata."

She waited, and there was nothing I could do but obey.

Stay still, Kiki. Please.

As I lifted my hand, Raikama plucked Kiki from atop my blanket. To my relief, Kiki didn't move. Anyone would think she was only a piece of paper.

"What's this?"

I bolted up. "It's nothing. Just a bird that I folded—please, give her back."

A mistake.

Raikama raised an eyebrow. Now she knew Kiki meant something to me.

"Your father dotes on you. He spoils you. But you are a princess, not a village girl. And you are far too old to be playing with paper birds. It is time you learned the importance of duty, Shiori."

"Yes, Stepmother," I said quietly. "It won't happen again."

Raikama held Kiki out. Hope flared in my chest, and I reached to retrieve her. But instead of handing her over, my stepmother ripped her in half, then half again.

"No!" I cried, lunging for Kiki, but Andahai and Benkai held me still.

My brothers were strong. I didn't wrestle against them as a sob racked my chest. My grief was overwhelming. To anyone who didn't know what Kiki meant to me, it might have seemed *too* much.

Raikama regarded me with an indecipherable expression: her lips pursed, those cold eyes narrowing into slits. Without another word, she tossed Kiki's remains onto the floor and left.

Andahai and Benkai followed, but Hasho stayed.

He waited until the doors were closed, then he sat beside me on the edge of my bed.

"Could you do it again?" he asked in a low voice. "Could you reenchant the bird to fly?"

I'd never meant to bring Kiki to life. All I was trying to do was make paper birds—cranes, since they were on my family crest—so the gods might hear me. It was a legend all Kiatans knew: if you made a thousand birds—out of paper or cloth or even wood—they could carry a message up to the heavens.

For weeks I'd labored alone—not even asking my brother Wandei, who was best at all sorts of puzzles and constructions, for help coming up with the folds to make a paper crane. Kiki was the first bird I'd succeeded in folding, though to be honest, she looked more like a crow with a long neck than a crane. I had set her on my lap and painted a red spot on her head—so she'd look more like the cranes embroidered on my robes—and said:

"What a waste to have wings that cannot fly."

Her paper wings had begun to flutter, and slowly, hesitantly, she lifted into the air, with the uncertainty of a nestling just learning to fly. In the weeks that followed, when my lessons were done and my brothers were too busy to see me, I would help her practice in secret. I took her out to the garden to fly among the pruned trees and stone sanctuaries, and at night, I told her stories.

I'd been so happy to have a friend that I didn't worry about the implications of having magic.

And now she was gone.

"No," I whispered, finally replying to Hasho's question. "I don't know how."

He drew a deep breath. "Then it's for the best. You shouldn't be dabbling in magic you can't control. If anyone finds out, you'll be sent away from Kiata for good."

Hasho lifted my chin to wipe my tears. "And if you're sent away, far from home, who will watch out for you, little sister? Who will keep your secrets safe and make excuses for your mischief? Not I." He smiled at me, a small, sad smile. "So be good. Please?"

"I'm already going to be sent far away," I replied, twisting from him.

Falling to my knees, I picked up the scraps of paper my stepmother had flung onto the floor. I held Kiki close to my heart, as if that would bring her back to life. "She was my friend."

"She was a piece of paper."

"I was going to wish her into a real crane." My voice fal-

20

tered, my throat swelling as I glanced at the pile of birds I'd folded. Almost two hundred, but none had come alive like Kiki.

"Don't tell me you believe the legends, Shiori," said Hasho gently. "If everyone who folded a thousand birds got a wish, then every person would spend their days making paper sparrows and owls and gulls—wishing for mountains of rice and gold, and years of good harvest."

I said nothing. Hasho didn't understand. He had changed. All my brothers had changed.

My brother sighed. "I'll speak to Father about your coming out to the Summer Festival when he's in a more charitable mood. Would that make you feel better?"

Nothing could make me feel better about Kiki, but I gave a small nod.

Hasho knelt beside me and squeezed my shoulder. "Maybe these next few weeks with Stepmother will be good for you."

I shrugged him away. Everyone always sided with her. Even the servants, though they might call her Raikama behind her back, never had anything ill to say about her. Nor did my brothers. Or Father. *Especially* Father.

"I'll never forgive her for this. Never."

"Shiori . . . our stepmother isn't to blame for what happened."

You are, I could almost hear him saying, though Hasho was too wise to let the words slip.

He was right, but I wouldn't admit it. Something about the way she'd looked when she'd heard I met a dragon left me cold.

"It can't be easy for her, being so far from her home. She has no friends here. No family."

"She has Father."

"You know what I mean." My brother sat beside me, cross-legged. "Make peace with her, all right? If anything, it'll make things easier when I ask Father to let you out for the festival."

I gritted my teeth. "Fine, but that doesn't mean I'm going to talk to her."

"Must you be so petulant?" Hasho prodded. "She cares for you."

I faced my brother, taking in his creased brow, the twitch of his left eye. All signs he was truly exasperated with me. Quietly, I said, "You don't believe me, do you? About the dragon."

Hasho waited too long before answering. "Of course I do."

"You don't. I'm sixteen, not a child. I know what I saw."

"Whatever you saw, forget it," he urged. "Forget Kiki, forget the dragon, forget whatever it is you did to make all this happen."

"I didn't *make* it happen. It just happened."

"Make peace with our stepmother," Hasho said again. "She is our mother."

"Not mine," I replied, but my words trembled.

I had thought of her as my mother, once. Years ago, I'd been the first to accept Raikama when Father brought her home, and back then, she had been fond of me. I used to follow her everywhere she went—she was so mysterious I wanted to learn everything about her.

"Where is your scar from?" I had asked her one day. "Why won't you pick a name?"

She'd smiled, patted my head, and straightened the sash around my waist, tying it into a neat, tight bow. "We all have our secrets. One day, Shiori, you'll have your own."

Magic. Magic was my secret.

What was hers?

CHAPTER THREE

I hated sewing. Hated the monotony of it, hated the needles, the thread, the stitching, everything. Not to mention, I pricked myself so many times the maids kept having to wrap my fingers until they were thick as dumplings. I almost missed my lessons. Almost.

The days crawled by, slower than the snails that clustered outside the papered window screens. I embroidered crane after crane, spending so much time on them that they began to haunt my dreams. They'd peck at my toes, their cinder-black eyes glittering, then suddenly turn into dragons with pointed teeth and mischievous smiles.

I couldn't stop thinking about the dragon—and the expression that crossed Raikama's face when Andahai had mentioned him. Like she wished I had drowned in the lake.

Who knew what went on in my stepmother's head? Like me, she had little talent for embroidery, but *unlike* me, she could sit and sew for hours. Sometimes I'd catch her staring vacantly at the sky. I wondered what she thought about all day. *If* she had any thoughts.

I ignored her as best as I could, but when I made mistakes in my tapestry, she'd come to me and say, "Your stitches are uneven, Shiori. You'd best redo them."

Or "That crane is missing an eye. Lady Bushian will notice."

Bless the Eternal Courts, her remarks never required a response, at least until today. Today she visited me with a strange request:

"The gold sash Lord Yuji gifted you to wear for your betrothal ceremony—do you know where it is?"

I shrugged. "It must have fallen into the lake with me."

My answer didn't please Raikama. She didn't glower or frown, but I could tell from the way her shoulders squared that it wasn't the answer she'd wanted.

"When you find it, bring it to me."

I lied that I would. Then she left, and I promptly forgot about the sash.

The morning of the Summer Festival, adults and children alike sauntered along the imperial promenade, clutching kites of every shape and color.

I longed to go. Today was the only day that Andahai let loose, that Benkai wasn't busy training to be a commander, that Reiji and Hasho weren't stuck studying with their tutors.

Even the twins, Wandei and Yotan—who were different as the sun and moon and always argued about everything—never argued on festival day. They came together to design and construct the most brilliant kite. All seven of us would help, and when we flew it across the sky, it would be the envy of everyone at court.

And all the food I'd miss: rabbit-shaped cookies filled with sweet red beans, skewers of rice cakes stuffed with fresh peaches or melon paste, sugar candies shaped into tigers and bears. How unfair it was that I had to stay inside and sew with Raikama!

Finally, when my stomach couldn't take it any longer, I worked up the courage to ask: "Stepmother, the festival is beginning. May I go? Please?"

"You may leave when your embroidery is finished."

I wouldn't be finished for another month. "It'll be over by then."

"Do not sulk, Shiori. It is unbecoming." My stepmother didn't look up as her needle swam in and out of the cloth. "We had an agreement with your father."

I crossed my arms, indignant. I wasn't *sulking*. "Don't you want to go?"

She turned and opened her sewing chest. Inside were hundreds of neatly wrapped balls of thread, yarn, and embroidery floss.

Raikama started putting away her threads. "I have never enjoyed such things. I attend only out of duty."

Outside the window, drums pounded and laughter

bounced. Smoke from the grills spiraled into the sky, children danced in their brightest clothes, and the first kites of the morning flitted high against the clouds.

How could anyone *not* enjoy such things?

I sat back in my corner, resigned to my fate. My brothers would bring me some of the best food, I was sure. But I wouldn't get a chance to talk to the visiting cooks or watch them at work. The only dish I had mastered was my mother's fish soup, but I expected to cook more—or at least supervise the kitchen—once I had to move to the North, region of the blandest cuisine.

I was so busy wishing I were at the festival that I didn't hear my father enter the room. When I saw him, my heart skipped. "Father!"

"I have come to invite my consort to attend the festival with me," he said, pretending not to notice me. "Is she ready?"

My stepmother stood, holding her embroidery chest. "Just a moment. Allow me to put this away."

When she disappeared into the adjacent chamber, Father turned to me. His expression was stern, and I put on my best apologetic face, hoping he'd take pity on me.

It worked, though what he said surprised me: "Your stepmother says you've made good progress on the tapestry."

"She does?"

"You think she does not like you," Father said observantly. His eyes, near mirrors of my own, held my gaze.

He sighed when I said nothing.

"Your stepmother has suffered many hardships, and it pains her to speak of them. It would gladden me greatly to see you think well of her."

"Yes, Father. I will do my best."

"Good," he replied. "Lord Bushian and his son will return in the autumn for Andahai's wedding. You will present your apology to them then. Now go and enjoy the festival."

My eyes lit up. "Really?"

"I'd hoped staying inside would calm your restless spirit, but I can see nothing will tame you." He touched my cheek, tracing the dimple that appeared whenever I was happy. "You look more and more like your mother every day, Shiori."

I disagreed. My face was too round, my nose too sharp, and my smile more impish than kind. I was no beauty, not like Mother.

Yet every time Father spoke of her, his eyes misted and I yearned to hear more. There rarely was more. With a quiet exhale, he drew back his hand and said, "Go."

I didn't need to be told twice. Like a bird that had finally been released from her cage, I flew out to find my brothers.

The Summer Festival was packed with hundreds of revelers by the time I arrived, but I found my brothers easily. They were lounging in the park, away from the manicured pavilions, the vermilion gates, and the white sand squares. The twins had crafted a brilliant turtle kite this year, and my other brothers were helping to paint the finishing touches.

The turtle's four legs jutted out of its shell, which was a patchwork of scraps from old silk scarves and jackets. Against the clear blue of the afternoon, it would look like it was swimming in the imperial garden's azure ponds.

I hurried to join them. Every year since we were children, we'd flown a family kite together during the Summer Festival. My brothers were all of marriageable age now, Andahai already engaged and the rest soon to be. It was our last time doing this together.

"You've outdone yourselves this year, Brothers," I greeted.

"Shiori!" Wandei spared me a brief glance, a measuring string in his hands as he checked the kite's final dimensions. "You made it. Just in time, too. Yotan was about to eat all the food we saved for you."

"Only so it wouldn't go to waste!" Yotan wiped the green paint from his hands. "You make me sound like a glutton."

"Shiori's the glutton. You're just the one with the big belly."

Yotan harrumphed. "It's only these ears that are big. Same as yours." He tugged at his twin's—which, like his, did stick out a little more than everyone else's.

I stifled a giggle. "Is there anything good left?"

Yotan waved at a tray of food they'd carried from the stalls. "All the best dishes are nearly gone." He winked and leaned close, letting me in on the stash of glutinous rice cakes under his cloak. "Shh, don't show the others. I had to bribe the vendor just to get this last plate."

Winking back, I popped a rice cake into my mouth. My shoulders melted as my tongue savored the chewiness of the rice dough, the powdered sugar dusting my lips with just enough sweetness. Greedily, I reached for another before Yotan could hide the stash again.

"Save some for the rest of us!" Reiji complained.

"I just got here," I said, snatching another cake. "You've had all day to enjoy the food."

"Some of us have been working on the kite," he replied testily. As usual, my third brother's nostrils were flared with discontent. "Besides, there's not much to enjoy. No monkey-cakes stall, no grilled fishballs. Even the sugar artist isn't as good as last year's."

"Let her eat," said Benkai. "You always have something to complain about."

While my brothers bickered and I feasted, my attention wandered past the magnolia trees to the lake—where I'd almost drowned. Where I'd seen the dragon.

Part of me itched to go and look for him.

"Come, let's hurry before the best food is gone," said Hasho.

"Pick up more grilled fish, will you?" Yotan called to us. My other brothers decided to stay back and help the twins with the kite. The competition started in half an hour, just enough time for Hasho and me to explore.

Children in masks squeezed between us, squealing as they ran toward the gaming tents to win porcelain dolls and silver-finned fish in glass jars. Back when I was their age, the games were what excited me most too. Now it was the food.

I inhaled, taking in the aroma of fried mackerel skewers and tea eggs, of battered shrimp and pickled bamboo shoots, of glass noodles dipped in peanut sauce. For a so-called glutton like me, heaven.

"Princess Shiori," the vendors exclaimed, one after another, "what an honor it is for my humble stall to be graced by your presence."

"Don't you think we should head back?" Hasho said after I'd gobbled up a plate of noodles and battered shrimp. "The competition's starting soon."

Father and Raikama were already strolling toward the central courtyard, where the kite competition would be held. On his way to join the emperor, Lord Yuji waved to Hasho and me.

"My, my, you're looking more like your mother every day," he greeted me pleasantly. "Young Bushi'an Takkan is fortunate indeed."

"Is he, now?" said Hasho. "Her looks are one thing, but her manners . . ."

I elbowed my brother. "Hush."

The warlord let out a throaty laugh. He had always reminded me of a fox, with sharp shoulders, little teeth, and an easy smile. "The North could use some of Princess Shiori's famous troublemaking." He clasped his hands, then gestured at my dress, plain compared to his opulent robes. "I heard you fell into the Sacred Lake not long ago and lost your father a fortune in silk."

"So I did," I said, and my tone took a tighter turn. "I'm afraid I also lost the sash you sent. I'm made to think it was quite valuable, given how it distressed my stepmother."

"Did it?" Lord Yuji said. "That is news to me, but worry

not, Your Highness. Sashes are easily replaced, and my sons and I only thank the gods you were found and returned home safely." He leaned close. "Though, between us, I am expecting a shipment of silk from my A'landan friends shortly— I am told red is your favorite color?"

"It is the color the gods notice most," I replied cheekily. "If I'm to be sent north, I will need all the attention they can spare."

He laughed again. "May the luck of the dragons be with you, then. Red it shall be."

As he left, I let out a sigh. Lord Yuji was generous and wealthy, and more importantly, his castle was just outside Gindara. Sometimes I wished I were betrothed to one of his sons instead of Lord Bushian's. If I *had* to be forced into marriage, at least I'd be closer to home—and not promised to some barbarian lord of the third rank.

"Alliances must be made," Father said whenever I dared complain. "One day, you will understand."

No, I'd never understand. Even now, the inequity of it made my stomach roil, and I stuffed my last rice cake into my mouth.

"You're eating so fast you're going to get indigestion," said Hasho.

"If I slow down, all the food will be gone," I replied between mouthfuls. "Besides, sewing takes up energy. Go on back—I know you're itching to watch Wandei test out the kite. I'm still hungry."

Without waiting for him, I traipsed down the aisles, heading for the rice cakes.

A fresh batch awaited me, neatly decorated in a large wooden bowl.

"Specially made for Princess Shiori," said the vendor.

I scooped it into my arms and grabbed a helping of sweet potatoes too, tucking the little sack under my arm. I made it halfway back to my brothers when I spotted a boy in a dragon mask lurking behind the grilled-fish stall.

His robes looked outdated, the sash too wide by a generation, and his sandals were mismatched. He was too tall to be a child, but he darted about the festival like one—or rather, like someone who wasn't supposed to be here. Oddest of all was his hair, streaked with green.

The kite competition would begin soon, and my brothers were waiting. But I wanted a better look at the boy's mask.

It was blue, with silver whiskers and scarlet horns. He was fast, scurrying about like a lizard, and even greedier than I was when it came to the food.

Everything in the vendors' stalls was free, offered by the craftsmen to advertise their wares, but it wasn't polite to take more than one or two plates at a time. This boy was taking at least five. How he managed to balance them on his arm was impressive, but if he kept up like this, the vendors would ban him from seeking more. And now he was angling after the fried lotus root.

I shook my head. *Novice.*

"I suggest you skip the lotus," I said, going up to him. "Everyone knows it's the worst dish at the festival."

I thought I'd surprised him, but he merely winked, a pair of red eyes glittering behind his mask. "Then I'll take yours."

Before I could respond to his audacity, Hasho reappeared at my side, finally finding me. "Shiori, are you coming back? It's nearly time for the kite cere—"

The boy's foot suddenly shot out, tripping my brother before he could finish.

Hasho stumbled. As he fell forward, grabbing me to steady his balance, a green sleeve whirled across my side and snatched the bag of sweet potatoes from under my arm.

"Hey!" I shouted. "Thief! Thief—"

The words hardly made it past my lips. Hasho and I toppled over each other, my half-eaten plates scattering across the street.

"Your Highnesses!" people cried. Hands outstretched to help Hasho and me up, a crowd gathering to make sure we weren't hurt.

I barely noticed. My attention was on the masked boy.

"You're not getting away so easily," I muttered, scanning past the onlookers. I spotted him edging along the outskirts of the gaming tents, then disappearing into the bushes. He moved even faster than Benkai, his steps so light they left no imprint on the soft summer grass. I started after him, but Hasho grabbed my wrist.

"Shiori, where are you—"

"I'll be back in time for the competition," I said, wriggling my hand away.

Ignoring Hasho's protests, I rushed after the boy in the dragon mask.

CHAPTER FOUR

I found him sitting on a rock, devouring a bag of honeyed sweet potatoes.

My bag of sweet potatoes.

Its scent wafted into the air, sharpening the hunger in my belly—and the anger rising in my fists.

I meant to accuse him of thievery, to sling a hundred different insults and curse him to the bottom of Mount Nagawi—but as soon as I saw him up close, different words came out of my mouth:

"Aren't you a little too old to be wearing a mask?"

He didn't look surprised that I'd followed him, or angry. Instead, a familiar grin slid across his mouth. I couldn't place where I'd seen it before.

"What is that?" he rasped, pointing at the wooden bowl under my arm.

"Rice cakes."

He took off his mask and reached for them. "Delicious," he said, crunching on the snack.

If not for the vibrant band of red around his pupils, so familiar yet so strange, I would have knocked the bowl out of his hands. But startled, I let go.

"Don't eat them all—"

Too late. Gone was the last sweet potato—and rice cake, too. I put my hands on my hips and flashed the boy my most irritated scowl.

"What?" He gave a half shrug. "Swimming all this way makes me hungry."

I was still staring at him, at the thick stripes of green wisped about his temples; it was a color I'd never seen before on anyone—even the pale-haired merchants who came from the Far West. His skin had little warmth to it, but there was a pearlescent sheen. I couldn't decide whether he looked bizarre or beautiful. Or dangerous.

Maybe all three.

"You're . . . you're the dragon! From the other day in the lake."

He grinned. "So you do have a brain. I was wondering, after you fell into the lake."

I met his grin with a glare. "I didn't fall into the lake. I dove into it."

"All for that bird, I recall. That *enchanted* bird."

Remembering Kiki sank my spirits. I dusted the crumbs from my sleeves and began to turn away from the lake.

"Where are you going?"

"Back to the festival. My brothers will be missing me."

He was at my side in an instant, his fingers catching my sleeve and pulling me down to sit. "So soon?" He clicked his tongue. "I found your bird for you and saved you from drowning. Don't you think you owe me some thanks? Stay a while. Entertain me."

"Entertain you?" I repeated. "There's a whole festival back there."

"It's all human games, nothing of interest to me."

"You're not even a dragon right now."

He wasn't. In his current form, he was a boy, a young man not much older than I. But with green hair and ruby eyes and sharp, clawlike fingernails.

"How *are* you human?"

"All dragons can do it," he replied, his grin widening. "I haven't practiced shifting into human form much until now." He blew at his bangs. "Always thought humans were boring."

I crossed my arms. "*I* always thought dragons were majestic and grand. You were hardly larger than an eel."

"An eel?" he repeated. I thought I'd made him angry, but he burst out laughing. "That's because I haven't grown into my full form yet. When I do, you will be impressed."

"When do you reach your full form?" I asked, unable to contain my curiosity. All I knew of dragons was from legends and stories, and those told little about dragon adolescence.

"Very soon. I'd say in a human year. Two at most."

"That isn't very long at all." I sniffed. "I can't imagine you growing *that* much in a year."

"Oh? Let's make a wager, then."

I leaned forward. My brothers loved making bets with each other, but they never let me join in. "What wager? Dragons aren't known for keeping their word."

"We *always* keep our word," he retorted. "That's why it's so rarely given."

I gave him a pointed look. "What are you proposing?"

"If I win, you invite me to your palace and cook a banquet in my honor. I expect a thousand dishes, no less, and all the most important lords and ladies to be in attendance."

"I only know how to cook one dish," I admitted.

"You've a year to learn more."

I made no promise. "If *I* win, you take me to *your* palace and throw a banquet in my honor. Same rules."

His grin faded, and he swept a hand through his long green hair. "I don't know if Grandfather would approve of that."

"It's only fair. Do you think my father would approve of me bringing a dragon boy to dinner?"

"Approve? He should be honored."

Honored? I drew a sharp breath. "No one speaks about the emperor that way."

"It's true," said the dragon with a shrug. "Humans revere dragons, but it's not the same the other way around. It'd be like I brought a pig to dinner."

"A pig!" I shot up to my feet. "I am not a pig."

He laughed. "All right, all right. Calm down, Shiori. It's a deal." He pulled on my arm until I sat again.

"And this is Kiata, not A'landi—my father would *not* revere a dragon," I huffed. "He despises magic—" I stopped midsentence. "How did you know my name?"

"That boy at the festival said it. Right before I tripped him."

"That was my brother!"

"Yes, and he seemed like a spoilsport. Aren't you glad you chased after me instead?"

I glared at him. "Tell me your name."

The dragon smiled, showing his pointed teeth. "I am Seryu, Prince of the Easterly Seas and most favored grandson of the Dragon King, Nazayun, Ruler of the Four Seas and Heavenly Waters."

I rolled my eyes at how conceited he sounded. Two could play at that game.

"Shiori'anma," I said haughtily, though he already knew it. "First daughter of Emperor Hanriyu, and most favored Princess of Kiata—Kingdom of the Nine Eternal Courts and the Holy Mountains of Fortitude."

Seryu looked amused. "So your father despises magic, eh? What will he think of *you*?"

I shifted sideways, uncomfortable. "What about me? I . . . I have no magic. There *is* no magic in Kiata."

"Magic is *rare* in Kiata," Seryu corrected. "Except for gods and dragons, of course. Oh, its sources may be dried up, but it's an element natural to the world, and even the gods can't erase *every* trace. That's why once in a rare moon, a Kiatan is born able to wield what is left. A human—like you. Don't deny it. I saw that paper bird of yours."

I swallowed hard. "Kiki is gone. My stepmother . . . destroyed her."

Seryu gestured at the pocket where I kept Kiki's pieces. "You can bring her back."

He stated it so matter-of-factly—the way I'd tell a cook that his shrimps were perfectly fried or his yams were well baked—that I blinked, my lips parting with surprise. "I can? No. *No.*" I shook my head. "I'm done with magic."

"What, don't you want to become an all-powerful enchanter?" He lowered his voice. "Or are you afraid your powers will corrupt you, and turn you into a demon?"

"No," I retorted. I sighed, reciting, "Without magic, Kiata is safe. Without magic, there are no demons."

"You do know what's in the Holy Mountains of Fortitude, don't you?"

"Of course I do." The mountains were right behind the palace; I saw them every day.

"Thousands and thousands of demons," Seryu replied conspiratorially, "and all the magic that your gods asked us dragons to help them seal up. Your emperor should *revere* the beings who helped to make his kingdom safe. Who *keep* his kingdom safe."

"The gods and the sentinels keep Kiata safe," I said. "Dragons are too busy gambling—and hoarding their pearls."

Seryu cackled. "Is that what they tell you now? Don't teach a dragon history, Princess, especially not magic history."

"Don't teach a human about our gods," I countered. "Are you even supposed to be here? The gods promised to keep to heaven after they took magic away from Kiata. Didn't the dragons say they'd keep to their lakes?"

"Sea," Seryu corrected. "We live in the Taijin Sea, in a glittering realm of shell and precious coral. Not some muddy lake. And dragons are not subject to the gods' rules. We never have been."

"Then why have your kind disappeared for so many years?"

"Because your realm is boring. My grandfather's palace alone would dazzle you out of your wits."

"I doubt that," I said dryly.

A thick eyebrow flitted up. "The only way you'll find out is if you win our wager."

"If I won, you'd find some way to trick me into staying in your 'glittering realm' for a hundred years. There's a reason you dragons have a reputation."

As Seryu grinned, not denying my accusations, I turned on my heel to leave. "Find some other fool to wager with you. That fool isn't me."

"What about your magic? It's a rare gift—rarer still in Kiata. You should learn to use it."

"And end up banished to the Holy Mountains?" I snapped, spinning to face him. "Demons take me, I'd . . . I'd rather sew all day! Stop following me."

"You're only saying that," said Seryu. "If you were really going back to the festival, you'd be running. You want to learn." He paused. "I'll show you how to resurrect your friend Kiki. Wouldn't you like that?"

My defenses crumbled. I did want to bring Kiki back, and I did yearn to learn more about magic. After all, if it had been absent from Kiata for so many years, there had to be a reason I'd been born with it—hadn't there?

The gods took magic away because it is dangerous, I reminded myself. *But the demons are already trapped in the* mountains, and all I want is to learn how to get Kiki back. What harm could it bring?

The future flashed before me, and I saw myself trapped in Castle Bushian, married to a faceless lord and confined to a room where I sewed and sewed until the end of my days.

If it *was* a choice between that and demons taking me, I'd choose the demons.

Besides, how often does one get to learn sorcery from a dragon? I knew if I didn't take this chance, I would regret it forever.

Seryu was still waiting, but before I could reply, a fleet of kites soared into the air. I was missing the kite-flying ceremony!

"Demons of Tambu," I cursed. "My brothers are going to be so angry with me. And Father . . ."

"Nothing you can do about it now," said the dragon. "You might as well enjoy the view."

Tempting, but I shook my head. "I've already gotten into enough trouble as it is." I started to go, then hesitated.

"One lesson," I said. "That's all."

The dragon's smile widened, revealing his sharp, pointed teeth. The look was not quite as feral as a wolf's, but it was enough to remind me that he wasn't human, no matter how much like a boy he looked.

"Here's a lesson for you before you go—" Seryu took the wooden bowl and spun it around on his finger. "Walnut wood has magical properties, did you know?"

I confessed I didn't.

"One of the little traces your gods left behind," he said

smugly. "Put something enchanted inside, and the walnut will conceal the object from prying eyes. It'll even contain the magic."

"What good is that?" I asked. "The bowl is barely larger than my head."

"When it comes to magic, size matters little." As a demonstration, he winked, and a flock of birds made entirely of water shot forth from the bowl and flew over the lake. At their highest point, they burst and evaporated in a puff of mist. "Might be useful for hiding future hordes of paper cranes."

I was about to tell him there were no future paper cranes when Seryu continued:

"Fold one when you're ready and send it into the wind. I'll know to wait for you here at this lake." He turned the bowl upside down on the ground, marking the spot where we'd met today so neither of us would forget it. "One last thing, Shiori—"

"What is it?"

"Next time, bring more rice cakes."

One lesson quickly became two, three, then five. I met Seryu every week, usually in the morning before my embroidery sessions with Raikama.

Each time, I brought different snacks for us to share, but he always liked the rice cakes best, especially the ones with chunks of peach inside, which were my favorite, too.

Today he had presented me with a bouquet of wilted peonies in return.

"Are you trying to woo me or insult me?" I asked dryly, refusing to take them. "You know Kiatans are superstitious about death."

"A senseless superstition," he dismissed. "These are for your lesson. Few can bring paper birds to life. I suspect you have a talent for inspiritation."

"Inspiritation?"

"You can imbue things with bits of your soul. It's almost like resurrection, but not quite so powerful. You won't be bringing corpses back to life. Or ghosts, for that matter. But you could probably get a wooden chair to dance on its legs, or revive a few wilted flowers—if you so desired."

He pressed the peonies into my hand. "Go on, try."

I can imbue things with bits of my soul, I repeated to myself. What was that even supposed to mean?

"Bloom," I told the flowers. Nothing happened. The stems crumbled in my palms, dried petals drifting to the ground.

Seryu chewed on a stalk of grass. "Didn't you hear what I said? Inspiritation, Shiori. Don't talk to the flower as if you're an undertaker. Think of something happy. Like chasing after whales or winning an argument against a tortoise."

We clearly had different ideas of happiness. Feeling silly, I searched my memories, skimming over sugared animals and kites, paper birds and snow-dusted cranes, before landing on my favorite memory: cooking with my mother. I used to sit on her lap in the kitchen and listen to her sing, her throat humming against the back of my head as we peeled oranges together and mashed soft red beans into a paste for dessert.

"Find the light that makes your lantern shine," she used to say. "Hold on to it, even when the dark surrounds you. Not even the strongest wind will blow out the flame."

"Bloom," I said again.

Slowly, before my eyes, the wilted peonies trembled with a raw, silvery-gold light. Then crisp new leaves sprouted from the stalk, plump and green. The flowers opened, their petals bright as coral.

My pulse thundered in my head, adrenaline pumping as if I'd just swum a race across the lake—and won.

"A bit of a cheat, using your voice, but they'll train it out of you if you go to enchanter school."

"I'm not going to enchanter school," I said, the bitterness in my words surprising even me. How could I go? Wondering whether Father would actually exile me—or have me executed—if he found out about my abilities had kept me up more nights than I wished to admit.

"Then I'll teach you," Seryu said. "I may only be seventeen dragon years, but I know more than the oldest enchanters in Lor'yan."

"Really."

"I do!" He glared at my skepticism. "Besides, you wouldn't want to study with an enchanter. They're all fixated on taking the emotion out of magic. They think it corrupts. But you liked how it felt, seeing the flowers come to life, didn't you?"

"Yes." *Yes* was an understatement. My heart was still

pounding in my ears, so fast I could hardly hear myself breathe. "Should I not have?"

"That depends on what you're trying to accomplish." Seryu gazed at my peonies, his red eyes unusually pensive. "Magic has many threads. The same enchantment cast with joy will have an entirely different result when cast with sorrow, or anger—or fear. Something to be wary of, especially with powers like yours."

"Powers like mine?" I laughed, making light of his seriousness. "Like making dead flowers bloom again, and bringing paper birds to life?"

"That's only the beginning. Your magic is wild, Shiori. One day, it will be dangerous."

"Dangerous," I mused. "Why, Seryu, you almost sound as if you're afraid of me."

"Afraid of you?" He scoffed, and with a whoosh of his arm, he summoned a tidal wave so high it dwarfed the trees around us. Then the wave fell, slamming into the lake—and drenching my robes.

"Seryu!" I shrieked.

He didn't apologize. "You'd do well to remember that I am a dragon, the grandson of a god," he growled before leaping back into the lake. "I'm not afraid of anything, least of all you."

I'm not afraid of anything. How often I had uttered the same words. But they were always a lie, and I had a feeling Seryu was lying, too.

CHAPTER FIVE

"Where have you been?" asked Raikama when I returned to work on my tapestry. "Late for the third day. Even for you, Shiori, this is unusual. I expect you to be more diligent about your work."

"Yes, Stepmother," I mumbled.

My tapestry was nearly complete, almost ready to be sent to Castle Bushian. I couldn't wait to be finished with it and have my days free again.

Except when I sat at my embroidery frame, I discovered my progress from this week had been undone. I gasped. "What—"

"Your lines were crooked," Raikama said, "and you missed a stroke on Bushi'an Takkan's name. Best to redo it all rather than risk offending his family again."

I gritted my teeth, anger boiling inside me.

Calm, I reminded myself, exhaling. *Calm*.

At this rate, I'd have to finish my tapestry at Castle

Bushian. I let out a groan. If only I could enchant my needle to sew without me.

Well, why not?

"Awaken," I whispered to my needle. "Help me sew."

To my astonishment, the needle fumbled to life, awkwardly dipping in and out of the silk. Then, as I gained faith in its enchantment, it started to dance across the frame in a symphony of stitches. I added three more needles to speed up the pace while I sewed too, keeping my back to Raikama so she wouldn't see.

All week we worked, until at last the tapestry—a scene of cranes and plum blossoms against the full moon—was finished. Once we were done, I gathered the needles in my palm.

"Thank you," I whispered. "Your work is complete."

The needles fell lifeless, and a sudden lethargy stole over me. I fought it off, rising triumphantly from my embroidery frame to tell my stepmother I was finished.

For what felt a very long time, Raikama scanned my work, but she was unable to find fault with it. "It will do," she allowed, though her eyebrows made a suspicious lift. "Once your father approves, I will ask the ministers to send it to Castle Bushian."

I nearly jumped with joy. Thank the Eternal Courts, that meant I was free!

Exuberantly, I put away my needles and threads. I wanted to find my brothers to celebrate, but magic was exhausting work—mentally and physically. I ended up dozing on my bed until Guiya, one of my maids, summoned me to dinner.

She was new, with blank eyes, a forgettable face, and an

48

exasperating obsession with dressing me, down to the last detail, in attire befitting a princess—a task my previous maids had long since given up. In her arms was a set of ornately tailored robes, sashes, and jackets I had no desire to wear.

"Your clothes are wrinkled, Your Highness," she said. "You can't leave your chamber looking like that."

I was too tired to care. Ignoring her pleas, I ambled to dinner, practically collapsing into my place beside Hasho and Yotan. I could hardly get through the first course without nodding off.

The cushions under my knees felt extra soft, and I swayed, lulled by the flowery aroma of freshly brewed tea. Hasho elbowed me when I slumped and knocked over my tea.

"What's wrong with you?" he whispered.

I ignored him, raising my sleeve as the servants cleaned the spill I'd made. "Father," I called, seeking his attention. "Father, may I please be excused? I'm feeling unwell."

"You do look paler than usual," Father said, distracted. His mind was elsewhere; meetings with the council had been running long, though Andahai and Benkai would not tell me why. He dismissed me with a nod. "Go, then."

My stepmother watched me strangely. "I will walk her out."

I looked up in horror. "No, I'm—"

"At least to the hall," she insisted.

She didn't speak until we reached the end of the corridor. "I've been thinking about that dragon you said you saw," she said in a low voice. "They are dangerous, untrustworthy beasts, Shiori. If you've come across one, you'd do best to stay far, far away. It is for your own good."

I hid my surprise. Had she actually believed me?

"Yes, Stepmother," I lied. As soon as I returned to my chambers, I collapsed onto my bed.

What did Raikama know—or care—about what was good for me? By the gods, she made it her mission to sow my life with unhappiness.

As my head sank into my pillow, and the sleep spirits came for me, I made a drowsy promise to myself:

Tomorrow I'd finally ask Seryu to show me how to bring Kiki back.

"Why are you so surprised she believes you?" said Seryu, chewing lazily on a fallen magnolia branch. "Dragons are real—everyone knows that."

"None of my brothers believe me, not even Hasho," I persisted. "And I'm not *surprised*—I'm *worried* she'll tell my father."

"If she hasn't already, I don't see why she would bother."

"You don't know Raikama." I dug my nails into the dirt, certain she was withholding the information to use against me later. The same way she'd disapproved of a match with Lord Yuji's son, and insisted on sacrificing me to the barbarians in the abysmal North.

"Maybe she's having you followed," Seryu said wickedly. His hair was entirely green today, and he sported horns I hadn't noticed before.

"Followed?"

He rolled onto his side, peering at something crawling over the bowl we used to mark our meeting spot. Then, with a claw, he picked up a water snake and held it close to my face. "Here's one of her spies."

I screamed, leaping to my feet. "Gods, Seryu. Take that away!"

"Relax. She's harmless. Just a little water snake." He wrapped the snake around his head, where it lounged over his horns. "See?"

I still wouldn't go near him.

"I was joking about her being a spy, Shiori," said Seryu. He made a hissing sound, and the snake's tongue darted out as if in reply. "She was just curious to see a dragon by the lake."

"You can speak to it?"

"*Her.* And yes, of course I can. Dragons and snakes are related, after all, and serpents of all kinds are sensitive to magic."

That I didn't know. "I don't like snakes. They bring up bad memories."

"Of your stepmother?"

"She has hundreds roaming her gardens," I replied by way of explanation. "My brother dared me to steal one once, and she caught me." My voice went tight at the memory.

"Snakes remind her of home," Father would tell the ministers who frowned upon her unusual pets. "Honor her wishes as you would honor mine."

It was what he told us children as well, and we had obeyed. At least until Reiji had dared me to steal one.

"You're the one who's terrified of snakes, not me," I told him. "Besides, I promised I wouldn't go into her garden without her."

"Are you afraid you won't be her favorite anymore if she catches you?"

"I'm not afraid of anything."

It was true. Raikama was fond of me. She wouldn't mind if I borrowed one snake.

The next afternoon, I stole into her garden, moving slowly so as not to startle the snakes. But their eyes—all yellow and wide and unblinking— unnerved me. I was only twenty steps into the garden when a small green viper started wrapping around my heel.

"Go away," I whispered, trying to kick it off.

But more joined, and soon a dozen snakes surrounded me. No, a hundred. They hissed and bared their fangs. Then a white snake hanging from a tree branch lunged for my throat.

With a scream, I jumped for one of the trees, climbing as high as I could. But the snakes followed, and my pulse spiked with fear. I braced myself for a fatal bite.

Suddenly the garden gate opened, and Raikama appeared. The snakes slithered back like a receding tide.

I was practically weeping. "Stepmother, please forgive me. I don't know how I—"

A withering glance was all it took for her to silence me. "Leave," she said coldly.

Never once had Raikama raised her voice at me. In shock, I nodded numbly, slid down the tree as fast as I could, and ran away.

"Ever since then, she's hated me," I said to Seryu with a shrug.

My nonchalance was feigned. To this day, I didn't understand why that moment had ruined everything between my stepmother and me, and I cared more than I pretended to. But no one, not even my brothers, knew that.

"Well, you have nothing to fear," replied Seryu, grinning. "If her snakes try to harm you, my pearl will protect you." He tilted his head at me. *We're connected, you and I.*

I could hear his voice, but his lips were still as stone. I jumped back. "How did you do that?"

"Like I said, my pearl will protect you. It links us, similar to the way you and Kiki are connected."

"Your pearl?"

"Yes, you'd have drowned if not for the tiny piece I put in your heart. Just enough to keep you out of trouble."

"You put a pearl in my heart!" I exclaimed.

"After you fainted. No need to sound so ungrateful— it saved you."

My alarm quickly subsided into curiosity. "So dragon pearls are magic."

"Are they magic?" He scoffed. "They're the very source

of our power—magic in its purest, rawest form. Demons and enchanters covet nothing more, since they enhance their abilities."

"Where is yours?"

"Here," he said, pointing at his chest. "I would show you, but its brilliance would blind you."

I mimicked his scoff to mock his ego. "Yet you chipped some off to save me?"

"I wanted to know what a pretty human girl was doing diving after a magic bird." He cleared his throat, his thick green brows knitting in confusion as I stared at him. "Not a sight you see every day. I figured a bit of the pearl might help you to shore. . . . Why are you staring at me like that?"

I wore a coy smile. "You just called me pretty."

A flush instantly colored his pointed ears. "I meant I thought you were pretty for a *human*," Seryu grumbled. "You'd be a hideous dragon."

A warm tingle smoldered in my chest, and I inched closer to him—just to see his ears redden more. "Luckily I'm not a dragon."

"Clearly," said Seryu, rubbing his ears. He glared. "Which is exactly why you can't go around telling anyone you have a piece of my pearl. It would be near impossible for anyone except me to take it from you, but enchanters are as greedy as they are resourceful. . . . Best not to take chances while I'm away."

"You're going away?" I exclaimed.

"Back into the Taijin Sea. My grandfather's court convenes in the westerly quadrant during the winter months."

"But it isn't winter."

"It is for us. Dragon time runs differently than in the mortal realm. A week for me is a season for you. I should be back by your spring."

"Spring?" I repeated. "But what about our lessons? And the cranes—you'll miss the cranes!"

The dragon's brow furrowed. "The cranes?"

"They visit the palace at the beginning of every winter," I explained. "It's tradition to greet them the first day they arrive."

"Just as it's tradition for the royal princes and princess to fly kites during the Summer Festival?" Seryu said wryly. "You humans have many traditions."

"You'll also miss my birthday," I said, suddenly glum. "It'll be my last one in the palace before I'm shipped off to marry Lord Bushian's son."

That caught the dragon by surprise. "You're going to be married?"

"Yes," I mumbled. I'd buried all the dread I felt about my betrothal for weeks, but now that Seryu was leaving, the reality of my fate stung.

"When?"

"I'll be sent to Castle Bushian before the end of spring. The wedding will be next summer."

The tension in Seryu's shoulders released. "Oh, that's plenty of time. Cheer up, I'll be back in the spring. In the meantime, work on your magic."

My fingers went instinctively to my pocket for the pieces of Kiki I still kept with me. "Show me how to bring Kiki back."

"You don't need any instruction. Just remember what I taught you."

Nervously, I placed the scraps of paper on my lap, four in total. All my enchantments since Kiki had been short-lived. The flowers I made bloom wilted once my concentration flagged, and the stick horses I made gallop collapsed as soon as I turned away. What if I resurrected Kiki, only to lose her again?

Kiki is different, I told myself as I carefully began to piece her together. *She's a part of me.*

After a minute, there she was. A little fragile, but mostly the same as before—with a beak that hooked slightly downward, two inky eyes that I'd dotted with careful strokes of my brush, and wings that creased in the center, so they curved like orchid petals.

Except the red ink of her crown had smudged and faded.

I scratched open a scab on one of my fingers, freeing a bead of blood that I pressed to the paper bird's head. As it darkened into crimson, I held my bird on my palm. I filled my thoughts with hope that she'd come alive again, and whispered, "Awaken."

A fine, silvery-gold thread of magic rushed past my lips and twisted across the bird's wings before settling there, as if stitched onto the paper. Then her wings flapped once. Twice. And she lifted, circling my face.

"Kiki!"

Kiki landed on my hand, her wings stroking my fingers. *That was quite possibly the worst nap I've ever had,* she grumbled, shaking her beak at me. *I dreamt I was ripped to pieces. I'm never sleeping again. Ever.*

"I can hear you," I marveled.

Yes, of course you can hear me! I'm your dearest friend, aren't I?

"Your desire to bring her back must have bonded you," mused Seryu. "Now you can hear each other's thoughts . . . though you might find the company of a dragon preferable to that of a paper bird."

Will she, now? Kiki twittered soundlessly. *I was her friend before she met you.*

I laughed, loving my bird's cheekiness. "Yes, but can you teach me magic while Seryu is away?"

"Unlikely." Seryu lounged back in the grass. "You could always ask your stepmother for help, though."

My laugh died on my lips. "My stepmother?"

Seryu shrugged. "Don't you know? She's a powerful sorceress. Magic emanates off her. Even when I was at your Summer Festival, I noticed it."

Raikama, a sorceress? Impossible!

"You must be mistaken."

"I would never mistake such a thing."

"I thought magic was a rare gift. How could Raikama have it too?"

"I said it's rare, not that *you're* the only one with it. And it's really not strange at all. Magic attracts magic. What *is* strange is that my grandfather let her cross the Taijin Sea. He guards Kiata's waters from foreign magic."

"Maybe he didn't know," I said, the spinning in my head coming to an abrupt halt. Could this be the secret that Raikama kept so carefully—that she had magic, like me? "You should ask."

"It isn't wise to pester the Dragon King about human matters. Or to alert him to a mistake made years ago. Besides, she is not an enchanter."

"What do you mean?"

"She isn't one of those greedy fools bound to a thousand-year oath, sworn to serve whichever master possesses their amulet. It isn't as grand as it sounds. Between masters, they have to spend their days in their spirit form, usually as some mangy beast without access to magic—or much intelligence."

"If enchanters are bound to such an oath, why do we fear them?"

"You don't, not in Kiata. They don't have any power once they cross the Taijin Sea."

"Why do we fear them *outside* of Kiata?" I corrected. I was curious.

"Because they're one breath from becoming demons. That is their punishment, should they break their oath. They're dangerous."

"And my stepmother isn't—dangerous?"

"Not in the same way," Seryu replied. "Her sorcery is wild and unrestrained—like yours. Powerful, to be sure, but you both suffer a mortal's short life-span." He didn't seem to notice my glare, and he went on. "The mystery is from where she draws her magic. She isn't native to Kiata, like you are.

She would need a source, a very great source, to emanate such power."

"Maybe she drinks snake blood," I said, rolling up my sleeves. "That would explain why she has so many."

"I don't think snakes are a source of magic."

"Well, if you won't ask your grandfather, then *I'll* have to find out." I shot Seryu a deviously smug look. "Sadly, you'll have to wait until spring to hear what I learn."

"A mortal's spring is but a few weeks away in dragon time. I can wait." Seryu grinned. "Now, I've already stayed longer than I should have. Not to worry, Princess. I'll return." He winked. "You've a tiny piece of my pearl, and I'll be needing it back."

When had he gotten so close? I could smell the sweetness of red bean paste on his breath. "Take it now, then," I offered, moving a small step back. My foot wobbled over a loose stone, and Seryu grabbed me by the elbow to steady me.

"Keep it." His eyes glittered as if he were carrying some secret. "You might need it."

He kissed my cheek, his lips softer than I would have imagined for a dragon. Then, without waiting for my reaction, he dove into the water.

"I'll see you in the spring!" he called with a wave, his tail splashing before I lost sight of him completely.

I picked up the walnut bowl we'd used as a marker of where to meet, brushed the dirt from its sides, and carried it home under my arm.

Spring suddenly seemed so far away.

CHAPTER SIX

With Seryu gone and my tapestry done, the rest of summer lumbered by. Lessons with my tutors resumed; the lectures on history, protocol, and language were tiresome, but I preferred them to sewing. I preferred anything to sewing.

Whenever I could, I made excuses to avoid my lessons. Harmless little lies, like telling my tutors that Andahai needed my help selecting a gift for his betrothed or telling the high priests that I couldn't pay my respects to the gods that afternoon because Hasho was ill and needed me to make him soup. But the truth was, my brothers were always busy, and no one ever asked for me. Not even Raikama.

For once I didn't mind, and I used my precious free time to spy on my stepmother.

After weeks of shadowing her, of sending Kiki to spy, all I'd learned was her palace routine. And what a monotonous routine it was! Breakfast with my father, then morning prayers, then a visit to her garden, where she fed her snakes and watered the chrysanthemums and swept the fallen wisteria petals. Then, worst of all, she sewed—for hours without end.

With a frustrated sigh, I flung a pebble into the Sacred Lake and watched the water ripple, then still. I sat and sank my ankles into the lake.

"She *can't* be a sorceress, Kiki," I told my bird. "Raikama has always hated magic."

Hated was an understatement, though I had never dwelled on why. Most people in Kiata hated magic. But Raikama's mysterious past did invite plenty of outlandish rumors about where she had come from, how she had met Father, and how she'd gotten her scar. Her fondness for snakes certainly didn't help the speculation. Once, a minister had tried to convince Father that Raikama was a demon worshipper—one of those heretical priestesses who came by the palace every year, throwing ashes at the gates and chanting nonsense about dark magic returning to Kiata. Father had exiled the minister and banned the priestesses from Gindara, but now I couldn't help wondering.

Could it be that Raikama hated magic because she was hiding her own?

I frowned. "She would have shown it by now. Seryu has to be wrong."

Try again tomorrow, suggested Kiki. *The dragon said she keeps her powers hidden.*

"He also said to practice *my* magic," I retorted. "Every hour I waste spying on her is a missed opportunity to improve my skills."

So is every minute you waste complaining, quipped Kiki, my unlikely voice of reason.

I let out another sigh, but the bird had a point.

"Ripen," I said to a budding berry, and it became plump enough that a kitebird dove to snatch it from my hand. "Skip," I commanded a stone, and it hopped across the lake until it was far from sight.

Such spells were easy, but things like trying to change the direction of the wind or call the larks and swallows to my fingertips—simple enchantments that should have been natural for any sorceress—made me fall asleep from the effort.

It's all right to feel bad about your lack of skill, Kiki said, trying to soothe me. Her sense of empathy was still a ways from being fine-tuned. *At least you can do* something, *unlike everyone else in Kiata.*

"Except Raikama." I flicked my fingertips into the lake, trying to make a tidal wave like Seryu had, but the water barely rippled.

You don't want to ask her for help?

"I'd rather drown in the Sacred Lake," I retorted.

That's a bit dramatic, isn't it? Kiki chided. When I sighed again, she poked at my cheek. *Why so despondent, Shiori?*

It didn't have to do with Raikama, not really. I had the rest of the summer to find out her secret; I was only in a rush because I was bored.

"My brothers taught me to swim in this lake," I finally replied. "We'd laugh so loudly we'd scare the ducks away. Andahai would pretend to be an octopus and attack us if we couldn't swim fast enough. I miss those times. I don't want us all to marry, to grow up and grow apart."

My brothers hadn't so much as asked for me this summer.

Andahai and Benkai were always in hushed meetings with Father and generals and ambassadors, Wandei was immersed in his books, Yotan was popular in court and constantly out with his friends, and Reiji and Hasho were currently engaged in a chess rivalry that allowed time for nothing else.

As I pulled my feet out of the lake, the wind pushed the current toward me. It was growing stronger, a sign that autumn was drawing near. I raised my arms, basking in the rush of cool air as it slipped into my sleeves.

No matter how many joyful memories I conjured up, no matter how loudly I shouted, I could not get the wind to listen.

How about that? Kiki suggested, pointing her wing at something floating in the lake. *Why don't you tell the wind to blow it toward you?*

I squinted. What could that be, glittering under a raft of moss and seaweed?

I scrambled along the shore and grabbed the longest branch I could find. Then I fished out the last thing I expected to see again.

"My sash!" I exclaimed.

It was the one I had worn when I jumped into the lake— the very one Raikama had asked me about. Its golden threads were soaked, the floral pattern was smeared with dirt, and the threads were tangled with moss, but it was otherwise intact.

I wrung it out, my thoughts churning. After spying on Raikama for weeks, I was half convinced Seryu was out of his dragon mind for thinking she was a sorceress. At least I'd find out why she'd wanted this silly sash.

Impulsiveness and curiosity—two of my fairest traits—had me bursting into her sewing room, waving it like a soldier's banner.

"Stepmother!" I said, displaying the damp and crumpled sash. "You wished to see this."

Raikama barely looked up from her embroidery. "Only because it was a gift from Lord Yuji. You've already offended one family, Shiori. Best not to insult another." She knotted her thread, then snipped it with a pair of scissors. "Have the maids clean it along with the rest of your things."

I turned to leave, and I would have thought nothing more of the incident—if not for the shadow that swept Raikama's face. Ever so subtly, a faint but unmistakable ring of gold flickered in her eyes.

The next morning, my sash was missing.

"Her Radiance wanted it," responded Guiya when I asked. She was staring at the floor, which was wise, considering that I was gaping at her in disbelief.

"So you gave it to her?" I exclaimed.

Guiya hunched her shoulders, trembling like a mouse. "N-no, Princess. Her Radiance . . . Her Radiance took it. Perhaps you'd like a red one?" She held up a richly wrapped bundle. "This just arrived from Lord Yuj—"

I dashed off before she could finish. By now, I knew my stepmother's schedule by heart, and she'd be in her garden. Perfect, since I knew all the ways to slip inside unnoticed.

I didn't venture deep; I was too daunted by the snakes. Sometimes I heard Father's chancellors gossiping about them, how the vipers were poisonous, some of them so deadly that a touch could kill. The memory of their scales against my skin still made me shudder.

Carefully, I toed off my slippers and held them under my arm as I waded into the shallowest part of Raikama's pond. There I hid under the rock bridge, crouching so long that my knees quivered, and the fish, thinking I was a lily pad, came to nibble at my toes.

After what felt like an eternity, Raikama arrived.

As soon as the guards closed the garden gate, she removed a ball of scarlet thread from within her robes. It looked almost like a red sun, except for the leaves clinging to its fibers.

I expected her to start talking to the snakes lounging on the footbridge near the wisteria trees, as she always did, or tending to her prized plot of moon orchids—the picture of which she often embroidered on her fans and shawls. Instead, she lifted her skirts to her knees and raised the thread above her head.

"Take me to the Tears of Emuri'en," she commanded.

The ball trembled, emitting a wash of reddish light as it bounced out of her hand into the pond.

Raikama waited at the edge of the pond. Its water had begun spinning furiously, parting to reveal a path at the center and a staircase below. Swiftly my stepmother descended.

I started after her, but serpents hissed, dropping from the trees and rising to block me.

Alarm washed over me, and I gasped, freezing midstep.

They were everywhere, some in dazzling colors I'd never seen before: turquoise and violet and sapphire. Others were black as night with scarlet stripes or ivory with brown speckles. But their fangs were all the same, curved like tiny daggers, their pupils menacing slivers.

They surrounded me, the same way they had all those years ago.

Shiori! Kiki called from the stairs. *If you don't hurry, we'll lose her.*

The water was starting to rush back over the stairs, but I'd still have to cross the snakes lingering on them.

Fear is just a game, Shiori, I reminded myself. *You win by playing.*

I tugged my slippers back on and charged toward the stairs. More snakes dropped from the trees, plopping into the water, but I didn't look back. Darkness caved over me, and I followed the glimmer of light down the stairs until I emerged on the other side.

It had to be magic that brought me out into the woods, far beyond the palace gardens. In fact, I couldn't even see the palace—only the Holy Mountains, so close they obscured the sky. If I was truly in one of the mountain forests, I was far from home indeed. But how I would get back was the least of my concerns.

Kiki tore into the trees, her fragile paper wings dancing in an invisible gust of summer wind. Far ahead, I could see the ball of thread bouncing through the thickets, its brilliant light painting the trees red. I ran as fast as I could, following

Raikama deeper and deeper into the forest—until, abruptly, she stopped.

Kiki bit my hair, pulling me behind a tree.

The ball had come to a dirt hole, full of twigs and leaves. It no longer trembled or glowed.

My stepmother set aside her sandals and removed the brass pin that held her hair in its signature coil. As her raven tresses tumbled down her back, she rubbed her temples. A streak of white hair appeared.

I frowned. That had never been there before. Not on the ageless queen.

Kneeling beside the dirt hole, she rolled up her sleeves and slowly loosened the layers of her robes until her shoulders were bare.

A light shone in her chest, dim at first; then it grew brighter until I had to shield my eyes. In Raikama's heart gleamed a broken orb, fractured in the center, like a moon cleaved in two. It was beautiful regardless, its surface dark as the night sky, yet its light as dazzling as dawn unfolding over the ocean. Mesmerizing to behold.

"That's it," I breathed. "The source of her magic."

Wonderful. Now let's leave, Kiki pleaded. *We've seen enough.*

"Not yet," I whispered, waving her away as I started to climb the tree. I needed to see more.

Water bubbled up from the center of the hole. A minute ago, it had been dry. Where was the water coming from?

I leaned closer, riveted. This *was* no ordinary pool—the

water was opaque and held no reflection. Could it truly be the Tears of Emuri'en—the tears that the goddess of fate was said to have shed as she fell from the heavens to earth? The gods had destroyed all such pools.

My golden sash lay over Raikama's arm, its slender cord undone. As she steeped it in the water, she spoke in a language I did not recognize. It was more rhythmic, the words lilting and round. Her voice sounded gentler, and for some reason, that made goose bumps rise on my skin.

"Do you understand what she's saying?" I whispered to Kiki.

It sounds like a spell. A perilous one. Kiki stabbed her beak at my cheek when I leaned closer. *Careful, Shiori! Gods, didn't anyone teach you that it's always the curious bird that gets eaten by the fox?* She moaned, *If only I'd been born to a more sensible sorceress.*

"Since when are you so worried about your life-span?" I retorted. "No fox will want you—you're made of paper."

Yes, but if you die, I die. So of course I worry about you. You'd dive into a fire if it meant getting answers.

"I see. You only care about me out of self-interest."

Naturally. A bird like me doesn't form unnecessary attachments.

Ignoring her, I squinted at the Tears of Emuri'en. Within the pool, ribbons of crimson streamed out of my sash—like blood. As they wove through Raikama's fingers, my stepmother's voice changed. Venom dripped from it, her tone harsh and deep.

"Andahai," she rasped.

Before my eyes, the ribbons in the water took on the shape of the crown prince, so lifelike that I flinched. I pursed my lips, suddenly missing my brothers—even Andahai. He could be dull and pigheaded, but if he ruled Kiata with half the care he gave us six siblings, our country would see its brightest days yet.

Then, as Raikama spoke their names, the rest of my brothers appeared one by one in the pool.

"Benkai." Tall and graceful, the brother I admired the most. He was the most patient of us, but that didn't mean he always listened.

"Reiji." He rarely smiled, and he spoke without thinking, not caring if his words stung. But if Hasho could put up with him, he couldn't be all bad.

The waters continued to swirl, and I tried to shake myself out of whatever enchantment Raikama must be casting, but she had not finished. There were still four children left.

"Yotan." The brother I counted on to say my bowl was half-full, not half-empty. The brother who put cicada husks on my pillow to make me scream and spiked my tea with enough chili to make me cry, but who always made me laugh.

"Wandei." The quiet one, who loved books more than people and would bury himself in thought if Yotan didn't remind him to eat and sleep. His inventions were a sort of magic in themselves.

"Hasho." My confidant. The gentlest, though he liked to tease me. Who even the birds and butterflies trusted.

Finally came my name.

"Shiori."

I lurched out of my daze. The ribbons turned black, clouding the water in the pool. Serpents—seven of them, more shadow than flesh—surfaced and swam to Raikama.

Kiki shot back into my sleeve. *Now, Shiori. We need to leave. Now!*

I heard my bird's warning, but I couldn't move. I was transfixed by the snakes.

They slithered up my stepmother, climbing her back and draping themselves over her neck.

Shiori, they whispered. *Die, Shiori!*

I had seen and heard enough. I scooted back off the tree branch and was beginning to scuttle down when I saw my stepmother's profile. Her eyes were yellow as a serpent's, and in place of her smooth skin, scales glistened—as white as winter's first snow.

I gasped and, missing a hold, fell off the tree with a hard thud.

Raikama spun.

"Who's there?" she called, covering her heart with her hand. "Show yourself."

Demons take me! I dove into the bushes. The leaves browned and wilted under my fingers, fear and nervousness making me unable to control my own magic.

I dared not even breathe, but my heart pulsed wildly in my chest. Eternal Courts, I prayed that it would not give me away.

"Show yourself!" Raikama said again, standing. I hardly recognized her, with her hair swirling about her in an inky mass and her tongue flicking out of her mouth, thin and forked. My stepmother was no sorceress; she was a monster!

In horror, I peeled away from my hiding place and began racing back. But an endless forest surrounded me. I didn't know which way was home.

It didn't matter. So long as Raikama didn't find me—

Someone grabbed my arm from behind.

"Shiori," my stepmother hissed.

I was too shocked to struggle. The shadowy serpents over her shoulder had vanished. Her face had gone back to normal, too, but the ivory gleam of her scales still spun in my memory, making me dizzy.

Kiki flew, slapping my stepmother with her wings, but Raikama batted her away with a powerful swing.

"Kiki!" I cried as my bird disappeared from view.

"You shouldn't be here," Raikama said angrily. "Look at me when I speak to you, Shiori."

I glanced up into her eyes. They glowed in a way I'd never seen before. Luminous and gold, so mesmerizing I could not look away.

"Forget everything you've seen here. You are exhausted— it was all a dream."

A wave of fatigue washed over me. My mouth stretched into a yawn, my vision swimming in and out—then I stopped. Blinked. I wasn't tired. And I hadn't forgotten why I was here.

My stepmother's lips dipped into a scowl. She grabbed my shoulder. "Forget everything you've seen," she repeated, her voice deep and sonorous. The water in the pool behind us rippled as she spoke. "Forget it and never speak of it."

"No," I whispered. "No, let me go. Let me go!"

I wrestled out of her hold, managing only a few steps

before she caught me again. Her strength, like her speed, shocked me. She easily lifted me off my feet, her long nails wrapping around my sleeves.

She held me up until my brown eyes were level with her yellow ones, and I screamed.

Kiki returned, diving to bite my stepmother's cheek. A scarlet gash pierced Raikama's skin. As she yelled out, I scrambled away, grabbing the ball of thread from her hand at the last second.

I ran from the forest. I'd seen all I needed to.

My father had married a demon.

CHAPTER SEVEN

I threw the thread high into the air and cried, "Take me home!"

At my command, the ball gave a great shudder and leapt away. I rushed after it, hardly able to blink for fear that I would lose sight of it cutting through the forest. Sweat drenched my temples, the summer heat clinging to my skin, but I didn't dare slow down.

I had to warn my brothers. Had to warn Father.

Finally I reemerged from my stepmother's garden, and I hurried into the palace.

What a sight I was. Leaves entwined in my hair, mud caking the embroidered hem of my robes. I'd even lost one of my slippers. The guards gawked, baffled by my dishevelment.

Nothing could stop me.

I barreled into Hasho's chambers, gasping, "She's—a—demon." I leaned against the wall, trying to catch my breath. "We've got to tell Father."

Hasho shot to his feet. He wasn't alone; Reiji and the twins were there too, engaged in a game of chess.

"Slow down. What are you talking about?"

"Raikama!" I gulped a lungful of air. "I saw her transform. She knows . . . she knows I was there."

Kiki burst out of my sleeve, and Reiji nearly overturned the chessboard.

"What is that?" he exclaimed.

"We have to tell Father," I repeated, ignoring him. "Where are Andahai and Benkai?"

"Here," answered Andahai. All of our rooms were connected, and he stood between Hasho's and Reiji's chambers, wearing a stern expression.

"What's with the commotion, Shiori?" He frowned when he saw my robes. "Did you fall into the lake again?"

I pushed past Andahai, turning to Benkai instead. He'd listen. He had to.

"She has a secret exit in her garden," I said, "and it leads to a . . . a place in the Holy Mountains of Fortitude. If we follow this ball, it'll take us there—"

My six brothers all wore identical expressions: creased brows, tucked chins, and pitying eyes. They wanted to believe me, but they didn't. Of course they didn't. I sounded like a raving fool.

"You . . . you don't believe me."

Reiji scoffed. "First you see a dragon, and now our stepmother is a demon?"

"It's true!"

"I know you don't want to get married, but surely there are better ways for you to get everyone's attention."

Benkai shot Reiji a warning look, then turned to me. "After dinner, Sister," he said kindly. "After dinner, we'll come with you to follow this ball of yarn, all right?"

"It'll be too late!"

"Shiori, Shiori," Hasho said, holding my shoulders. "You're trembling."

I twisted out of his hold, still reeling. "Father married a demon. We have to tell him. We have to—"

My tongue failed me. Raikama had appeared at the door. Gone was her serpent face, the white streak in her hair. Even her skirts were no longer wet.

But her presence was different: more powerful, more commanding. And the gash my bird had given her had healed in less than an hour!

As Kiki rushed back into my sleeve, my brothers immediately swept into the appropriate bows—but I lurched for the closest sword rack. Hasho blocked me and gripped my arm so hard I cringed.

Raikama's eyes bored into mine. "I would like to speak with Shiori."

"Perhaps after dinner, Stepmother," replied Benkai. His shoulders had tensed and broadened, but although he was the tallest of my brothers, with at least a head over Raikama, somehow she towered over him. "We're already late to—"

"The six of you will leave first."

To my surprise, my brothers did not argue. Hasho let go of my arm, and he started for the door.

I grabbed a jade-hilted sword and chased my brothers, blocking Yotan and Wandei. "No, stay!"

The twins halted their steps, looking confused.

"Shiori," rang my stepmother's voice. "Drop the sword."

It fell from my hand, and I gasped. I couldn't move. My body was rebelling against my every command, rooting my feet to the ground and my arms to my side.

Fight, Shiori! Kiki cried, biting my hand from inside my sleeve. *You must fight!*

Raikama touched my shoulder. "Look at you. You're hardly in any shape to come to dinner. Go quickly now and change. I will make up an excuse for your father."

Her eyes flickered yellow, and a rush of cold tingled over my mind and body. Suddenly my anger at her was dulled, my memories of what I'd seen in her garden no more than a haze, a dream. All I wanted to do was obey, to go to my room and change so I'd be on time for dinner.

I'd wear one of my red robes. Red was my favorite color, and Father always said I looked best in it. Or maybe I'd wear that red sash Guiya had mentioned.

I jerked, my hands balling into fists. Raikama was doing it again. She was trying to enchant me!

I shoved Hasho as hard as I could, waking him, then I tugged at Benkai's and Andahai's arms, shouting to my brothers, "Don't look into her eyes! She's trying to control us! She—"

"Enough."

The word cut into the air like a knife. The slew of accusations died in my throat, as if someone had stoppered it with a cork.

Benkai grabbed the sword I'd dropped and pointed the blade at Raikama.

My stepmother barely flinched. Her eyes glowed yellow, the way they had when we'd been alone in the woods. "I would advise putting down your sword," she said softly.

Benkai's arms trembled, muscles straining, and his face drained of color. Something drove him to lower his weapon against his will.

"Demon!" Andahai cried, brandishing his sword at Raikama. "Yield!"

Andahai, too, did not make it even one step before he suddenly dropped his weapon. The rest of my brothers launched themselves at her, but they might as well have attacked the air. For all it took was a lift of her chin, and none of them could move.

"Run, Shiori!" Hasho managed to rasp. "Send for Father!"

I flew across the room, my hands groping at the doors, but they would not budge. "Guards!" I screamed, but the windows blew open, and a blast of wind rushed inside, swallowing my cry.

I staggered, the wind pushing me back until I slammed against Hasho's dresser. As I crumpled, pain bursting inside me, a nightmare unfurled.

"Sons of my husband, I do not wish to harm you," Raikama said quietly to my brothers, "but your sister has discovered the secret I hide most dearly, and I can see there is no way to cleanse the memories from your mind. You leave me no choice. It is for all our sakes that I must do this."

The light in her chest hummed and shone even brighter than before, fanning out across the room until it enveloped my brothers.

They began to change. Their throats first—so they couldn't scream. Black feathers coated their necks, stretching up to the long beaks sprouting from their noses and lips. I heard bones break and muscles rip as their arms lengthened into glossy white wings, and their legs thinned, becoming knobbed like stalks of bamboo. Their eyes rounded and deepened, and, last, six crimson crowns festooned the tops of their heads.

Cranes, my brothers had turned into cranes!

They flew wildly about me. Screaming, I picked up a fallen sword and charged at Raikama.

She whirled, dodging with a quick side step before she seized my wrist. With the same tremendous strength she'd wielded in the forest, she lifted me. My sword clattered to the ground.

"Bring them back!" I spat, struggling against her. "Bring them back, you monster!"

I might as well have pleaded with Sharima'en the Undertaker, but in my madness I thought I saw a glimmer of pity in her eyes, an ember of feeling.

I was wrong.

"*Monster,*" my stepmother repeated softly. Lethally. The scar on her face glimmered in the lantern light. "They called me that once. They called me many worse things."

As I twisted and squirmed, her perfect lips curved into a

grimace. "Of all the people I met in this new life, I thought you might be the one to understand. But I was wrong, Shiori." She lifted me high. "Now you must go."

Before she could cast her curse, my brothers swooped. In a fury of sharp beaks and powerful white wings, they attacked our stepmother. Furniture flew, and amidst the chaos, I kicked Raikama in the chest and knocked myself free.

I fled to my room, slamming the door behind me. I had to stop her. But how? Not with my zither or embroidery needles, and certainly not with my calligraphy brushes.

My mousy maid was there, cowering in the corner. I'd never been so happy to see anyone in my life. "Guiya," I shouted, practically shoving her out the door. "Run, tell my father. Tell him Raikama is—"

Guiya's hands were behind her back, as if she was hiding something. A dagger, I sorely hoped. When she saw me, she lurched forward. "Shiori'anma—"

That was as far as she got. Suddenly her throat constricted and her eyes turned white, rolling back until her body went slack. Guiya slumped to the ground, unconscious.

Demons of Tambu! I had but seconds until Raikama appeared at the door.

I tried to shake Guiya awake. No luck. No dagger on her either. Only a handful of what looked like black sand— probably charcoal for tinting my hair and lashes. Useless.

I whirled, scrambling deeper into my bedroom. On my desk were the paper cranes I'd folded. Hundreds of them. I hurled them into the air. "Come alive, and help my brothers."

At my command, their pointed beaks lifted and their

paper wings flapped. Within seconds, they rocketed behind Kiki.

They surrounded Raikama at the doorway, but they might as well have been gnats. She raised an arm, and a brilliant light flashed from her heart—then all at once my birds dropped, as lifeless as a pile of stones.

Only Kiki still flew. She hid behind my hair, her wings trembling so violently I could practically hear the little bird's fear.

"So you do have some magic in you," my stepmother said, cornering me. "This would have been easier if you didn't."

Hate gave me strength. I threw the walnut bowl from Seryu at her head, hurling it harder than I had anything before in my life.

But Raikama caught it in one hand. She held it on her palm, and a glow pooled within it, shadowy snakes crawling over the brim and wrapping themselves around my neck.

Muscle by muscle, I stiffened, immobilized by the snakes squeezing me tighter and tighter, until not even a wheeze could escape my lips.

"Stop," I gasped. "Let . . . them . . . go. . . ."

"You wish to speak?" My stepmother's yellow eyes glowed. "Then be wary of what you say. For so long as this bowl rests on your head, with every sound that passes your lips, one of your brothers shall die."

Raikama raised my chin so our eyes met. I expected her to laugh at how helpless I looked, but her expression was unreadable.

"As of now, your past is no more. You will neither speak nor write of it. No one shall know you."

She set the bowl upon my head. As the wooden sides fell over my eyes and nose, I opened my mouth to scream, but her curse arrived faster than my voice, and a world of blackness folded upon me.

CHAPTER EIGHT

I woke facing the empty sky, my back against crisp green earth. Tall bunches of grass brushed against my cheeks and ankles, and the wind carried a bitter chill that was twining its way into my bones.

I pulled myself up, breathing hard.

This wasn't home. I was on the top of a hill, no palace in sight, and in place of Gindara was the sea. I could see it from every direction, the gray water lapping the shore.

Raikama had stranded me on an island. One, from the looks of it, in the Far North. The moon was as large as my fist and still shone in the morning sky.

Anger swelled in my chest, but I balled my fists, pushing it away. I'd be angry later. Right now, I needed to get out of here . . . I needed to find my brothers and return home. I scanned the landscape below, noticing specks of rusted red and brown along the shore: fishing boats—a faint promise of civilization.

I hiked up my tattered skirts and scrambled down the hill.

Before long, I heard horse hooves stuttering against a dirt road.

What luck! I thought, racing in their direction. I flailed my arms, and started to open my mouth to shout out to them. I'd simply tell them I was Princess Shiori, the emperor's daughter. They would be more than pleased to bring me home.

But the coarse laughter of men—and the flashes of steel blades carelessly wielded in their hands—stopped me midstep.

"Hey, you!" one yelled, spotting me from afar. "Girl with the hat—halt!"

Fear swooped in my gut. I'd heard plenty of stories about the perils of Kiata's roads, bandits being the most dangerous of all.

I disappeared into the bushes. A hundred steps in, I shed my outer robe so I could move faster. My teeth chattering from the cold, I ran, following the pallid rising sun above me, so small and white it looked nothing like the sun I was used to seeing at home.

When the hill was far behind, and but a mound against the gray-blue sea, I slowed to catch my breath. The bandits hadn't followed, thank the Eternal Courts, and I'd come across a flooded rice field. A village couldn't be far off.

Searching for a path, I raised my hand to shield my eyes from the sun. But when my fingers brushed against wood instead of skin, the bandit's words came thundering back to me.

Girl with the hat, he had yelled.

My heart gave a lurch. There *was* something on my head.

Not a hat. A bowl, wooden and unyielding. Try as I might, I could not take it off. Was this Raikama's magic?

I knelt by my reflection in a shallow pool, staring at myself. The bowl was deep, covering my eyes and my nose—yet I could see perfectly, as if the wood were no more substantial than a shadow. That wasn't the case for my reflection: no matter what angle I tilted my face, the bowl covered my eyes and obscured everything above my lips.

A hard lump formed in my throat as the burning heat in my chest returned.

Father wouldn't recognize me like this. No one would.

I'll write to him, I told myself determinedly. The moment I reached the nearest village, I would send a letter telling Father where I was. We'd find my brothers, and someone— some enchanter somewhere—had to have the power to undo what my stepmother had done.

Then, against the gray clouds gathering in the east, six birds soared across the sky. My heart leapt to my throat as I remembered my stepmother's curse.

"Brothers!" I yelled. The word tasted like ash, but I didn't stop to wonder why. I cut across the rice field toward the sea, flailing my arms.

The birds flew on.

No, no, no. They had to see me! They couldn't go.

"Come back! Brothers!"

Panicking, I tore off my slipper and flung it at them. My shoe arced into the air, a blur of bright pink barely higher than the trees around me. It had no chance of scraping the sky.

"BROTHERS!" I pleaded one last time. "Please!"

At last the birds stopped. I dared hope that they'd seen me.

No. They were falling. Plummeting. Flightless, as if someone had clipped their wings. It happened so fast all I could do was watch, horror twisting in my belly.

I rushed to the beach, almost screaming when I came upon the six birds lying lifeless in the sand. But my breath caught before I could make a sound: six ghostly serpents, each as transparent and dark as a shadow, glided out from beneath the dead birds' wings. The serpents reared up, rising to the height of my waist and meeting me with their ominous yellow eyes.

"This is your only warning," they hissed. "Next time, it will be your brothers who perish—one for each sound you make."

Their work done, they faded into oblivion.

And to my horror and relief, I saw that the birds weren't cranes at all, but swans. They weren't my brothers, but they were dead—because of me.

Six swans, one for each of the six words I had spoken.

For so long as this bowl rests on your head, with every sound that passes your lips, one of your brothers shall die, my stepmother had said.

A well of grief opened in my throat as I suddenly understood Raikama's curse.

I wanted to shout. To yell. To cry. To show myself that it wasn't true. That it was a terrible, terrible mistake. But the six dead swans, their eyes black and glassy, their long white necks twisted and bruised, assured me it was not so.

I crumpled to my knees, a silent sob burning in my lungs.

My stepmother had broken me. She'd cast me away from my brothers, my family, my home. Even from myself.

Tears trickled down my cheeks. I wept until it hurt to breathe, and my eyes were so swollen I could not tell the sky from the sea. I didn't know how long I sat there, rocking myself from side to side, but as the tide began to rise, I finally did too.

Wits, Shiori, I told myself, wiping my cheeks dry with my sleeve. *Crying will do you no good. Languishing out here, despairing over what's happened, is exactly what Raikama wants.*

She wanted me to suffer, maybe even to die.

You can't break the curse if you're dead. You'll certainly die if you spend all day out here, wallowing about like some self-pitying fool.

Wits, Shiori, I repeated. I needed food. I needed shelter and money. All things I'd never had to worry about before.

I fumbled at my waistband, at my neck and my wrists and my long fluted sleeves.

There was nothing. No coral necklace, no jade pendant, no bracelet strung of pearls. Not a single coin or even an embroidered fan I could pawn off.

For the first time, I regretted not letting my servants deck me with jewels or adorn my hair with gold pins and silken flowers.

I searched all my pockets, even the ones inside my innermost robe. Nothing.

Then, out of the last pocket, something came fluttering.

Kiki eased herself out of the fabric, bending her neck and wings to smooth out their wrinkles. She landed on my lap, her paper face somehow expressing concern.

Kiki! I cried in my thoughts.

She heard me, and she opened a wing to stroke the flesh of my palm. That simple caress was enough to bring tears to my eyes again, this time with relief. I wasn't alone.

I cupped her in my hands and pressed her against my cheek.

I can't speak, I told her. Even my thoughts sounded wretched. *My words . . . they bring death . . . they killed the swans.*

My paper bird was quiet for a moment. Then she said, surprisingly gently, *What are words but silly sounds that tire the tongue? You don't need them to find your brothers. You have me, and you won't be alone, not as long as we search together. No more tears until we find them, all right?*

Kiki's promise moved me. I hadn't expected so much from my bird, and I held her against me, keeping her safe as the waves crashed around us.

"Find the light that makes your lantern shine," Mama would say. Now, more than ever, Kiki was that light.

All right, I agreed.

By the way, Kiki said, settling on my palm, *I think those bandits back there were actually fishermen.*

Why didn't you say anything?

I was stuck in your pocket.

At that, I smiled. A little bit of my old strength returned.

Together, we found Tianyi Village, the only village on this island. With my chin high and nose to the sky, I walked the streets with the air and dignity of a princess. But no one cared how daintily I walked, how gracefully I gestured, or how proudly I could move my lips without speaking. All they saw was my torn and muddied dress, my dirty feet, the odd bowl on my head. All they understood was that I could not speak. And so they spurned my silent entreaties and turned me away.

It's just a matter of time before Father finds me, I reminded myself grimly. Gods, I hoped Guiya was still alive. She *had* to have heard my brothers fighting against Raikama—she would tell the guards, who would tell the emperor, and Father would force Raikama to undo the curse. All I had to do was survive until then.

Except how did one survive on nothing? I tried begging, but no one would help a strange girl with a wooden bowl stuck on her head. I tried writing in the dirt for food, but no one could read. Children gathered to mock me, and some villagers threw stones, calling me a demon, but I couldn't speak to defend myself or look them in the eye. After three days of being ignored and spat on, of sleeping outside with nothing but rainwater to fill my belly, my hopes deflated.

Hunger made me desperate. Desperation made me bold.

When the next dawn arrived, I sneaked out to the gray-watered bay, where all the fishermen docked their vessels, and unknotted the rope to one of the shrimping boats.

I didn't notice a woman's dark profile looming over me—until it was too late.

"No one steals from Mrs. Dainan," she hissed, raising a fishing pole. Before I could react, it came whacking down on the wooden bowl on my head, so hard that my ears rang and the world spun.

I collapsed.

CHAPTER NINE

I scrambled to my senses and tried to get up, but Mrs. Dainan beat the bowl on my head again. "It would have been smarter for you to swim off the island, girl. That bucket's not even fit for catching shrimp."

She pushed me toward the gray waves crashing against the docks, daring me to jump in. When I didn't, she harrumphed and grabbed my chin, studying the sooty hollows of my cheeks. "Just as I thought. No demon would be as pitiful as you."

She threw her apron at me. "You work for me now. Any tricks, and I'll tell the magistrate to cut off your hands for trying to steal my boat. Understand?"

Hunger sharpened in my gut as I bunched up the apron in my hand. It was stained with oil and brown sauce, and dried grains of rice that I could have licked right off the cloth.

Just for a day, I promised myself before I trudged after her. I glanced at the empty sky, imagining six cranes threading through the clouds. *Just for a day.*

I'd soon lose count of how many times that promise was to be broken.

⁓

"Lina! Lina, get over here, you stupid girl!"

Lina. Even after two months, I still wasn't used to the name Mrs. Dainan had given me, but I didn't mind it. It was better than *thief* or *bowlhead* or *demon*—then again, I supposed none of those would have been good for business.

"Lina! I'm waiting."

What Mrs. Dainan lacked in height she made up for in vociferous anger. Even earthquakes couldn't outdo the thunderous power of her ire. She'd been in a bad mood lately; the autumn drafts made her bones ache, and she took the pain out on me.

I only wondered what I'd done this time.

Setting my broom to the side, I approached her, preparing myself for a public rebuke. I bit the inside of my cheek—a painful reminder not to speak.

"Mr. Nasawa ordered a cup of rice wine, not plum wine," Mrs. Dainan rumbled. "This is the third time in an hour you've mixed up orders."

Not true. Mr. Nasawa, a fisherman who regularly came to Sparrow Inn, had most definitely asked for plum wine. I glared at him, but he averted his eyes. As much as he liked causing trouble for me, I suspected he secretly feared me.

"Well?"

A month ago, I would have gritted my teeth and gestured

that she was wrong. Would have ended up with a mark on my cheek and no dinner.

I knew better now. Now I showed my defiance in other ways.

Sorry, I gestured, lowering my head another inch. I was starting to take Mr. Nasawa's cup of plum wine when Mrs. Dainan smacked the side of my head with the heel of her hand.

The bowl sitting on my skull thrummed, sending me staggering back. The cup thumped onto the ground, wine splashing the hem of my skirts.

I gathered my balance as Mrs. Dainan rounded on me, tossing a broom at my face. "Useless girl," she spat. "Clean up the mess."

"Why even bother keeping her?" drawled Mr. Nasawa. "Look at her, with that bowl on her head. I've never seen anything so ill omened."

"Let her be, Mrs. Dainan," one of the other fishermen muttered. "She's a good cook. The best you've had yet."

"Yes, let her get back to work. Old Nasawa did ask for plum wine. Even I heard it!"

Not wishing to quarrel with the customers, I reached for my broom and swept up the shards of the shattered wine cup.

How I went from boat robber to tavern cook was a blur. Even more confounding, it was already midautumn; the browning maple trees outside the inn were a constant reminder of my broken promise.

I swallowed, guilt festering inside me. I hadn't meant to stay for long, but Mrs. Dainan worked me so hard that I collapsed on my cot every night, drained of energy and too tired to figure out a plan to leave. Come morning, the cycle only repeated itself. Besides, where could I go with no money?

You could ask one of the fishermen to lend you a boat, Shiori, said Kiki, reading my thoughts. *Many of them like you.*

She fluttered inside my pocket. I wished I could let her out, but I couldn't leave her alone in my room, not when Mrs. Dainan made a point of searching it every few days unannounced.

Kiki looked for my brothers each day, but she'd had no success, not even in getting word of Father. Tianyi Village was so far from the mainland that little news made it here.

I pushed my way into the kitchen to check on the large pot simmering on the stove.

Preparing the morning soup was my main task at Sparrow Inn, the reason Mrs. Dainan wouldn't cast me out. My soup was good for business.

It was my mother's recipe. She died when I was three, but I had carried the warmth and flavor of the soup deep within me—the memory of poking into the pot for chunks of meat and picking out combs of fish bones, of decking my spoon with a bracelet of onions and savoring the soft crunch of the radishes and the orange splashes of carrot. Most of all, I remembered the way she would sing little songs she made up as we worked in the kitchen.

Channari was a girl who lived by the sea,
who kept the fire with a spoon and pot.
Stir, stir, a soup for lovely skin.

Simmer, simmer, a stew for thick black hair.
But what did she make for a happy smile?
Cakes, cakes, with sweet beans and sugarcane.

After she died, I still sneaked into the kitchen to help the cooks make Mama's soup. It was the only dish they allowed me to prepare, probably out of pity, and I became good at it. It was what my brothers requested whenever they weren't feeling well, and despite them being strong, sturdy boys who rarely fell ill, there *were* six of them. I took every bruised ego and scraped knee as an opportunity to hone Mama's recipe.

Whenever I made it, I felt close to Mama—and happy. *Almost* happy, which was all I could ask for these days. It was the only time I forgot about the wretched bowl on my head or that I had been cursed into silence. Or that my brothers were out in the world somewhere, their spirits trapped in the form of cranes, lost to me.

Besides, if I didn't cook, then Mrs. Dainan did. Her recipes tasted like paper, bland and practically inedible. She would have served stew with donkey dung if it meant saving money, but most of the time she reboiled the leftover bones for a week, throwing in half-rotting vegetables and, I suspected, dishwater.

Naturally, she was furious when she caught me adding extra carrots to the soup and seasoning the rice with the broth of fish bones. But the fishermen took note of how the meals suddenly tasted better than before, and how the rice was fluffy instead of soggy, and how the vegetables crunched under their teeth and freshened their breath. Business swelled, and Mrs. Dainan stopped lecturing me about squandering her ingredients. Instead, she raised prices.

I didn't like her, but it wasn't easy for a widow to run her own business. Her struggles showed in the deep grooves on her face, which made her look far older than she must have been. She wasn't kind, but in her own way, she protected me—at least from her customers.

A soldier grabbed my skirts as I emerged from the kitchen, pulling me toward him. "What's under the bowl on your head?"

I swung my broom into his face. *Don't touch me.*

"Why, you—" He rose angrily, but he was so drunk that he swayed, unable to keep his balance. He tried to throw his wine at me, but he missed. "Demon! Demon!"

Mrs. Dainan spoke up. "Leave her alone. My last girl was more of a demon than this little shrimp. She's not very bright, but she can cook. You enjoyed your soup this morning, didn't you?"

"Then why the bowl?" the soldier slurred.

"She's just ugly, is all," Mr. Nasawa said. "So hideous her mother glued it to her head to spare the rest of us from seeing her ugly face."

Mrs. Dainan, Mr. Nasawa, and the soldier shared a laugh, and I stopped sweeping, my vision blurring with anger. My stepmother had done this, not my mother. It sickened me to think a monster like Raikama was still married to Father, still Kiata's honored imperial consort. My nails dug into the broom handle.

There had been more men like this soldier at Sparrow Inn

lately. Drunk and belligerent, traveling through Tianyi Village on their way to defend the North. Every time a new one passed through, a wave of unease settled over me. Gods, I prayed Father was not preparing us for war.

As if Mrs. Dainan could sense my distraction, she turned sharply, wagging a bony finger at me.

"Stop eavesdropping, Lina," she barked. "We're low on firewood. Go get some."

I grabbed my cloak by the door and exchanged my broom for an ax.

Still fuming, I planted myself in front of the nearest woodpile. The chore used to tire me after only a few swings; the ax felt so heavy it took two arms to lift. Now I hefted it easily in one hand.

With every swing, I let out my anger.

It was no coincidence that Raikama had left me in the most isolated part of Kiata, with no way of getting home.

Had she always used her magic to make us do what she wanted? Was that how she had charmed Father into marrying her? Her, a foreign woman from a faraway land, with no money or title to her name.

Part of me wanted to think it was so, but I knew it wasn't.

I would have noticed her eyes when she summoned her power, yellow as the summer chrysanthemums that bloomed in our gardens. I would have noticed the stone in her heart, shimmering like obsidian in the moonlight.

Most of all, I would have noticed her face. Her true face. Ridged and hideous, with ivory scales—like a snake's.

The wind lashed at the bowl on my head, mocking me.

There was nothing I could do. I was stranded, alone, with no voice, no face, and no magic.

A hundred times, I'd tried making the dead grass under my shoes green again, tried making the rotten tangerines Mrs. Dainan bought from the market plump and juicy again. Tried folding birds and fish and monkeys out of whatever I could get my hands on—to bring them to life. Once, it had been as simple as a word, a thought, a wish. Every day I tried and tried again, refusing to give up.

But whatever magic I'd had was gone. Little more than a dream.

One last swing, and the wood cracked and groaned. I stepped out of the way as the log split in two, and wiped sweat from my brow.

Maybe magic wasn't the answer. Maybe I had to find another way.

I raised my ax to the next round of wood and gathered my strength.

Curled up on a straw pallet, with Kiki in the crook of my arm, I dreamt of my brothers. Every night I saw them: Andahai, Benkai, Reiji, Wandei, Yotan, and Hasho. Six cranes with crimson crowns.

Sometimes I called out to them, and they fell, one by one, in a flash of red—with a serpent's bite on their black-feathered throats. I would wake drenched in sweat, my body violently shaking. Other times I dreamt they were searching for me, flying over distant lands I did not recognize. Those dreams had a vivid clarity, and I prayed they were visions. That my brothers were alive and safe and hadn't forgotten themselves—or me.

Tonight I dreamt of Raikama.

The trees in our garden had turned a burnished shade of yellow, their leaves singed with a blush of red.

Day after day, my brothers returned to the palace. They flew, squawking cries that sounded vaguely like my name.

"Shiori! Shiori!"

It was against the law to kill a crane on imperial grounds, but the soldiers grew so alarmed by their daily appearance that they shot pebbles at the birds when they tried to land in the gardens. Yet my brothers were not deterred.

Finally, one day, the cries grew so loud that my father himself came to view the six cranes soaring above his palace.

"Strange," he mused. "Usually the cranes only visit in the winter. Come look." My stepmother joined him. "They're different from the birds that ordinarily visit."

"Different? Husband, you can read the faces of birds now?"

"No." My father made a sad little laugh. "But

their eyes . . . they almost look human. So doleful. Almost as if I've seen them before . . ."

At that, my stepmother stiffened. "They're turning violent," she replied. "The largest one attacked a guard today, and another flew into my garden. They're wild cranes. Have the guards shoot them if they come again."

Before my father could protest, the flecks of gold in my stepmother's eyes shimmered, and his face went slack. He nodded mutely, as if thinking, Of course you're right.

The next time my brothers came searching for me, she made them forget too. "Fly south," she said. "Forget your sister, and join the others of your kind."

No! *I wanted to scream.* Don't listen to her!

But away the six cranes flew, and I could not tell whether my stepmother's enchantment had touched them or the archers had frightened them off.

When I woke, my back was moist with sweat, and my legs were sore from kicking in my dreams. But my mind was sharper than it'd ever been, as if it had finally pierced the veil of fear Raikama had cast over me, and whittled my sorrow into steel-hard mettle.

I'd languished here long enough. It was time to make Raikama pay for what she had done. It was time to find my brothers.

CHAPTER TEN

Mrs. Dainan was in the kitchen, watering down the rice wine and tossing this afternoon's leftovers into the vegetable stew I'd made for dinner.

"What is it, Lina?" she asked impatiently.

Yesterday's nightmare had bolstered my courage. I outstretched my hand, making a gesture for money.

Mrs. Dainan scoffed. "You've some nerve, asking me for money. Why should I pay a thief?"

I didn't take back my hand. I'd been here for two months, and during that time, I'd more than made back whatever her shrimping boat was worth. She knew it. I knew it.

The handle of her broom came crashing down toward my head. I saw it coming and dodged, but it still hit my shoulder.

Pain shot up my collarbone, and I pressed my lips tight so I wouldn't cry out. The possibility that I might accidentally make a noise frightened me far more than Mrs. Dainan's strikes.

"Thief that you are, you think anyone else will take you

in?" she jeered. "Maybe I should sell you to the brothel. But who would want you with that ridiculous thing on your head?"

I clenched my fists to keep from reacting rashly. I needed to endure this just a while longer. My nails bit into my palms as I calmed myself.

"What do you need money for, anyway? You've no home, no family." She closed the window shutters with a clatter. "Now get out before I—"

Her rebuke was cut off by the sound of hooves cantering to a stop. A horse neighed outside the door.

Mrs. Dainan sniffed and straightened her collar before opening the door. Seconds later, her back curved into a deep bow, her arms fluttering and her voice rising to an obsequious pitch I didn't know she was capable of.

"Ah, welcome. Welcome, sir."

An imperial sentinel had entered the inn.

My breath caught in my throat, and I quickly grabbed Mrs. Dainan's broom, pretending to sweep while I moved closer to eavesdrop.

Historically, sentinels were knights trained to battle demons, aiding the gods in driving them back into the Holy Mountains of Fortitude. Now that such threats had supposedly been put to rest, sentinels protected the imperial family and kept the peace wherever they were stationed. Some trained all their lives for the honor; it was one of the few ways a poor man could change his fortune.

This sentinel was young, but even then he was likely earning at least ten gold makans a year. Enough to have a few silvers in his pockets.

What are you doing, Shiori? I scolded myself. *Fantasizing about robbing a sentinel?*

"Lina!" Mrs. Dainan was yelling. "Where are your manners? Fetch our new guest here some of your delicious soup. And a cup of tea."

I hurried to obey. When I returned, the sentinel was seated in the corner by the window, far from the other guests.

He kept his helmet and armor on, but I would have recognized him as a sentinel even if he'd worn rags like mine. He had the look: the stiff posture, the proud shoulders chiseled from years of rigorous training, the solemn eyes absent of mischief or cunning. I'd met a thousand just like him.

"Are you coming from Iro or Tazheni Fortress?" Mrs. Dainan asked, warming her tone to one that I had never heard before. She made a show of folding the hot towel she set on his table. "Many soldiers have been gathering there. Good for business, but not so good for Kiata, I'd gather."

"I'm passing by."

The sentinel's response was curt, a sign he wanted to be left alone. But Mrs. Dainan chattered on. "Making your way home, then?"

"The emperor has been searching for his children," allowed the sentinel. He wasn't much of a conversationalist. "I was asked to join the inquiry."

The hairs on the back of my neck bristled.

"Ah yes." Mrs. Dainan pretended to sympathize. "The poor princes and princess. Well, we haven't seen them. No news here!"

This the sentinel already seemed to know. He removed a

battered-looking book from his knapsack, opening it to deflect further questions from Mrs. Dainan. Then he tilted his chin at his cup of tea, already empty.

"Lina!" Mrs. Dainan snapped before turning to attend to other customers. "More tea."

I poured quickly, wondering what had led an imperial sentinel to this far island in search of my brothers and me. Was there a way to tell him who I truly was? Could I trust him?

He barely noticed me, his gaze trained on his book as he reached for the soup. While he drank, I peered over his shoulder. He wasn't reading; he was flipping through old drawings in a sketchbook. Some had little notes by them, but I couldn't see—

"It isn't polite to read over people's shoulders," he said, startling me.

He set down his soup and looked up. At the sight of the bowl on my head, curiosity flickered across his face. I was used to the reaction, and braced myself for a slew of questions I couldn't answer.

They didn't come.

"You must be the cook," he said instead, gesturing at his bowl. "Mrs. Dainan wasn't exaggerating about your soup. It's exceptional. The flavor, the fish, even the radishes. Reminds me of home."

I nodded, but I didn't really care what he thought of my soup. I wanted to ask him how my father was, how long he'd been looking for me. Whether my stepmother was still at his side.

Most of all, I wanted to scream, "I'm Princess Shiori!" I

wanted to shake him by the shoulders until he recognized me. I wanted to order him to take me home.

But I did none of those things. I simply bowed my head and retreated to the kitchen.

After all, who would believe that the Princess of Kiata was a serving girl in the middle of Tianyi Village with a wooden bowl stuck to her head, so poor that she could not afford a comb for her tangled hair or straw slippers to walk out in the fields?

No one would. Least of all this sentinel.

You could ask him for money, a desperate voice inside me suggested. *A silver coin is nothing to him. It'd be the world to you.*

I would gladly beg if it meant finding my brothers. Even if it meant shedding what little pride I had left. But begging would be futile. Mrs. Dainan would see me and take the coin away.

That little voice dug deeper. *So you'll rob him.*

Yes. If that was what it took to find my brothers, I would do just about anything.

Dusk took its time to arrive, with shadows falling over the inn and the burnished light of sunset filtering through the cracks in the narrow corridors.

While everyone was eating dinner, I hauled my mop and a bucket up the creaky steps to the guest rooms to wash the floors and change the lantern candles. My last chores before I could take my own meal and end the day with sleep.

I saved the sentinel's room for last. Mrs. Dainan had given him the best chamber, which didn't mean much: only that he had a window that faced the water, a teapot that didn't leak, and a stool that didn't wobble when one sat on it.

Usually I kept the door open while I worked. But tonight I closed it. Firmly.

Gathering my courage, I began to search his room.

The sentinel hadn't brought much. His cupboard was empty, and he'd kept his sword at his side—likely his money too. But I didn't need much. Just enough to buy my passage south.

On the clothing rack hung his bow. It looked expensive, carved of the finest birch and painted a deep, rich blue. But I wasn't foolish enough to try and sell a sentinel's weapons.

His cloak, however, folded up neatly on his cot, was a different story. Sadly, it was more ragged and torn than it'd looked. Holding in a sigh of frustration, I shoved my hands into its pockets. Nothing inside.

I spun, ready to give up—until I saw he'd left behind his knapsack, in a shadowed corner. Unexpected, for a man who seemed so careful.

The contents of the knapsack confirmed my judgment of his character: there was a gourd for water, a copper tinderbox, a bundle of muslin with a fine bone needle and a knot of thread, extra woolen socks, and an excessive number of books. There were volumes on poetry and classical painting and history. And there was the sketchbook I'd seen him with earlier—filled with drawings of mountains and crescent boats on a river, and a little girl with pigtails holding a rabbit. The art was pleasing, but I was here for makans, not paintings.

Then . . . at the bottom . . . something soft . . .

It was the slipper I'd been wearing when Raikama cursed me! The one I'd thrown into the sky after I thought I saw my brothers.

The slipper was little more than a rag, yet I would have recognized it anywhere—the bright pink silk, the finely embroidered cranes, the stains from grass and pebbled road. I held this last remnant of my past and wondered about the sentinel. How did he come across this?

Curious to know more, I dug deeper into his bag. In one of the side pockets were two thin blocks of wood, tied to hold something that was clearly important.

I grabbed it.

My fingers worked quickly, unraveling the cord. Between the blocks were the remains of a scroll. My brow furrowed with confusion. A letter in A'landan?

I opened it wider, wishing I'd paid more attention to my language tutors. Unlike Kiata, whose mainland and many islands had been united for millennia, A'landi was an enormous country divided into dozens of contentious states. Our faiths and traditions overlapped in many ways, but that didn't mean I could read the language fluently.

Thankfully, the message was simple:

Your Excellency,

Four Breaths appears an elegant solution, but I fear it is no longer necessary—

Four Breaths? I frowned. I'd heard of the poison before. Its recipe was a secret among only a handful of the most skilled assassins, highly prized because even its smell was noxious—putting its victim into a deep sleep. When ingested, though, it was deadly.

Someone had once tried to send Raikama a sachet of incense laced with Four Breaths, but she'd detected it almost immediately, earning Father's admiration.

"It smells sweet," she had taught my brothers and me. "Like honey. Assassins will always mask the scent. And they use very small doses, for the poison leaves gold traces on the skin when inhaled, and blackens the lips when drunk."

Thinking back, it was no shock that a snake like Raikama had a talent for discerning poisons. If only we had known.

I returned my attention to the letter. A section of the middle was ripped out, dried blood staining the edges, but another fragment remained at the bottom of the message:

The princess and her brothers are gone from the palace. I will meet you and the Wolf, as agreed, to discuss our next course of action.

A shiver raced down my spine. Who was the Wolf, and what did he want with my brothers and me? I put the letter back between the blocks of wood, certain I had come across some dark scheme to hurt my father—and Kiata. Could that be why Raikama had cursed my brothers and me? To strip my father of his defenses and leave the kingdom vulnerable to attack?

What was this sentinel doing with such a message?

The lanterns trembled. At first I thought it was Kiki, returning from her daily search for my brothers. But then I heard footsteps tromping up the stairs.

I jumped. After throwing the scroll back into the knapsack and quickly blowing out the lantern light, I rushed for the door, but it was too late.

The cold sting of a blade nipped my neck.

I froze, recognizing the sentinel's lean silhouette against the wall.

"*You*," he said, a note of surprise in his voice. He took a harsher tone. "Turn around slowly."

My heart thundered in my ears while I obeyed. If he was a real sentinel, the sword at his side would be sharp enough to cut through bone. And he would be well within his rights to kill me.

He scooped up the scroll, noticing straightaway that someone had tampered with the cord, and shook it at me. "What were you doing with this?"

I met his gaze stonily, my lips thin and closed.

"I won't ask again."

I pointed at my throat, indicating that I couldn't speak. Then I extended my hand, palm out, to explain that I'd been looking for money. I made ocean waves—*money, to leave the island.*

The sentinel lowered the dagger, understanding. "I saw the innkeeper strike you. Is that why you wish to leave?"

All I did was dip my head. He was observant, this one. I'd learned to be too, through my silence.

"I see."

He tucked the scroll back into his knapsack. "It's a good thing I caught you," he said sternly, but the edge in his tone had been sanded off. "Carrying this around would only get you killed."

I tilted my head. *Why is that? What does it say?*

"For someone who can't talk, you have quite a way of making your thoughts known." The sentinel closed his knapsack. "My business is my own, and none of yours."

I studied him. Despite his harsh tone, I wasn't afraid of him. He could have killed me just now for going through his things. But he hadn't. That was enough for me to deduce that the letter wasn't intended for his eyes. He'd told Mrs. Dainan he was looking for the royal children. He must have stumbled upon it during his search.

A dozen questions burned on my tongue. I wanted to ask him for news of home and my father. I wanted to demand that he tell me everything he knew. But first, I needed to tell him who I was.

All of me shook, delirious with elation, as I started to write my name on my palm. Miracles of Ashmiyu'en, finally someone had come who could read!

Then invisible snakes hissed in my ears. *Remember,* they warned. *No one shall know you.*

I stilled, the bowl on my head heavy as stone. Even this far from home, Raikama's curse ensnared me.

The hissing stopped as the sentinel took off his helmet. His dark hair, tangled and unkempt, curled at his ears, and a stray lock fell over the peak in his hairline. It made him look less menacing, less like a hardened warrior and more like a weary traveler in need of a wash and a shave.

He looked up. "Still here? Any other thief would have fled by now." A pause. "I take it you're not much of a burglar, if you've the audacity to rob a sentinel. Your first time?"

I hadn't meant to answer, but my hand shot up, two fingers raised.

"Second time, then." The corner of his mouth lifted, almost into a smile. "You're honest. Not like your mistress."

I wasn't. My brothers had once called me the princess of liars. But I supposed I had changed over the past months. So much had changed.

"Mrs. Dainan called you Lina. Is that your name?"

I hesitated. Shook my head.

"I didn't think so. It's pretty, but somehow it doesn't suit you." I waited for him to explain what he meant, but he didn't. "What *is* your name?"

At the question, I pursed my lips. My fingers made the first stroke of my name before I thought better of it.

"Don't want to tell me? That's all right." His voice had become gentle, almost pleasant. There was a certain musicality to it, every word clear and unhurried.

Unusual, for a sentinel. The ones I'd met in the palace were always gruff, more expressive with their swords than with their words. Then again, what other sentinels did I know who carried around a sketchbook and read poetry?

A silver coin appeared between his knuckles. "Here, take this. Make good use of it."

My eyes flew up. It was more than enough to get me south to find my brothers.

I grasped at it, but the sentinel held it out of reach. "Wait until after breakfast before you leave," he said, as if extracting a promise.

My shoulders tensed, and my face went blank. *Why?*

"Better to begin a journey on a full stomach than an empty one. I'm speaking for myself *and* for you."

I pointed outside. *You're leaving too?*

"Tomorrow morning," he confirmed. "My mission has been something of a failure, but your soup was an unexpected comfort. I swear, there must have been magic in your pot— today was the first time I can remember actually enjoying radishes." Humor twinkled in his earthy eyes. "I would like very much to try them again and make sure it wasn't a fluke."

I couldn't stop myself from returning his grin. What a silly young man, disliking radishes so much he worried my soup might be a fluke. Just thinking about it made me laugh in my head.

Very well. One more breakfast couldn't hurt. But afterward, I too would be off—to find my brothers and break our curse.

Once the coin was in my hand, I fled his room, forgetting my mop and bucket. Excitement bubbled in my chest, and I could hardly keep myself from skipping to my room.

Maybe, just maybe, my luck was starting to turn.

CHAPTER ELEVEN

The next morning, a second sentinel arrived at Sparrow Inn.

I didn't bother going out to greet him. I was stirring my pot of fish soup, inhaling the aroma, and paying extra attention to the radishes.

My toes tapped to an imaginary beat, and I sang in my mind:

Stir, stir, a soup for lovely skin.
Simmer, simmer, a stew for thick black hair.

I was happier than I'd been in weeks.

Sunshine tickled my nose, and I set down my ladle to scratch it. Then I studied my silver makan, watching the light reflect off its edges. I still couldn't believe the sentinel had given it to me. I would have to get his name before he left; Father would reward him for his generosity once I was safely returned home.

After my soup was served, I would leave. By tonight I would be far from this place.

But as I set the soup bowls onto a tray, the new sentinel's blade slammed against the outer wall, and clay tiles shuddered down the roof.

"You dare try to cheat me?" he roared.

"F-f-forgive me, m-my lord," pleaded Mrs. Dainan. "I wasn't thinking."

My song came to a fragile halt, and I glanced outside, peeking through the window shutters to see what was happening.

"Order your guests to come forth into the hall," commanded the sentinel. "I want everyone present."

Who was this man? The mail adorning his arms and legs was a deep blue, their chains so delicately crafted they looked like tiny fish scales. Gold-spun cords held together steel plates of armor around his torso, polished to the point that I could see Mrs. Dainan's reflection in them—she was on her knees, bowing as though her life depended on it. It probably did.

He looks important—like a lord, Kiki observed. *You should go up to him.*

And do what? I retorted. *Didn't you see how he hacked at the wall?*

Mrs. Dainan tried to cheat him because he's rich. I would be upset too. Quick, he's coming inside.

The door swung open, making the soup on my tray shudder. Unable to contain my curiosity, I crept outside the kitchen to see what was happening.

Into the inn the young lord strutted, kicking dirt from his boots as the guests hastily fell to their knees. His eyes were a dark, slippery lacquer, and thick muscles corded his neck as he surveyed the inn. Then, with a grunt, he swept to the other side of the crowd.

He's looking for someone, I realized.

Maybe a bandit? Kiki suggested. *Or a runaway servant?*

I didn't reply. This man was no ordinary sentinel. He was a *high* sentinel, likely the son of one of Father's warlords. Was he here for my brothers and me?

With a sharp breath, I plucked Kiki off my shoulder and hid her in my sleeve. I started to retreat back into the kitchen, but the lord heard me.

He whirled, pressing his blade's edge against my neck. "Show your respect. I will not ask again."

I'd never knelt to anyone except Father. Working in the inn had worn down my pride, but whatever shred I had left refused to let me stoop to this cruel stranger. I looked up at him defiantly, and a flicker of anger passed over the young lord's face.

"Take that bowl off your head."

Without warning, the flat of his sword smacked my head, and I stumbled, dropping my tray. Soup spilled, hot splashes licking my ankles. I bit my lip until the heat passed, but I didn't move to clean the mess.

When I clambered back to my feet, the young lord raised his sword again. Consternation—and the slightest glimmer of fear—lingered in his narrowed eyes. He'd been expecting the bowl on my head to break.

"What manner of demon are you?" he demanded.

"Her name is Lina," rang a familiar voice from behind me, "and she's not a demon."

It was the sentinel who had arrived yesterday. He fixed his gaze firmly on the newcomer. "Have you come all this way to find me, Cousin, or are you here to bully innocent villagers?"

Cousin? I did see a resemblance, now that I knew to look. The two men were of similar height and build, sharing the same proud shoulders and unwavering eyes. But they might as well have been spring and winter, so different were their demeanors.

"It is a sentinel's duty to protect Kiata from demons," the lord bristled. "I know a demon when I see one. Dark energy surrounds her."

"Enough of this superstitious nonsense. There are no demons in Kiata. You are a high sentinel, not a high priest. Put away the sword, Takkan."

Takkan?

Startled, I scrutinized the lord as he sheathed his sword. Emblazoned on his scabbard was a rabbit on a mountain, surrounded by five plum blossoms—and a white full moon.

My stomach somersaulted. Even though I had never paid attention to my heraldry lessons, I knew *that* one. It was the Bushian family crest.

And Takkan . . . Takkan was a name I'd spent years avoiding. The name of the boy I was supposed to marry.

The world rattled into focus. This *was* my chance. All I had to do was show him I was Princess Shiori, the emperor's daughter. Within days, I'd be back in the palace.

But my wits held me still.

I'd met Takkan once. Just once, when we were children. I didn't remember anything about him—what he looked like or sounded like—but everyone always assured me that Lord Bushian's heir was earnest and kind.

Lies. The Takkan I saw before me now did not look kind. His black eyes were hard and cold, and there was something threatening about the way he moved, like a hound on the hunt.

"Not a demon, you say?" said Takkan with a sneer. "Demon worshipper, then. Even worse." He stalked across the room, addressing the villagers. "You've all heard of those so-called priestesses of the Holy Mountains. Keeping their dark magic secret from even the gods. This little mite looks like she could be one of them. What dark spirits could she be hiding under that bowl?"

"That's enough," said the other sentinel, irritation edging his voice. "That's just a tale, and she's just a girl. She meant no harm."

"Just a tale?" Takkan repeated. "Funny of *you* to say so, Cousin."

The sentinel merely glared.

No one knew what business the two had, but the whole inn had gone quiet, and the air was thick with tension. I was barely aware of the dozen villagers around me, all with their faces pressed to the ground as if the walls were crumbling.

I stirred uneasily, shifting my balance from one foot to the other. I was sure Takkan would punish his cousin for his impertinence.

Instead he spun away, as if forgetting me entirely. "Gather your things," Takkan growled to the sentinel. "I'm to take you home."

As Takkan stormed away, I slipped back into the kitchen and scooped up what soup remained in the pot. I poured it into a bowl, almost spilling it once again as I hurried out the kitchen door.

I had not expected Takkan's cousin to be right outside.

He caught me by the arm, steadying me before I crashed into him. "In a rush to leave?"

I wasn't startled, merely nervous for the soup. It was all there was left.

I held out the bowl. *For you.*

"Thank you." He raised it to his lips, then hesitated and lowered the bowl.

"Do you wish to come with us?" he asked, so quietly only the two of us could hear. "We're headed south to Iro. Have you heard of it?" Wistfulness touched his voice. "It is beautiful . . . the most beautiful place in Kiata when it snows."

His offer moved me, but the irony nearly made me laugh. Of course I knew of Iro—the prefecture of Castle Bushian. I swore my tutors had been bribed to tell me daily of its magnificence. How Iro was surrounded by mountains and the Baiyun River—an oasis in the dismal North. All useless attempts to mollify me about my betrothal.

Yet when the sentinel spoke of its beauty, I believed him. His voice was thick with homesickness—and raw with a wonder that could not be feigned. I almost wanted to see it for myself.

"It isn't far," continued the sentinel, "just past the North Sea Strait, on the mainland. I could find work for you in the castle if you wished. Your life would be easier than it is here."

I shook my head. Much as I liked him, my mission was to find my brothers. Besides, I wanted nothing to do with his cousin Takkan.

Disappointment tugged at the young sentinel's mouth, but he drank the entire bowl of soup. "It was no fluke," he said, chewing deliberately on the radishes.

I took his bowl, assuming he was finished and would leave, but he unknotted a tasseled blue charm from the fan on his belt. On it was a small silver plate with the word *courage*. "If you do find yourself in need of work, show this at the castle gate. The guards will not hesitate to admit you."

He offered me the charm, but I wouldn't take it. It was a thoughtful gift but utterly worthless to me. I reached for his dagger instead—sheathed beside his sword.

"You want that?" Surprise, then mirth, touched the sentinel's warm eyes. "You're a brazen one. All right, keep it. But stay off the roads at night—bandits grow bold, with many of the sentinels away looking for the royal children."

He hesitated, then attached the charm to its hilt before giving it to me. "Try to be careful."

Our fingertips touched, and my heart gave a little skip. I'd never gotten his name.

But when I looked up again to ask, he was already gone. I went to the window, watching his horse until it disappeared down the narrow road beside the sea. Once he was gone, I slid the shutters closed and didn't give the sentinel another thought. There was too much to be done, now that I had the means to leave.

That night, when everyone was asleep, I loaded an empty rice sack with as much as I could carry—some pickled vegetables, salted fish, freshly griddled shrimp. I wished I'd had time to prepare food that would last me the full journey, but I couldn't be choosy.

Come dawn, when Mrs. Dainan woke and discovered there was no soup simmering on the stove, I would be long gone.

CHAPTER TWELVE

I bought a boat from a fisherman in Tianyi Village. He had to think me addle-brained for sailing away on the cusp of winter, but he taught me how to cut the sea with my oars, how to read the wind to navigate south, and how to throw a net to catch fish.

Meanwhile, his wife tucked a blanket and a box of fried fishcakes and boiled eggs into the boat. Their daughter also tied a charm—a little red doll with two beads as eyes—for protection. When I found them, hours later, the unexpected kindness nearly brought me to tears. But I'd promised Kiki no tears, not until I found my brothers.

A few hours before dusk, I left the island at long last, helming a boat barely long enough to fit me lying down, and with one sail that juddered against the wind.

Doesn't look like it'd hold up well against a storm, Kiki said, voicing my worries.

The sky's clear, I replied as I rowed. *There's no storm ahead.*

Winter was my greater concern. The cold chased us south,

a perpetual rime of frost stinging my face. Every night I prayed to the gods, asking them for just two things: that I'd find my brothers, and that I wouldn't freeze to death in my sleep.

I kept close to shore, letting the sail do most of the work. Only when the weather was fair and the winds were strong did I dare row across the North Sea Strait. Dawns blended into dusks, and I spent so much time surrounded by water that I began to dream in blue.

Sometimes I called out to Seryu in my mind, hoping he'd hear me and dramatically leap out of the sea in his dragon form. He could command the currents to stop fighting my boat, or he could make the water a little warmer. But he never appeared, and I soon gave up.

When I wasn't rowing, I kept my hands busy to distract myself from the cold. I didn't have paper, so I folded bits of dried kelp into the shapes of birds, melting wax from my candles to hold them together.

What are you going to do with all those birds? Kiki asked.

I shrugged. *It's something to do.*

Oh, good, said Kiki. *I was worried you thought you could make a wish. You said once you'd wish me into a real crane. I'd rather stay made of paper, thank you.*

Why is that?

Look what trouble having a pulse has gotten you into, Shiori. Kiki tsked. *Your betrothed almost gutted you with his sword—can you imagine how painful that would've been?* She shuddered. *You couldn't even tell him who you were.*

Yes, well, I thank the great gods I skipped our ceremony. I shuddered too, but for a different reason.

To think that everyone used to sing Takkan's praises. I *knew* my tutors had been lying to me.

I'd asked Father once, "If Takkan is so wonderful, why doesn't he ever come to court to visit?"

Father had replied that a boy like Bushi'an Takkan wouldn't fare well in Gindara.

Certainly not. He was a brute, just as I'd pictured him, and I finally felt vindicated for hating him all these years. I just couldn't believe Father had been willing to marry me to that barbarian; he really must have been under Raikama's spell.

I'd be perfectly happy if I never heard the name Bushi'an Takkan ever again, I declared to Kiki.

Once I returned home, I would ask Father to annul the engagement.

If I ever returned.

On the ninth sun after I left Tianyi Village, I reached Kiata's mainland.

I was cold and tired and starved, but the sight of land spurred a burst of energy in me, and I plied my oars into the water and forged ahead.

I navigated the shoreline slowly, taking in the craggy mountains bordering the forest, some so high they pierced the clouds. The forest itself was vibrant, for unlike in Tianyi, the trees here had only begun to lose their leaves. They dazzled my eyes with their raiments of emerald and gold and ruby and stretched as far as I could see, seemingly without end. This was the Zhensa—the never-ending forest.

As I rowed closer, a chorus of birds exploded from the trees into the sky.

Have you seen her brothers? Kiki called out to the birds. *They're six cranes with crimson crowns.*

The birds eyed Kiki, surprised that a paper crane spoke to them. Then they chirped their replies.

They say they haven't seen any cranes come this way, Kiki translated.

I turned to Kiki, amazed. *You can speak to them?*

She shrugged by lifting a wing. *How else do you think I've been looking for your brothers all this time?*

While I listened, Kiki called out to the butterflies and the bees, even the mosquitoes that pestered me at night. *Have you seen six cranes with crimson crowns?*

Always the answer was no. And always Kiki would relay the animals' same response: *But we'll look out for them and tell them to find you if we do.*

So it went, until finally, just as dusk was about to fall, we drifted onto the Baiyun River. There, a beaver was working on his dam.

Kiki listened to his grumbles and barks. *He says the river bend is just around the corner and that we should pull ashore there. There's danger ahead.*

Thank you, Mr. Beaver, I gestured, and Kiki communicated my question: *Have you seen six cranes pass by?*

Six cranes? Like those? He looked to the sky.

My breath caught in my throat. Soaring above us were six cranes, their crimson crowns stark against the ashen clouds.

I jumped to my feet, waving my oars. The boat jerked, and as I stumbled to catch my balance, my brothers flew on.

Brothers! I flailed. *Kiki, tell them I'm here!*

But Kiki's attention was elsewhere. The beaver had disappeared, as had the butterflies. A cascade of water surged ahead.

Watch out, Shiori!

My bird rushed in front of me, shouting and shrieking words that I could barely hear. Water pounded my little boat from every direction, the waves tossing us about.

We spun, caught in an unyielding current, rushing forward toward—

A waterfall!

Terror gripped me. There were no boulders to jump onto, no shore within reach. I pulled the rudder as far as it would go to turn my boat around, but the water was too violent, propelling me forward with alarming speed and sweeping away my oars.

We careened toward the falls.

Tell my brothers I'm here! I shouted to Kiki in my mind. *Hurry!*

While my bird vaulted into the sky, the river became a torrent, threatening to engulf me. I gripped the sides of my boat as it rocked against the waves. The little red doll, the fishing net, my blankets—everything was washed away. I would be next.

A veil of mist obscured the waterfall, but I could hear it. I could feel it, too, the cold spray in my face, the strong current that would soon bring me to my end.

The boat teetered on the brink before shooting over the falls. My stomach plummeted, but for a moment, I was flying. I could see a rainbow at the bottom—a beautiful last sight, I supposed, with the water cascading all around.

No, I *was* flying! Strong white wings beat against my back, and flashes of crimson darted in the mist, accompanied by furious squawking.

My brothers—my brothers had come for me!

They threaded their necks under my arms and legs, biting my drenched robes as they lifted me. They soared so fast and so high that my feet dangled over the waterfall and my stomach clenched from the height.

But I wasn't afraid. I cupped Kiki in my hands, knowing she was just as content as I was to see my brothers' wings skim the clouds.

Finally I had found them. And they had found me.

CHAPTER THIRTEEN

We flew until the last glimmers of sunlight sank behind the horizon and darkness stained the sky.

My brothers landed before a cave molded into the mountains, marked by a narrow ledge under a canopy of branches and leaves. Moonlight crept over the forest, and as it touched my brothers' crimson crowns, one by one they became human again.

It was not an elegant transformation. I waited in the corner, biting down on my lip as my brothers' limbs stretched and their muscles strained until all six crumpled in a heap, breathing as though each gasp were their last. But when they finally rose, the tears I'd held back for all these months welled in my eyes. Tears of joy and wonder and relief that we were together again.

An embrace came from every direction, and my brothers began talking at once.

"Where have you been?"

"We've been looking for you for months!"

"We would never have recognized you, Sister. Thank the great gods your little bird screeches like a crow!"

But one question rang louder than the others:

"What is that bowl on your head?"

Andahai shushed everyone with a clap. "Enough, Brothers. I know we're all excited to see Shiori again, and relieved that she's alive and well. But maybe we should give her a chance to speak."

At that, I lowered my head sadly.

"What's the matter, Sister?" Hasho asked. In the two months since I'd seen him, his hair had grown noticeably longer, as it had with my other brothers. Badly shaven beards sprouted from their chins and cheeks, and mysterious scrapes peeked out from their torn sleeves and pants. There were other changes too. Less obvious ones, like the shadows clinging to their broadened frames, the glassy hollowness in their eyes—as if their time as cranes was chipping away at their humanity day by day.

I couldn't evade telling them about my curse any longer.

I tapped my throat, then shook my head.

"What's the matter, Shiori? You . . . you can't speak?"

It wasn't that I *couldn't* speak. I *must not* speak.

But none of my brothers understood, and I didn't know how to explain.

Even as I tried, they weren't paying attention. They were exchanging looks with one another, looks that I could not read. Reiji grunted, his expression darkening. He was the only one who had not welcomed me back.

"Raikama thought of everything," Benkai murmured.

"What about that bowl on your head? Is that also our stepmother's mark?"

Wandei approached, his head tilted methodically. "Surely there has to be a way to take it off." He tried pulling it, gently at first, then with more strength. "It won't budge."

"Let me try," Yotan said, coming up behind his twin to try to yank it off. He scratched the mole on his chin, puzzled. "Have you tried cutting it?"

I exaggerated a nod, dipping the bowl low. I'd tried everything—every knife in Mrs. Dainan's kitchen, and every tool I came across while in Tianyi Village. The bowl was indestructible.

Kiki chose that moment to fly out from behind my hair. Her pale wings flapped crisply, newly dry after our encounter with the waterfall, and my brothers backed away.

All except Hasho.

Kiki landed on his raised hand, resting on the curve of his thumb. She remembered my youngest brother, the only one who'd known my secret.

"Good to see you, Kiki," Hasho said politely. "I hope you've been keeping Shiori out of mischief these last two months."

My brothers had seen Kiki the day our stepmother cursed us all, but they'd never gotten a chance to ask me about her.

"She has no string," Wandei marveled.

I'm not a kite, Kiki said dryly, though my brother couldn't hear.

Reiji's eyes narrowed with distrust. He put on his usual grimace. "It's magic."

"Of course it's magic," said Hasho. There was a warning in his tone. "Don't, Reiji. We've been through this before...."

I frowned at my brothers. What was going on? *Been through what?*

"Magic is forbidden," argued Reiji. "This . . . this paper bird is trouble."

I'll show him trouble! Kiki nipped his nose.

Reiji lunged to catch her, but Kiki was too fast, shooting up and quickly returning to my shoulder.

"It's your fault we're cursed," Reiji accused me, his nostrils flaring with resentment. "If you hadn't angered Raikama, then we would still be at home, still be princes, not forced to spend all our days as birds." He gestured spitefully at his bruises and ragged clothes.

"So you'd rather we never found out that Father married a demon?" Yotan spluttered.

"What good came of it? We didn't get a chance to tell him. Now he's alone, with *her,* and we can't even protect him."

My heart sank. Countless nights I had lain awake, blaming myself for what had happened. I didn't regret following Raikama and learning what she really was. But what if I had run to Father first, and not my brothers? What if I had been more careful, had listened to Kiki and not gotten caught?

What if I had never agreed to learn magic from Seryu?

I could have done a hundred things differently, but it was too late now.

I retreated to the corner, hoping to disappear among the shadows. My brothers, still arguing, barely noticed.

"You think our sister is a demon like our stepmother?"

Yotan exclaimed. "You must be more bird than man, Reiji, for your wits to be so scrambled!"

"Father forbade magic for a reason," Reiji said tightly. "Our *ancestors* forbade magic for a reason."

"So you would have our sister banished?" asked Hasho.

"I would have her tell Father the truth instead of getting us all cursed!"

"Enough." Andahai raised a hand to stop the arguments. In the past, that was all it took for my brothers to listen, but Reiji still sizzled with anger.

"Enough, Reiji," Andahai warned. "Shiori is returned to us, and we go forward together. Understood?"

When Reiji finally nodded, my eldest brother exhaled.

Hasho found me in the corner, and he took my damp cloak, hanging it up and exchanging it for a thin blanket, which he wrapped around my shoulders. "Come outside," he said. "Let Reiji calm down."

We stepped out onto the ledge, and I sucked in the brisk air. Trees rustled below, and crickets chirped against the howling wind. Stars shimmered in the evening sky, but I could no longer see the moon.

"We missed you, Shiori," said Hasho. "Reiji, too, though you must be patient with him. The curse has been . . . difficult, especially on him. He knows you did the right thing. He's just taking longer than the rest of us to accept it."

I looked up at my youngest brother. His eyes were the same gentle ones I had always known, yet now there was a sadness that wasn't there before. Seeing it made my heart sit heavier in my chest.

Hasho's shoulder brushed against mine. "Perhaps there is some good to come of this curse. The six of us are learning to work together. Now that we've found you, it'll only be a matter of time before we defeat Raikama." He gave me a half smile. "We must stay together if we are to break her enchantment."

Hasho and I returned to the cave, and the first thing I did was seek out Reiji. He loitered by the hearth, watching lotus root and chestnuts boil. When he saw me, he started to turn away.

I didn't let his attitude dishearten me. I approached his side, waiting until, little by little, his shoulders—tight with tension—relaxed.

Reiji released a quiet sigh. "I would never want Father to banish you, Sister," he said, "whether or not you have magic."

It wasn't an apology, but it was enough for now.

I touched his hand, showing that I understood.

Hasho broke between us with a smile. "Come, let us celebrate your return. We don't have much by way of food." He gestured at the paltry supplies in the back of the cave— a sack of bruised oranges, a smattering of chestnuts, and a set of broken clay cups. "But beginning tomorrow, we'll have to double our efforts, knowing your hearty appetite."

Already my stomach was grumbling, but the stew boiling in the pot wasn't finished cooking, and I had questions.

I pointed at their arms and legs, then at the moon outside. *You turn into men at night?* I asked, mouthing the question that had been nagging at me since their transformation. I'd been worried they were cranes forever.

Benkai was the one who answered. "Yes, but it isn't the consolation you might think, Shiori. Our minds are sharper than most cranes, but the days blur together when you're a bird, and we don't always remember that we'll transform at dusk. It's especially dangerous when we're flying—several times, we've almost fallen from the sky. . . ."

His voice trailed, and he folded his long arms over his legs.

But when you're men, you can try going home. I drew the character for men and home on my hand. *Father will—*

"Father won't recognize us. No one does. The curse follows us even when we are men. If we try to give any indication of who we really are, we turn back into cranes."

The curse followed me too. I'd tried to write my name to that sentinel, but Raikama's snakes warned me away.

"We have no hope of reaching Father," said Andahai grimly. "The nearer we are to home, the more powerful our stepmother's enchantment becomes. Even if the moon is risen, we won't turn back into men." My brother's tone darkened. "What's more, Raikama has ordered the guards to shoot any cranes that venture too close to the palace."

"Yotan was nearly killed the last time," Reiji said, his jaw tightening. "He took an arrow to his wing."

Remorse rushed over me, and my arms wilted to my sides.

"Don't worry about it," Yotan said quickly. "It was weeks ago, and I'm already much better."

Hasho pushed a bowl of food into my hands. "Eat. It always lifts your spirits."

"Yes, let us celebrate our reunion tonight," said Andahai. "Now that you're back, we won't have to suffer Hasho's cooking anymore."

My youngest brother made a face. "I'll be glad to relinquish the task to you, Shiori. You'll finally have your wish of learning to cook."

Digging into my bowl, I nodded mutely. My brothers had no idea I'd spent half of autumn toiling at Sparrow Inn. I'd changed so much since we were last together. Even in the few hours since our reunion, I could tell the same was true of them.

Dinner was a boiled stew of whatever my brothers had in the back: the lotus root and chestnuts and some unappetizingly brown pieces of meat I could not identify. The skin was slippery and tough—if I hadn't been so famished I probably would have spat it out. But the meat itself wasn't bad. Somewhere between a bird and a fish.

"Frog," Yotan said bluntly as I struggled to chew. He grinned. "We thought you'd prefer it to worms and spiders."

I forced a swallow. *Tasty,* I lied with a smile.

As we ate, Kiki buzzed from brother to brother. She'd already charmed the twins, and once or twice I observed Reiji's grimace fading, though his glower quickly returned when he realized I was looking.

Only Andahai sat alone, rolling an orange in his hands. He had hardly eaten.

What is it? I motioned. It wasn't like him to be so melancholy.

"It's nothing," Benkai answered for him, but I caught my oldest brothers exchanging a glance.

I started to look for a stick to write with in the dirt when Benkai touched my shoulder. "He's simply relieved you're back."

I glanced at Andahai. It'd been years since I had seen my oldest brother in anything but his princely silks. He was the crown prince, heir to Father's kingdom. The brother who bore the responsibility of our entire country. The one who protected us and listened to us, who mediated our arguments and tended our injuries.

For the first time in a long time, he looked like my brother first and the crown prince second. Aggrieved that he couldn't do anything to save us from Raikama's curse.

I brought my bowl and sat with him.

The curse, I gestured, making my hands into wings. *I want to hear more.*

"Not tonight," Benkai said, ever wise. "Tonight we celebrate, all right, Shiori? Our stepmother has wrought enough sorrow. We cannot let her shadow darken our precious hours of light. Not another word about the curse."

Not another word. Easier done than they thought.

As always, it was Hasho who soothed me. He scooted close, offering me half his food, which I refused to take until he scooped it into my bowl. "We spent weeks preparing this cave for you, Shiori," he said quietly. "We hoped more than anything to find you. And now we have."

Now you have, I echoed.

I'd dreamt of this moment for so many weeks, of how happy I'd be when my brothers and I were reunited. Now that it had at last arrived, I couldn't celebrate.

Smiles flashed at me, wooden sticks clanged rhythmically against the flat stones my brothers were using as plates, and Yotan made whuffing sounds on a flute he had fashioned. But as I mustered a smile, I couldn't shake the feeling that something was wrong.

My brothers were hiding a secret. One they were afraid to tell me.

If only they knew I felt the same way.

I pursed my lips tight, holding in my curse. Whatever their secret was, I knew mine was worse.

The night passed quickly. I didn't remember falling asleep, but my brothers' movements woke me. They were tiptoeing to the mouth of the cave, with roughly made pouches slung around their necks.

I sprang after them. *You're leaving?*

"Dawn is nearly here," Hasho explained. "We'll be gone until sundown—to find you something to write with, and to scout for news. Stay here and don't wander too far."

I grabbed Hasho's sleeve. *Take me with you.*

"We'll be faster without her," said Andahai when my youngest brother hesitated.

Hasho made an apologetic grimace. "Wait for us. We'll talk tonight."

The sun peeked out over the horizon. As soon as the light touched their skin, they began to turn. Their human eyes blackened into beady crane eyes, and their flesh bristled with feathers. Finally their arms lengthened into wings, and their shouts of "Until tonight, Shiori!" were replaced by the cries and trumpets of cranes.

I ran after them out of the cave, watching my brothers leap off the ledge into the sky. Once they were gone, I kicked the dirt, angry to be left behind.

Kiki landed on my shoulder. She suppressed a yawn. *Is this going to be a daily tradition? I could have used a few more hours of rest without all that squawking.*

I gave her a wry smile. *You slept the entire night.*

Nearly dying will do that to you. She shrugged a wing. Kiki never ceased to surprise me with how alive she was. *You didn't want to go with them?*

They wouldn't let me. They said to sit still and get some rest. That we'd talk tonight. I kicked at the dirt again.

Only rocks considered sitting still a virtue. Demons take me before I called it one of mine.

I grew bored after an hour. My brothers had created a small but practical living space in the cave: a hearth in the center lined with stones—Wandei's work, I guessed—and a meager stash of firewood. A mostly empty sack of rice along with the broken pot we'd used last night to boil chestnuts. There was even a book or two, the pages yellowed and weatherworn. But the last thing I wanted to do was read.

I practiced throwing the sentinel's dagger at a plank of wood. Only a few throws landed successfully, but I wasn't deterred. It helped to imagine Raikama's face as my target.

By midmorning, I was restless. *I'm going for a walk,* I announced to Kiki.

Your brothers told you not to wander too far.

It's not wandering if I know how to get home.

We weren't as high up in the mountains as I'd originally thought. The ledge was narrow, but there was a path down-hill. While I descended, I kept one eye on my footing and one eye on the view below.

The forest unfolded across the horizon, and there was no village or town in sight, only the Baiyun River, if I recalled my geography lessons correctly. Wherever my brothers had gone, it had to be quite a distance.

The river's waters were calm, and I wished I hadn't lost my little boat—especially the fishing net inside. If my brothers were going to make a habit of leaving me behind, I could have at least caught some trout or carp for dinner. It'd be better than that frog stew Hasho had made.

Kneeling, I tested the water, stifling a gasp at how cold it was.

Ripples danced from my fingertips, and as the water cleared, I faced my reflection. It wasn't the first time I'd seen myself since Raikama had cursed me, but every time, I recognized myself a little less.

Even with the bowl on my head, I could tell I looked older. My mouth didn't curve as easily as it once did, and my shoulders were broader, hardened by months of labor.

No longer was I the girl who rolled her eyes at her brothers or squealed over rice cakes and sugared animals on sticks.

Now I carried a dagger everywhere, even in my dreams.

I took off my shoes and stepped into the river, digging my toes into the mud.

Seryu, I called in my mind. And waited.

I waited until the cold numbed my ankles and the fish came up to nibble at my toes. Kiki flew circles around me, teasing the fish until one nearly nipped her wing off.

I tried again: *Seryu?*

Silence.

What was I expecting? For the dragon to burst forth the moment I called his name?

Seryu was deep in the middle of the Taijin Sea, probably lolling about in a palace carved of pearl and shell. He'd warned me he wouldn't return until spring.

Feeling foolish, I turned back for the cave, almost wishing I had never left.

My brothers returned with beakfuls of fish and a basket overflowing with lettuce, tangerines, and half-eaten steamed buns. No paper or brush or ink, but they'd brought me new clothes—a cloak, a pair of mismatched socks, and gloves for the harsh winter ahead.

I gaped at them, gesturing at their own ragged clothes.

Hasho shrugged. "No one sees us at night."

No one sees me in the day, either, I thought.

I'd been waiting all day for their return, anxious for my questions to be answered. Without a brush and ink, I settled for a more inventive way of communicating. I threw water over a patch of dirt and smoothed out the mud.

I hadn't written in months, and my hand shook as I pressed the tip of my dagger into the damp earth.

Take me home?
The guards won't shoot me.

At the question, my brothers' smiles faded. "It's not so simple, Sister."

My brow knotted with confusion. What wasn't simple? We were together again, finally, after nearly all of autumn apart. They could fly, meaning we could easily reach the palace in a matter of days. Why were they so reluctant?

"Our stepmother has made things a bit more difficult for us. For one, Father wouldn't recognize us, even if we were right in front of him in our human form."

Bile rose to my throat. That dream I'd had of my stepmother's glowing yellow eyes piercing into Father's . . . had that been real?

How do we defeat her?
Is there a way to break her enchantment?

"Yes, but it won't be easy," Andahai replied, rubbing his narrow chin. "Every day these last two months, we searched for you. We had no idea where Raikama had sent you. We split up and traveled to A'landi and Agoria, even to Balar."

"We didn't find you," Benkai said, taking over the story.

"But we did meet an enchanter—he said that the only way to break our curse is to take away our stepmother's magic."

I would have snorted if I could. That wasn't helpful.

How?

Andahai hesitated, which worried me. My eldest brother was never at a loss for words. That he was nervous now made me nervous.

He straightened, but the way his eyes darted at the others made my gut sink. I had a feeling I wasn't going to like his next words.

"It appears that Raikama is in possession of a dragon pearl," he said slowly. "And you, Shiori, you will have to steal it."

CHAPTER FOURTEEN

The edges of my vision blurred, my brother's words ringing in my ears.

It was not out of alarm or shock that I was reeling. No, everything had suddenly become clear. That day I'd followed Raikama to the Tears of Emuri'en, I'd been looking for the source of her magic. I'd seen it—that mysteriously broken orb my stepmother kept hidden in her chest. It had glowed with power, like a bead of sunlight.

So, that had been a *dragon* pearl.

I touched my heart, where the fragment of Seryu's pearl rested, long forgotten. Then I rose to my feet, frantically circling my hands to ask: *How do I get it?*

"Sit, Shiori," said Andahai, covering the mud with his hands before I could write. "Hear us out first."

I sat, but I gripped my dagger hard, dozens of questions itching to get out.

"You need to weave a starstroke net," Andahai said. "It's the only thing powerful enough to subdue a dragon's magic."

I frowned. I'd never been the most diligent student of Kiatan lore, but *that* story I knew.

"It grows on the top of Mount Rayuna, in the middle of the Taijin Sea," my brother went on, ignoring my troubled look. "No one has ever been able to get near it, let alone touch it—not without magic."

I glanced at my other brothers, who were all gazing at the ground. We were thinking the same thing. Countless fools had tried in the past to gather starstroke, but its leaves were sharp as knives, and the mere touch of its thorns was said to be like a stab of fire. Yet the greater danger was the Dragon King himself, who was known to guard Mount Rayuna. Anyone caught gathering the nettles would be at his terrible mercy.

"But we can fly," said Andahai, "and you . . . Raikama said you have magic in your blood."

At the mention of our stepmother, I looked up in bewilderment.

"She wasn't lying about that, was she?" Yotan asked.

I grimaced. *No.* But I wasn't sure how that would help us here.

"Then you should be able to use this." Benkai held out a straw satchel, worn and box-shaped, with a sturdy strap and two wooden buckles. Plain and unremarkable, it looked like any old bag a poor villager might carry. But when I lifted the flap, I saw that it was lined with strips of dark wood. Walnut, if I were to guess.

"The enchanter gave it to us. He said its depths are boundless, and that only someone with magic can see its contents. It will help you contain the starstroke's power while you weave the net."

I threw the satchel to the side.

He just happened to have this in his possession?
Who is this enchanter, anyway?

"Master Tsring is a famous seer in A'landi." Benkai paused, returning the satchel to my lap. "He's the one who found us and helped us. We were hoping he could locate you." His gaze fell on the bowl resting atop my head. "But he said your magic was blocked."

An accurate statement, but I still didn't like or trust this Master Tsring.

What does he want in return?
The pearl, once we're finished with it?

"He wants the net," replied Hasho. "It'll be of no use to us after we break our curse. It's a fair trade."

Hardly. I crossed my arms. From a glance at Reiji, my least trusting brother, I could tell they had already argued over this point.

"Let us worry about the enchanter later," Andahai said firmly. "For now we focus on the starstroke net. Are you up for the task, Shiori?"

What choice did I have?

I am. I threaded my arm through the strap of the satchel. *Of course I am.*

"Wait." Wandei exhaled, reminding us all that he was the only one who had not spoken. "You never told us, Sister, why it is that you must not speak."

I closed my eyes, wishing he hadn't asked.

Using the dagger to point at my throat then at my brothers, I mouthed:

Because you'll die. For every word I utter, every sound I make—one of you will die.

My brothers' faces went ashen, and they looked at each other, passing something unsaid. The most telltale sign that they were hiding something from me was the frown Andahai wore. He elbowed Benkai, shaking his head.

What was going on?

"Perhaps we are asking too much of you, Shiori," said Andahai slowly. "Weaving the net will be painful; it will cause you much agony. I would not wish to multiply your burden."

I sprang to my feet. *My burden?* I gestured wildly. *Every morning, your bodies are ripped apart as you turn into cranes.* I had watched Hasho try to hold in a scream as Raikama's enchantment consumed him. I had seen Yotan's face blanch as the colors of dawn began to paint the sky.

And me? For all my complaining, all I had to do was wear a silly bowl on my head and hold in my voice.

My curse was easy compared to theirs, and I would gladly take on any burden if it gave them relief.

"Let's wait until tomorrow," said Hasho. "We aren't in any rush to break the curse."

Not in any rush? My head jerked up, certain that was a

lie. I glowered at Hasho. My youngest brother used to be the one who kept *my* secrets. What was he concealing now?

Reiji spoke up, his nostrils flaring. "We need to tell her. It'd be wrong for us to leave for Mount Rayuna without her knowing."

"Reiji," Andahai cautioned. "We agreed—"

"*You* forced us to agree. She has to know."

I grabbed Hasho's arm. *Tell me.*

Hasho's eyes were trained on the ground, not a good sign. "We . . . ," he stumbled, "we told you that we need to weaken Raikama with a dragon net and t-take her pearl to break the curse."

Yes. I was growing impatient. *Yes, I know all this already.*

"We haven't told you what to do once you have the pearl," said Andahai, his narrow face becoming tired and drawn.

Now he had my attention.

"You must hold it in your hands," he said slowly, "and speak our stepmother's true name."

Her true name? I furrowed my brow. That was easy enough. I could simply ask Father once we returned to the palace with the net.

Realization dawned. I had to *speak* her name.

I couldn't break their curse if I couldn't speak. So long as this wretched bowl rested on my head, any word I uttered would bring death.

The air squeezed out of my lungs. One of them would have to die.

I stabbed my dagger into the mud, staggered by the cruelty of Raikama's curse.

"If it comes to that, all of us are willing to take the risk," Benkai said quickly. "Aren't we, Brothers?"

I'm not! I shouted by shaking my fists. I shot to my feet, only to sink to the ground once more. *I'm not.*

"Now isn't the time to despair, Shiori," said Yotan, wrapping his arm around my shoulder. But even his eyes, which so often danced with merriment, looked resigned.

Thinking to cheer me up with food, he passed the remainder of last night's stew to me, but I only stirred the bowl numbly.

"The six of us will gather what information we can about her name," said Andahai, taking my silence as a cue to move on. "You focus on crafting the net. In the spring, we will fly to Gindara again and break our stepmother's enchantment."

In the spring? I blinked, scraping the end of my spoon into the mud.

Will we be ready by then?

"We have no choice," said Benkai grimly. "We are at war, Shiori. With A'landi."

The words thudded in my ears. *At war?*

"Father has no more heirs now that we are missing, and Raikama has no child of her own. The khagan of A'landi's northern states has declared Kiata's throne ripe for the taking, and he has been bribing some of our most powerful allies to turn on Father. Father's called all the great lords to Gindara to repledge their fealty."

I glanced at my younger brothers, all solemn-faced. Only yesterday we had been hugging each other with joy. How quickly that joy had been replaced with a cold and terrible dread.

No one would betray him.
All the houses are loyal.

Benkai's expression did not inspire confidence. "Greed is a great motivator," he said thinly, "and there's talk of the khagan having an enchanter."

"He's called the Wolf," Andahai said, and I started, recognizing the name. "You've heard of him?"

Only from a letter I found.
It must have been intended for the khagan.

I wrote what I could remember, except the words I hadn't been able to translate. "Do you know who it was from?"

I shook my head with regret, imagining now it must have been from the lord who had betrayed Father. I dipped into my stew and ate a spoonful, swallowing hard. *Tell me about the Wolf,* I mouthed.

"Master Tsring warned us about him," said Andahai. "The Wolf was his student before he revealed his true nature. He is treacherous and cruel, and very clever."

But why come here?
He would have no magic if he stepped into Kiata.

"One doesn't need magic to be dangerous, Shiori," Benkai replied. "A reputation is all it takes to spread fear. And fear is a mighty weapon."

"Or," said Wandei slowly, "perhaps the seams that keep magic from Kiata are fraying. The gods have been silent for centuries. It could be they've decided it is time for magic to return to Kiata. Look at our stepmother—and you."

I felt immediately ill. My fingers stiffened around my spoon, and I set down my stew. I had lost my appetite.

"Don't worry yet," said Hasho, trying hard to comfort me. "If luck is on our side, A'landi's states will fight among themselves, and the khagan will forget about us. At the very least, winter will give Father more time to prepare."

And me time to break our curse, I thought.

If anyone was a seer, perhaps it had been Mama—for naming me Shiori, meaning "knot." A symbol that I was the last of her seven children, the one who would bring my brothers together, no matter how fate conspired to pull us apart.

We were seven, and seven was a number of strength. An uneven number that could not fold unto itself, large enough to withstand many threats, yet small enough to stay devoted.

I looped the satchel's strap over my shoulder and looked each of my brothers squarely in the eye.

Whatever it took to stop Raikama and break the spells she'd cast upon us, I would do it. Even if it took months or years, even if I incurred the gods' wrath and made enemies of the dragons.

Take me to Mount Rayuna.

CHAPTER FIFTEEN

The next day, we left for Mount Rayuna.

With Kiki securely tucked inside my sleeve, I clung to the edges of the wooden basket Wandei had designed for transporting me. It was more secure than holding on to their necks, but my stomach still swooped whenever we dipped through the clouds.

Four of my brothers bit ropes attached to the basket, while one flew ahead to navigate, and one stayed in the back to keep watch. We were so high that the rivers looked like ribbons and the mountains like wrinkles across the earth.

Along the way, my brothers told me all they had learned of starstroke and the dragons that kept it, with Kiki translating. Dragons had not always been omens of good fortune, nor had they always been infrequent visitors to land. They were mercurial and violent, often indulging in their power to wreak chaos in the seas. Worst of all, they had answered to no one—not even the gods.

To temper their strength, the gods forged starstroke from

a trio of magics: strands of fate from the goddess Emuri'en's hair; the blood of stars from Lapzur, the source of an enchanter's power; and demonfire scoured from the Tambu Isles, birthplace of demons.

As starstroke grew wild all over Lor'yan, the dragons retreated into the sea, hiding there until the gods pleaded for their help in divesting Kiata of magic and sealing the demons within the Holy Mountains. In exchange for their help, the Dragon King demanded that the starstroke be contained to the summit of Mount Rayuna. There, he kept a watchful eye out for any who might try to steal it.

Thieves, such as my brothers and me. By the Eternal Courts, I prayed that we were so insignificant—six cranes and a magicless girl—that he would not notice us.

There! I cried, pointing ahead. *I see it.*

Steam curled from Mount Rayuna's summit, as thick as the clouds. Molten rivers hissed, streaming down like liquid gold, and powerful winds gusted, forcing my brothers to drop me off lower on the mountain.

I scanned the summit, taking inventory of the glimmering bushes of starstroke. There had to be hundreds, if not thousands, studding the mountaintop. I would have to work quickly and finish before dusk—before my brothers turned back into men. Mount Rayuna was not a place I wished to be stranded.

Hasho approached. The black edges on his wings were the thickest, like broad strokes of ink under the fold of his snow-touched feathers. His eyes were most like mine even when he was a crane. Brown with flecks of amber.

He says that if at any time you change your mind, Shiori, to tell me. Kiki glanced down at Mount Rayuna, askance, before she relayed the rest of Hasho's message. *I'll find your brothers, and they'll take you home.*

I shook my head. I wouldn't change my mind.

He also wants to know if you want one of them to stay with you.

Here on Mount Rayuna, where wild magic grew rampant, I did not dare have anyone accompany me to fetch the nettles. Certainly not my brothers.

I shook my head firmly and passed Kiki to Hasho. If a paper bird could have scowled, she would have. She flittered back onto my shoulder, hissing, *I'm coming too.*

But—

I'm a paper crane, Shiori, not a real one. If something happens, you can fold me back to life again.

Not without my magic, I wanted to reply, but I nodded to avoid frightening her. I let my satchel fall to my hip, its presence strangely comforting as I embarked up the mountain.

It wasn't a hard climb, though the ashes made the trek slippery. Often I kicked against objects too brittle to be stones, too hollow to be branches. I prayed they weren't bones.

I was halfway to the summit when the ground shook, and I stumbled against a rock pillar.

Emuri'en's strands! Kiki gasped. *That wasn't the Dragon King, was it?*

Just a quake. I braced myself until the tremor passed. *I think.*

Kiki beat her wings faster, narrowly evading a spurt of

lava from one of the rocks. *All this fire is going to scorch my tail! What was I thinking, coming with you? Hurry up, Shiori. I don't want to stay here a minute longer than we have to.*

It wasn't hard to find the nettles. Their leaves, silvery green with dark red veins, were spiked, and their thorns were as sharp as teeth. They grew in clumps scattered around the summit of Mount Rayuna, their thick stems glowing with demonfire and swaying to gales of blistering wind. That they could survive in such conditions, let alone thrive, reminded me that these were no ordinary nettles.

I approached the first bush with caution. From afar, the nettles looked no brighter than the molten streams sizzling down the mountainside. But the closer I drew, the more intensely the starstroke glowed. A wash of heat prickled my face, and I used my bowl as a shield. Even then, my eyes watered.

Your brothers said you don't have to go through with this, Kiki reminded me. *I can tell them if you—*

It's not so bad, I lied, mustering a smile. *Just like slicing a thousand onions.*

In spite of my bad joke and brave words, I bristled with fear. I could feel my heart jumping in my chest, a sharp pain throbbing so hard it hurt to breathe.

It was the tiny fragment of Seryu's pearl, glinting under my collar for the first time—a warning not to go any farther.

It's repelled by the starstroke, I realized.

Can it help us? Kiki asked, sneaking into my thoughts.

No, I couldn't access its magic while I was cursed, but I

didn't need to. If being near starstroke made *my* tiny pearl ache, I grinned just thinking of what it would do to Raikama.

Wrapping my satchel's strap around my hand, I reached for my dagger and hacked at the nettles.

The blade might as well have been cutting at stone. Not a nettle fell. Not even a leaf.

Frustrated and out of breath, I staggered back. Even with the strap covering my skin, my hand hurt as if pricked by a thousand fiery needles. I balled my fist, trying to keep in the rising pain.

Kiki circled me frantically. *Shiori, Shiori! Are you hurt?*

No. I sucked in a breath, unwrapping my hand as I approached the bush of starstroke again. *I think I have to pull them out by hand.*

By hand? No, Shiori, that'll—

I wasn't listening to Kiki's warning. *Fear is just a game,* I repeated to myself, over and over. *You win by playing.*

I yanked the nearest stalk.

A scream boiled inside me, nearly surging out of my lungs. I bit down on my tongue, throttling up the sound inside me. My vision swam, and as blood gushed through my teeth, all I could see was six lifeless swans on the beach.

When I finally caught my breath, my face was wet with tears. I'd hurt myself plenty of times working in Mrs. Dainan's kitchen, but the pain of touching starstroke was like nothing I had ever felt before. The jagged leaves cut into my skin like knives, and the thorns—the thorns were like stabs of fire.

But it worked. Thin silvery roots, like spiderwebs, burst from the earth. I threw the plant, roots and all, into my satchel.

The burning eased as soon as I let go of the starstroke. I clenched my fist, then opened it, looking at my palm, raw with scorch marks.

Enough, Shiori, Kiki pleaded. *You'll die if you keep this up.*

It'll be easier the next time, I assured her, even though I knew that was a lie.

Pain didn't get easier. I just had to get stronger.

I ripped off my sleeve and crammed it into my mouth. My voice had shriveled up inside my throat, unused for months, but I wasn't going to take any chances. Any sound would condemn my brothers.

I ignored Kiki's protests and attacked the second patch of nettles. I pulled at a larger bunch this time, using both hands to rip the roots from the earth. I'd need hundreds to weave a net that could capture Raikama's pearl.

Every time I tore one of the nettles, I thought of my father, my brothers, my country. I pictured Father torn apart with grief, unable to trust anyone around him, convinced that one of the warlords had captured his children, when it was really the person he trusted most—Raikama.

I couldn't let Raikama win.

Eventually Kiki stopped telling me to give up and instead reminded me to rest. I had to, even if I didn't want to. Too many times, I lurched to the side to retch from pain or to cradle my blood-streaked hands.

I stuffed the nettles inside my satchel. I had probably

gathered enough fill over a dozen, but the enchanter hadn't misled us about the satchel's endless depths.

Crawling away from the bushes, I blew on my hands. The pearl still throbbed in my chest, but I was nearly finished.

"Shiori!"

I stilled. I would have recognized that voice anywhere. But no, it couldn't be.

"Shiori," Seryu rumbled. "What are you doing on Mount Rayuna?"

Now I turned, searching among the nettles.

"Behind you. In the water."

Kiki flittered before the pool, which bubbled with heat and spurted every few minutes with small geysers.

I could not see Seryu, but our minds touched, his words buzzing in my ear as if he were next to me.

"You must leave this place," he said. "Get out now."

I can't. Go away, Seryu. Unless you're here to help.

"Help with what—why are you here?"

She's been cursed, Kiki cut in.

"Cursed?" the dragon exclaimed. "What—"

I can't tell you, I interrupted. *She'll kill my brothers if I do.*

"Who will? Your stepmother? She cannot punish you for your thoughts, Shiori. What is this curse?"

Raikama turned her brothers into cranes, Kiki burbled, *and the only way to break her spell is to—*

I closed Kiki's beak with my fingers. *That's enough. I'll tell him the rest.* I swallowed hard, knowing my friend wouldn't like what I was about to say next.

It's to weave a dragon net.

I could feel Seryu tense. "So you *have* come for starstroke." His voice was strained. "Just what dragon are you trying to ensnare?"

Not a dragon. My stepmother. She has a dragon pearl.

"A dragon pearl!" Seryu repeated. "That's impossible. No human possesses a dragon pearl."

You gave me a part of yours.

"Only a sliver. Even then, it was a tremendous risk. No dragon would give more, not without Grandfather's blessing. It would have to be stolen." He paused deliberately, as if to remind me of my surroundings. "And you are the first mortal in centuries to venture here."

He made a low growl I was glad I couldn't see. "You'd better leave. If my grandfather senses someone stealing starstroke, he will be furious. I'll try to distract him, but it might be too late. You must go. Now."

I scrambled to my feet. *Wait, Seryu. When will I see you again?*

"When the tides are highest, my dragon magic is at its peak. Stop by the nearest river after the next full moon and call for me. I'll come to you then. Now hurry and leave this place." A hint of fear edged his voice. "My grandfather's wrath is no trivial thing."

Once he vanished, a deafening *crack* lashed the sky.

Then the mountain roared.

CHAPTER SIXTEEN

Fires leapt up, steam hissing from the ground. The earth shuddered, and like insects, the black rocks began to scatter and swarm down and down, taking me with them.

Brothers! I shouted in my mind. Kiki shot up from my shoulder, flying off to find them.

I slid down the mountain, scrabbling for a bone or a pillar or anything to grab hold of. But the mountain was sliding with me. Spires of rock crumbled as it quaked, and smoke billowed up into the sky.

A pit of lava seethed below, bright as the liquid sun. I wished I hadn't looked down. Powerful as Seryu's pearl was, I didn't think it could resurrect me. Not while I wore this bowl on my head. *Especially* not if I melted.

My brothers were squawking for me, but they were searching from above the clouds of smoke. I had fallen too far for them to see me.

I rolled onto my stomach, wrapping my arms around a

crumbling stone. My hands hurt too much for me to hold on long. *Kiki,* I cried. *Kiki.*

If ever I was grateful for my bond with the magic bird, it was now. I could almost sense her diving toward me, screeching at my brothers to follow.

They broke through the clouds, fighting pasts blasts of scorching wind. Their white wings were bright against the blowing ash and fire.

Hasho and Reiji grabbed my collar and flung me into the basket. But as we swerved away from Mount Rayuna, leaving it far behind, in my delirium, I thought I heard the thunderous growl of a dragon.

We fled across the Taijin Sea, racing the storm. Lightning lashed the sky, thunder crackling not far behind. Then came the rain.

It spilled from gravid clouds, each plop as heavy as a grain of rice. As the raindrops poured into my basket, my brothers careened, their wings folding as they struggled to carry me through the storm.

We dipped below the clouds, the ropes that held my basket twisting as my brothers grappled against the wind.

I clutched the edges of my basket, ignoring the burning pain in my fingers.

Don't let us die, I'm too young a bird to die. Kiki was praying to every god she knew, but all I could do was stare at the sea. Something was hurtling through the water, a creature long and serpentine.

Thunder boomed, earth-shatteringly loud. It made the waves rise, and the winds double in strength. In alarm, Wandei and Yotan let go of the ropes holding my basket. For the longest second of my life, I flailed against the violent wind as the basket's sticks and branches came apart under my hands. The sea thrashed hungrily, and by the time the twins picked up the ropes again, I was shivering with fear—and revelation.

That wasn't thunder, I realized, still watching the waters below.

It was the roar of a dragon.

His whiskers were like lightning bolts, white and crooked, and the icy boulders of his eyes flared with menace.

Nazayun, the Dragon King.

From the depths of the Taijin Sea, he rose in all his terrible splendor—a tower of violet and sapphire scales. Benkai let out a high-pitched screech as the dragon swung his claws toward us.

My brothers dipped, narrowly missing the Dragon King's attack.

He wants the nettles back, Kiki shouted. *If you don't return them, he will kill you!*

King Nazayun wasn't exactly giving me a chance to return the nettles. He struck relentlessly, my brothers just barely dodging each attack. We couldn't outfly the dragon for long—not while my six brothers had to carry me by a rope in their beaks.

I tugged on Yotan's wing. Wandei's too. In spite of their

159

differences, the twins were closer with one another than any of our siblings. Even now, their wings beat in harmony.

I gestured to the Dragon King. *Take me to him.*

Kiki began to translate, then her beak lifted in horror. *What in the gods, Shiori? No!*

I wasn't listening. I was already hooking one arm over Yotan's neck and the other over Wandei's.

It was reckless. I could hear Andahai's shouts as Wandei and Yotan carried me out of the basket, my legs hanging over the raging sea. Kiki's were a little harder to ignore.

Shiori, this is madness. Think of me. I'll die if you die! Haven't we talked about caution as the creed of the wise? Shiori!

Pinching my bird's wings, I thrust her into my sleeve for safekeeping. Then, with a nod to my brothers, I jumped onto the Dragon King's head.

I landed on one of his horns and slid down to his eyebrows. Pain sliced into my hands as I clung to his bristly gold hair, thick as I imagined a bear's fur to be. Before I lost my grip, I opened my satchel.

Light spilled out, dazzling the dragon's pale eyes.

I have need of a starstroke net to break a terrible curse, I shouted with my thoughts, not sure if he could hear them. *One enacted by my stepmother, the Nameless Queen. Please, she has a dragon pearl in her heart, and I need it to save my brothers—these six cranes. Grant us safe passage across the Taijin Sea. I will return the starstroke when I have broken the curse.*

I lowered my collar, revealing the glimmering fragment of Seryu's pearl inside my heart.

King Nazayun's eyebrows slanted with recognition, and the waters trembled. For a moment, I thought my gamble had worked.

But I was mistaken.

With a roar, he dove back into the sea, taking me with him.

Nothing could have prepared me for the Dragon King's might. I tumbled off his brow, my terror reflected in his gleaming sapphire scales before I went into free fall. Waves crested over the dragon like mountains. The wind flung me across the sea.

I braced myself for the crash, but it never came.

Wooden branches cracked under my back as strong, feathered wings batted us away from immediate peril.

Your brother Andahai says that was very stupid, Kiki chided me as I rolled onto my stomach in the basket.

She didn't have time to relay any further reprimands. Benkai directed us into the headwinds, and we rushed across the Taijin Sea, trying to outrun the Dragon King before he realized I was still alive.

But a new danger presented itself as the clouds shifted, unveiling the sun.

It was sinking, minutes away from dusk. If my brothers couldn't reach land in time, they'd transform in midair over the roiling sea.

We had to act quickly. The most important thing was my satchel of starstroke. Benkai was the most athletic of my brothers, the fastest and strongest flyer in his crane form. I shoved the leather strap into his beak, waving for him to take it to the shore.

He didn't hesitate. His neck dipped slightly under the weight of the satchel as he sped toward the shore. He'd make it. I knew he would.

I just wasn't so sure about the rest of us.

Lightning chased us, long and crooked like dragon claws, sent by Nazayun himself. The bolts thrashed the sky, some striking so close that I could smell the smoke they left curling behind them, like ribbons of bone.

The shore appeared, and I could see the hem of the Taijin Sea foaming against the pebbled sands. *Just a few more seconds of light,* I prayed.

The sun did not hear me. She stretched her amber arms, burnished with a sleepy glow of the rising stars, across the sea one last time, making the tides gleam. Then the last rays of daylight sank beyond the horizon, and as night fell, so did we.

Terror clotted my throat. The wind threw me out of my basket, and I heard myself scream inside my head. In every direction, my brothers spun away from me, the moonlight hitting the fluid contours of their faces as their shrieks turned into human cries.

Hasho struggled to hold me. I grasped at his feathers, but he trembled uncontrollably as my stepmother's dark spell seized his body.

His eyes hollowed, legs bent into a crouch, and face contorted with pain. His long black beak shrank into pale lips and a slightly hooked nose, frail bird bones reconstructing themselves into human ones, muscles thickening into arms. Lungs gasping as if he couldn't breathe.

When he hit the water, he still hadn't finished changing. I knew it'd be the same for the others.

I gulped a breath a mere blink before the sea devoured me too.

It was a miracle that my bones didn't shatter. They certainly felt like they had. I couldn't tell how deep I sank. Eerie stripes of moonlight illuminated the water, passing over my body like ghosts.

While my hands flailed, my legs instinctively kicked, propelling me upward. I swam for the surface, my head growing light and heavy at the same time. My lungs pinched tight, my heart pumping madly to keep me alive.

I kicked harder. Out of the corner of my eye, I saw Reiji struggling to grasp a piece of debris. I grabbed him, pain spasming through my hands.

I wrapped my arm around his neck, kicking both of us to shore, where Kiki and the rest of my brothers were waiting.

The twins greeted Reiji and me, but Andahai and Hasho were crouched beside Benkai. My second brother had collapsed on the sand.

I ran to him. *Benkai!*

Hasho propped him up, and Andahai shook him until, finally, Benkai spat sand and seawater.

I wasn't the only one who collapsed with relief.

"You scared us, Brother." Andahai punched Benkai in the shoulder. "We thought you'd died."

Benkai managed a smile. "It'll take more than the Dragon King to kill *me*." Seawater dripped from his hair onto the thin robe over his shoulders. "But if we keep away from the Taijin Sea for a while, I won't complain."

I threw my arms around him, laughing silently as I hugged him.

"You're hurt," said Hasho, seeing me flinch as I withdrew from the hug. He took my arm. "Benkai, quick. Come take a look."

It's nothing. I hid my hands behind my back, away from my brothers' inspection, but Benkai was firm.

"Let me see, Shiori."

With great reluctance, I held out my palms, and Hasho and Benkai both inhaled sharply.

This morning, my hands had been those of a young girl. Callused from my hard work at Sparrow Inn, with some cooking burns that were still healing—but otherwise smooth and unblemished. Now my skin was raw, bubbling with silver and red veins that mirrored the starstroke's leaves. The burning pain had subsided, but simply curling my fingers still hurt enough to make me clench my teeth.

It'll pass, I gestured with a shrug. *It's already getting better.*

Not believing me, Hasho ripped his sleeve and wrapped my hands. He held my shoulders, half smiling at me.

What is it? I mouthed. *Do I have kelp in my hair?*

"You look like her," said Hasho, his eyes fierce and proud. "Mama."

I did? My brothers had never said that.

"Only a little," Reiji replied. "Mama was more beautiful. And infinitely less impulsive."

I glared at him, but a slight smile—one that wasn't

unkind—spread across his face. "You're yourself, Shiori. The knot that holds us together, whether we like it or not."

Then he and my brothers did something they had never done before: they bowed, lowering their heads in respect.

Get up, I mouthed, ushering them to rise. *Honestly— Kiki, can you tell them to get up?*

My paper bird tilted her head to the side coyly. *It's not my place to tell the princes of Kiata what to do.*

Only the princess?

Only the princess.

The lightning had ceased, leaving jagged scars among the starry patchwork of night.

I searched the heavens for stars I recognized. There weren't many: the Rabbit—friend to Imurinya, the moon lady. The Hunter's bow and arrow, which belonged to Imurinya's husband. And the Crane, the sacred messenger of fate.

The Crane was a constellation of seven stars northeast of the moon. I traced it with my finger, the way I did when I was a child. Father had named those seven stars after us seven children.

Andahai, Benkai, Reiji, Yotan, Wandei, Hasho—and Shiori.

"No matter where life takes you," he would say, "you will be like those stars—connected by the light you shine together."

Though it was cold on the beach, and we were drenched with rain and seawater, somehow I felt warmer than I had in a long, long time.

CHAPTER SEVENTEEN

If there was anything good to come of being cursed, it was that in one short week, my brothers and I grew close again, as close as we'd been when we were children.

Though winter loomed over our little cave, the skies dismal and gray, our spirits were anything but. Yotan and Benkai told ghost stories by the fire, Wandei chased after Kiki and tried chiseling birds of his own out of firewood, and I supervised while Andahai and Hasho cooked.

Sometimes during our meals, we shared our earliest memories of Raikama. I contributed little—I was the youngest, after all, so my recollections were the least clear. But it was also shame that kept me silent; I'd been the fondest of Raikama when she first came to Kiata, a fact I wished I could erase forever.

Or maybe I already had. It was odd, but I hardly remembered why I'd ever loved my stepmother. It was as if someone had turned those memories into sand and blown them away from my past. Truth be told, it was probably better that way. I didn't miss them.

"She isn't from Kiata, that much we know," said Wandei logically. "If Father met her abroad, he must have brought ships with him. An entire crew of men. There will be records of her arrival, or at least of her birthplace."

"A woman with her beauty cannot simply have appeared out of nowhere," Yotan agreed.

You forget that she's a sorceress, I reminded them, poking my words into the dirt. *She might not always have been beautiful.*

"But she most certainly had a name. A family. A home." Hasho paused. "It's a start."

It *was* a start, but I was more preoccupied with the ending. A day or two after we returned from Mount Rayuna, when the pain in my hands had subsided, I sought out Benkai to show me how to use my dagger.

There had been a reason I'd taken the dagger from the sentinel, and it wasn't merely to break chestnut shells or hack starstroke. Benkai was a high sentinel, and my other five brothers were skilled warriors—one day soon, we would have to return home to the palace, where Raikama's magic reigned strong.

Teach me, I begged silently.

Andahai stepped between us. "A dagger isn't going to do much against Raikama. Even Benkai missed when we tried to fight her."

"Let your hands heal so you can begin work on the

starstroke," Yotan agreed. "The net is our best chance of defeating her."

"Take a rest, Shiori."

"You're all coddling her as if she were a silkworm," said Reiji. "She just stole starstroke from the Dragon King. She can handle a knife!" He rose, dusting his torn trousers. "I'll teach her."

The others and I looked at him, startled. Of all my brothers, I hadn't expected *him* to take my side.

Without another word, he led me to the back of the cave, and our training began. Eventually Benkai joined, and by the end of the night we were sparring.

"You've grown stronger, Shiori," Benkai said, surprised when I held my own against him.

Two months of toiling for Mrs. Dainan, cleaving cabbages and melons with her dull knives and hauling firewood in the cold, had helped.

If only all that could have prepared me to deal with the pain of the starstroke.

The next day, when my brothers left to gather supplies for winter, I tackled the nettles at last, spreading them over the cave to determine my course of action.

No blade could pierce the nettles, let alone cut them. In their raw form, I couldn't weave the stems together to make a net, and I certainly couldn't sew them together—not with their fiery thorns and razor-sharp leaves.

A trio of magics, I repeated to myself after hours of agonizing with Kiki. If three magics had really created these cursed nettles, all I could see was the demonfire—the blinding light that encased every stalk. Where were the strands of fate and the blood of stars?

"Try removing the leaves and the nettles," Kiki suggested. "You can hardly touch the starstroke otherwise."

It wasn't as easy as pruning roses, that was for certain. The thorns and leaves were like teeth and claws. Removing the leaves was the easier task, for they snapped off with a few scrapes of my blade. As long as I was careful not to touch their jagged edges, my fingers usually managed to escape unscathed. The thorns, on the other hand, were stubborn magic. They could not be removed unless I pounded at them with rocks that I collected along the mountainside. Pounding them off was slow, arduous work.

But I was indeed to be rewarded. Demonfire armored every vine of starstroke, but once the last leaf was cut and the last thorn chipped off, the nettles transformed. The demonfire sank into the fibrous stalk, muting the nettles' dazzling light. Within minutes, the starstroke became a skein of coarse, loose threads, glimmering violet and blue and silver like stardust against the twilight sky.

The blood of stars.

I cradled the threads in my battered hands, half in awe, half in disbelief. This one reedy string had taken all day to achieve. I would need hundreds more before I had enough to weave a net. At my current pace, it would be well into winter by the time I was done.

Still, I'd learned to rejoice in even the smallest victories.

That evening when my brothers returned, I showed it to them. We celebrated by roasting chestnuts and feasting on purple yams, and counting the stars until we fell asleep.

If only such good times were meant to last.

As the days passed, I could feel myself slipping back into old habits. More than once, I almost snapped at Andahai aloud, almost laughed at one of Yotan's jokes, almost cooed at the nestlings Hasho brought into the cave.

My voice, which I had trained myself to forget when I was at Sparrow Inn, was dangerously loosening from my throat. That could not happen.

I started pretending to be asleep when my brothers returned in the evening, started to feign indifference when they offered to fly me into the clouds. I withdrew from dinner early, didn't laugh at Yotan's jokes, and told Benkai and Reiji I was too tired to spar.

Being alone was easier. Working with the starstroke alone was easier.

Each night my hands healed just enough for me to attack the day's work again. I handled the nettles with care to avoid the worst of their wrath. When I was feeling brave, I practiced touching the thorns and the leaves, teaching myself to hold in my gasps and cries.

Pain doesn't get easier, I reminded myself when I flinched. *You just have to get stronger.*

Slowly, the practice made my tender skin grow thick and resilient, and by the end of the month, I could grab an entire stalk of starstroke without so much as a wince. But I knew it wasn't enough for just my skin or my voice to be strong. All of me had to be, if I wanted to break our curse. My heart, especially.

That evening, I stood outside the cave to observe the moon. It had grown plump over the month. Soon it'd be full, and I would see Seryu again. I hoped he had gleaned something useful from his grandfather.

"You want to consort with a dragon?" Andahai exclaimed when I wrote my brothers about the impending meeting. "Have you forgotten it was a dragon that nearly killed us?"

That was Seryu's grandfather, I mouthed, but my eldest brother didn't understand. He didn't want to.

I tried again, starting to scratch in the mud: *He can help—*

Andahai snatched my writing stick from me. "You are not to meet with him," he said. "I don't care what your reasons are. A dragon's only allegiance is to himself. We cannot trust anyone."

I searched among my brothers for an ally, but found none, not even in Hasho.

"My decision is made, Shiori," Andahai said. "You are not to leave."

"Andahai's right," Benkai said gently. "Our priority must be discovering Raikama's name. But perhaps when we are back, we can come with you."

My head jerked up. They sounded like they'd be away for longer than a day.

"We'll be gone a week," Benkai confirmed. "Maybe longer, if our journey takes us outside Kiata."

"There is plenty of food for you," said Yotan, trying to

make me feel better. "And you'll have the nettles to keep you busy."

Where are you going?

"We will begin in the South," Andahai said. "Snakes are cold-blooded creatures. It is unlikely that Raikama came from the North."

A fair assumption. Yet it stung that they hadn't consulted with me first. I reached for my writing stick to ask more about their route, but Andahai immediately presumed I was trying to ask to go with them.

"You'll only slow us down. Wandei doesn't have time to make another basket for you. Stay in the cave and keep hidden."

Keep hidden? I crossed my arms, both exasperated and insulted at once. I thumped my fists on my chest. *I can fend for myself.*

"Maybe against Reiji, but Benkai lets you win. Bandits won't."

Hasho agreed. "Promise us you'll stay in the cave."

"We've prepared everything that you need," said Andahai. "Food, water, a space to work on the nettles. Don't leave unless it's a dire emergency. Cavorting with dragons is *not* a dire emergency."

I hadn't come all this way just to languish in a cave, weaving starstroke from dawn to dusk. I had come to break the curse.

Anger flared in my chest but I bowed, thanking my brothers for their thoughtfulness and flashing them my meekest smile.

Not one of them noticed that I made no promise.

In the morning, as soon as my brothers left, I grabbed my satchel and hurried to the river to meet Seryu.

Didn't you hear what your brothers said? Kiki exclaimed, flying after me. *Stay in the cave!*

I skipped over a fallen log, jumped into a pile of orange and yellow leaves. *Did you really believe I'd listen to them? Raikama has a dragon pearl, and who better than a dragon to help us?*

Gods, things on Mount Rayuna had been so rushed I hadn't even had a chance to tell Seryu the most terrible part of the curse: that I had to utter Raikama's true name—and lose one of my brothers.

I forged on. *Seryu can help us, I know it.*

Not today, Kiki pleaded. *There was a skirmish in the forest this morning. The flycatchers told me. Soldiers.*

Soldiers? I slowed, surveying the trees rocking in the wind. Their branches were sparse, gray with the coming winter. The percussion of leaves crunching and sweeping was only squirrels and foxes at play. *My father's men?*

Some were, some weren't.

Where are they now?

Kiki flittered higher, chirping something to the other birds. *South of us.*

I relaxed. *So if we keep heading west to the river, we should miss them.*

No! Kiki fluttered. *If you keep heading to the river, you'll get closer to them. They're on the move too, Shiori. You should turn back to the cave.*

And miss meeting with Seryu? I shook my head. Not a chance—I had too many questions for the dragon. *Stop worrying, Kiki. I'll be careful.*

Over the last week, the trees had lost their splendor, their limbs graying with frost as their leaves fell upon the earth in coats of brown and burnt orange. It made for a bleaker, entirely different-looking forest, but I knew my way to the river. Its waters were fierce today, and I followed the roar of rapids until at last I reached its banks.

Seryu! I shouted with my mind. *I'm here!*

No sign of the dragon. He hadn't specified a time for us to meet, so I knelt on the soft dirt, tossing pebbles into the river and staring down blue-dappled lizards perched on the rocks beside me. Above, Kiki hovered anxiously.

Will you calm down? I asked. *There's no one around.*

I leaned back in the grass. If Seryu was going to take all day, then *I* was going to take a nap and let my tired fingers rest.

A lizard crawled over my stomach, hopping onto my satchel.

You're hungry, aren't you? I asked it silently. *I am, too. I should've thought ahead and packed a snack.*

Maple leaves tumbled over my face, their edges crisp and browning. I blew them off my nose and started to roll onto my side, but the lizard was still on my satchel. Its muscles had gone taut, and it jerked its head up, the last movement it was ever to make.

A snake struck, swallowing the lizard in one bite.

I shot up to my elbows, kicking away in fear.

The snake lurched toward me, its mottled head high, two round yellow eyes ensnaring mine.

"Shiori," it hissed.

I went immediately still.

"So this is where you've been hiding." The snake flicked out its tongue, thin and forked. Those yellow eyes darted to the enchanted satchel on my hip. "Her Radiance warns you not to interfere with the spell she has cast. There are events in motion you do not understand."

I swung at it with my dagger, and as it dove back into the leaves, I sprang to my feet and ran.

I didn't know which way I was going; I wove through the wash of orange and gray and brown. Kiki screamed something, but my heart was pounding too loudly in my ears to hear. I figured she was telling me to go faster. Only when my legs started to tire and my throat began to burn did I look back.

The snake was nowhere to be seen, thank the gods. I leaned against a tree to catch my breath.

That was close, I breathed, expecting Kiki to laugh with me.

But she wasn't there.

Kiki? I cried, spinning. I didn't look where I was going and stumbled. Over a dead body.

I wheeled back in horror.

Two cloudy eyes peered up at the sky, still wide with shock. The blood was bright against a scattering of dead leaves and spilled from a neat slash to the abdomen. It was a recent death; the birds and insects hadn't gotten to him yet.

Shiori! Kiki screeched. *The hunters!*

Twigs snapped. Footsteps crunched in the fallen leaves.

I froze. My knees locked as I crouched, hiding behind a bush. But I forgot about my breath. It frosted in the air, the steam curling up and giving away my presence.

"Who's there?" yelled a man, not far.

The shouts grew closer, and I went very still, everything sharpening into focus. I'd run the wrong way. I couldn't hear the river anymore, and—no, no. I cursed my terrible luck.

An arrow shot out from behind the trees, whizzing so close my ears rang, temporarily deafened.

"Lord Hasege, it's a girl!"

I bolted, my heart beating twice as fast as my steps.

There's four of them! Kiki screeched. *Watch out! Behind the bushes—*

A hunter leapt out, low, his knife angling for my leg. My first impulse was to scream, but luckily, fear closed up my lungs. I scraped away, only barely.

Another one! On your side!

Another hunter knocked me to the ground. It happened so fast that I tasted dirt before I felt the ringing in my head, but I quickly scrambled to my feet.

I dove into the bushes, skidding across leaves and tumbling down little mounds. It felt like I had been running for hours, but I could still see the dead bodies peeking out from beneath the foliage. It couldn't have been more than a minute before I heard footsteps again.

There were four of them, just as Kiki had said. Only they weren't hunters, not with their feathered helmets and leather armor. They were sentinels.

"When you're overpowered by an opponent, flee," Reiji had told me during our lessons. "Benkai will tell you to stay and fight, but winning is not about honor. It's about surviving to fight again."

I was trying. But the tallest one—the leader—was fast. Strong, too. I narrowly ducked the tip of his sword as it came slicing toward my face. Thinking myself victorious, I let my guard down; I didn't see his foot sweep out to throw me onto my back.

The earth thudded under me, and I bit my cheek not to cry out in pain. By the time I rose, three arrows were pointed at my head. The leader lifted his helmet.

Takkan.

The cruel stare he gave me was the same as before. Black eyes, hard and unyielding. Crooked smile, so cold that my stomach turned to ice. Yet something was different. His armor was plain and unadorned—no deep blue chain mail—and the scabbard of his sword was bereft of the Bushian crest.

"Hold your weapons," he ordered as his men rounded on me. Three fellow sentinels, but to my disappointment, not one of them was the kind soldier from Sparrow Inn.

"I remember you: the kitchen wench who wouldn't bow," Takkan sneered. "Your timing is suspect, demon. I knew you were no cook."

He held me up by my neck and forced me to look at the bodies fallen in the forest. "Look around: your companions are dead. Soon you will be too."

Arrows stuck out of their ribs, gashes bright red with

death. All seven were robed in brown, camouflaging themselves with the woods. Assassins.

Everything was ringing, the trees rustling in the wind, my pulse drumming in my throat. I kicked air, and my fingers clawed uselessly at my neck. *I'm not with them.*

Takkan didn't understand. Neither did his men.

"I can't even see her face," grumbled one of the sentinels. "Can't she speak?"

Takkan squeezed my jaw so hard it hurt. He shook me. "Where is my cousin, demon? Speak, or this breath will be your last."

Was he talking about the soldier at Sparrow Inn?

"She doesn't look like she's with the A'landans," said another sentinel, studying me. He was the oldest of the four, his pewter-colored hair tied into a topknot. "We should let her go."

"Let her go? I've met this minx before." Takkan shook me again, harder this time. "Where is Takkan?"

I looked up, disoriented. I could have sworn he had just asked me where Takkan was.

But you're Takkan, I thought, my mind reeling in confusion.

"The girl's a wildling, not an assassin," said the older sentinel again. "Hasege, we don't have time for this. Release her and let us be on our way."

Hasege?

Whatever this false Takkan's name really was, it did not matter. I grabbed an arrow from his quiver and dragged the pointed end across his face.

Hasege let out a roar, and I head-butted him in the skull. It was the best use I'd ever made of the bowl on my head. He dropped me, and I snatched my dagger, twisting away from the sentinels.

I wasn't fast enough. He seized my wrist, squeezing it until my heart leapt with pain and the dagger fell out of my grasp.

He caught it in his other hand. Blood trickled down to his chin, clotting in the dark bristles of his beard. He was pressing the blade against my neck when he let out a deep laugh.

"Look what we have here," he said, showing his men. "Takkan's dagger."

Takkan's dagger? My thoughts churned wildly. But that . . . that meant that the sentinel at Sparrow Inn was . . . was . . . Lord Bushian's son. My betrothed.

My head hurt too much to make any sense of it, and it didn't help that Hasege dug the dagger deeper into my skin, the metal's sting cold and biting. "So you *have* seen him."

I kicked at the three sentinels, knowing it was useless to try and make them understand, but I was desperate enough to try anyway. *He gave it to me.*

The older one, the one who'd suggested letting me go, frowned. "She has Takkan's emblem." The sentinel pointed at the knotted tassel on the dagger, the one I'd thought a useless decoration. "She is under his protection."

Hasege darkened. "Would he offer to protect a spy? I think not. More likely she stole the tassel from him."

"We ought to release her."

The emblem dangled before me, a blur of blue, and for

the first time, I saw it clearly. All these weeks I had ignored it for the dagger, never noticed that the other side of its silver plate was emblazoned with Takkan's name and family crest: a rabbit on a mountain, surrounded by five plum blossoms—and a full, white moon.

Gods, it was true. The sentinel at Sparrow Inn *was* Takkan! If Lord Bushian's son had given me his protection, no sentinel could harm me without grave consequences.

Hasege's gaze hardened. A beat too late, I realized he had no intention of letting me go. By the time I started running, his men seized me. I tried to kick and punch, but ropes bound my hands together, and someone forced a gag into my mouth.

The sentinels threw me to the ground. I landed against a hard rock and winced from the pain. As the wind whined against their blades, I went rabbit-still, awaiting the blow that would end me.

It never came. Someone threw me on top of a horse. Before my legs finished swinging down, Hasege slammed the pommel of his sword into the bowl on my head—and the edges of my world faded into oblivion.

CHAPTER EIGHTEEN

"You say you found her in the woods?"

"Yes, my lady. North of the Baiyun Pass." A delicate pause. "She slashed Hasege—"

"In the face. Yes, I've heard the story."

As the voices drew closer, and footsteps thudded down the dungeon, I perked up. It'd been five dawns since I'd arrived in this miserable place, but I recognized the man's voice. He was the same sentinel who had spoken up for me against Hasege and his hooligans in the woods.

Silently, in the dark of my cell, I pressed my ear against the wall to listen more closely.

The lady harrumphed, a sound deeper than her voice. "Tell me the truth, Oriyu. Could she really be a spy?"

"Unlikely. She had Lord Takkan's emblem—"

"Yes, a fact none of you bothered to tell me! Now let me inside. I want to have a word with her."

The door rattled open, and I peered at the lady from under my wooden bowl. Could she be Lady Bushian? The light from her candle was weak, so I couldn't see her features clearly, but I made out a sturdy figure in plain blue brocade and a thick woolen shawl. Gray marbled her tightly waxed hair, and a pale jade bracelet glimmered from one of her wrists. But what caught my attention was the satchel hanging over her shoulder.

My satchel.

"You're not asleep," she said, seeing my fingers twitch. "Sit up. And don't pretend not to understand; the guards have already informed me that you're smarter than you look."

Obediently I got up, only to lunge for my satchel.

Oriyu blocked me, and I tripped over my bound legs. "You'll have to answer some questions before you get your bag back."

I sank weakly against the wall. I'd waited days for someone to interrogate me, or whip me for scarring Hasege's face. But no one had come. I'd been utterly forgotten, lucky if the guards remembered to bring me one meal a day. The hunger had been worse than the waiting.

Now, suddenly, I was to be interrogated?

"I've been told you cannot speak," said Lady Bushian. "You will answer with a nod or shake of your head. Understand?"

I nodded once. Satisfied, Lady Bushian motioned at the ropes over my wrists and ankles. Oriyu only cut my legs free.

"Get up and follow me," said the lady, picking up her skirts. "This place is hardly suitable for an interrogation."

Seeing as I had no choice, I wobbled after her.

"You certainly don't look like a spy" was all she said before Oriyu opened the prison door.

Sunlight stung my eyes, and teeth chattering, I hugged my arms over my chest, startled by the brutal cold lashing at my cheeks. And the mountains! I didn't recognize any of them. I had to be farther from my brothers than I'd thought.

I started mining my memory of my old geography lessons, but once I saw the embroidered banners hanging from the castle walls, I knew exactly where I was. The one place I'd been trying to avoid for over a decade: Castle Bushian, the imperial fortress of Iro.

The stronghold of the North was just as I had imagined: grim and bleak, with barren courtyards and parched gardens surrounding a lifeless castle with gray-tiled roofs. Even the air smelled heavy, of sandstone and woodsmoke. My hopes of escape melted, as if they were made of ice.

We were about to enter one of the fortress's guardhouses when a young girl with two braids and persimmons sticking out of her pockets ran toward us, her face flush with excitement.

"Is that her, Mama?" she cried, breathless. "Is this the girl who—"

"Megari!" Lady Bushian chided. "I distinctly remember telling you to stay inside the castle. You'll catch cold out here. You should be resting."

"You can't expect me to rest *all* day." Megari beamed in my direction. "I wanted to meet the girl who fought Hasege. May she join us for lunch?"

Lady Bushian immediately frowned. "How did you hear about that?"

Megari grinned at Oriyu, who pretended to look away

and adjust his helmet. "Oriyu told me. He said she had Takkan's dagger, too! Please, Mama, may she join us?"

"It would hardly be appropriate."

"But she's hungry. Aren't you?" Megari's eyes sparkled with mischief. She looked to be no older than ten, and the hem of her dress was striped with mud. I liked her immediately.

When her mother wasn't looking, I answered Megari with a small nod. I wasn't just hungry. I was famished.

Megari tried to slip one of her persimmons into my shawl, but Oriyu cast us both a stern glance.

"I'll get you some later," she whispered, following her mother and me into the guardhouse before Lady Bushian could forbid it.

Inside, a young woman was seated primly on a wooden stool. She clutched a scarlet umbrella and was dressed entirely in white except for an ebony belt embroidered with mountains. Her round face, powdered and accentuated by a mole on her right cheek, looked kind—but once she raised her eyes, I saw that they were sharp as thorns.

"Zairena?" Megari breathed, turning to her mother. "What is *she* doing here?"

Lady Bushian glared at her. "Manners, Megari. Or Oriyu will send you back to your room."

"Is this the thief you wanted me to meet?" Zairena asked, bowing demurely. "The child who stole Takkan's emblem?"

My eyes narrowed. *Child?* I couldn't have been more than a year younger than she was. And I didn't *steal* the emblem.

"Oriyu claims Takkan gave it to her," said Lady Bushian

tightly. "When and why, we shall soon find out. Hasege said she was with assassins he encountered in the Zhensa, but my nephew is hardly a trustworthy source of news. I hate to ask, Zairena, but does she look familiar to you?"

Zairena leaned forward to scrutinize me, resting her chin on her umbrella. "No, no. I would have remembered one such as her, with that strange bowl on her head. I have faith that all the bandits who attacked my parents are dead. Lord Sharima'en has such a way of claiming the wicked." She paused. "Though perhaps there *is* something wicked about her. Hasege did tell me about this girl. He said she tried to kill him."

"No, she didn't!" Megari argued. "Mama, she's not an assassin. She can't—"

Lady Bushian's shoulders tensed. "I will decide the girl's fate," she said, drawing out a dagger from her side. Takkan's emblem swung from its hilt, and mud encrusted its silken cords.

"Two weeks ago, my son told me he was going hunting with Hasege. He took five of Iro's best sentinels with him. Hardly the appropriate entourage for a simple hunting trip."

"Takkan's never been a very good liar," Megari muttered.

"Their mission took them deep into the Zhensa Forest, where assassins ambushed them. They were separated, and Takkan has not returned." Lady Bushian's cold gaze met mine. "And in the forest where he went missing, my nephew found you—with this." She dangled the emblem before me. "Did you steal it from my son?"

I shook my head vigorously.

"Am I to believe he gave it to you?"

To think I'd wanted Takkan's dagger, not the emblem. I swallowed hard.

Yes, he did. I nodded firmly.

"When?"

That was a harder question to answer without the use of my voice. I put up my fingers. *Four, five, maybe six weeks ago?*

"Why?"

I pursed my lips, then scooped the air and stirred. *He liked my cooking.*

Lady Bushian shook her head, not understanding.

"She gave him food," Megari guessed when I pretended to drink from my cupped hands. "She cooked for him."

Lady Bushian raised an eyebrow as I confirmed this with a nod. "You cooked for him," she repeated.

Soup, I mouthed, pretending to feed myself.

That, Lady Bushian seemed to understand. She gripped her son's dagger tightly.

Oriyu spoke up: "She was alone when we found her. Hasege . . . attacked her, in spite of my opposition. She cut him in self-defense."

"I see." Lady Bushian's eyes were like her son's, their depths easy to underestimate. "What did you say her name was, again?"

"Hasege called her Lina."

"Lina," echoed Lady Bushian. "A simple name. But I cannot decide if she is a simple girl. Time will tell, I suppose. Oriyu, free her."

As the sentinel cut the ropes at my wrists, Zairena's lips puckered as if she'd tasted something sour.

"Lady Bushian," she said in a low voice, "are you certain it's wise to allow her to stay? I fear there must be something amiss with her."

She stared at the bowl on my head, making it clear exactly what was amiss. "What if she harbors dark spirits or brings ill luck to the castle?" She twirled her umbrella. "I didn't want to say it earlier, but Hasege warned me that she . . . she might be a demon."

Megari snorted, reminding us of her presence. "Hasege would call his own mother a demon if it suited him. There are no demons in Kiata."

"That's where you're wrong," Zairena warned the girl. "All the demons are sealed up in the Holy Mountains, and though they can't leave, they call out to the weak, compelling them to commit their evil deeds. I worry that this girl could be possessed."

"That's nonsense."

"Respect your elders, Megari," Lady Bushian said, shooting her daughter a warning look. She turned to Zairena, reassuring her. "I trust my son more than my nephew. Takkan mentioned meeting a cook in Tianyi Village. What he did not mention was that she couldn't speak."

"Cannot speak?" Zairena touched the mole on her powdered cheek. Her tone oozed with pity. "I see. It would be like Takkan to feel sorry for such a girl. He has your compassion and generosity."

"Yes, I thought he'd inherited my honesty as well," Lady Bushian replied dryly. "But it seems he's been taking lessons from his sister."

"He's a very poor student, Mother," quipped Megari. "You have nothing to fear."

"Don't I?" Lady Bushian's lips thinned. "We'll see if—*when* he returns."

The word *when* came out strained, and in spite of my resolve to remain indifferent, I felt a twinge of concern. My own mission was too urgent for me to concern myself with Takkan's troubles, but now that I knew it was he, not Hasege, who'd been the kind sentinel from Sparrow Inn, I certainly didn't wish him dead.

Lady Bushian composed herself and turned to me. "Winter is upon us, and you will stay until it passes. In the kitchen, I've decided. Oriyu will show you to the servants' quarters. Now go."

I wouldn't budge. Not until she returned my satchel.

"The bag, Lady Bushian," said Oriyu. "I believe she wishes it returned."

"What's inside?" Zairena asked.

"Nothing," replied Lady Bushian, drawing her eyebrows together. "Absolutely nothing."

Thank the gods, that enchanter hadn't lied about the bag's powers. I practically snatched the satchel from Lady Bushian's outstretched arms. Clasping it in both hands, I fought the urge to make sure the nettles were still inside.

"Poor child," said Zairena, shaking her head as I held the

satchel tight. "It must be of sentimental value—all she has left in the world."

I relaxed my grip. I needed to appear less attached. The last thing I wanted to do was attract suspicion to my satchel.

Zairena patted my shoulder, drawing so close I could smell the incense suffused into her robes. "You aren't alone, Lina. I know how you must feel."

Before I could push her away, she withdrew and addressed Lady Bushian: "Allow me to walk Lina to the kitchen and acquaint her with the staff." She draped her cloak over my shoulders. "She looks like she could use a hearty meal, and it is the least I can do."

"Are you certain?"

"It would be no trouble at all."

"You've grown into such a charitable young lady," said Lady Bushian in praise. "Megari would do well to learn from you."

Megari rolled her eyes, and under the cover of my bowl, I did the same. At least I wasn't the only person who recognized a two-faced viper when I saw one.

As if on cue, a twisted smile bloomed on Zairena's lips once we were alone.

"You've charmed Lady Megari," she said, opening her umbrella and raising it aloft. "But that charm won't work on me." She turned on her heel and pointed at a stone structure opposite the castle. Smoke billowed from its chimney, and fire glittered in the windows.

"That is where you'll work," she said, then turned

abruptly, guiding me toward a brick storehouse not far from the dungeon. A servant was waiting outside, holding a wooden bucket along with a folded blanket and a stack of robes—my new uniform, I assumed. After a hasty bow to Zairena, he thrust the items into my arms and scurried back toward the castle.

Zairena opened the storehouse's back door. With relish, she gestured into the cellar. "And this is where you'll sleep."

My back went rigid. This was not the servants' quarters, as Lady Bushian had promised.

Inside, a narrow wooden stairwell led to a cavernous chamber filled with sacks of rice and, from the smell, barrels of salted fish. There was no sleeping mat, no hearth, not even a place for me to heat a kettle.

Zairena arched a thinly painted eyebrow. "What, you thought you'd stay in the castle with the other servants? We can't have you bringing ill fortune into the castle. Besides, no one wants to be near you with that *thing* on your head." She paused. "Except the rats, of course; they like to visit now that the weather has turned cold."

Anger stirred in my heart. I was no fool: I would freeze sleeping in this place. Likely even fall ill and die.

"Hurry and wash," Zairena said, stabbing the end of her umbrella into the ground. "Chiruan is expecting you in the kitchen."

Wash? With what?

There was no water, only barrels of freshly caught fish scattered among the ones of those that had already been salted and dried. The smell was rancid.

Before she left, she lifted her cloak from my shoulders. "You won't be needing this anymore."

A chill instantly seeped into my bones, and Zairena shut the cellar door, leaving me in the dark.

At least it was quiet here. Secluded, too.

I peeked into my satchel. Bright light fanned out, illuminating the room. Everything was still inside, the fragile threads of starstroke sparkling as if stained by the blood of stars, the raw nettles still burning with demonfire.

I took one careful step down, then another and another. The wooden stairs were old, some cracked and splintered. Cobwebs clung to my hands when I touched the walls, and I shook them off, repulsed.

Rats squeaked, emboldened by the shadows, and I staggered against one of the barrels of fish. Demons take me, I hated rats. Not as much as I hated snakes, but close.

I opened my satchel wider. A sharp light spilled out, and the rats skittered, frightened by the dark magic I'd brought here. A small triumph.

I shivered as I dressed. It was still day and already it was freezing in here. That did not bode well for the night. Or the rest of the winter.

Something rustled outside, scraping against the wall.

Kiki? I called.

No, it was just an ordinary bird. Likely a raven or a crow.

Worry preyed on me. All week I'd called for her, stretching my mind as far as it could go, but Kiki never responded. Had Hasege found her and destroyed her? Or had she flown to my brothers, looking for help?

Strands of Emuri'en, I hoped she was safe.

I shut my satchel, and as the light from the starstroke dwindled, I raced back to the stairs before the rats regained the courage to come out again.

On the last step, I turned back, my eyes adjusting to the shadows and my ears picking out the skittering roaches and rats. Critters, unbearable cold, and rank smells—those I could deal with. This place was undesirable, which meant no guards, no maids. No one would come into the cellar, especially at night.

Little did Zairena know it, but she'd given me a sanctuary, a new workplace. Until I found a way to reunite with my brothers, it would have to do.

CHAPTER NINETEEN

The promise of warmth and food had me hurrying to the kitchen. The wooden building radiated heat, and inside, the cooks shouted orders for sesame oil and ginger while servants gossiped, stacking lacquer trays and porcelain cups and copper kettles. But when I entered, all became silent. The servants dropped their plates and waved charms to ward off demons; the cooks shut the lids over their clay pots and grabbed their knives.

It seemed that Zairena had already sent word of my arrival.

I lifted my chin. *Let her try and make my life miserable. I'm not staying long anyway.*

Only the head chef, Chiruan, acknowledged me. "If Lady Zairena hadn't warned us you were a demon, I'd mistake you for a fish," he grunted, throwing me a washcloth. Short and wide, he had the build of a barrel, the sturdiness of a brick, and the belly of a bear. He was strong, too, and the cloth landed on my arm with a slap. "You reek, girl."

I sniffed my hands. He was right: I *did* smell.

After I wiped my hands, he tossed me a pouch of rice wrapped in dried reed leaves, again throwing it with force. "Eat quickly, then get to work."

I retreated to a corner and wolfed down the meal, savoring the bits of salted pork and pickled cabbage. All too soon the rice was gone; my sharp pangs of hunger were only half-satisfied. But there would be no more food until dinner.

My work wasn't so different from my chores at Mrs. Dainan's inn: I swept the kitchen and the pantry, washed the dishes, and scrubbed burnt rice off the bottom of the pots. When Chiruan sent me out to fetch wood from the storehouses, I searched the fortress for a way out.

Castle Bushian was one of Kiata's smallest strongholds—I could walk the entire perimeter in half an hour—but one of the best defended, situated atop a craggy hill. High stone walls surrounded the castle, except on the east, which bordered the Baiyun River. There were towers festooned with archers, and two gates—one on the north side and one on the south—manned by plenty of guards.

Getting out wouldn't be easy. But surviving the Zhensa in this cold would be even more difficult. Already, frost slicked the surface of my wooden pails.

Winter was here.

One morning, the kitchen was practically empty when I reported to work, but Chiruan was at the stove, steaming a cake over the fire. It smelled heavenly, warm and sweet, a hint of ginger wafting across the room.

"Persimmon cake, Lady Megari's favorite," said Chiruan,

cutting three slices onto a blue porcelain plate. He set it on a wooden tray, beside a basket of fresh fruits beautifully decorated with a sprig of plum blossoms.

"She's taken to her bed the past few days, but whenever she requests cake, it's a sign she's on the mend. She specifically asked for *you*, Fishgirl, to deliver it."

His tone was devoid of insult or judgment, which surprised me. As did Megari's request. *Me?*

"It is not my place to question Lady Megari, only to attend to her wishes. Her room is on the uppermost level of the castle, in the East Mountain wing, left corridor. She should be practicing her music at this hour, so follow the sound of her lute if you become lost."

Chiruan returned his attention to the iron pots whistling over the fire. Dinner, I presumed.

"Don't linger," he said sharply. "This is not a respite from your chores, and if the maids see you on their way back from the orchard, I will not defend you."

I grabbed the tray, nodding to show I understood.

"Wrap a scarf around your head so the guards don't see the bowl. They'll ask fewer questions that way."

Chiruan's foresight turned out to be correct. Although the guards inspected my tray of persimmon cake, no one questioned my presence inside the castle.

The halls were narrow, barely wide enough for two to walk side by side, and the paneled walls were wooden and sparse, unlike the gilded doorframes and painted murals in the imperial palace.

As I followed the soft strumming of a moon lute upstairs,

a room with open doors caught my eye. Inside were two embroidery frames, a loom, and a spinning wheel. Not unlike Raikama's old sewing room.

"This way!" Megari exclaimed, peeking out from her room down the hall. "I worried you were lost."

I hurried inside and set the tray on one of her lacquered tables. Megari watched me inquisitively, her hands clasped behind her back. A gentle flush tinged her cheeks, but her breathing was short and there were shadows under her eyes. I hoped the cake would help her feel better.

"Wait, don't go," she said as I turned for the door. "I've been wanting to talk to you all week."

I bowed my head and pointed toward the kitchen building. *Chiruan is waiting for me.*

"Sit, sit," she insisted. "It's an order."

Megari waited until I sank into one of her silk pillows. I could have fallen asleep then and there, if I hadn't been so worried that I stank of fish.

She reached for the plumpest fruit in the basket. "Have a persimmon. This year's crop is the sweetest yet. I would know, since they're my most favorite fruit. Take some cake too."

Thank you. I tucked the persimmon into my pocket, but the cake I wolfed down in three ravenous bites. My stomach growled so loudly I was thankful the curse only penalized my tongue for speaking. Otherwise, my brothers would be long gone.

"Eat more," said Megari. "Mother and Father always say that courage is the Bushian creed, but in times like these I wish it were more like 'Keep to yourself and drink tea.'

Maybe then my oaf of a brother wouldn't have us all agonizing over what's happened to him."

I stopped chewing. Swallowed.

"No, you should eat. I've been stuffing myself with persimmons and cakes, trying not to worry about Takkan. But I shouldn't. Worry, I mean." Megari straightened, though her shoulders still trembled. "He promised to be back before the Winter Festival, and he never breaks a promise. He's too afraid of me to even try."

I offered her a brave smile. I knew what it was like to worry about brothers.

The last time I had spoken to Takkan, he had asked me to come to Iro. It was beautiful, he'd said. His eagerness to return home was plain to see. He would not have kept away by choice. Not without word to his family.

Not unless something terrible had happened.

"I feel better now that you're here, though," Megari said, perking up a little. Her small shoulders still shook, but she reached for one of her dolls and hugged it. "I have a feeling I know why he gave you his emblem. You're like a girl out of one of his stories."

My smile turned inquisitive. His stories? Takkan didn't strike me as a spinner of tales, but what did I know about my former betrothed? I hadn't even been able to recognize that his brute of a cousin was traveling under his name.

"I suppose it's my duty to watch over you until he's back," said Megari. "Gods know what horrible lies Hasege and Zairena have spread about you, with that bowl on your head. You can't take it off, can you?"

I twisted my lips, expressing the obvious.

"That's unfortunate." The little girl sighed. "It's odd, you know—Zairena wasn't always a bully, not like my cousin. Now they're like two blossoms on the same rotten branch."

Megari rose. "Mama will keep Hasege in line at least, but these days, Zairena could set the whole castle on fire and Mama wouldn't blame her."

I spread my arms in question. *Why is that?*

"Because her parents were killed by bandits deep in the Zhensa. Mama was devastated—Lady Tesuwa was her best friend."

That explained the white robes; Zairena was in mourning.

"I heard you were found in the Zhensa too," said Megari, opening her desk drawer. "Were you on your way home?"

I didn't know how to answer so she could understand.

She took out a sheet of parchment and offered me a brush and ink she had already prepared. "Can you write? If you tell me where you're from, I can ask Oriyu to send you back. Or you could point to a map."

I hesitated. At Sparrow Inn, I'd considered telling Takkan who I was, but Raikama's curse had stopped me. My stepmother couldn't know I was in Iro. Did I dare try again with Megari?

My wrist tensed, the starstroke burns making it hard for my fingers to hold something so delicate, but I ignored the pain.

I am

I lifted my hand, not daring to continue. It was a test, these two innocent words. I waited with my brush hovering over the paper. Nothing happened, no foreboding shadows. No snakes.

Was I finally out of Raikama's reach?

I dipped my brush into the ink eagerly. There was so much to say. I could tell her to bring me back to my brothers, or that my stepmother was a sorceress. Or that my brothers had been turned into cranes . . .

But as I started to write, the ink splattered, spreading impossibly . . . into the shape of a nebulous black serpent.

The brush slipped from my hand.

I'm sorry, I mouthed, blotting the precious pages with my sleeve. The serpent had vanished, but ink had spilled all over her desk.

"It's only a spill," said Megari.

It was no spill. My hands curled into fists as a wave of heat washed over my face. There would be no writing to Father, no soliciting Megari's help. Nowhere was I safe from Raikama's curse.

The serpent still burning in my memory, I scrambled for the tray I had brought. I needed to leave, to get back to the kitchen, but the doors suddenly opened from the other side, and in strode Zairena with a pot of steaming tea.

"Eating cakes again, Megari?" She swept right past me, as if I didn't exist. "Aren't you tired of persimmons by now? Persimmon cake, persimmon soup, persimmon tea. The last time you ate so much, you were sick for days."

"I was tired, not sick," Megari said flatly. "And it's my favorite fruit."

"Yes, and I'd say you've had enough of it." Zairena surveyed the crumbs on the plate with a wrinkled nose. "Besides, what does an A'landan like Chiruan know about making sweets? The only desserts worth eating are from Chajinda."

Zairena set down the tray and poured a cup of tea for the young girl. "Perhaps when winter is over, I'll send for monkeycakes. I could use a taste of home."

Monkeycakes were Chajinda's most famous dessert. Even my brothers, who didn't have a predilection for sweets, always sought them from the stalls at the Summer Festival. I liked them, too. They reminded me of the cakes my mother used to make. Cakes I doubted I would ever taste again.

Megari lowered her moon lute cautiously. "Will you, really?"

"Yes, but only if you finish your tea. You're on the mend, Megari, so long as you eat your vegetables and stop inviting wild girls into your chambers."

I'd finished cleaning the spill, and Zairena at last acknowledged me with a glare. "She's a demon worshipper. Didn't you hear your mother?"

Megari struck a loud, jarring chord. "My mother didn't say that. Hasege did."

"Just as well."

"Hasege's an idiot. You used to think so, too."

"When I was your age," Zairena said tersely. "Then I learned to have more respect. Hasege is out there risking his

life to search for your brother. He might be Takkan's only hope of making it home alive."

Megari's shoulders fell, and Zairena refilled her tea. "That's a good girl. Now, continue practicing your music. I'll see that Lina returns to the kitchen."

Before Megari could protest, Zairena grabbed me by my sash and dragged me out.

Once we were down the hall, she snatched the persimmon from my pocket. "Stealing, are we?"

She lifted a hand to slap me, but I'd had enough of that from Mrs. Dainan. I caught her wrist, holding it high, and her eyebrows shot up with shock.

There we stood, in the middle of the cramped hall, locked in a furious standstill. I raised my chin, daring her to call for the sentinels.

What I didn't expect was for her to drop the persimmon. It fell to the hard wooden floor, and she smashed it with her foot, pressing down with all her strength. When she stepped away, all that remained was a mess of pulp.

Stunned, I let go of her hand, and she spun on her heel, knowing that in some unspoken way, she had won.

Snow fell that evening, the first I had seen, but not the first of the season. A reminder that my birthday, the first day of winter, had passed during the week I'd been in the castle dungeon. I used to start counting down the days and weeks as soon as the Autumn Festival passed, but this year I had completely forgotten.

I closed my eyes, pretending I was home and imagining the celebration banquet—the musicians and dancers, the entire palace smelling of pine and cedar, the roofs decorated with carpets of snow. I imagined arriving in a festive palanquin with plush silk satin cushions, attired in a scarlet jacket with a long brocade sash, and a headdress woven with silken plum blossoms and all the flowers of winter. And the food . . .

Braised pumpkin with pork and ginger, rice cakes with pureed red beans, sea bass marinated in sweet wine with pickled carrots . . . It was so real in my mind I could practically taste the dishes. But my belly wasn't fooled, and the only guests at my birthday "banquet" this year were the rats squeaking around my slippers.

To celebrate, I set aside the starstroke, giving my hands a day of rest. I lay in the fish cellar watching moonlight pierce the gaps between the bricks and catching the flecks of melted snow that slid through the roof slats.

Only a few months ago, I had to remind everyone I was sixteen, not a child. If I were ever to return, I doubted anyone would make that mistake again. These last few months had stretched on like years. I could hardly believe I was only seventeen.

Halfway through the night, something tickled my nose. I swatted at my face, thinking it was a fly.

Is that how you greet me, Shiori, when I've come all this way to wish you happy belated birthday?

Kiki!

I bolted up. My little bird perched upon my hand, and I cradled her close to my chest. *I missed you so much.*

I followed you, but— She showed me her wing, which had become bent. *From the storm.*

Oh, you poor thing. I straightened the crease, thumbing the silvery-gold etchings on her wing, so delicate they looked like feathers. *There, good as new.*

Kiki beat her wings gratefully, but when she spoke, her voice wobbled. *I worried that boor of a sentinel might have killed you.*

He didn't, thank the Eternal Courts. But you'll never guess where he brought us.

She rotated her neck and wrinkled the tip of her beak. *To the fishmonger's?*

I laughed silently. *Welcome to my belated birthday banquet,* I thought in my most festive voice, *hosted this year in Castle Bushian's most luxurious fish cellar.*

This is Castle Bushian? she exclaimed.

Ironic, isn't it? I thought wryly. *But I thank Emuri'en that you're here. I could use some help getting out of this place.*

Getting out? The cold will kill you, Shiori. You should stay here until winter is over. Stay and finish the net, then reunite with your brothers in the spring.

There's still time, I insisted. *The Zhensa is right outside Iro. They can't be too far.*

There's a reason the Zhensa is called the never-ending forest. Kiki burrowed herself into my hair, her voice close to my ear. *Think, Shiori. What good is reuniting with your brothers without the net?*

They'll be looking for me—

I'll spread word among the creatures of the forest that you're well, she interrupted. *Your brothers should be searching for Raikama's name, not worrying about keeping you safe. You're a distraction to them, just as they are to you.*

How are they a distraction to me?

Look at your hands. Kiki brushed a wing against the scars on my palm. Even that made me wince. *Will you be able to finish the starstroke net without making a sound?*

Yes. I nodded staunchly. *I will.*

That is because you have a strong will. But you'll need more than that to beat this curse. You'll need a strong heart, too. For all the joy your brothers bring you, you wouldn't be able to laugh with them or joke with them or talk to them at night, and in the day, you'd torture yourself with guilt when they became cranes. You'd be miserable, and the last thing you'd want is to work on the starstroke. She threw up her wings, her way of showing disbelief. *Besides, do you really want to spend all winter cooped up in that cave?*

Deep down, I knew she had a point. Now that winter was here, the cave would be even colder than my cellar. But my heart was set on finding my brothers again and breaking our curse together. Nothing could sway me.

You think this fortress isn't a cage? That my tasks here aren't a distraction? I retorted. *Everyone treats me like a monster, Kiki. I can't even go to the river to look for Seryu. I won't stay, not while there's still a chance.*

Kiki sniffed. *Stubborn girl. It's a bad idea, I'm telling you so. If you attempt to escape, the best possible outcome is to end up back in the dungeon again. Don't say I didn't warn you.*

I won't, I replied silently, pulling the blanket up to my shoulders.

I was seventeen now. Wise enough to know that the only one to blame for my decisions was me.

CHAPTER TWENTY

The luck of the dragons was not on my side. The next day and the next, it snowed and snowed, then rain came and turned the world into slush as the winds howled through shrunken trees outside my cellar.

But it wasn't the weather that prevented me from leaving. The real problem was the gates. All I needed was the crack of an opening so I could slip out, but the iron doors remained stolidly closed and locked.

Who do you think is going to come in and out of the fortress during this storm? Kiki posed.

Still, I didn't give up, and on the third night, my patience was rewarded.

I was pounding my nettles, chipping off their jagged leaves and whittling off their fiery thorns, when the drums boomed.

At first I mistook the sound for thunder. But a rhythm emerged, making the walls shudder. I stopped to listen.

Three more beats. Silence. Then the drums started again, faster this time.

I sat up, my muscles tensing. *Kiki, do you hear that?*

Kiki leapt off my shoulder and squeezed through the bricks to peek outside. *Torches are going up on the watchtowers. I don't know what it means, but the guards are lowering the bridge over the river. Something's happening.*

What good fortune! If the guards were lowering the bridge, that meant someone was coming in. This could be our opportunity to escape. Hurriedly, I gathered my nettles into my satchel, slung it over my shoulder, and slipped outside.

Do you have a plan, or do you mean to wander aimlessly? Kiki asked tartly.

I have a plan. Mostly. *You know the stable I pass every day on my way to the kitchen? I'll steal a horse and ride out while the gate is still open.*

That's a terrible plan! Kiki exclaimed. *They'll shoot you down before you even pass the gate.*

I have to try.

I kept to the shadows as I scuttled across empty courtyards, dipping into the bushes when I saw movement ahead.

Just like Kiki said. Guards, soldiers, even sentinels—all rushing to the north gate. Some had even brought their horses.

They were moving fast, and the gate was already rumbling, the heavy iron doors grating against the earth. Archers sprang from the watchtowers, and horsemen rounded the fortress walls as rain washed down, churning the slush on the ground into muddy pools.

Beyond the gate was complete darkness.

Finally I acknowledged that this had been a terrible, terrible idea.

Now you see? Kiki whispered harshly. *You think you can just dance out of the gate in this storm? Let's go back to the cellar before someone sees you. Come on.*

I bit my lip in defeat, hesitating only a moment before I picked up my feet and started to plod back to the fish cellar.

Behind me, the guards yelled at each other, pulling the gate open. "Make way—Lord Takkan has returned!"

My pulse quickened in counterpoint to my halting steps. Takkan was back?

Arrows whined through the sky, heading for the fortress. I only caught flashes in the torchlight. Then they landed, chipping the castle's stone walls and stabbing the tiled roofs. More than a few skipped across the ground, landing not far from my feet.

I jumped back in shock. The fortress was under attack!

Kiki darted into a guardhouse for cover. As my bird hid on the wooden slats above the window, I crouched outside the door and squinted at what was happening.

A horse charged through the gate, its rider crying out words I could not discern. There were two men on the mount, and I thought I glimpsed Takkan, but I could not be sure.

As the storm intensified, the sentinels swiftly worked to close the gate. But men on the other side still funneled through the crack, their horses splashing against the wet ground.

Assassins.

There had to be over a dozen of them, their blades gleaming.

Rain pounded on my head, drowning out the sounds of the unfolding fight, but I crawled back inside the guardhouse.

I pressed my cheek against a pillar. Outside, men fell. Lanterns shattered.

Fear crept up to my throat as Kiki shrank behind my hair. *Never thought I'd say this, Shiori, but I miss the fish cellar.*

I grabbed a stool, breaking off a leg to use as a weapon, and hid under the window. Flying arrows made the lanterns flicker; they were so close I could hear them slice through the rain.

"Help!" a sentinel outside was yelling. "Oriyu? Hasege?"

His cry was lost in the storm, the alarm bells, and the clamor of battle, but I heard him. I peeked out, recognizing the sentinel's horse as the one that had burst through the gate. An arrow shaft jutted out of the mount's flank, and now the sentinel was easing his companion off its back.

"Help! Lord Takkan is wounded."

My toes curled in my shoes. I had to do something. I had to help.

Shiori, don't. Kiki yanked my hair.

I was already darting out. *Here,* I waved to the warrior, and grabbed Takkan by the legs. Together we hobbled back toward the guardhouse—evading arrows and falling debris.

We laid Takkan on a mat, his face twisted in pain.

I tried to ask what had happened, but to no avail.

"Don't just stand there, girl," barked the sentinel. "Help me remove his armor."

I obeyed. I took off Takkan's gauntlets, his boots, his sword, my fingers lingering only the briefest second over the carving on its sheath. His family crest, I could tell, even in the shadows. A full moon wreathed in plum blossoms.

Carefully, we removed the steel-plated armor and the leather padding over Takkan's torso. My hand jumped to my mouth when I saw the blood. It was bright even in the murky light, and there was so much . . . so much I couldn't see where it came from.

The sentinel drew a sharp breath. "It's worse than I feared," he rasped, positioning his fingers to stanch the blood. The wound was just left of Takkan's heart, a deep stab. "You'll have to get the doctor. Tell Lady Bushian—"

An arrow pierced one of the wooden beams above us, and I jumped. But it was the suddenness of it that had startled me. I regained my composure almost instantly, plucking the arrow out.

"Never mind, you'll be killed out there if you go. You stay."

The sentinel himself was injured—I could tell from the gashes on his armor and the blood smeared across his bare scalp—but his injuries were not as grave as Takkan's. He rolled Takkan onto my lap and set a small lantern beside us. "Keep his side elevated and maintain pressure on his wound while I seek help. His life depends on it, do you understand?"

Yes. I didn't even notice him leave. Blood pooled where I pressed down on Takkan's wound, red and vivid and seeming to have no end. The air had a sharp tang of copper, one that made my stomach twist and churn.

He grunted every time I increased pressure, which was both a relief and a distress. I had Kiki catch rainwater with her wings and dribble it over his parched lips, but I wished I could do more for him.

That's Radish Boy, isn't it? Kiki quipped. *He looks different.*

I swept Takkan's hair out of his face and touched his cheek, moist and cold. He looked younger than I remembered; his hair had been trimmed, his cheeks and chin tidied of stubble. Handsome by any measure, though most girls in court would find him too rugged. Were he anyone but Lord Bushian's son, even *I* would have found him handsome. But we couldn't change our bloodlines.

In Tianyi Village, I'd thought him a stranger. A dutiful sentinel who'd taken it upon himself to search for the royal children—as many others across the kingdom must be.

This was the first time I'd seen him and known who he was: Takkan, my betrothed, the boy I'd despised . . . simply for existing.

How many times had I selfishly, horribly prayed that he might die—that his ship might be lost at sea or that he might fall into a well—just so I wouldn't have to marry him?

Maybe I *did* deserve to have this bowl on my head, to never be allowed to speak again. To be sent far away from my family, with little hope of finding my way home.

I patted his cheeks, trying to slap him into consciousness. *Come on, Takkan. You can't die. Not here, not on my lap. You have to live—live, and when I break my curse, I can tell Father to unknot our strands and you'll be free to marry whomever you'd like. You don't want your fate tied to mine, I promise.*

I leaned over him, pressing harder against his wound. *You'll find some nice lady who loves the snow and the rabbits*

211

and wolves and whatever it is you Northerners love. Come on, I pleaded. *Please don't die.*

Both our lives might have ended right there and then if Kiki had not noticed the assassin creeping up in the darkness.

Shiori! she shouted.

I scrambled for Takkan's blade. I didn't have a chance to unsheathe it before the assassin struck.

My back slammed against the wall, the edge of the assassin's sword screeching against my hopeless scabbard. I grasped the hilt tightly, pushing back as hard as I could. My fingers were slippery with blood, my elbows digging into the walls. I couldn't see the assassin's face, but he had to know that one more strike was all it would take to end me.

Kiki!

My bird already knew what to do. She bounced onto the assassin's nose and covered his eyes with her wings.

The assassin lashed out wildly, and I ducked. His blade sliced against the bowl on my head—a useful shield, it turned out. He cut at the air, his sword swinging into the wall and catching between the slats of wood.

I rejoiced too quickly. As Kiki flew back to my side, the assassin grabbed one of the slats and knocked me down.

His hands found my neck, and panic shot up through my chest. I kicked and punched, but it was no use. Air squeezed out of my lungs, and white spots danced in my vision. All at once my mind locked itself—I was drowning in the Sacred Lake again, trapped. Dying.

From the corner, Takkan suddenly groaned. He kicked at

the lantern rolling on the ground. With a rush, it came rattling toward me.

Its rusted handle was the most delightful thing my fingers had ever grasped. Without a second thought, I smashed it against the assassin's skull.

The flames spread quickly over his cloak, and he yelped. Ran outside into the rain. Within seconds, an arrow found its way into his back. He collapsed, dead.

Great gods, I nearly collapsed too. I breathed in and out, recovering from my shock. Then I remembered—Takkan was awake! I crawled back to him, terror clutching my heart when I saw that his movement had opened his wound further. Blood spilled onto the floor, and as I rolled him back into my lap, he reached for my hand, grasping my fingers weakly.

"Close," he whispered. "Close it."

His eyes shut again, and I choked back a silent cry. The blood wouldn't stop, no matter how hard I pressed on his wound.

Demons take me, what should I do?

I whirled, scanning my surroundings for some way to help him. Swords of all sizes, a whetting stone, a small jug of rice wine under one of the blankets. What was a guardhouse without medicine or supplies? I searched his pockets. Nothing.

His knapsack, Shiori!

His knapsack—the bag I'd searched when he came to Sparrow Inn. Had there been a needle and thread inside?

My shaking hands grew slippery with sweat. The copper

tinderbox, his canteen . . . I tossed those items behind me. There! I almost missed it—a bone needle, tucked into a roll of muslin. For once in my life, I threaded the needle on my first try. Then I held it between my fingers, my heart racing as I brought the two ends of Takkan's torn flesh together.

Rain dribbled from the cracks in the wooden roof, pattering against my head as I rolled up my sleeves. At the last minute, I stuffed my apron into Takkan's mouth.

I had no idea what I was doing, but I had to clean the wound somehow. I opened the jug of rice wine and poured it over his wound, squeezing his fingers as he jolted. I was sure I'd just hurt him like mad, but he barely let out a whimper. Like me, he knew how to be quiet.

I didn't know what I was doing, other than closing the gaping wound before me. I'd never had the steadiest hand, and my fingers were even less deft now, after my weeks of battling starstroke nettles. But I doubted Takkan would care about the beauty of my stitches.

The first stitch was the hardest. Poking through skin was nothing like embroidering silk. Skin was thicker, more slippery, more tender. Takkan's fingers twitched, a comforting sign that I wasn't killing him.

I sang my little song in my head as I worked.

Channari was a girl who lived by the sea,
who sewed with a needle and some twine.
Stitch, stitch, stitch, the blood away.
Breathe, breathe, breathe, the night to day.

My spontaneous lyrics weren't very good, but the rhythm helped calm me and kept me going, even when my fingers shook and fumbled the needle. I lost count of how many times that happened.

At last I was done. Blood stained the thread, and some still oozed out between the stitches, but I'd stopped the worst of it.

Takkan's heart thumped under my palm. Beat by beat, it steadied.

Thank Emuri'en, I hadn't killed him.

I leaned back, my body sagging with relief. Outside, the rain had abated. The battle seemed to be over, and a spell of quiet had fallen upon the fortress. I finally released the breath I'd been holding, only to gasp a new one a few seconds later.

Footsteps were approaching.

"A'landan assassins," reported a gruff voice from outside. I stilled so I could listen better, my gaze fixed on the armored figure unfurling from the shadows. "They followed Takkan and Pao into Iro."

Shiori, is that—

Kiki didn't have to finish. My stomach curdled with dread.

Rounding toward the guardhouse, his face bathed in torchlight, Hasege appeared.

"One was captured," he continued, flicking his blade free of blood, "but he has committed himself to Lord Sharima'en rather than speak. Where is my cousin?"

I stopped listening. I was already gathering my satchel. I couldn't risk anyone seeing me with my starstroke, least of all Hasege.

"You there!" he yelled as I darted out of the window. "Stop!"

I ran as fast as I could, jumping over the wide puddles across the stone courtyards. The torches had long since gone out, extinguished by the rain, and I hurried back in near darkness.

Hours later, I sent Kiki for news of Takkan.

She came back with nothing.

CHAPTER TWENTY-ONE

He wasn't dead. Not yet.

That much I learned the next morning. Every few hours, the servants brought soup to Takkan. Thick herbal concoctions that made my nose wrinkle and my eyes water. From the long faces the servants wore each time they came back, I gathered they weren't doing much good.

That was all I knew about how he fared; the kitchen had gone quiet in the wake of his return. There was little gossip, and even less news—worrisome but also reassuring. No news meant he wasn't dying. I hoped.

I kept sane by busying myself with chores. The storm had worsened, which meant fewer trips to the storehouses and more time in the kitchen. I offered several times to prepare my soup for Takkan, but no one understood, so I tried to be useful in other ways. But no matter how quickly I finished mopping and scrubbing, Chiruan's shrimp-eyed cooks, Rai and Kenton, wouldn't let me near their worktables, not even to wash the rice.

"This rice will touch the mouths of Lady Bushian and her household," Rai barked. "We can't have it reeking of fish."

When I tried to wash the fish, they whisked that away from me too. "They might have let you cook in Tianyi Village, but not here. This is a lord's manor, Lina. Can't have your filthy spirit contaminating his food."

Chiruan watched from his corner, his eyes disapproving, but he never said a word.

The worst was at lunch, when all the other servants gathered at the long table in the anteroom. Every day when I went up to get my food, Rai swatted my hands away.

"Demons don't need to eat," he said. "Certainly not meat or vegetables."

Kenton was just as bad. "You want extra food, Lina? Here." He scooped a ladle of water into my bowl, then snickered.

I glared at him, thinning my lips and sucking in my cheeks to form a monstrous expression that seemed to petrify the cooks. It was a small way of getting back at Rai and Kenton. Often I fantasized about rolling them in sticky rice and locking them in the fish cellar—an offering to the rats.

I was sitting alone at the table when Chiruan set a bowl of steamed rice in front of me, then a small dish of carrots and mushrooms and a bowl of soup.

"Don't mistake this for pity, Fishgirl," he said gruffly.

I stared at him, moved by the unexpected gesture. *Thank you.*

"But, Chiruan," Kenton protested, "Lady Zairena said—"

"This kitchen is my domain!" Chiruan shouted, startling us all. "Not Zairena's. Not Hasege's. *Mine*. Fishgirl is under my command. Understood?"

"Understood," everyone murmured, and lunch began.

Three bites into the meal, a lady with a scarlet umbrella appeared outside the window, approaching the kitchen. Her head was wrapped in scarves to block the rain, and I held my breath, hoping against hope that it was not—

Zairena.

"Close the windows!" the servants whispered. "Quickly!"

They scattered, all seeming to know the purpose of her visit. They dashed to the pantry, gathering ingredients, while Rai and Kenton fetched a teapot, a sieve, and a stone mortar.

"Lady Megari must be unwell again," Chiruan muttered, setting down his bowl. Smoke had begun to cloud the kitchen, and he fanned the flames. "The girl's got a stomach weaker than a butterfly's lately. Shame, her spirit's so strong."

I started to open one of the windows, but Chiruan stopped me. "Don't. Lady Zairena says the outside air will spoil her tea." He exhaled sharply, betraying a mixture of irritation and respect. "It's a special brew, taught to her by the priestesses in Nawaiyi. Does wonders for Lady Megari."

Under my bowl, I arched a skeptical eyebrow. Nawaiyi *was* famous for its healing temple, but I had a difficult time believing its pious priestesses had taught Zairena—of all people—their arts.

Zairena entered through the sliding doors, making for the bronze kettles rattling over the stove. A small pouch dangled from her wrist, and she ground its contents in the stone mortar before brewing her special tea. No tea I knew of required the attention of five servants.

"Have this brought to Lady Megari," she instructed one. "And bring me another bowl. No, not that one, you fool." She shoved the girl out of the way. "One with a lid." She made a show of dramatically arranging the tray. "*This* is for Lord Takkan."

For Takkan?

"Have you seen him, Lady Zairena?" one of the maids asked worriedly. "Is he better?"

"He drifts in and out of consciousness," she murmured, loud enough for me to hear. "His fever has broken, but he's refused all food. Even water. Lady Bushian is beside herself."

Concern tugged at my heartstrings, and I peeked over my shoulder to see what Zairena was preparing for him. A soup, it looked like.

"Chiruan, have you any more dried red dates and fork root?"

Chiruan disappeared into the pantry and returned with a large red lacquer box I'd seen at his side once or twice. A cloud of faintly familiar smells wafted into the air: spices and herbs from across Lor'yan.

I made the mistake of appearing curious. Rai caught me staring and blocked my view. "Intrigued by the old man's recipe box, I see. Must be the spices."

Kenton snickered. "He's got some in there that'll make a perfect incense against a demon like you."

I ignored the cooks, crouching by the buckets to finish my scrubbing.

"I have no more need of assistance," Zairena was saying to Chiruan and the other servants. She rolled up her sleeves and stirred her pot. "I've disturbed you all enough. Go, finish your lunch." A pause. "Except you, Lina. Come here."

I rose slowly.

Zairena wore a wolf's smile as she stirred her pot. "I heard you were famous in Tianyi Village for your soup. I plan on making Takkan a broth that might whet his appetite, something lighter than all those herbal soups Chiruan has been sending to the castle."

Her spoon clanged against the sides of the pot, an unwelcome percussion. But that was not why I flinched. Did she actually mean for me to help?

"You know how hot it gets in the kitchen, laboring over a soup. Already a terrible thirst ails me." Her gaze landed on my lunch, growing cold on the table, still practically untouched. "Kindly fetch me some fresh water."

Fresh water? I started for the well behind the cooking ranges.

"No, no. The water there is warm—and dirty, with all those bits of charcoal and rice floating about the trough. I should like clean, cold water. The well by the southeast bridge has some I find especially refreshing. Bring a few buckets back, will you?"

Could she be serious? Rain was falling in sheets, so hard I could have caught bucketfuls of water from the sky before I reached the southeast well. But no one spoke up for me.

"Why the pout, Lina? The cold and the rain should not bother one such as you."

Resentfully, I kicked my skirts and obeyed.

My robes became soaked within seconds of my stepping outside. I ducked into the stables as the storm worsened, banging my hip against one of the horse troughs. Straw floated in its waters, and I made a silent snort.

Gods, how satisfying would it be to throw a bucket of horse water at Zairena's face!

But as I prepared to go back out into the rain, the trough's murky water swirled, and a dry, familiar voice boomed from within: "Only for you, Princess, would I suffer the indignity of having to be heard from a horse trough."

It was the last voice I expected to hear, especially coming out of the horse trough, and I jumped back, startled.

Sure enough, it was Seryu! His ruby-red eyes sparkled through the floating pieces of hay, the outline of his green hair a familiar comfort.

"You're harder to track down than the sons of the wind, you know that?" the dragon admonished. "Here I was, worried that Grandfather had changed his mind and thrown a lightning bolt into your brothers' cave. Instead it turns out you've found yourself a castle."

I'm resourceful, I replied through my thoughts, recovering an air of my old self. *Always have been.*

I put my finger to my lips, glancing around to make sure we were alone. *I'm sorry about the river. I ran into soldiers.*

"I know," he answered. "I was angry at first, until I heard

your brothers searching for you. Who knew six cranes could squawk so loudly, and over the Taijin Sea?"

That was odd; Hasege *had* taken me far from our hideaway in the forest, but I could still see the Zhensa from my window if I looked hard enough. *Why can't they find me?*

"Why indeed." The tension in his voice was palpable. "Your stepmother's magic is strong, far stronger than even I thought. When they are men, she summons serpents to deter them from seeking help. And as cranes, whenever they come close to finding you, strong winds throw them off course, toward the sea."

My fists clenched at my sides. I knew firsthand how dangerous the winds could be for my brothers.

"I tried calling out to them," Seryu continued. "I made contact with two of your brothers. The young one, who talks to animals even after he's turned back into a man—"

Hasho.

"—and the handsome one. He's best at hunting."

Benkai. I inhaled, relieved to hear that my brothers were well. *You've been watching them.*

"Only when they cross the sea. I have no bond with your brothers, and they have no magic in their blood; it makes communication difficult."

But you'll try again? Promise me you will.

"A dragon doesn't make promises to a human," said Seryu pointedly. "Especially not one who steals starstroke from Mount Rayuna without telling me."

I'm sorry, Seryu. Truly I am. I paused, gripping the side

of the horse trough and leaning closer to his reflection. *But please. If you won't make the promise to a human, make it to a friend.*

The water grew still. Then Seryu snorted, and I could tell he'd given in. "The others must be right. Imagine me, Grandfather's favorite, bearing the brunt of his anger. For a human." Seryu's voice became soft. "I must really be fond of you."

My cheeks heated, but relief flooded over me. I would have hugged the dragon if he had been here, but he was not. *Thank you.*

"Don't thank me yet." His red eyes glittered. "Your stepmother will find other ways to thwart me. Her greatest power is in convincing others to do her bidding."

This I knew. I remembered the yellow tinge in her eyes when she used her power. I wondered how often she had used it on my brothers to make them love her, on my father to make him listen to her. I shuddered. I prayed it had never worked on me.

"I'm starting to believe she really does have a dragon pearl," Seryu continued.

She does. I crossed my arms. *I saw it. She kept it in her heart, like you. It was how she turned my brothers into cranes*—I touched the walnut bowl on my head—*and cursed me with this.*

"I wondered what that was," said Seryu dryly. "I thought it some strange human hat. Well, it explains why your magic is muted. Why our connection through the pearl is faint."

There's more: I must not speak—or tell anyone who I am, even through writing.

"Then I'll do it for you."

No. Only you and Kiki can know since we're connected. No one else. I won't run the risk of Raikama punishing my brothers.

The water swirled, and Seryu's expression was unreadable. "Tell me about her pearl."

It was like a drop of night, I recounted, *dark and broken. When she called upon its power, it made her face change into a snake's.*

The water stilled as Seryu considered this. "Her true face, then," he murmured. "One cannot lie to a dragon pearl, particularly if it is not one's own. But for the pearl to be dark and broken . . . that is something I've never heard."

Maybe your grandfather will know. Could you ask him without saying anything about my curse?

"He won't speak to me," Seryu said. "Last time I tried, he cut my whiskers and tossed me into a whirlpool. But someone else will annoy him soon enough. In the meantime, I will search for your brothers and send them to fetch you."

No, don't. Once out, my words surprised me just as much as they did Seryu. Earlier this week, I'd been willing to risk my life to be reunited with my brothers. But I was starting to see the wisdom of Kiki's argument to stay put.

They have their mission. I have mine. I swallowed. *We're better off apart.* The admission came more easily than I expected it to, free of guilt and heartache. *Or maybe we're better off never breaking this curse.*

"What are you saying?"

At this point, I didn't know. I was exhausted, my mind

numb from worrying about Takkan and my brothers, my body drained from working on the starstroke and in the kitchen. For the longest time, I had willed myself not to think about our curse, but now, half-freezing in the rain with my robes soaked and my spirit weakened, I let my darkest fears surface.

I have to speak my stepmother's true name to break our curse. But if I speak, one of my brothers will die.

"That *is* an unpleasant dilemma," answered the dragon.

Help me, Seryu. Can you remove this bowl from my head? It's the only way I can regain my magic.

The waters rippled, and I felt an invisible force touching the bowl on my head. It tugged and tugged, until finally Seryu let out a growl of defeat.

"Let me think on it, Shiori," he mumbled. "You finish the net before my grandfather changes his mind about letting you live. I'll send for Kiki when I have news about your stepmother. I am confined to the water until spring, and it'd be better if you could come to the river. Can you manage?"

The river was outside the fortress walls. I didn't know if I could sneak out, but I'd find a way. I nodded.

"Try to stay out of trouble until then, all right?"

What makes you think I'll get into trouble?

"You're right, I might as well ask a moth to stay away from a flame."

It was a lighthearted joke, but I was not in the mood for humor.

Without a goodbye, I left Seryu for the well and hurried back to Zairena, my buckets as heavy as my heart.

That evening after dinner, Zairena's soup returned to the kitchen. Untouched.

Given how she'd treated me, I should have delighted in her failure, but I was too worried about Takkan. He would die if he couldn't regain his strength.

The kitchen was in an uproar. Rai and Kenton were tasked with preparing all of Takkan's favorite dishes, and Chiruan resumed making his herbal soups. Whenever I glanced over at the head chef, he had his lacquer box out, poring over recipes and herbs. None of them seemed to work.

Demons take me, I had to do something.

You've already done something, said Kiki that night when we were alone in the fish cellar. *And look, you almost got yourself killed.*

I almost got myself killed by trying to escape, I reminded her. *Not by helping Takkan.*

Why do you care so much about him? Because he's your betrothed?

I glared at my presumptuous little bird. *That's the last reason why,* I told her staunchly. *I don't care about him. But if he really got himself hurt searching for me . . . then I have to at least try to save his life.*

You've grown a conscience in the past few months, Shiori. Does that mean you'll grow one, too?

My bird made a chirp of displeasure. But she twittered no retort, and I hurried out of the cellar and into the pantry. Late-night trips to the kitchen had been how I'd survived the last few weeks on Rai and Kenton's meager meal portions. But this was the first time I'd slipped inside to cook.

Not every ingredient I needed was available in the winter—no cabbage or onions, and the supply of carrots was low—but I would make do. Takkan had said he thought that there was magic in my pot, but he was wrong. I didn't have magic. All I had was hard work and care. Both, I needed now more than ever. Luck wouldn't hurt either.

I kindled a fire, sparks flying as the flames illuminated the kitchen. With a clang, I set my pot over the stove and began to work.

CHAPTER TWENTY-TWO

Three times now, I had secretly exchanged Chiruan's soup for my own—just a bowl's worth so no one would grow suspicious. It went into the castle on a crowded tray full of Takkan's favorite dishes. My spirits deflated each time the maids came back, shaking their heads that he had touched none of it, but I didn't give up. I'd keep making it until it worked—or until I was caught.

On the fourth morning, the maids didn't come back. Instead, a sentinel stormed into the kitchen, his boots covered in snow that had fallen overnight.

It was Pao, the warrior who had left Takkan with me when they'd returned. His hair was so short he was nearly bald, and there was rice on his face, clinging to his stubbled chin—a sign he must have been sent here from breakfast—but no one dared point it out.

"Who prepared Lord Takkan's soup?" he demanded.

"I did." Chiruan crossed his arms, but his brow wrinkled with worry. "What's the matter?"

Pao ignored him. "I ask again: Who prepared Lord Takkan's soup?"

The kitchen fell silent. The wash boys stopped slurping their morning porridge, the cooks dropped their knives, and Chiruan wiped his hands on his apron.

Slowly I set down my mop and came forth.

"Get back," Chiruan said, waving me away. "I don't need a scapegoat. This is my kitchen."

I wouldn't back away. I lifted my chin so Pao would understand I had done it.

Recognition flickered in the sentinel's deep-set eyes. "You." He gave me no hint of my fate. "Come with me."

My heart thumped in my chest. Maybe my soup hadn't even reached Takkan, or maybe it had given him indigestion. Had he choked on a stray fish bone, and that was why I was being called? Had I killed him?

Terrible scenarios unfolded in my imagination as Pao escorted me into the castle. It didn't help that the corridors were long, seeming to stretch endlessly. Finally, I heard Lady Bushian's voice trilling from what had to be the dining chamber, and Pao motioned for me to wait outside the door.

"Will you give up this ridiculous search?" she said, sounding aggrieved. "You were nearly killed. And don't tell me it was a hunting accident."

A murmur, too quiet for me to hear. I dared hope it was Takkan.

"If you'd wanted me to be calm, you wouldn't have gone out without my permission! I was willing to overlook you stealing Hasege's armor to investigate the Northern Isles, to humor this obsession with finding Princess Shiori. But then you go off again, barely two weeks later, without telling me? All because you found a slipper near Tianyi Village?"

My chest tightened. It was Takkan, and that was *my* slipper.

"I'd rather not discuss this at breakfast, Mother. Please."

"Do you think A'landan assassins would have been so careless as to leave a slipper in the fields?" Lady Bushian pressed. "They're trying to draw you out. To kill you—as they nearly succeeded in doing."

"They would have no reason to want me dead," Takkan said evenly, "unless they believed I'd found something."

"Yes, Pao told me about the letter you found. He said that you found it on yet *another* assassin who tried to kill you."

I stole a glance at Pao, who shifted his balance uneasily.

"I don't care what was in the letter. Or how important it was for the emperor to read it immediately."

"Mother . . ."

"The royal children have perished. Even His Majesty has accepted that." Lady Bushian slammed something onto the table. "Can you imagine what it was like for me to see you brought home half-dead? You aren't to search for the princess again—I forbid it. Do I have your word, Takkan?"

Pao knocked, muffling Takkan's reply. I wouldn't have chosen this moment to enter the dining chamber, but the sentinel opened the doors, and I had no choice but to follow.

Inside, Takkan sat at the head of the table, his hands wrapped around his bowl. His face was pale, his frame drawn and weary. But he looked better. Far better.

I bowed, addressing Lady Bushian first, then Takkan, who gave me a warm smile. "I thought I recognized that soup."

Megari tilted her brother's bowl to show me that it was empty.

"It's the only thing he's eaten all week," she said. She impersonated Takkan's deeper voice. "Sooouuuup. Fiiisshhh sooouuuppp." She chuckled as he made a face. "I hope you made a big pot, Lina. He's going to drink it all at this rate."

I hadn't made a big pot. But that could easily be changed. I dipped my head graciously, then twisted toward Pao. Takkan was well again, and my endeavor had been successful, complete with personal thanks from the young lord himself. I assumed Pao would take me back to the kitchen.

Not yet.

"I asked Pao here to send for you," said Takkan, still smiling, "but he has a habit of taking orders too seriously. I hope he didn't give you a scare."

Pao made a half smile. "Sir, if you'd seen the stitches she left on you—*I* was the one in for a scare." He eyed me. "I take it your cooking is better than your suturing."

A sniff came from Zairena's direction, and I lowered my head.

Yes, it is.

"You have my thanks as well, Lina," said Lady Bushian, sparing me the briefest of glances. "We are grateful for your help."

"Indeed, Lina." Zairena looked up. "Why don't you take some persimmons back with you?"

It was a dismissal, one I was more than ready to accept.

I'd done what I needed to for Takkan. Our strands could be uncrossed.

"There's no need." Takkan gestured at the long lacquered table. "Have as many as you like. Join us for breakfast."

Me? I balked. I glanced at Pao, who raised his chin a hair, as if to say, *Go on.*

I took the empty seat beside Zairena, trying not to gloat at her tight, strained smile. Takkan's at least was real.

"I realize now that I never properly introduced myself," he said. "I am Bushi'an Takkan of Iro."

Yes, I already knew he and Hasege had traded places to thwart assassins. What I didn't know was why A'landan assassins were after him. Lady Bushian had implied it had to do with Takkan searching for me, the princess. But I sensed there was more.

"Lina," said Takkan, snapping me out of my thoughts, "you have already met my mother, my sister. And Tesuwa Zairena, our guest."

Zairena suddenly rose. "Please excuse me. I realize now I neglected to thank the gods for Takkan's recovery." Her words sounded utterly contrived, but she reached for her umbrella nonetheless. "I will be quick; it merely does not sit well with me to leave them unthanked."

"Go on, Zairena," said Lady Bushian. "We will be here when you return."

I barely noticed her leave. My attention was on the food, and it took all my restraint not to throw myself at it. I helped myself to a little bit of each dish: a dollop of steamed egg custard, a spoonful of braised lotus root, and five or six pickled bamboo shoots. I pretended not to notice Takkan chuckling at my gluttony while his mother wrinkled her nose.

"That's the third time she's gone to pray this morning," Megari observed. "Perhaps it'd be more convenient if she took her meals in the temple."

"Megari!" chided Lady Bushian. "And you, Takkan, it was her quick thinking that saved you. She spent all night redoing the stitches on your wounds, and with her eyes closed to preserve her modesty. Do you not recall?"

I recalled stitching Takkan's wounds—when the blood coating his chest was so bright and thick that I could not tell where his flesh began. If *I* had closed my eyes to preserve my modesty, he would have died.

"With all her goodness, she should be a priestess," Megari muttered. "Can we donate her to the city temple? I'm sure she'd be happier not having to run back and forth to the temple all the time. And why does she always have to bring her umbrella?"

"Her umbrella is for the rain," said Lady Bushian brusquely. "If you keep up such talk, I'll make *you* go pray to the gods. You know very well there was a storm when Zairena's parents died. It's perfectly reasonable for her to loathe anything that reminds her of that awful day."

"But she carries it even when it's not raining," Megari protested. She tugged on Takkan's sleeve. "You noticed it too, didn't you?"

"Not everyone revels in seeing the sun like you do, Megari," he replied. "Though it certainly wouldn't hurt Zairena. She's become so pale since the last time we saw her."

"That's powder," Lady Bushian huffed. "And the last time you saw her, you were all children, chasing rabbits like uncivilized beasts. At least Zairena has the sense not to do that anymore." Lady Bushian harrumphed at them, then focused her attention on Takkan, fussing over his health and only acknowledging me when absolutely necessary. Every time, she avoided looking at the bowl on my head.

I was only halfway finished with my breakfast when Zairena returned, too soon to have visited the temple and come back. I wondered where she had really gone.

"Such respect you have for the gods, Zairena," said Lady Bushian, welcoming her back. "If only my children were so devout. Ashmiyu'en must have listened to you and seen to Takkan's swift recovery."

Zairena touched her cheek, radiant from the praise. "The goddess of life is compassionate. The priestesses taught me to revere her above all."

"We ought to thank Lina as well," Takkan said, his gaze finding mine and holding it with intensity. "If not for her, I'd have been dead by the time the physician arrived."

The certainty in his voice made me suck in my breath. What did he remember about that night? He'd been awake long enough to help fight off the assailant. Had he seen Kiki flittering over my shoulder, urging me to keep calm as my shaking fingers sewed his wound shut?

"I owe you my life," he said, bowing his head in deep gratitude. He turned to his mother. "From now on, Lina is my guest here, free to come and go as she pleases."

I exhaled. *What?*

"Your guest?" Zairena repeated, echoing my surprise. "She's a . . . a cook. Not to mention, Hasege's prisoner."

Takkan's tone hardened. "I am in charge of the castle while my father is at court. Not Hasege."

"Is she to eat with us too," Zairena spluttered, "and sleep in the fortress?"

"You talk as if she's a frog," said Megari. "Just because she can't speak doesn't mean she can't understand you, you know."

"Megari," said Lady Bushian severely.

"*She's* the one being rude, not me."

Zairena's dark eyes filled with regret. "You must forgive my outburst. My concern for Takkan's recovery has me out of sorts." She smiled so sweetly I bit my cup's porcelain lip, wishing she would choke on a bone.

"What I meant was—perhaps it would be more comfortable for Lina to remain with the servants. That is, after all, what she is used to."

Is it? I met her gaze evenly. *I wouldn't know, given that I've been sleeping among barrels of dead fish.*

There was a threat behind Zairena's words. I knew she was expecting me to refuse Takkan's offer. Any proper servant would have bowed and graciously uttered that it was reward enough to sit at breakfast with her superiors.

But I wasn't their servant. And I certainly wasn't scared of Zairena.

"There's a room near me," Megari volunteered. "Warmest in the castle."

That was all I needed to convince me. I didn't want to be

a guest in the castle. Didn't want to have to attend meals and have my comings and goings observed and analyzed. Didn't want to be any closer to Takkan than I already was. But after a week in the fish cellar, I'd have happily curled up in a bed of glowing coals if it meant a night without freezing my fingers off. I gave a nod.

Then, completely aware that Zairena was watching with a scowl, I reached for one of the persimmons in the center of the table and took a long, satisfied bite.

My new room was around the corner from Megari's, decorated with porcelain pillows covered with sheaths of blue and green silk, a writing desk carved of fir, and a hanging scroll of pressed gingko leaves. There was a circular window too, overlooking a vista of Rabbit Mountain, famous for its two peaks resembling a rabbit's ears when covered in snow. It felt like a luxury to stretch my arms without hitting a wall and to breathe without wanting to vomit from the smell of fish. Best of all, there were no rats.

Had I ever slept in a chamber as large as this? The life I had once lived—with three chambers for my personal use and an entire room simply for storing my robes—felt like a distant dream.

Aren't you glad you stayed? Kiki asked. *Imagine having to go back to that drafty cellar. Or your brothers' cave.*

It is nice, I allowed.

Generous of Radish Boy. I'm starting to like him already.

I twisted my lips at her. *You're a fickle one. I seem to recall someone who didn't want me to waste my time brewing soup for him.*

Kiki sank into a cushion, lounging against the soft silk. *How was I to know he was such a generous soul? Maybe you ought to have married him after all.*

It's not generosity, I thought stiffly. *I saved his life. He's showing his gratitude. I would've done the same in his position.*

Would you, now? Would you have given yourself a silver makan, too? I can't see you rewarding a robber, Shiori.

He felt sorry for me. That's why he gave me money.

Suit yourself. All I'm saying is, he doesn't seem quite like the barbarian you pictured.

I ignored her, stowing my satchel under the bed, then searching the cupboards. In them was an array of robes a servant must have selected while I'd been at breakfast. I found a simple navy dress and an earthy green sash that fit nicely.

It was the softest, cleanest material I had worn in months, and after I changed, I untangled the knots out of my hair and wilted onto the nearest chair. I would have fallen asleep right away if a slender writing brush on the desk hadn't caught my eye.

There were ink sticks too, and a stone for grinding and mixing them into liquid, but, curiously, no paper. Disappointing, but perhaps it was for the best. After what happened in Megari's chamber, I knew better than to try and write for help.

Someone's silhouette appeared on the other side of my

doors' paper panels. Once I saw who it was, I bolted up and started to bow.

"No bowing," said Takkan. "Please."

Some color had returned to his cheeks since breakfast, but he smelled of medicine—of gingko and ginger and orange peel.

He walked inside slowly. "I warn you, Megari will be sneaking into your room often."

I rubbed my hands. *Because it's warm?*

"For the view." He planted himself on a stool beside my hearth and regarded the mountain outside. Pride rippled in his voice. "Beautiful, isn't it?"

Snow painted the peaks of Rabbit Mountain, even whiter than the scrolls of clouds hanging in the sky. It looked less like a rabbit and more like an egg with two ears, to be honest. Then again, maybe I was still hungry.

"It's most beautiful when the moon appears between the two peaks," Takkan said, pointing. "If you're lucky, you'll catch the moonlight shining down on the Baiyun River. It lights up the entire valley. We say that's when Imurinya is watching."

Imurinya, the lady of the moon. She was said to have spent her childhood on Rabbit Mountain. There used to be paintings of her in the palace, but Raikama had them taken away.

"Legends contain vestiges of magic," my stepmother would say. "Best forgotten."

Now I understood why she detested fairy tales. With all her snakes and wicked power, she could have stepped out of one herself.

"No one seems to think very highly of Iro," Takkan went on, "especially in the winter: 'The people are too harsh, the weather is too cold, the food is too bland.' Maybe all that is true, but this place grows on you . . . if you give it a chance."

I smiled politely. Everyone thought their hometown was the most beautiful. And while my view was a magnificent one, it did not move or impress me. All I saw was snow. Never-ending snow that dusted the tiny city below and blanketed even the forest beyond.

"Not convinced?" Takkan said. "For a girl from Tianyi Village, you're a tough one to please. That's not where you're really from, though, is it?" He paused. "If you tell me, I could help you find your way home."

I stared at the floor and gave a half shake of my head. This was my home, for now.

"Stay as long as you wish, then. But I would feel better if I returned this to you." Takkan held out his dagger. The familiar blue emblem—newly cleaned and scrubbed—dangled from its hilt. His voice tensed. "I was told Hasege thought you stole it."

His mouth became a hard line, a trace of fury ticking in his jaw. "It was unforgivable, what he did. He's been sent away."

I shrugged to show him that I wasn't afraid of Hasege. The only person I truly feared was Raikama.

While I set the dagger on my desk, Takkan lingered. "One last thing," he said, reaching into his pocket. He held out a side-stitched book, newer and finer than the sketchbook I'd found in his knapsack. "It's one of mine. I like to draw . . . as you so keenly noticed while breaking into my room." A small smile. "I thought you might find it useful."

I took the book with both hands. All the pages inside were blank, and rolled along the spine was a drawstring pouch, large enough to hold a bottle of ink and a brush. At Takkan's thoughtfulness, I let down my guard. Just a little.

Thank you.

"I remembered how you tried to write me your name at Sparrow Inn. Will you write it now? Your real name?"

My shoulders tightened, and Takkan quickly withdrew his request.

If there was disappointment, he hid it well. "Your past is your secret to keep. I won't ask you again. But I do hope you will at least share some of your thoughts."

It was my turn to hesitate. No inky serpents would leak from my brush as long as I didn't allude to my past—that, I understood about my stepmother's curse. Everything else was fair game.

Wait. I did have one request.

I wrote slowly, my characters coming out splotchy and almost illegible. I'd never had beautiful handwriting, no matter how my tutors forced me to practice and my brothers made fun of it, but with my swollen fingers, it was even worse.

Want work in kitchen.

"You'd like to keep working in the kitchen?"

I gave a vigorous nod.

"Who am I to stop you?" he said, amused. "I've a feeling,

Lina, even if I commanded you to eat with us every day and night, you'd find a way to do what you wished instead."

It was true.

With a flare of my old mischief, I replied,

Cook radishes. Lots.

As the sound of his laughter filled my new little room, for a moment I was glad I had stayed in Iro.

But remaining in Castle Bushian was a means to an end. Once I finished my net, I'd leave. Spring would be here before I knew it, I told myself, knowing full well it was a lie. If there was one thing I understood about the North, it was that the winters here were long.

Very long.

After being welcomed into the fortress with a suitable room of my own, the last thing I expected was to miss my smelly fish cellar.

I had hot water at my disposal, a bronze brazier that kept the room warm, and cupboards full of coats and robes.

I should have been pleased at this turn of events.

But no.

On the first night, once everyone was asleep, I naively opened my satchel, and it was as if I had released demon-fire: the starstroke's flaming light spilled out of the bag and snaked through the cracks between my wooden doors, illuminating the dark, empty halls.

I quickly shut it, breathing hard.

What was I thinking? That no one would see its light? That no one would hear me crushing its thorns? The walls were paper-thin; I could hear Megari practicing the lute even though she was on the other side of the corridor.

Magic burst from the nettles, beams of demonfire and flashes of color from the blood of stars. If anyone found the starstroke, I'd be imprisoned and, most likely, executed.

I'd have to go back to the cellar, I realized grimly.

Sneaking out of the castle was easier than I thought. Pao turned a blind eye when he saw me come and go. I had earned his trust, it appeared. Either that, or he assumed I was leaving to make soup. A good guess, since I always returned with the stench of cod and mackerel.

In the cellar I stayed, long into the night, my fingers working until they were so stiff I couldn't make a fist. Kiki helped, pecking my cheeks to keep me awake.

My pace was improving. I loosened four strands of starstroke from its armor that night, my best yet. I braided their iridescent threads before setting them carefully back into my satchel. Then I turned to a fifth strand.

Only when the cold had numbed the fiery ache of my hands, and my eyes could not stay open a second longer, did I finally creep back to the castle and drift off to sleep.

CHAPTER TWENTY-THREE

The next day, the cooks, the maids, the wash boys—everyone who had called me Demonface behind my back—all greeted me warmly. Rai and Kenton welcomed me into the kitchen with a new apron, cleaned and pressed. And at lunch, sweets and skewered meats topped my bowl.

"So it was our Lina who saved young Lord Takkan."

"Well done, well done."

"We really thought you were a demon worshipper. Lady Zairena was so convincing. . . . We hope you don't take offense."

No, I didn't take offense. But I gathered their praise and smiles and tucked them in an imaginary pot and shut the lid. Growing up at court had taught me to discern my real friends from those who would desert me if ever my fortunes changed.

Chiruan was the only one who said nothing. He offered me a bowl of pickled cabbage and minced pork over rice, as he did the others, but he was silent until I finished eating.

All too aware of his scrutiny, I rose and returned to my stool in the corner to debone some fish. Chiruan followed.

244

"Go back to the castle," he said. "You're a guest of honor now. What are you still doing here? And handling fish I did not give you permission to touch!"

Paying him little heed, I placed the fish into the bucket by my side and reached for a new one. It was a question I couldn't answer, not in a gesture or a mime.

Every night, I worked myself to exhaustion, pounding the starstroke. Even when the thorns fell off in fine piles of gray dust, sometimes a few needle-thin barbs would cling to the naked vines, a painful surprise when I grasped them. I would have to pick them out from my fingers before I could finally sleep. And when sleep did claim me, so did the night-mares. Falling cranes with human eyes and human screams. Girls with snake faces. Broken pearls that swallowed up entire kingdoms. Such images haunted my precious rest.

Only in the kitchen was I free of them.

I wouldn't give it up.

Though he couldn't see my eyes, Chiruan seemed to understand. He took my fish and passed me a cloth to clean my hands. "You may wash the rice" was all he said.

And so, with that simple task, I began my apprenticeship in his kitchen.

I would have spent all my time learning from Chiruan if I could. Over the next few days, I received additional duties along with washing the rice: cutting ginger and blending sevenspice, beating egg custards and steaming bread. By the next week, I was learning to make noodles, and I found that kneading the dough soothed my aching hands. I loved it, and couldn't stop talking about it with Kiki.

But the kitchen was a distraction from my real task. I was halfway finished with removing the thorns and cutting the leaves from the starstroke, which meant that soon the worst would be over. Soon I would need to begin spinning it.

My first week in Iro, I'd spied a spinning wheel in Lady Bushian's leisure room. Every afternoon, she gathered there with a small circle of friends to paint, play tiles, and listen to Megari play her moon lute.

I'd never been invited, but I started lingering in the dining room after lunch, staying so long that Lady Bushian had no choice but to ask me, out of courtesy, if I wanted to join her upstairs.

As Oriyu parted the doors into the leisure room, my impatience became painful. When no one was paying attention, I stole a look inside. The spinning wheel was still there—centered between two tall folding screens patterned with rabbits and the moon.

"It's Zairena's." Lady Bushian had caught me staring. "A handsome instrument, isn't it? It's carved of birch and elm. Her mother left it to her. Zairena seems to have inherited her talent at the wheel, but I was never good at such crafts."

Neither was I, I thought as I stepped aside so Oriyu could escort Lady Bushian into the room. But she didn't move. Her jaw was tight, reminding me of Takkan when he was about to speak an unpleasant truth.

"A moment, Lina," said Lady Bushian quietly. "It warms

me how much my children have taken to you, and you are most welcome in the castle. But I am relieved that you have seen the wisdom of retaining your duties in the kitchen."

I went still. What was she trying to say?

"What I mean is, you are my guest because Takkan believes you saved him. And I would ask that as my guest, you do not forget your place."

A surge of heat rose to my cheeks. *Do not forget my place?*

Her tone was even, the inflection of each word too rehearsed to be natural. "I have been told that you visit Megari's chambers—"

Only once! I thought. *And on her invitation.*

"—and that Takkan has come to yours."

I bit my cheek, trying to hold in the absurdity of it all. Did she think I was attempting to seduce her son? The thought alone made me wish I could snort. The last thing I wanted to do was win over my former betrothed—a mere lord of the third rank—and live in this intolerably frigid wasteland. I had a curse to break, and a home to return to.

It was all true, but my face grew hot with shame. *Listen to yourself, Shiori,* I thought. *You're lucky that this "lord of the third rank" took you in. Otherwise, you'd still be at Sparrow Inn. Or someplace worse.*

Lady Bushian must have read my glumness as a reaction to her rebuke, for she sighed.

"I don't mean to sound harsh," she said, a little less coldly than before. "Iro is a small fortress, and news travels quickly within its walls. Given your . . . unusual circumstances, it would be wise to take care. For your sake. Am I understood?"

For my sake. Really, she just didn't want her children to be seen gallivanting about Iro with someone who looked like a demon worshipper.

Fighting to stay calm, I managed a nod.

Not a beat too soon, Zairena arrived, with a basket of persimmons and several of Lady Bushian's friends behind her. From the smug smile on her lips, I was sure she had heard everything. I was even willing to wager that *she* had inspired Lady Bushian's rebuke.

The reason, I couldn't fathom. There was no flush in her cheeks or infatuated smile when she spoke to Takkan, signs I'd noticed in the girls flirting with Yotan or the boys who sought attention from Benkai. Or did she actually worry that I was a demon worshipper? A few girls at court had left to study with high priestesses and had returned mind-numbingly devout. But Zairena seemed too conceited to be overly religious.

Maybe she just disliked me because she was no longer the only special guest at the fortress.

"These are the last of the season," she said, setting the basket on a low table. "I thought we all could use a snack."

The other ladies immediately rose to take one. "How thoughtful, Zairena."

"Take as many as you wish. I already set aside a few for dear Megari."

While everyone thanked Zairena for her generosity, I sank into my chair, too aggravated to eat. No one would meet my eyes, only confirming that all had heard Lady Bushian's humiliating remarks.

"I saved a few for you, too, Lina," said Zairena, passing me a parcel of persimmons wrapped in a swath of striped cotton. She smiled a little too sweetly. "A belated welcome to the castle."

While I set the gift to the side, Lady Bushian ushered Zairena to the spinning wheel.

"Show us what you've been working on," she said. "We are all eager to see what the priestesses taught you in Nawaiyi."

I leaned forward, eager too.

Zairena rolled up her sleeves and sat at the wheel, cranking it a few times before she began feeding in straw-colored fibers from her free hand. Gradually, a lustrous golden thread began to unspool.

Lady Bushian's friends gasped with delight.

"It certainly is beautiful," said one, "but why not buy thread from the market? It would be much easier."

"Indeed it would," Zairena agreed, "but not golden thread. The color is difficult to find these days, given that we might be going to war with A'landi. My father's carriage was carrying shipments of this very dye when we were so cruelly attacked." She swallowed visibly, her round face paling. "Spinning it on my mother's wheel makes me feel close to them."

"What will you do with the thread when you finish?"

Zairena held up the spool, and her voice rose with pride. "I will send it to the Nameless Queen."

At the mention of Raikama, I snapped to attention.

"The emperor himself heard about what happened to my parents. He must have felt badly for me after suffering his own loss, and told Her Radiance about my threads. She's placed an order for forty spools to make new ceremonial robes. That is why I must spin all day, so I may send it to the palace before the Winter Festival."

Forty spools of golden thread—for a new ceremonial robe? In all my years living with Raikama, never had I seen her take interest in her attire, let alone personally buy anything. Certainly not threads, sparkly or not.

Zairena was lying.

I was sure of it, but I said nothing. Instead, I watched her work the wheel, trying to memorize the way she drove it with one hand and fed the spindle with her other, producing a stream of fine silky thread.

It doesn't look so hard, I thought, mimicking her motions behind my sleeves. *How fast it spins. I could be finished in a few nights.*

"Come, why don't you try," Zairena said, rising so Lady Bushian's friends could have a turn at the wheel.

"Why, it is like spinning gold!"

Zairena beamed from the praise. "If I have any thread left, I'll weave sashes for everyone."

She sounded like she was in a generous mood. I rose to join the crowd around her wheel.

May I try? I gestured.

To her credit, Zairena's smile did not falter. "I would not recommend it for you, dear Lina. Spinning is a delicate art, for nimble fingers." She gestured publicly at my hands, and even Lady Bushian recoiled at the sight of my scars.

"I would rather spare you the pain."

My fingers had gone through so much they *wouldn't* feel the pain, but I had no way of communicating that. Zairena had a voice; I did not.

I gave a curt nod, fuming as Zairena draped a sheet of muslin over her spinning wheel. The hour for leisure had ended, and not a moment too soon.

"Once your hands have healed, perhaps you too would like to make something for the emperor's consort," Lady Bushian said kindly. "Her Radiance has been grieving all winter for the lost children."

I nearly laughed at the irony of her comment, well intentioned as it was. But I restrained myself, gave a vigorous shake of my head, and rose to leave.

"Lina, don't forget your persimmons," said Zairena, placing the parcel into my arms. She waved to Oriyu, who waited by the door. "Return my spinning wheel to my room."

At the request, Oriyu's brow wrinkled like a prune. The sentinel was not a maid, and transporting goods from one room to another was not one of his duties. But I had a feeling Zairena had noticed how intently I watched her spin and made the request to needle me. I needed to be more careful around her.

As the sentinel lugged it away, I stole one last glance at the spinning wheel. I would find a way to use it soon enough.

CHAPTER TWENTY-FOUR

Four persimmons.

Each one was firm and plump, and perfectly edible, but Zairena's insult was hardly veiled. Any gift given in fours was a wish for ill fortune to the recipient.

I used to laugh at such superstitions, but that was before Raikama's curse. Now I needed all the luck I could get.

I folded them back into Zairena's muslin sheet and slung them over my shoulder, not wanting anything to do with them.

I'll drop them off at the temple, I decided, spotting its pointed clay roof across the courtyard. It was small and unattended, the entrance marked by two stone braziers and scarlet pillars framing the wooden steps. *Or throw them back into the orchard.*

The weather gods decided for me. Thunder rumbled from far away, promising rain. I ran for shelter under the temple's sloped veranda.

As I climbed up the temple stairs, the door flew open. "Lina!"

Surprise at seeing Takkan made me jolt, and the persimmons catapulted out of my grasp and rolled down the stairs.

There went my offering. I didn't think they had fallen *that* hard, but every single one was bruised, the amber skin nearly black from impact.

Takkan knelt, helping me retrieve the persimmons. "Offerings to the gods?"

They were. My mouth slanted, my expression for wry humor.

Hastily, I grabbed the fruits and bowed, then made for the stone steps down. I'd rather face the rain than stay in the temple with Takkan.

"Wait, Lina—"

I fluttered my hands at the altar, stooping to show deference. *I don't wish to disturb your prayers.*

A clap of thunder punctuated my gesture, and Takkan looked up. The clouds were suddenly darker. Heavier too, as if armored for battle.

"The dragons are out to play," he said as the first sprinklings of rain loosened from the sky. "You should stay inside until they're finished."

I hesitated. *What does that mean?*

He let out a short laugh. "It's a story I used to tell Megari."

Curious now, I lingered at the door and wheeled my hands. *Explain.*

"Everyone knows that seeing a dragon is a sign of good fortune. I told her that lightning comes from dragons scratching

the sky, and thunder is the sound of their cries as they play."
Takkan's dark eyes twinkled with humor. "I thought it'd get
her to stop barging into my room in the middle of the night,
demanding that I tell her stories and keep her company. But it
seems to have backfired on me. Now during every storm, she
comes to my room, counting the thunderclaps and lightning
bolts. She's accumulating luck to wish for a shorter winter."

I smiled, holding in a laugh.

"You like the story?"

Against my will, I did. It sounded like a joke Yotan would
have played on me.

"I think that's the first time I've seen you really smile,
Lina." He cocked his head, a grin tilting his mouth. "Except
when I gave you that silver makan."

How can you tell?

"You have a dimple when you're happy," he said, seeing
my twisted lips. He touched his own left cheek to mirror
mine.

I was impressed he had noticed. Did he usually observe
such things?

The sprinklings of rain turned to fat plops pattering
against the temple roof. The cold made the scabs on my
hands itch, and I wrapped my scarf around my fingers tighter
to stop myself from scratching.

"Come inside," he said, opening the door wider, "before
the rain gets heavier."

I shouldn't. I motioned with my hands, not knowing what
to do with them. *Chiruan* . . .

"Come inside," he repeated, not understanding my gestures. "Since you're here, I want to ask you something."

My hands fell to my sides. Curiosity was my greatest weakness.

Rain drummed on the roof as I followed him into the temple. Joss sticks burned, incense rising to my nostrils. I glanced at the offerings on the altar, taking in the fluted bottles of wine, the vessels of boiled rice and bowls of persimmons and unripe peaches, the hanging copper coins and embroidered charms to ward off ghosts and lost spirits.

On one of the ceremonial tables was the pink slipper he'd found near Tianyi Village. *My* slipper. Beside it, the apology tapestry I'd embroidered.

"It was sewn by Princess Shiori herself," Takkan intoned. "An apology for missing our betrothal ceremony."

I knew what it was. I just never thought I would see it again.

Emotion swelled in my throat. I wanted to brush my fingers over the crane eyes I'd struggled to sew. They looked like little black bulbs, some knotted too big, others too small. The red-capped heads were all different sizes, some lopsided and others with crooked necks. I'd never been much of an artist, and it showed.

All I'd thought about while I worked on the tapestry was seeing Seryu again, and when he'd give me my next magic lesson.

What I would do to return to those times. To give Father the embrace he always resisted and ask him about my mother.

To hear my brothers laugh so loudly the sound bounced all the way from the other end of our hall to my chambers.

"And this," Takkan said, picking up the slipper. "This is what she was wearing the last day she was seen. I found it near Tianyi Village, hundreds of miles and a sea away from the imperial palace. Not far from Sparrow Inn, as it were." His voice had drifted into a low whisper. "Did you ever see her . . . while you were there?"

My composure faltered. Was this what he'd wanted to ask me? I bit the inside of my cheek. It would have been easy to lie, but I didn't want to.

I cast my gaze to the ground, played dumb.

"Of course you didn't. I'm sorry I asked." Takkan set the slipper down. "It's just odd that no one knows what happened to her. Whether she and her brothers were killed, or taken from Kiata by our enemies."

Why did he care so much about what had happened to me? Lady Bushian had called it an obsession, but we'd never spoken. I'd even snubbed him at our betrothal ceremony. Why risk his life to search for me?

Look closer, I wished I could say. *I'm here. I'm here, Takkan.*

But I knew the power of my stepmother's curse. Even if he were the most observant man in Kiata, all he would see was a girl with a wooden bowl over half her face.

I reached for my brush, uncovering my hands just enough to write:

Why assassins hurt you?
Because search for princess?

He settled his gaze on me, his eyes chillier than I'd ever seen them before. "Do you remember that letter you found in my knapsack?"

How could I forget? He'd nearly slit my throat for it. I tugged the end of my scarf as he explained what I already knew: that he'd found it on an A'landan spy, someone who meant my brothers and me harm.

"I was able to trace it," Takkan said finally. "To Lord Yuji."

Lord Yuji! My knees knocked with surprise, and if I hadn't been leaning against the altar table, I might have stumbled over my own feet.

"I left Iro to send word to His Majesty," continued Takkan. "That's when Yuji's assassins came for me. They're the ones I encountered in the Zhensa, the ones who nearly killed me. Who *would* have killed me, if not for you and Pao."

As the news sank in, anger welled in my chest. So *that* was why Yuji wanted Takkan dead. The warlord had always reminded me of a fox, the way Raikama was like a snake. Demons take me, if the two were conspiring together against Father . . .

"Soon all of Kiata will know of Yuji's treachery," said Takkan thickly. "And Shiori . . ."

I lifted my head. *What of Shiori?*

"The letter I found was only a fragment, but Yuji mentioned that the missing princes and princess were gone. Not dead. *Gone.*"

Yes, I remembered it too.

"That's why I think she's alive," Takkan said softly, turning to the statues of the seven great gods. "Every day I pray she is. Shiori and her brothers. Their loss has already broken His Majesty. I pray they will be found before it breaks Kiata, too."

I nodded to show I agreed, but under my bowl, heat prickled my eyes. I pictured Father half racked with grief, half bewitched by my stepmother. Just the thought made my heart ache.

Gods, protect my father, I prayed. *Gods, protect Kiata. Keep them safe; keep them whole. If anyone should suffer, let it be me. Not my family. Not my country.*

A shroud of darkness had fallen over the temple. There weren't many hours of light in Iro, and already dusk was upon us.

"It seems the dragons have finally gone back to the sea," murmured Takkan as the rain abated.

I'd completely forgotten about the storm. I started to pick up my bruised persimmons, but the cold had numbed some of the tender spots in my fingers and I forgot to be careful. A spasm of pain shot up my hand, and I winced, gritting my teeth until it passed.

"What is it?" Takkan asked worriedly. "Are you hurt?"

No. No. I drew my hands behind my back. I pretended to shiver as I wrapped them. *Just cold.*

"You don't need to cover your hands, Lina. I've seen the burns."

Of course he had.

Takkan tilted his head. "May I?"

I hesitated, Zairena's ridicule still fresh in my memory. If Takkan were to recoil . . .

Then what? I reprimanded myself. *What do you care what he thinks? What do you care what anyone thinks?*

I *didn't* care. I proved this to myself by yanking the scarf from my hands.

Indifferent, I am indifferent to Takkan. My mind chanted this refrain, but my eyes roved over his face as he inspected my fingers, a silvery latticework of cuts and burns. I could tell it upset him, seeing my hands hurt this way—more than the bowl on my head or that I refused to speak. A dozen questions perched on the lift of his brow. But his lips didn't twist with disgust, nor did his eyes soften with pity. I didn't think I could bear his pity.

"Your fingers won't heal properly," he intoned, "not when you have barbs still in your flesh. I could remove them for you now, but if you prefer to see the physician—"

No. I did not wish to see a physician. I did not wish to see anyone.

Takkan frowned. "Lina," he said firmly, "your choice is either me *or* the physician. Otherwise, you won't be working in the kitchen, not with your hands like this."

I felt a stab of annoyance and crossed my arms. *Are you commanding me now?*

"Don't look at me like that. It won't do you good, cooking with an injury. The longer you go without help, the longer your hands will take to heal."

His eyes were adamant, one thick eyebrow slightly raised as if to dare further disagreement.

Much as I hated to admit it, he was right. I had done my best to take the barbs out every night, but my fingers were no longer deft at such precise work, and a few stubborn ones remained. They bothered me more than the cuts and burns.

I twisted my lips, then laid my palm flat for him to begin. Go *ahead*.

"Would you like a handkerchief or something to bite down on?"

I wanted to laugh. A few barbs would hardly be enough to make me whimper, let alone scream. Instead I shook my head.

Holding my hand still, he removed the barbs, slowly and steadily. His hands were so gentle it almost tickled.

I looked away, watching incense burn beside the altar. Usually its smell, a smoky marriage of sandalwood and jasmine, made me sleepy, but not here. Not while the sticks burned in front of my slipper and tapestry. Not while Takkan was holding my hands. I turned back to him, so focused on his task that he barely noticed me.

Funny, I used to flirt with the boys at court by sitting this near to them. Flashing coy smiles and brushing my elbows against theirs was a game for me at festivals and boring ceremonies Father made me attend. I liked seeing the effects of my attention—whether it made their breathing quicken or their ears redden, whether they immediately began to recite poetry or tried to claim my hand. But with Takkan, I didn't dare. It wasn't a game with him.

When at last he finished, he reached into his pocket for a wooden container of balm, the same he carried for his wounds. A familiar whiff of medicine stung my nose, herbal and sharp.

"Try this," he said helpfully. "Rub some on your hands every morning, and when the pain keeps you awake at night."

Thank you. I turned for the door, eager to finally leave.

Outside, the rain had set into a soft, powdery snow, and torches lit the fortress grounds, their flames quivering against the wind like fireflies.

"Wait, Lina," said Takkan, clasping the other end of the sliding door. All traces of his earlier pride had vanished, and his voice had gone solemn. "They told me you were found in the middle of the Zhensa. I swore not to ask you about your past, but if someone has hurt you, or if you are in trouble . . . tell me. Please, don't hide. I'm a friend."

My heart grew suddenly heavy, and I was glad he couldn't see my eyes. They would have given me away. Slowly, ever so slowly, I made the slightest nod.

I hurried out, the snow falling soundlessly on the top of my bowl. If Takkan called after me, I couldn't hear. All I heard was the slosh of snow under my shoes.

All the way to the kitchen, Takkan's promise haunted me. If he had only been that simple sentinel from Sparrow Inn, I would have trusted him in an instant. I would have wanted to be his friend.

It was too late to leave and search for my brothers. Whatever the gods were scheming—bringing me to Castle Bushian and reuniting me with my former betrothed—I had no choice but to find out.

CHAPTER TWENTY-FIVE

A blizzard beset Iro, putting my work back by a week. I went mad waiting for the snow to stop and tried to pound the nettles in my room, covering the milky paper of my doors and windows with dark cloth and wrapping my rocks in a cloak to muffle the sound. But I soon gave up. I couldn't chance being caught.

"No one's permitted out of the castle," Oriyu said when I pretended I needed to go to the kitchen. His nose twitched. "Not even you."

Did you see how he sniffed at you? Kiki complained as we returned to our room. *As if you reeked of fish.*

I do usually reek of fish, I thought back, rubbing my hands. *What happened to the nice one?*

As soon as she asked, we spotted poor Pao by the south gate, looking miserable at having to be outside during the storm. The snow had turned into sleet, and thunder rolled across the sky.

I was in such a hurry to get back to my room I didn't

notice dim lantern light wobbling through the paper panels until I came to my doors—and found them slightly ajar.

Someone's inside! Kiki warned, flying to her hiding place behind my washbasin.

I gritted my teeth, hating that I couldn't prevent the shiver that coursed down my spine. Gods, I hoped it wasn't Zairena.

I kept one hand on my dagger, and with the other, I slid open the doors.

A figure crouching by the window shot up. "Lina!"

It was dark, but I recognized that voice. *Megari?*

"You're back!" she cried. "I wanted to watch the snow over Rabbit Mountain, and you have the best view, but you never answered the door, and then the storm got worse. . . ."

Another burst of thunder. It boomed so loudly the windows shook. With a shriek, Megari covered her ears, her shoulders shaking as she buried her face in my robes.

"The dragons must be out to play," she muttered as lightning flashed.

I smiled. I was glad Takkan had told me that story.

The dragons are out to play, I repeated. I wondered what Seryu would think of that.

Gently, I tugged Megari's hands from her ears. I lifted her face from my robes, tilting her head up so she could read my lips.

It's all right. It can't hurt you. I brought out a short stack of paper and began to fold a sheet by the lantern light.

As the beginnings of a crane took shape, Megari watched, mesmerized.

I placed the paper crane on my palm. *Like it?*

"Yes! Will you show me how to make one?"

She learned the folds quickly, and she clapped with delight when she made her very own bird. Thunder rolled, farther away this time, and Megari glanced at the window.

"I'm not always afraid of thunderstorms," she said, summoning a hint of pride. Her voice faltered. "Only the really bad ones. Takkan and I watched the last storm together—and I counted every lightning strike. I didn't even cover my ears when there was thunder."

At the mention of Takkan, my concentration faltered and I made an incorrect crease. It'd been easy avoiding him these last few days. Sometimes I saw him during meals, but like me, he was always quiet. Funny, he seemed to talk most when he was alone with me. I supposed he simply felt it polite to fill the silence. I wasn't much of a conversationalist these days.

Together Megari and I sat by the window, watching the lightning. We raced each other to see how many cranes we could fold before the next crack of thunder, and we counted the number of lightning bolts.

Slowly her eyelids began to droop, and the wings of her latest bird fell too, as she forgot to lift them after she made her final fold. I swept my hand over her eyes, the way my mother did to help me sleep.

I'd never had a sister, but if I had, I would have wished for one like Megari.

I kissed her forehead and laid her on my bed. While she slept, I rested my head against the window and searched the sky for the constellation of the Crane, but there were too many clouds. So I counted the strikes of lightning to six—

one for each brother. My eyelids closed by the time I reached Hasho.

When I woke, my blanket was spread neatly over my body, covering even my feet.

Megari loomed over me, fully dressed.

"The storm's over!" she declared, her moon lute bouncing against her back. "Wake up! It's already past breakfast."

Once I rolled to my side, she opened the windows. The storm *was* over, but battered clouds still hung in the sky, gray and torn.

"Look, look what survived the blizzard!" she said, pointing toward a patch of pink-blossomed trees by the river. I had to squint to see them, but once I did, they popped out against the landscape of melting snow. "See that? Plum blossoms! I'll bet they just bloomed—the thunderstorm must have been lucky after all. Let's go, Lina. It isn't far—just outside Iro, down the hill. We could be back before lunch."

My head tilted with caution. *What about your mother?*

"We can't tell Mama. She'll say no because it's too cold, that there's assassins and wolves and a thousand other reasons—"

I hesitated. *Wolves?*

"We're not going far out enough for wolves." Megari laughed at my concern and threw my cloak over my shoulders.

"Come, Lina," she said, towing me by hand toward the door, "we'll be the first to see the blossoms. I'll bring my moon lute and play until my fingers freeze. It'll be beautifully romantic."

I touched her braids. Only a few months ago, I'd been just like her. Young, and wanting to treasure every moment because I feared it'd be the last. Impatient, for a year felt like an eternity. Now I felt older than the moon.

Go on, urged Kiki, stretching behind a vase. *You could use the excursion.*

Will you come?

And stay in your pocket all day? Kiki snorted. *I think not.*

Megari was still pulling on my sleeve. *All right,* I mouthed, kicking my satchel under my bed.

"Yes!" she cried, and she let out a squeal that warmed my heart.

Together we found Pao, who let us out of the fortress. We capered down the hill, often losing our balance against the ice. I lost count of how many times we fell on our bottoms and had to pull each other away from freezing puddles. It had been so long since I'd had a carefree moment like this. Megari's happiness was infectious, and I couldn't stop smiling.

"I haven't gone to Iro in months," Megari said, pointing at the city below. "There's a road from the castle to Iro, but it's covered in snow and ice. I hope it clears before the Winter Festival."

A smattering of soldiers' camps dappled the hillside below the fortress, but Iro itself was smaller and quieter than I'd imagined. I saw merchants carting goods along the icy roads, and a man selling roasted chestnuts, but the streets, white with snow, boasted little other traffic. No mansions or villas, no outdoor markets or arched bridges or boats rowing along the river. Only a handful of red gates in the watery sun.

It was everything I would have hated as Princess Shiori.

Now I found it idyllic.

I held out my hand to catch the clumps of snow falling from the tree branches. As they melted on my palms, I watched children poke sticks at the frozen river winding through town. The sight of the Baiyun River made me hang back. Had Seryu finally made amends with his grandfather? It had been weeks, and I'd heard nothing from him.

"That's Rabbit Mountain," Megari said, pointing at the snow-covered peaks above. "Legend has it that any rabbit who climbs to the top gets to live on the moon with Imurinya. In the spring, the valley has hundreds—*thousands*—of rabbits. Takkan and I used to try and catch them, but Mama would never let us raise one. She said it would be too much work, and that we'd only be sad if Chiruan made rabbit stew one day."

She chattered on: "She wouldn't let us climb to the top either. We tried to drag Zairena with us once when she was visiting, but she loved looking at the rabbits so much we never made it to the top. Who would have guessed she'd become the tiger she is now? I would have invited her today if she were more like her old self. I think she's happier spinning at her wheel anyway, making those silly threads for the empress."

Empress consort, I corrected automatically in my head. But yes, I was secretly glad Megari hadn't invited Zairena.

"Besides, you're much more fun than her," said Megari,

hooking arms with me. We were nearing the plum trees. "I could see all the rabbits running to you and trying to jump onto your hat, Lina. It must be excellent for keeping out the snow and the sun."

I smiled, touched by the girl's cheerfulness. *Yes, it is.*

"It does get sunny on Rabbit Mountain in the spring— and crowded sometimes, when everyone comes for the view. But it's still my favorite spot in Iro. You'll see. When the trees flower and the mountain turns green, it's like a place out of dreams. Only Takkan seems to like Iro best in the winter."

Why is that?

"Because that's when he gets to work on his stories. They're all over his desk." There was a conspiratorial lift in her eyebrow. "I've been trying to get him to tell one this year at the Winter Festival, but he's as stubborn as his horse. I'll bet *you* could get him to, though . . . since you saved his life."

Now I straightened. I knew that tone. I had practically invented it when I wanted something from my brothers.

"Oh, everyone would love it so much. It's tradition for someone from the family to open the Winter Festival with a performance. It's a way for us to make the people of Iro happy. Father used to recite poetry, and Mama used to dance. Now I play my lute, and when we're lucky, Takkan . . ."

Her voice drifted as she glanced nervously about the trees. I looked around, too. What was she looking for?

Megari grabbed my arm. "There they are! The plum blossoms!"

The grove was small, only a dozen trees at most, but it *was* beautiful. Rose-kissed petals sailed across the wind, floating onto the soft, untouched snow. Not far away, I heard the river warbling—and a horse neighing.

"You're late," said Takkan, closing his sketchbook. "You said you'd be here playing on your lute before I arrived."

"Takkan!" Megari jumped into her brother's waiting arms. He spun her in the air, stopping midway when he noticed me.

"I brought Lina along—is that all right? She hasn't seen the plum blossoms."

Takkan greeted me with a smile. "Is that so?"

I didn't smile back. I wasn't unhappy to see him, but I did wonder what Megari was scheming.

Behind the trees, his horse nickered and grumbled, kicking up snow that flew in our direction.

"Easy there," Takkan said, trying to calm him down. "Admiral. What's gotten into you?"

Admiral snuffled, and his huge eyes blinked fearfully. I stepped back. I had a feeling he was reacting to me.

"I should have brought some persimmons," Megari said, stroking the horse's thick mane. "There, there, that's a good boy." She nuzzled him. "I'm still trying to get my big brother to change your name to Noodles. Admiral is such a stodgy old name."

"He's a sentinel horse, Megari, not a rabbit."

"Sentinel horses can have personalities too. See, he likes it."

"I think he just likes you."

"Then he has good taste."

With a laugh, Takkan tended to Admiral, and Megari hooked an arm around one of the plum trees and spun, catching stray petals as they fell. She snapped off a sprig and handed it to me. "A keepsake, Lina. Until spring."

I touched the blossoms to my nose, inhaling their sweet fragrance. I tucked the sprig carefully into my pocket.

"Sometimes I wish the Winter Festival were here instead of in town." Megari sighed. "Can you imagine having the lantern lighting among these trees? It'll be scenic enough by the river, I suppose. Oh, you'll love it, Lina. It'll be so cold you can't feel your nose, but there's no night as wonderful. And then there's the fireworks."

"I thought you didn't like fireworks," said her brother.

"I don't," Megari quipped. "They're loud and everyone else loves them too much. But I'm willing to face my fears for the sake of the festival. Unlike you, Takkan. So much for courage being our creed."

"This has nothing to do with courage," Takkan said sternly. "No matter how many times you ask, I'm not going to change my mind."

Change your mind about what? I gestured.

Before Takkan could stop her, Megari pivoted dramatically and hopped onto a tree stump.

"Hear me, friend Lina: my brother, Bushi'an Takkan of Iro—who has eluded assassins and bandits and fought valiantly on behalf of Emperor Hanriyu—is shy. He has been ever since he was a boy. He had no friends, not even Pao. And he would climb trees to hide from crowds—"

"Megari! Get down from there!" Takkan raked an embarrassed hand through his hair.

I wished I could laugh. One started to ripple up from my belly, and it tickled to hold it down. But I settled for a smile, the widest I'd had in a long time.

"He's also afraid of monsters. Eight-headed ones with striped fur and white hair—" Megari jumped off the stump, grinning wickedly as her brother's cheeks turned a fierce shade of scarlet. "Do you remember how Hasege said he saw one on the roof? You stood guard for weeks, looking out for a monster you made up in your own story!"

"That was a cruel joke," Takkan said, his exasperation growing. "And I'm not afraid of monsters."

"You're afraid of singing for the festival, though."

Megari was brazen, I thought, chuckling at how mortified Takkan looked. Like he wished the river would sweep him away.

You sing?

"Does he sing?" Megari repeated. "The priestesses used to say that Takkan could summon the larks and swallows with the sound of his voice, just the way I can calm the raging winds with my moon lute."

"Coincidentally, those priestesses also say Mama has diamonds spilling from her lips whenever she donates gold makans," said Takkan dryly. He faced me. "They exaggerate, Lina. Grossly."

With a shake of my head, I reached into my pocket, fumbling for my brush and writing book.

I want to hear. Never met a singing warlord.

A faint smile touched Takkan's mouth. "Just how many warlords have you met, Lina?"

I put up both my hands to indicate dozens. Hundreds. It was the truth, but of course Takkan thought I was joking.

None sing. None indebted for saving life.

He groaned. It was a shameful blow—even I knew it. Thankfully, he was a good sport.

"Megari put you up to this, didn't she?" he said, turning to his bright-eyed sister.

The girl shrugged. "You're always saying history ignores Iro. Someone has to sing of all the battles we've fought so they'll be remembered."

"I meant for you to sing them, Megari. You're the musician, not I."

"Come, Takkan, you sound like you'd rather go to battle than sing one measly song with me. Lina isn't expecting larks and swallows to flock to the temple, you know. Not during the winter, anyway."

I nodded, reassuring him.

"All right," he finally agreed. "If feeling a little ill in front of several hundred people will make you happy, then it's a small price to pay. One song."

Megari jumped, clapping with glee. "We'll have to practice so you don't make a fool of yourself in front of Lina."

"*You* should practice before it gets too cold," Takkan said. "Didn't you say you wanted to play among the plum blossoms, or was that a ruse to get Lina and me to come here with you?"

"It was a ruse for me to get you to sing at the festival, Brother. I knew you wouldn't say no, not in front of Lina."

Megari took out her lute and plopped onto a fallen log. Her face lit up with joy as soon as she began strumming.

I leaned against a tree and listened. Music had never been high on my list of life's enjoyments. Playing the zither had been a chore I ranked as only slightly more desirable than sewing.

But I'd been wrong. I had underestimated music.

Megari plucked a yearning chord, and my heart ached fiercely, as if its own strings had been tugged. What I wouldn't give to dance along to Yotan's flute again or to sing with my mother in the kitchen. Those were happy times, like this moment now. Too soon, Megari's song would become a memory as well.

Takkan appeared, leaning against the other side of my tree and listening to his sister play. Had he been there the entire time?

When he saw me glancing at him, I quickly looked away. But it was too late. He rounded the tree until we were side by side.

I started to move toward another tree, but Takkan whispered, "There's a story behind this song. Hear how Megari's mimicking the river?"

She swept her fingers over the strings. Yes, it sounded like water rushing and trickling.

"The song is about a girl riding down the Baiyun River in a chestnut shell," Takkan said. "She was the size of a plum, so small she battled cicadas with needles and hopped onto kitebirds to fly away from her enemies. And she wore a thimble on her head so no one would know she was actually a daughter of the moon lady."

A *thimble on her head?* I showed my skepticism with twisted lips. *Did you make this up?*

"You don't like it?"

I shrugged. It didn't make any sense. Why a thimble over her head if she was a daughter of the moon lady?

"It's not my best." Takkan chuckled. "But I sometimes wonder if you're one of them, Lina. A daughter of the moon. I've decided that must be why you don't want anyone to see your eyes. They'll blind us all with their brightness."

He was teasing, using his stories to coax me out of my shell. Demons take me, it was working. I picked a blossom from my sleeve and blew its petals into Takkan's face. It made him laugh, and I smiled. I took in the smudges of ink and charcoal on his rolled sleeves, the windswept hair neatly gathered at his nape, his dark eyes, somehow brighter every time I saw them. Kiki was right. He wasn't so much the barbarian I'd pictured.

It didn't mean I liked him, of course.

But it couldn't hurt to like his stories.

***

It had just begun to snow when we saw the wolves. They loped down the hill, stalking across the snow-white ledges—their eyes pale and merciless.

Megari's grip on my arm tightened. We turned for another path, but the rest of the pack was on its way, appearing from the direction we were headed. Soon we'd be surrounded.

"Lina," Takkan said through his teeth as he passed me Admiral's reins. He reached for his bow and quiver of four blue-feathered arrows. "Take my sister back to the castle."

"Back to the castle?" Megari repeated. She let go of my sleeve. "No, you're not staying behind to—"

Takkan cut her off, picking her up and setting her on Admiral's back.

For Megari's sake, I climbed onto the horse too, digging my heels into his sides to urge him to ride away.

"Lina! We can't leave Takkan. He's injured. You have to turn back—"

My mind was screaming the same. I'd never seen Takkan in combat before. I had no doubt that he was skilled, and that no man would want to make an enemy of him. But no matter how competent a warrior he might be, he was still weakened from his injury. He couldn't fight an entire pack of wolves alone.

I jumped off, slapping Admiral to carry Megari back to the castle without me. She'd be faster without my weight to bear, and she knew the way. I landed in the snow, and Takkan pulled me to my feet. From the hopeless flicker of his dark eyes, I could tell he thought me a fool for staying.

But at least I was a courageous fool.

The wolves encircled us, emboldened by my small dagger and Takkan's heavy breathing. They growled, their gray coats glistening with snow. Their fangs were so large they jutted out from their lips.

"Stay close," said Takkan, pressing his back against mine. The air was thick with menace, as tense as the bowstring straining under his fingers. I bit my lips shut, more afraid that I would gasp aloud than that their white teeth would end me.

A howl came from beyond the hill—and then the wolves attacked.

Takkan released his arrows, shooting with the precision of a gifted marksman. Each arrow found its home in a wolf's belly or chest. If there had only been four wolves, the battle would have been over. But more arrived, coming from behind the trees and up the hill.

He drew his sword.

I was the more vulnerable prey, but the wolves ignored me completely. They howled, dodging my attacks and kicking me away. All they cared about was Takkan.

They were going to kill him.

Blood pounded in my ears as the fight drew uphill, crashing through the undergrowth. I tackled one of the wolves rushing after Takkan, but its powerful legs kicked me aside and I tumbled uselessly down.

Below, one wolf skulked along the edges of the hill. At a glance, he looked like the others: his fur was a light bristly gray, his ears pointed and alert. But he was smaller than the other wolves, and he was watching the fight from afar. Every time Takkan killed one of his pack, he let out a terrible cry. He was the one who had howled to begin the attack.

I crawled toward him, scraping along the undergrowth.

There was a gold cuff on one of his forelegs. Unusual for a wolf.

I leapt onto his back, my feet skidding against the snow as he tried to throw me off. Fangs snapped at my face, and the world spun, the sky a gray-blue blur as the wolf tried to slam me against the hill. But I held on.

He smelled like smoke, and his eyes were murky yellow like those of the other wolves, yet they snagged the light in a way that made me look twice. He snarled, trying to shake me off, but I held on, blindly brandishing my dagger.

He pinned me down in the snow, about to finish me with his claws. But I stabbed my blade into his flesh, twisting deep until it pierced bone. The wolf let out a deafening cry. Blood gushed from the gash in his gray fur.

I thought he would charge again in revenge, but his yellow eyes swept over me, taking me in. His gaze was menacing even for a wolf. And oddly calculating.

With a sweep of his tail, he whirled and bolted up the hill, howling for the rest of the wolves to retreat.

Takkan ran to my side, breathing hard. There was blood on his face, and his cloak was torn beyond repair. But he wasn't hurt and neither was I.

He dropped his sword in relief. "That was . . . the most reckless, most foolish . . . bravest thing I've ever seen."

Stop talking. I pulled him into the snow with me, and for a moment we lay there, half recovering our breath, half laughing that we were miraculously alive.

Before long, a horse galloped toward us. It was Megari on

Admiral, the bow in her sash becoming undone as she charged our way. Her face was streaked with tears, but she wore a scowl fiercer than any wolf could have made. She jumped off the horse and threw a fistful of snow at her brother.

"Don't you dare send me off like that again!"

"And let you get eaten by wolves?" Takkan shielded himself from his sister's attacks. "Better I get eaten than have Mama kill me at home. You are her favorite, you know."

"I know." Megari wrapped her arms around her brother's waist. "But it's only because you're so dense." She pretended to punch his ribs. "Throwing yourself at a pack of wolves when anyone sensible would have run."

Brother and sister laughed.

The ghost of a laugh escaped my lips, too. Barely a sound. But a dreaded shadow writhed from the top of my bowl: an invisible serpent slithering down into my pocket.

I thrust my hand inside, pulling out the sprig of plum blossoms Megari had given me. Its leaves and flowers had gone black.

Whatever joy I'd tasted quickly fled. My heart sank. For a precious instant, I'd forgotten the dark curse looming over me.

When Takkan and Megari weren't looking, I dropped the sprig, letting its withered buds fall into the snow.

I did not smile again the rest of the way home.

CHAPTER TWENTY-SIX

It jolted me to see Hasege back at the fortress. He stood beside Pao, guarding the gates, and greeted Takkan, Megari, and me with a scowl.

"So it's true. You have taken up with the demon girl."

Takkan's reply was the coldest I had ever heard: "You've returned early, Cousin."

"Have you lost your senses, Takkan? War is coming, and you send me away when I should be defending the castle—all for this demon?"

"Call her demon once more, and you will not be welcomed back in Iro. Not ever again."

Hasege's lips thinned. He wouldn't look at me, as if unnerved by my presence. The scar I'd given him gleamed in dusk's violet light, crooked and pale and ugly.

"I caution you, people will talk. Iro is already in disgrace after your broken betrothal—why do you think more soldiers are being directed to Tazheni Fortress than here? Now you humiliate us further by making a houseguest of this . . . this

279

evil spirit! No wonder they say the dead princess rejected you because you were unworthy."

There was a hiccup in my breath, and a mix of anger and shame stirred in my chest. That hadn't been why I'd run off from the ceremony! Was it truly what everyone was saying?

At my side, Takkan had stiffened noticeably. "I care naught for Gindara's gossip. But you will have more respect for Shiori'anma."

"Respect as she had for you? I only hope that while I've been away, you've ceased wasting everyone's time looking for her. On this, your father would agree with me. Even Lord Yuji has given up."

"Has he?" Takkan said grimly. Taking his sister's hand, he strode past Hasege and turned to Pao. "We encountered wolves on our way home. I want the area scouted."

"Wolves?" Pao's dark brows slanted into a frown. "Wolves have not been spotted near Iro in years."

"They attacked on the hill, not far from the western edge of the river's mouth."

Hasege laughed. "You think even wolves are Yuji's assassins now, Takkan? They're only beasts, and you escaped intact. You truly *have* lost your senses."

I watched Takkan, wondering whether he'd noticed that smallest wolf. The one with the cuff on his foreleg . . .

Takkan's eyes were stony. "We cannot rule out the possibility that Lord Yuji sent them. It is possible he has given up on finding Shiori'anma, but he remains a traitor. A dangerous one."

"Hasege and I will ride out to investigate," Pao said quickly. He nudged Hasege. "Come."

"No," replied Hasege. "I'll go alone. You escort the women inside."

There was no need. Lady Bushian was already at the gate, running toward her daughter.

"Mama!" Megari cried. "It was my idea. I wanted to see the plum blossoms, and—"

"Not another word," said Lady Bushian. She cast me a glare that would have made even the wolves whimper.

I trudged numbly back to my room. My robes were torn and my skirts were soaked, but I couldn't stop thinking about the wolves' attack and how the plum blossoms had withered. I could hardly see straight. Too late I realized my footsteps had led me toward Zairena's room instead of my own.

"Hasege has returned, have you heard?" her maid was telling her. "Will you greet him? He's talking with Takkan outside—"

"Hasege can wait."

Zairena spied me at the door and opened it wide. "Have you come to say goodbye, Lina?"

Goodbye?

"You think you can put Megari in danger and remain in Lady Bushian's good graces?" Zairena laughed. "I wouldn't be surprised if she asks you to leave."

My jaw tightened. I kept walking, but Zairena blocked me.

"Where are you running off to? There's no need to hide, not when you have that bowl on your head." She clasped the sides of the bowl, trying to pull it off.

I twisted out of her grip, inwardly cursing the fortress's narrow hallways. I wasn't in the mood to deal with her. My robes were drenched, my fingers in dire need of rebandaging.

Zairena stepped aside. "Ah, I've struck a nerve, haven't I?" She tilted her head, touching the mole on her cheek. "What *are* you keeping under that bowl, Lina? I so hope it's something worth all the trouble."

I shouldered past her. *Trouble* was an understatement.

I stopped attending meals in the castle. I even skipped my lessons with Chiruan. He had promised to cook sevenspice tofu and crab in silken egg custard—two dishes that had become my favorites. But since my trip to see the plum blossoms, I had no heart to learn.

Despair welled up in me, and I buried my face in my hands. Countless nights of wielding enchanted nettles with knife-sharp leaves and scorching thorns hadn't made me utter a sound, but in one fleeting moment with Megari and Takkan, I had almost ruined everything.

I had nearly gotten my brothers killed.

When I grew tired of pacing my chambers and moping alone by the window, I wandered the fortress. Eventually I found a pavilion cloistered in the gardens, and I took solace on its veranda, warm and secluded. With all this unrest and talk about war with A'landi, the pavilion looked like it had been forgotten, the stone steps leading to the doors piled high with snow. I started a fire in the brazier and huddled beside it, watching the lanterns sway from the frost-touched eaves.

To pass the time, I folded cranes. Tiny ones, a fraction of Kiki's size, since paper was precious.

You haven't moped about like this in ages, Shiori. Kiki flapped her wings, depositing snow onto my nose. *Nothing happened. No one was hurt. Why so sad?*

I didn't look up.

Cheer up. Sing that silly song of yours. You can't languish about all day. You have a curse to break.

My starstroke net was the last thing I wanted to think about. When I waved Kiki away, she grunted and flew off. After half an hour, I grew worried and started to put away my paper birds to go look for her. Then, out of nowhere, Kiki came diving toward me, ducking into the basket. At the same time, a familiar figure rounded the corner.

"I see you found the famous moss pavilion," Takkan said, brushing off leaves clinging to the benches. "No wonder I couldn't find you, hidden in the back of the garden. I thought you would be in the kitchen, but Chiruan says he hasn't seen you since yesterday."

He'd been looking for me? My brow pinched, but I still didn't look up. Didn't acknowledge him. I pretended to focus on my cranes, trying to signal that I wanted to be alone.

"This was supposed to be a teahouse," Takkan went on, "but Mother gave up on the idea. Now it's a good place to do some quiet thinking—or practice singing where only the birds can hear." A wan smile. "Or *fold* some birds. Will you make a wish once you have a thousand?"

I swallowed hard, answering his question only in my thoughts. By now, I had probably already folded well over five hundred. In the beginning, my goal had been to make a wish. A silly, fanciful wish. Now I knew better than to depend on old tales.

No, I folded them for myself. It'd become a habit of mine, to give my hands something to do and make me feel a little less lonely when Kiki was away, spreading word about me to my brothers.

Though I didn't respond, my silence would not deter Takkan. He searched in his knapsack for a sticky rice dumpling wrapped in bamboo leaves and twine.

My head lifted.

"You always reach for these at dinner," he said, unwrapping one. I recognized the dumpling as my handiwork; the twine was crossed in all the wrong spots, pinching the leaves too tightly. Much as I liked it, I still hadn't mastered the dish.

My stomach growled, mutinying against my resolve to ignore him. I redoubled my attention on my cranes, not even looking up as he offered the dumpling again.

Kiki rustled from inside my basket of cranes, crawling to my elbow and biting my arm. *Eat, Shiori.*

I'm not hungry.

Not hungry? After all the trouble I take to find him and bring him here? He almost saw me!

You led him here? I pretended to brush snow from my sleeves. *I thought you would tell me to ignore him.*

When have I told you that? She bit my arm again, as if that would knock sense into me. *You conjured me out of hope,*

284

Shiori. Do you think you can break your brothers' curse in despair? Go, go spend time with him.

"What are you keeping there in your sleeve, Lina?" Takkan asked good-naturedly. "If it's cakes, I'll take this dumpling back."

My resistance melted, but mostly because I was hungry. I accepted the dumpling and devoured it in three bites, the sticky rice clinging to my teeth as I chewed. I wiped my mouth and let out a contented sigh.

"Tea?"

No. I'd only allow myself to be bribed once.

I crossed my arms, looking up. Takkan was eating a dumpling too, and a canteen of tea was on the bench beside him.

He looked different today. Instead of his armor, he wore a long navy jacket I'd never seen before, crossed at the collar, with buckwheat-colored trousers and a thin black sash. It made him look less like a stiff-backed sentinel, more like someone I would have wished to be my friend. I wondered if he thought of us as friends.

"I would have come to look for you earlier," he said suddenly, "but I've been away with the sentinels—hunting for wolves."

I crumpled the dumpling leaves in my fist. *Wolves?*

"We found their den," said Takkan. "The others have concluded that they were merely wolves, nothing suspicious—and certainly not part of a coordinated attack by Lord Yuji and his allies. But I am not so convinced."

Pulling down his hood, he took the step below mine. He

spoke very quietly. "You were with me, Lina. Did you notice anything unusual about the wolves?"

I pursed my lips tight, relieved that he had seen it too. *About one of them, yes. The smallest one with the yellow eyes.* I reached down to my ankle, indicating that he'd worn a gold cuff.

"I saw it," murmured Takkan, "and I can't stop thinking about it. Lord Yuji's ally has an enchanter named the Wolf—one that's bound to him by an amulet he wears."

Enchanters, I remembered Seryu telling me, were sworn to serve whomever possessed their amulet.

"When I brought it up with the others," Takkan continued, "they thought I was out of my mind for thinking . . . for thinking there was something strange about the wolf we saw. For thinking that it could have been—" He hesitated.

Magic? I traced over my palm.

"Yes," he whispered. "Magic."

Takkan inhaled. "I don't know much about magic, Lina, but I've heard stories from outside Kiata. In every one, enchanters are cunning, often more so than their masters. The Wolf, I sense, will be no different."

He laughed at himself softly. "Listen to me, counting on secondhand tales to inform my strategy. Everyone is focused on defeating the A'landans, but here I am, worried about the Wolf. It's a good thing I'm not on the emperor's council, or the commander of the army. No wonder the others think I've gone senseless."

I leaned a little closer, showing him I didn't think that. Not at all.

286

He lowered his voice. "Sometimes I think magic never left Kiata. Not fully. I would even go so far as to wonder whether the princes and princess themselves were ensorcelled—it is the only way to explain how no one has been able to find them." His lips thinned. "But maybe I'm just fooling myself. Winter here has a way of muddling one's reason."

I shivered, suddenly cold. Takkan was so close to the truth, yet he didn't even know it. My fingers squeezed the unfinished crane still in my grasp.

I made one last crease on the bird, then opened its wings and showed him.

"What is it, a dove?"

No.

"A swan?"

I tapped the bird's head.

"A crane?"

Yes. I folded another sheet into a crane. Then another and another until I had six, set out in a misshapen circle. It was the most I dared to show him.

"Six cranes," said Takkan. "I'm afraid I don't understand."

Of course he didn't. It was unfair, making him play this guessing game. Leading him on as if there were a reward at the end of the trail.

Guilt and frustration swept over me, and I gathered the cranes and tossed them high. Down the stairs they flew, their heads bobbing in the wind as they landed on the snow. But one did not fly and instead landed on my arm. As I picked it up by one wing, Takkan took the other. Our fingertips were so close I could almost feel the warmth of his skin.

287

I drew my hand away and turned to the tea, which I'd declined. It had gone cold by now, but it didn't taste bitter as it washed down my throat. It was still fragrant, and the trace of its lingering warmth soothed me.

Takkan held the last crane on his palm. "They're important to you, aren't they? The cranes."

That, at least, I could answer. I nodded.

"Do you know how they came to have that red crown on their heads?"

No. Tell me.

"Everyone knows that Emuri'en used to be the greatest of the seven gods," Takkan began, his voice deepening as he recounted Kiata's dearest legend. "She made the ocean out of her tears and painted the sky with her dreams. And her hair outshone every light and star in the universe. So radiant were her tresses that the sun asked for a lock and wore it as a necklace to illuminate the world."

Takkan's voice rolled like the rich thrum of the zither's lowest notes. "With the earth now bright, Emuri'en watched the humans who dwelled below, and she grew to love them. But she could see that humans were weak—susceptible to greed and envy. Every morning, she cut her hair, dulled its brilliance by dyeing it red—the color of strength and blood—and tied different mortals together, binding their fates with love. But with each strand she cut, her power grew weaker, so she drew upon the clouds to make a thousand cranes—sacred birds to assist her in her work."

He took out the two strands of twine used to wrap our rice dumplings and held one under the crane's beak.

"Over time, she gave away so much of her power that she could no longer remain in heaven, and she fell to earth. Her cranes tried to catch her, but as they dove, they spilled her red dye upon their foreheads, creating the crimson crown that is still there today." His voice softened. "When Emuri'en saw, she smiled one last smile, and she made them promise to continue her task, connecting fates and destinies.

"The thousand cranes flew to heaven, praying that she be revived. Though the gods themselves wished their sister to return, they could not bring her back. So instead they took the last strand of her hair and planted it on earth, in hopes that she be reborn one day. And she was, but that is a story for another time."

He picked up a second crane from the ground, tucked the other strand of twine under its beak.

"To this day, cranes carry the strands of our fate. They say that each time two people's paths cross, so do their strands. When they become important to one another or make a promise to one another, a knot is tied, connecting them."

He knotted the two strings together at one end and lowered his voice. "But when they fall in love, their strands are tied together at both ends, becoming one." He tethered the second end of the twine so it became a circle. "And their fates are irrevocably joined."

It was the end of his tale, and he offered the knotted strings to me.

I hesitated. "If fate is a bunch of strings, then I'll carry scissors," I used to tell my tutors when they'd teach us about Emuri'en. "My choices are my own. I'll make them as I please."

Easy for a princess to say, but I was a princess no longer.

Too late, I reached out to Takkan. A gust of wind swept the strings from his grasp.

They fell onto the snow, and I jerked to pick them up before the wind stole them. But either I was too slow or the wind was too quick. Our strands of fate twisted off into the air, fluttering above the roofs, then far, far away.

Heavens knew what would become of them.

CHAPTER TWENTY-SEVEN

I was in the kitchen when I heard screaming. The shrill pitch cut through the din of Chiruan's chopping, the steady hiss of the kettle, and the clatter of the cooks' pots as they prepared lunch.

I lowered my knife, wiping it on my apron as I glanced at Chiruan. *What's happened?*

"Go take a look."

I grabbed my cloak and ran outside. Already there was a crowd by the garden across from the north gate.

I noticed Hasege first, guiding Zairena through the men and women. She carried a fan made of black silk and beaded tassels. It was raised, covering everything but her eyes.

Had she been the one who had screamed? No, she couldn't be. Her chin was raised, her sleeves folded neatly at the cuffs—she was walking slowly, as if toward the temple for a prayer ritual.

What's she doing here? I wondered. *What's happening?*

Zairena closed her fan and knelt, her white robes

camouflaged against the snow. I stood on my toes, keeping one eye on Kiki, who had flown out of my sleeve to get a better glimpse of what was happening.

Then I saw it.

A dead sentinel lay in the snow. Under the weak winter sun, shadows clung to his still form, and someone had covered his eyes with a thin sash, but I recognized him immediately.

My heart leapt into my throat. *Oriyu.*

His veins were blue against his pale skin, his gray hair matted to his temples. But it was his lips that caught my attention.

His lips, Kiki gasped. *They're . . . they're—*

Black. I crossed my arms, shivering. I didn't need years of study with the priestesses of Nawaiyi to know what the poison was. Four Breaths.

Her fan rising yet again, Zairena gave Takkan a solemn nod.

"Four Breaths," she said to the rest of us in her gravest tone. "Within an hour of drinking, the victim's lips turn black, and death quickly follows."

Zairena turned to the maid at her side, the one who must have discovered the dead guard.

"Go now to the temple. Cleanse your spirit of this terrible murder. I will come with you—we must pray that Oriyu's soul finds peace and does not linger to haunt us."

The crowd parted for them, and I used the opportunity to push my way toward the corpse.

I kept my head low, weaving through the crowd until I could see Hasege and Takkan.

"He will be buried tonight," Hasege announced gruffly. "The assassin will be found. Now return to your work."

The crowd dispersed, but I remained. The sentinels were searching Oriyu's body, and I wanted to see what they found.

Hasege waved a torch in front of my face. "You're not welcome here."

"Let her pass," said Takkan, stepping between us. His face was drawn, and his usually light movements were heavy with grief. I felt for him. Oriyu had been his friend. "Perhaps she will see something we missed."

"She could be the assassin," Hasege said harshly. "She isn't from Iro, and she has no family to speak of. Look at that bowl on her head. She is concealing something—"

"I've told you before she is under my protection."

Hasege lowered the torch to let me pass, but an uneasy silence followed. I could tell that many of the men agreed with him and didn't like me. They cast me narrow glares, their jaws clenched as I approached Oriyu.

Pao, at least, made space for me.

"He had fire-watch duty two nights ago," he was murmuring. "Oriyu hadn't slept in days, so I took his shift and told him to rest. When he didn't appear for his next watch, I assumed he'd been asked to go searching for the wolves again."

My fingers dug into the snow as I took in Oriyu's blackened lips, his wrinkled robes, the pile of armor Pao and the others had removed. Nothing.

I inhaled. The incense on his clothes was strong, and oddly sweet.

I waved to Pao, made sniffing sounds, then pretended to fall asleep. Four Breaths could be inhaled, I tried to explain.

Breathe poison to sleep, I wrote into the snow. **Then eat. Die.**

Pao frowned. "You think the assassin fed it to Oriyu while he was asleep?"

I couldn't be sure, so I shrugged. It was a guess.

There were hundreds of soldiers outside in barracks, but the sentinels kept track of every person who came and left the fortress. That would make it easy enough to trace the assassin. Unless—

Hasn't left? I wrote.

As Pao relayed my deduction, the others met my idea with glowers and frowns. My ears picked out their discussion easily: What did I, "a mere slip of a girl," know about murders and poison? Other, more creative names for me were uttered, until Takkan silenced them with a glare.

He had been quiet. His dark eyes shone, lit by torch fire, as he studied his friend's dead body.

Under my sleeves, gooseflesh rose on my arms. I was sure he was thinking of the letter he'd found near Tianyi Village. If Lord Yuji had indeed found a way to produce Four Breaths, he could cause much trouble indeed.

Takkan bent to unwrap Oriyu's scarf from his neck, folding it neatly at his side. He began to remove his friend's gloves and inner robes.

"Takkan, what are you doing? We've already—"

Takkan ignored the sentinels. "Pao, hold a lantern."

Carefully, Takkan searched his friend's corpse, turning

him onto his side. "There," he said at last, tracing a web of faint golden veins under Oriyu's arms. There were more on the back of his neck, but almost entirely faded.

"Lina was right. It appears Oriyu *did* inhale Four Breaths before he was given a fatal dose."

"What good does that do us?"

Takkan rose. "We will seal the fortress," he said firmly. "No one may enter or leave until we uncover the assassin."

"Seal the fortress?" Hasege said incredulously. "Are you saying you actually believe the girl? Only a fool would stay."

"A fool, or someone very clever. Someone we know and trust. We can take no chances."

"At least send a few of us to search outside the fortress," said Hasege. "Or do you not even trust your own men? Your own kinsman?"

Takkan's response was chilled. "If one of my kin has a history of dishonoring the Bushian name, then he is not worthy of my trust."

Hasege threw me a spiteful glare. He was trying hard— and failing—to contain his anger. "How do we even know the assassin was *in* the fortress to begin with?" he growled. "Oriyu could have been poisoned while he was out hunting for wolves. A fool's errand *you* ordered, because you believe Lord Yuji sent them to kill you."

Takkan's expression darkened. "Are you suggesting that I am to blame for Oriyu's death?"

"Now, now, Cousin. I am not casting stones. I'm merely considering all the possibilities. As you yourself are fond of doing."

Takkan held his cousin's gaze. "Let us consider the possibilities, then. Why would anyone seek to poison Oriyu twice? First by putting him into a deep sleep, then by feeding him a lethal dose?" He spoke slowly, considering each word. "I would wager that the assassin had another target in mind, and Oriyu was exposed to the poison by mistake. Once the assassin found out, he murdered him—and hoped that the cold would erase all traces of Four Breaths on his skin."

"I say the assassin mistook the old man for you," argued Hasege, "and now he is blundering his way back to Yuji's camps as we dither here, wasting time instead of chasing after him."

"This was no botched attempt on my life," Takkan said, picking up Oriyu's scarf. "We are assuming the assassin *is* an assassin. There are easier ways to kill a man than with Four Breaths. Other poisons are just as lethal, just as quick. No, Four Breaths is unique because it can make its victims sleep like a numb moon, rendering them vulnerable to capture."

"Someone like the emperor?" Pao said.

"Or the royal children."

As a chill came over me, Hasege's mouth twisted into a cynical smile. "Really now, Takkan, you aren't tying Oriyu's death to that letter you found, are you?"

"It cannot be a coincidence."

"Let's say the assassin is indeed in the fortress," said Hasege. "Who would he seek to harm if not you?"

"We will not know until we find him," Takkan replied grimly. He raised Oriyu's scarf. "Oriyu did not burn incense regularly. We start there, find out where it came from. Question everyone in the fortress."

Takkan turned his back to Hasege to face the other sentinels. "Whatever the assassin's affiliations, we must find him . . . before he takes another life. Understood?"

One by one the sentinels bowed, murmuring their agreement. I glanced at Hasege; he was thin-lipped, his black eyes smoldering. He did not bow.

The sentinels filed out, three of them carrying Oriyu away, and the others going with Takkan back into the castle. Hasege alone headed for the gates to order that they be closed until further notice.

I watched his heavy steps sinking into the snow. Something in the air had changed. A veil of uneasiness and distrust had settled over the castle.

There was a traitor among us.

That night, I was so angry I barely felt the cold. I opened my satchel, taking out the nettles and spreading them before me like tresses of fire. After all these weeks, my body had developed an unexpected tolerance to the thorns, and though my hands burned and blistered under their scorching heat, at least the pain had become manageable.

Which only meant that my mind could focus on other things—like the traitor in the castle. Like my stepmother.

Do you think your stepmother had something to do with Lord Yuji's uprising? asked Kiki.

She has to be involved, I thought back, nicking a thorn off the starstroke. *Why else would she send my brothers and me far away? To overthrow my father's rule. Maybe Yuji is her lover, and all this time she's been plotting to put him on the throne.*

But as soon as I thought it, a chord of uncertainty twanged in my gut. Plenty of men had coveted Raikama over the years, but she was fiercely loyal to Father. She always had been.

Or did I think that because she had ensorcelled me?

Of course she had, I thought to myself with a scoff. She had probably enchanted all of us into becoming her puppets, into loving her.

An ache arose in my chest. It was like a ghost inside me, the shell of a feeling that surfaced through the cracks of my memory to remind me that I'd genuinely loved Raikama once—even if I couldn't remember why.

Because it was part of her spell, I rebuked myself, irritated that I had let my anger at Raikama dissipate, even if for only an instant. I clenched my fists.

She's a snake, I told Kiki fiercely. *She told me that herself once. I didn't understand back then, but now I do. She's poison, and she's trying to destroy Kiata.*

My paper bird looked up askance. *Then why bother with you and your brothers? Why not just kill you and overthrow your father all at once? She certainly has the power to do that.*

It was a question that had troubled me for months. It'd been a barb in my hand, one that I kept pushing in deeper the harder I tried to take it out.

She's poison, I repeated, refusing to discuss it further.

But inwardly, I began to wonder. Ever so briefly, I'd let go of my hate for Raikama—for the first time since I'd been cursed. I could have sworn that during that moment, whatever enchantment was clouding my memories had felt weaker.

No, it had to be my imagination. Why would Raikama use her magic on my memories? What answers could my past possibly hold?

It made no sense, yet I couldn't stop wondering. I couldn't stop digging at the gaps in my memory. And that night, in my dreams, I began to remember.

"Andahai said someone tried to poison Father last week," I said, catching Raikama alone in her chamber. She was combing her hair and humming to herself—until she saw me. "He said you made an antidote that saved him. How did you make it? Did you use your snakes?"

She deliberated, the same way I did before deciding whether or not to lie. "Yes, with my snakes. Sometimes, but not often, poison is the cure for poison. It's a medicine in disguise."

"Can I see them? Oh, please. Hasho brings home toads and lizards all the time, but he can never find snakes. And I've never gone into your garden."

"It'd be dangerous, Shiori," Raikama said. "Some of my snakes are poisonous. They might bite a troublemaker like you."

It was an affectionate joke, but her tone was

strained. A more thoughtful child would have changed the topic. That child was not I.

"Don't you ever worry that they'll bite you?" I inquired.

"Poison has little effect on me. My snakes know better than to try."

"Why doesn't it have an effect on you?"

She laughed, teasing. "Your curiosity will be the doom of you one day, little one."

"Why?" I pressed.

A pause. "Because I am one of them," she said finally. She set her comb down, her eyes round and luminous. Then when she blinked, they became yellow—like a snake's.

I woke, almost jumping out of my bed. The memory should have chilled me, but in some strange and incomprehensible way, it didn't.

Because for the briefest of instants—I missed her.

CHAPTER TWENTY-EIGHT

Come the end of the week, I raised my rock one final time, holding it high and with great ceremony above the nettles. Down I struck, grinding into the last thorn until it broke off with a snap.

At last it was done. The worst was over. No more jagged leaves, no more fiery thorns. Demonfire still glinted through the starstroke, like aftershocks of lightning, but it no longer blinded me with each flash. Now every strand shone with effervescent luster, a kaleidoscope of lights and colors.

I could have stared at them all day. But my work was not done.

Back in my chambers, I tested the starstroke fibers in my fingers. They felt coarser than they looked, almost like straw. They were loose like straw, too. Without their casing of demonfire, the strands fell apart easily. They needed to be twisted together.

They needed to be spun.

At first I thought I could be clever and assemble my own

spindle out of a writing brush. I wound the starstroke fibers around and around—trying to mimic Zairena with her spindle. But it was impossible. The thread came out lumpy and coarse, and it would take weeks, if not months, to finish my work this way.

I needed Zairena's spinning wheel.

The problem was that ever since she'd caught me staring at it in Lady Bushian's leisure chamber, she had kept it in her private quarters.

She'd love nothing more than to catch me spinning enchanted nettles, I muttered silently to Kiki. *She already thinks I belong in the dungeon. Imagine how gleeful she'd be at the prospect of my head on a spear.*

What alternatives do you have? Kiki asked.

Not many, I admitted, dressing for the kitchen. *I'm going to start by making her some cakes.*

Cakes? echoed my bird, wrinkling her beak. *Really, Shiori?*

Yes. Whenever I got Hasho into trouble, I always made it up to him with food. Food is the best peace offering.

Maybe for you, said Kiki, still skeptical. *Someone like Zairena would prefer jewelry.*

Well, I don't have money for jewelry. I have access to the kitchen, and Zairena said she misses the desserts from her province.

So, cakes.

Not just any cakes. Monkeycakes.

Monkeycakes were so named because the snow monkeys were known to sneak out of the forests to steal them. They were round and orange and stuffed with peanuts, usually served on sticks to resemble furred feet on bamboo. I'd spent plenty of Summer Festivals watching the vendors from Chajinda make them, and I was confident I could replicate their recipes.

Maybe a little too confident.

I used carrots to dye the rice flour, but it ended up looking more peach than orange. After I pounded the dough and peanuts with a wooden mallet, some cakes ended up with too much peanut, and some with too little. Grilling the cakes, too, proved tricky. The dough kept sticking to the pan, and I burned the edges instead of making them crispy.

My next batch, I learned from my mistakes and watched the cakes more carefully. Mother had made a similar treat for me once, using coconut along with the peanuts. She'd held my hands with a wooden spoon over the fire.

"Sing our song once, then flip," she'd say. "Sing again, then flip."

Channari was a girl who lived by the sea,
who kept the fire—waiting for her sister.
What did she make for a happy smile?
Cakes, cakes, with coconut and dates.

I had nearly finished grilling the second batch when Takkan and Pao entered the kitchen. Fresh snow laced their cloaks, and the outside chill had brought a flush to Takkan's nose and cheeks—a sight I found more endearing than I wanted to.

303

"A bit early for dessert, isn't it?" he greeted. "How are Pao and I supposed to search for assassins when you tempt us with these smells?"

He reached over the grill, but I swatted his hand lightly. *They're still hot.*

"May I have one of those?" Pao asked, pointing at my plate of sacrificial cakes—the ones I had burned.

When I gave him the entire plate, his serious face almost opened to a smile. Almost.

"You've made yourself an ally for life," Takkan joked as Pao drifted to the edge of the kitchen to eat. Pao was starting to remind me of my brothers. His ears stuck out like the twins', and his smiles were hard-earned like Andahai's.

But Takkan? I hadn't yet made up my mind about my former betrothed. Somehow, it didn't feel right comparing him to my brothers.

He drew close, hovering over the pan, and I suddenly became glad for the crackling fire under my monkeycakes—a credible explanation for the wave of heat that had come over my face.

Have you found the assassin? I mouthed hastily, pointing at Oriyu's scarf, which Takkan had folded over his arm.

"No, Pao and I are still looking. We've been questioning everyone in Iro, but to no avail." He waved at my cakes. "Thoughtful of you to send us off to work today with snacks."

They're not for you, I started, but Takkan reached for one over the grill.

He let out a cry. "That's hot."

I crossed my arms, holding back a laugh. *That's what you get for your impatience.*

Takkan was still holding the cake, tossing it from hand to hand to let it cool. Finally he bit and chewed.

I fluttered my hands eagerly. *How is it?*

"Now who's being impatient?" he teased. His mouth was full, and the words came out muffled. "I've barely finished chewing the first bite. I'll need a second to form an opinion."

He took another bite, keeping his expression perfectly neutral and not divulging any opinion at all.

Takkan grinned. "I've always loved a good monkeycake."

I relaxed. *They're recognizable? Not too sweet? Not too thick?*

He didn't understand my questions, but he relieved my worries by reaching for another one. I let him have it before I nudged him away from the grill and pointed at Pao. *Share with him.*

"Who are the rest for?"

I batted my hand like a fan to indicate Zairena.

Takkan raised an eyebrow. "Zairena? Did she ask you to make them today?"

No. I lifted a shoulder. *Why?*

"She said that they taste best when you eat them in the snow." Takkan held his cake out the window, and as the snow landed on it, little tails of steam curled off the grilled surface. "Monkey tails."

I smiled. They did look like monkey tails.

It was hard for me to imagine Zairena being such a

whimsical child, but I knew firsthand how much one could change after a great loss. Maybe there really was a chance of becoming friends.

Takkan offered me the steaming cake. Who would have guessed Zairena was right? The snow hardened the cake's glutinous skin faster, making it even crispier.

I nodded my approval.

"Now I'll just take a few more with me. For Pao, of course." He winked, stacking cakes into his pockets. "Come, I'll walk you back to the castle."

I dreaded seeing Lady Bushian even more than I dreaded seeing Zairena. Ever since Megari and I sneaked off to Rabbit Mountain, I'd been doing my best to avoid her. I knew she blamed me for nearly getting her son and daughter killed.

So when she welcomed me into the leisure chamber, I couldn't have been more surprised. "You've been avoiding me, Lina," she said sternly. "Skipping meals and dipping into the shadows whenever you pass me in the halls."

Under my bowl, I blinked. Had I been that obvious?

"Courage is the Bushian creed."

"Mother . . . ," intervened Megari, "she fought the wolves with Takkan! I don't think you need to lecture her about—"

"Hush, Megari. Unless you wish to be next." Lady Bushian straightened, gathering her poise and refocusing her gaze on me. "Next time you disobey my rules, you come face me right away. My anger does not fade with time; it grows. And you are *extremely* lucky that Takkan sneaked out also. If he hadn't been there with you two when the wolves attacked . . . well, neither of you would be under this roof. Am I understood?"

I dipped my head. It seemed Takkan hadn't told his mother about the wolf with the gold cuff.

"Good. Now, what is that you have? Cakes? Did you make them to try and appease me?"

I merely smiled, glad I couldn't answer.

"Come, bring them inside."

Zairena was at her weaving loom. A little frown beset her lips, probably displeasure that Lady Bushian had decided not to cast me out after all. I set the tray in front of her, forcing myself to smile.

"Monkeycakes!" Megari exclaimed. She plucked one, stuffing it into her mouth in a similar fashion to her brother. "Mmm."

Zairena took a cake, sniffing it. "They do look like monkeycakes. You've some ways to go before you master the recipe, though, Lina. The edges are burnt—and what sort of color is that? Snow monkeys are orange, not pink."

I parted the window shutters. White light brightened the chamber, and a brisk breeze carried in through the iron latticework. Zairena shot to her feet, immediately opening her fan to cover her face.

"Just what do you think you're doing?" she exclaimed. "It's freezing outside. Megari will catch cold."

I tilted my head in confusion. I was holding the cakes outside the window—just like Takkan had shown me.

"Monkey tails!" Megari cried.

Steam spiraled up from the orange cakes, and Megari grabbed two and passed one to her mother and the other to Zairena. "Eat it quickly, before the steam goes away!"

The monkeycake crunched under Megari's teeth, but Zairena wouldn't touch hers. "I prefer not to indulge in sweets," she said, finally setting down her fan.

"Aren't they your favorite?" said Megari.

Zairena held her composure, calmly sipping her tea. "People change. Besides, they're already cold." Her nose made the slightest twitch. "Look at them, all burnt and uneven. I wouldn't even serve such cakes to my dog."

"You don't have a dog," Megari retorted. "And you used to eat them off the snow when you dropped them."

Lady Bushian sent her daughter a warning look.

Megari sniffed. "Well, that only means more for everyone else. Thank you for making them, Lina."

I mustered a smile for the little girl. But as I set my cake to my lips, I suddenly lost my appetite. Zairena had lied about the cakes, just like she had lied about the threads for Raikama.

Strange things to lie about, cakes and threads. When I chose to lie, it was to hide the truth. Zairena's behavior almost made it seem as if she didn't know the truth.

As if she were an impostor.

It was just a twinge in my gut, nothing more. It wouldn't be wise to jump to conclusions, but then again, I had never been one for wisdom.

I told you already, not everyone is as affectionate about food as you are, Shiori, Kiki said, hopping onto my shoulder to keep up with me as I stalked down the hall toward Zairena's room. She bit my hair, trying to pull me back before I acted rashly. *Don't you think you should at least wait until night?*

Then she'll be sleeping—in her room!

Not every night. Not since Hasege's returned.

I stumbled in my step and blinked at my little bird. What a snoop she was! *You're certain of this?*

More certain than you are that she's an impostor.

You didn't think to tell me?

I only just heard from the guards, said Kiki, buzzing close to my ear. *I don't spend all my days listening to human gossip.*

Maybe you should, I thought back, changing course for my own chambers. *It's turning out to be useful.*

Kiki cast me a look of displeasure, but her chest puffed up with pride.

That night, while Kiki led the guard on a merry chase about the fortress grounds, I slipped into Zairena's room. It was twice the size of mine, but had only a partial view of Rabbit Mountain. One of her white robes was draped over a folding screen to dry, and her black sash was flung carelessly over a stool. Strong incense burned in front of a personal altar, with an offering of fruits and rice wine, and her parents' names written on slabs of wood.

I fanned the air and planted myself in front of her chests. Inside were letters, most from Zairena's mother to Lady Bushian, and scrolls from the Temple of Nawaiyi, commending Zairena for her diligent studies. And a painting of her.

Kiki flew in, and I cocked my head at her, seeking her opinion. *Odd, isn't it? Carrying around a painting of yourself.*

Kiki scoffed. *She loves herself. Are you surprised?*

No, but I was still suspicious. I studied the picture. It certainly looked like Zairena. The same rounded chin and pointed nose, the single plait down her back, the mole on her right cheek.

It was unmistakably her.

I set it back, my spirits dampened. But I wasn't finished with my search.

I moved to her drawers. There were jars of willow bark for helping Megari's stomach ailments, talismans and charms to ward off demons and for safe travel, an incense pot, an array of cosmetics, and far too many scarves and fans.

And in her chests, only threads, threads, and more threads. The golden ones had already been sent off to Raikama—Zairena had made a show of wrapping the box and had talked about nothing else for days—but there was a bottle of the golden dye left.

I held it up. The color *was* luminous, but that didn't change my mind about Raikama. My stepmother might spend her days at the embroidery frame, but she had about as much passion for sewing as I did for snakes.

Carefully, I twisted open the bottle's stopper and sniffed. The smell was pungent, like concentrated ink with a strong dose of bitter tea. No trace of sweetness. I ripped a page from my writing book and smeared some on the paper.

If it's poison, it will turn black soon enough, I told Kiki. *But heating it can speed up the process—like cooking.*

I raised the page to a candle and waited. The dye dried and glistened, becoming smooth and only more golden. Not black.

Not poison? Kiki asked.

No, I confirmed, half-disappointed and half-relieved.

So Zairena wasn't the assassin. Maybe my dislike for her was clouding my logic.

At least barging in here hadn't all been for nothing. Zairena's spinning wheel stood in the corner of her room, covered by the muslin sheet.

I approached it tentatively. If she caught me using it for my starstroke, I'd be thrown back into the dungeon. Cast out for being a sorceress. Burned at the stake, with my soul never allowed to find peace.

But if I didn't spin the nettles, my brothers would remain cranes forever.

Between the death of my brothers and my own, I would pick mine with no hesitation.

Good thing I'd brought my satchel. I lifted the sheet and reached for an empty spindle.

Keep watch, I told Kiki.

The last thing I needed was for Zairena to catch me spinning starstroke in her room.

CHAPTER TWENTY-NINE

Night after night, I sneaked into Zairena's room to work. By the end of the week, I was so tired that my eyes burned and I practically swayed with every step. But I was nearly finished. I *would* be finished tonight.

The starstroke danced off my fingers, its coarse fibers gliding onto the wheel and working themselves onto the spindle, turning into something finer. Something magical.

As the fibers melded into one continuous thread, a red strand braided itself into the starstroke—Emuri'en's strand of fate. My heart sang the first time I saw it, and even after I'd returned to my room, I couldn't sleep out of excitement. Now, on this last night of spinning, my heart was heavy for reasons I didn't want to think about. Raikama's curse was starting to weigh on me, and I just wanted to be finished.

I was more careless than usual, forgetting to exchange the spool for an empty one, my fingers occasionally sliding off the wheel as my foot cranked it unsteadily. My eyes strained against the glow of the nettles, but my fingers worked even as my mind drifted. When I finally emptied my satchel of the very last vine, and the spindle was full of thick and glistening starstroke, I let out a sigh of relief, allowing myself a moment to admire my work.

Then I covered Zairena's wheel and cleaned up any trace of my trespass. The incense didn't help; it was so heavy it was making me sleepy. I rubbed my eyes. *Help me, Kiki.*

As Kiki flew to pick up a fallen strand of starstroke, she let out a low whimper. *My wing! Look at it, it's ruined.*

Gold dye stained Kiki's paper wing, seeping into the silvery-gold feather patterns along the edges.

Come, it isn't the end of the world. I'll wipe it off. I had opened the window for a handful of snow and was rubbing it onto Kiki's wing when footsteps squeaked against the wooden floors outside.

I scooped Kiki up and pressed my back against the wall. When the footsteps passed, I hurried out of the room, cursing the fortress's hallways for being so narrow.

Zairena was at the stairs, and she spun as soon as she heard me, a frown darkening her expression. "What are you doing skulking about?"

Her hair was loosened from its usual braid, her sleeves were wrinkled, and her lips were slightly swollen. I raised my chin at her disheveled appearance. *I could ask the same of you.*

I strode for the stairs, but Zairena wouldn't move. "You have no business in the North Garden wing. Were you in my room?"

She grabbed my wrist and shook it, as if I'd stolen jewelry and hidden it in my sleeves. "Show me what's inside the bag."

My heart thundered in my ears. *Here, open it yourself.*

Zairena flung the satchel open. Inside was as empty as the dark side of the moon.

I thought it would appease her, but Zairena only seemed more infuriated. She thrust the satchel back into my arms. "Watch yourself," she hissed. "We hang thieves here, but I'd prefer to see you burn."

As she stalked away, I calmly retied my sash.

Do you want me to poke her eyes out for you? Kiki asked, flying out of my bowl.

Tempting, I muttered. *But no. She isn't worth it.*

She isn't terrifying, not like your stepmother. But I've got a bad feeling, Shiori.

I yawned, too tired to care. Zairena had been making threats all winter. She was like a snake with no venom. Her bites couldn't kill.

They would hurt, though.

The next morning when I arrived in the kitchen, ready for work as usual, Rai and Kenton blocked me at the door. They huddled together like a pair of catfish, their whiskers long and uneven, and their minds too empty to think for themselves.

These few weeks we'd built a civil, if not warm, way of working together in the kitchen. Rai had even started letting me dip into his stash of sugar, and Kenton had finally admitted that my fish soup was better than his. Why did they glare at me now?

"We have no need of you today, Lina," they said harshly. "Go home."

They started to close the door, but I ducked between them and dashed to the back, where Chiruan was steaming eggs.

He acknowledged me with one of his usual grunts. "You should leave," he said without looking up. "Come back in a week, when things have settled."

When what has settled? My confusion multiplied, and I expressed it with my hands.

Another grunt, and his nostrils flared. "Of course you wouldn't know what's happened." He lowered his voice. "The young mistress was ill yesterday. Zairena blames it on those cakes you baked. You aren't to enter the kitchen, not until Megari recovers."

She thought I poisoned Megari? I shook my head violently. *That's ridiculous.*

Chiruan turned to the lacquer box at his side, the one where he kept his spices and recipes, and sprinkled a pinch of peppercorns into the dish simmering by the eggs. "Don't look so crestfallen, Lina. Lady Bushian and Lord Takkan both ate the cakes. I'm certain the young lord at least will vouch for you."

Chiruan gestured for me to leave, but I wouldn't budge. I wasn't crestfallen, I was furious! And worried. *How is she?* I asked, tugging at my hair to indicate Megari's pigtails.

"She'll be well. Her stomach is weak, and this sort of

thing comes and goes. Lady Bushian will understand that you had nothing to do with it."

I was boiling with rage. All this simply because Zairena thought I had stolen into her room?

"It'll pass in a few days, Lina," Chiruan said, misreading my anger for fear. "Go apologize to Zairena for whatever you've done to offend her."

Apologize? Had all his spices gone to his head?

"Yes, apologize. These nobles need their toes tickled and their egos stroked, Lady Zairena most of all."

I pursed my lips tight. *Absolutely not.*

In an unusual act of sympathy, he said, "You're a hard worker, Fishgirl. I'll make sure no one takes your spot washing the rice when you're gone. Now heed what I say and hurry on. Don't make an enemy of Zairena."

I threw off my apron and hurried away, but not to apologize.

Chiruan was wrong—I had enemies aplenty. One more wouldn't hurt.

Talismans hung from the latticework on Megari's doors, little charms that chimed and tinkled when I slipped inside.

Takkan was already there, sketching in one of his books. He looked up to acknowledge me, raising a finger to his lips. Megari was asleep.

I tiptoed toward her, biting my lip as I took in her small,

pale face. Her fingers were splayed over the folds of her blanket, her breathing slow and soft. Under her arm, peeking out of her blanket, was a round-eyed doll with silk flowers in its hair. It seemed to smile at me no matter where I moved, like its owner.

"She's resting," Takkan whispered. "Her stomach made her ill, but she's convalescing now."

I nodded, but my shoulders were still heavy. I started for the door.

Takkan followed. "You look upset, Lina," he said once we were outside. "Is it the rumors?"

I looked up at him, surprise parting my lips. He had heard?

"I know they are not true. So does my mother." He tucked his sketchbook under his arm. "Come with me. I want to show you something."

Pao was guarding the doors we approached, two sliding screens decorated with a gilded full moon and Rabbit Mountain in ivory. The sentinel's head tipped with curiosity when he saw me, and a beat later I understood why.

Takkan had brought me to his chambers. They were neat and sparse, unlike Megari's. His sword hung on a rack, his armor and helmet in an open closet. To the left, by the windows, there was a desk surrounded by books and tall stacks of paper.

"That's what I wanted to show you," he said, leading me to the desk. "I thought you might appreciate it."

Nearly a dozen paintings rested on the low table, all

inscribed in Takkan's neat hand. They depicted moments from Kiata's most beloved legends.

"It's meant to be a gift for Megari when I have enough stories," he said sheepishly. "I fear by the time I finish, she'll be too old for them."

One can never be too old for stories, I thought, tracing over the painting of Emuri'en. The cranes with scarlet crowns that looked so startlingly like my brothers. The impossibly long hair that intertwined fates and sometimes changed them.

It was beautiful.

I knelt, studying painting after painting. There was the moon lady with her hunter husband, and one of Lord Sharima'en, the god of death, with his wife, Ashmiyu'en, goddess of life. There were stories about dragons chasing tortoises, and bamboo cutters who encountered magical spirits in the trees. But there was one painting that didn't belong.

It was at the bottom of the pile, and I tugged at it gently while Takkan let in more light from the windows.

He'd illustrated a girl with long black hair and rich vermilion robes. She was carrying a potted orchid, and above her flew a kite, blue as painted porcelain. Something about the scene made sorrow bloom in my chest, though I could not place why. *What is this?*

A shadow passed over Takkan's face. "That's not for Megari."

For whom? I mimed.

Takkan took a deep breath before responding. "Princess Shiori."

The name thudded in my ears. *Oh.*

The girl *did* look like me. My brothers were even there, six young princelings in the background. I reached for one of the brushes on his desk and wrote in my book:

You knew her?

"I had no choice in the matter," Takkan said stiffly. "Our betrothal was arranged when we were children. Father always said it was a great honor to our family, given that we've never been as powerful as those who live closer to Gindara. It came as a surprise, one we couldn't turn down."

Had he wished he could turn it down? I'd been surprised too. "A lord of the third rank?" I'd complained more than once. "If I'm going to be sent all the way to Iro, can't he at least have a villa in Gindara so I can visit?"

I swallowed the memory, filled with shame.

Takkan went on: "I'd heard plenty about her. That she was rebellious and impatient, full of mischief and a liar. But everyone who knew her loved her. They said she had spirit, and a laugh that no one could resist.

"So I wrote her letters. I wanted to get to know her, but how do you introduce yourself to a princess?" He laughed, but there was little humor in his tone. "Mother suggested I write her stories, and so I did. They were about myself, life in Iro—with little drawings. The winters here are long, so I had plenty of time. I was told Shiori was curious, so I'd try to end each story on a suspenseful note, hoping she would write back to ask what happened next." Takkan had wound himself tight, telling me this story, and now his shoulders finally bowed, and he folded himself over his knees. Quietly, he said, "But she never did. I don't think she even opened them."

I was glad for the bowl on my head, because I couldn't look at him.

I remembered those letters. Every few months, my maids brought one to my chambers, each envelope thicker than the last.

"At least he has beautiful handwriting," I'd said the first time, seeing my name in Takkan's hand. But I didn't read any of them. Didn't even open them. Part of it was out of petulance, but mostly . . . mostly, I hadn't wanted to face my future. My bleak, horrible future, married to some bleak, horrible lord.

If I could go back to the palace now, those letters would be the first things I searched for.

Rude, I mouthed, pounding my fist on my palm. *You must have been angry.*

"I was angry," admitted Takkan. "I was even planning to tell her so when I met her, but . . ." He sighed. "But she made me change my mind."

Now my brow furrowed. For the life of me, I did not ever remember meeting Takkan—except when we were children, barely old enough to have memories.

When did you meet her?

"My family was in Gindara during the Summer Festival one year. I tried to find Shiori to introduce myself, but the

320

royal children were occupied. There was a contest—just for them, organized by Lord Yuji." At the name, Takkan tensed. "He'd given the six princes and princess each a pot of soil the month before. Orchid seeds were sown in each one."

I remembered. A test—for "moral character," Yuji had said. Andahai, Benkai, Wandei, and Hasho had passed; they'd watered the plant every day, but not even the slightest bud had sprouted. Yotan had broken his pot in a fight with Reiji, and both had admitted it, so they had passed as well—for their honesty. But I . . . I had failed the test because my pot had bloomed with orchids.

They'd been purple, the same color as the expensive dyes merchants sent us for our winter robes. Vibrant as a splash of twilight. I remembered being surprised—and delighted—by how beautifully they had grown. I should have questioned how they had blossomed so quickly, and how the flowers had taken on exactly the color and shape I had imagined.

I now knew it was because of my magic.

"There was no seed in the pot," Lord Yuji said, baring his little teeth as he smiled, "only crushed orchid petals at the bottom of the soil. It was a game, Shiori'anma. I'll not pass judgment on you for planting a new flower into your pot."

"But I didn't," I protested.

"Admit you cheated, Shiori," said Reiji. "We know you to be the princess of liars."

"I didn't cheat!" I cried. My face heated with humiliation. Everyone was staring. "I'm not lying."

321

None of my brothers believed me. Not even Hasho.

I spun away, refusing to be wrongly shamed in front of the entire court. I ran to the back of the courtyard and hid behind a magnolia tree, nibbling on cakes I'd stashed in my sleeves.

Before long, a boy I didn't recognize offered me a handkerchief. He was thin and gangly, his robes too short and his hat sliding off his overly waxed black hair. Probably some courtier's son who'd been ordered to search for me in exchange for my father's favor.

He looked amused—and somewhat relieved that I was eating, not crying.

"Monkeycakes?" he greeted. "They're exceptionally good this year, but a little messy." He touched his mouth, a polite indication that I had crumbs all over.

I snatched the handkerchief from him and wiped my lips. I was about to order him to go away when he knelt beside me and said solemnly:

"I believe you—about the flowers."

He'd caught me at my weakest. My shoulders sagged. "I watered them every day. I talked to them, the way Chef talks to his herbs to get them to grow faster."

"It was a mean trick Lord Yuji played on you."

"Lord Yuji?" I repeated, twisting a lock of hair

as I ruminated. "Why would he trick me? He wants
me to marry one of his sons."

The boy flinched. He asked hesitantly, "Do you
want to marry Lord Yuji's son?"

"I don't want to marry anyone," I declared. "But
better one of Yuji's sons than that barbarian fool in
the North. At least I'll be closer to home, so I can
spend as little time with my husband as possible."

"I see. So it's not because you dislike your be-
trothed."

"I dislike that he exists." I sniffed, folded his
handkerchief, and handed it back. "Thank you . . .
I didn't catch your name."

The boy smiled, his demeanor oddly sunnier.
"My name isn't important." A kite floated over his
shoulder, exquisitely painted with a flock of cranes
flying above a mountain with two peaks. He held
it out to me. "Do you like it? I painted it myself."

"It's nice, almost as good as Yotan's work. Are
you entering it into the competition?"

"There isn't time. My father and I have to leave
before dusk. We live far from here."

"Who's it for?"

He took out a brush and started writing. His
calligraphy was neat and precise, but I didn't have
the patience for him to paint someone's name on
the kite. My temper was already hot from Lord
Yuji's contest, and I took his kite and ran with it.

For a boy with spindly legs, he was fast. He caught up with me quickly, and in my surprise, I accidentally let go.

The kite soared high and out of reach. I started after it, but the boy drew me back. "Let it fly."

We watched it soar high above the trees, and my heart sank as the kite grew smaller, until it was but a dot in the sky. Tears welled in my eyes, and I hated myself for crying in front of this boy I didn't know. For losing his kite, too. For ruining everything I touched.

"I'm sorry," I said, feeling terrible.

His eyes were dark and serious. "Don't be. Kites are meant to fly, some higher than others."

"It's a lucky one, then. The rest of us are bound by our strands." I let out a miserable sigh and wiped at my eyes. Then I turned to the boy. I meant to speak imperiously, but my words came out wobbly and guilt-ridden: "You said it was a gift. I could help you paint another one. I'm not very good at art, not like Yotan—"

"I'd like that," the boy said eagerly, shedding some of his awkward formality.

He smiled again, his disposition even sunnier than before, and in spite of my tears, I couldn't help smiling back. I folded my arms across my lap, about to sit on the grass to start our painting when, at that moment, someone approached from behind.

The boy stiffened immediately, becoming shy and withdrawn. "On second thought, please don't concern yourself over it." He bowed, excusing himself as Hasho came into view. "I'm glad I finally met you, Shiori'anma."

All this time, that boy had been Takkan! He looked different now. No longer the gangly, timid boy with too much wax in his hair. Then again, I wasn't the same girl either.

I sucked in my breath, coloring with shame. Even my brothers hadn't believed me about the flowers. Why had Takkan, who barely knew me? Whose letters I had tossed aside and never read. Whose friendship I had spurned.

"After I met her," Takkan was saying, "I never wrote to her again."

Why not?

"Because I had the answer I was looking for."

I tensed, sure that Takkan had hated me. The answer would hurt, I knew, but I couldn't help asking:

What was that?

"My parents think of marriage as a duty to one's family and country," Takkan said, by way of response. "I think of it as a duty to one's heart. Food feeds the belly, thoughts feed the mind, but love is what feeds the heart. I hoped, with my letters, that Shiori and I might grow to make each other's hearts full. That we might be happy together. After I met her, I thought yes—yes, there was a chance."

My heart quickened and skipped, doing all sorts of leaps in my chest I had never known possible.

"Maybe I was fooling myself." Takkan held up the painting of me with the kite. "I was going to give this to her after our betrothal ceremony, but she chose to jump into the Sacred Lake rather than meet me."

It was the first time I'd seen Takkan actually look pained.

His shoulders tensed. "My family became the ridicule of Gindara, and I told my father that we should leave right away. Princess or not, no person of good character would act so disrespectfully."

The painting drooped in his hands, and my stomach sank with it. I'd wounded Takkan by running away from the ceremony. Not once had I wondered what it must have been like for him, to journey across the country to meet me. He must have been so disappointed. And hurt.

"After I returned home, I wished I had at least given her a chance to explain herself," Takkan confessed. "I wished I hadn't left so angrily. But I was too proud to write her."

He put aside the painting, his back to me. "Then she disappeared," he said softly, "and I will always regret that I didn't stay. Maybe things would have been different for her if I had."

My breathing had gone shallow, and before I could stop them, tears pricked my eyes. I wiped them hastily, but I must have missed a spot, for Takkan offered me his handkerchief. Just like he had all those years ago.

"Are these tears for the princess, Lina?" he asked gently. "Or are they for yourself?"

At the question, I looked up. My brush slipped from my grip, and Takkan and I both bent to pick it up. Our fingers touched, clasping either end of the stick.

He looked down at our hands. Mine trembled, and he covered it with his, steadying me.

"I wish you would speak to me," he said. "Sometimes, the way you move your lips, I swear that you can. Even if I'm wrong, I wish I could at least see your eyes."

His eyes startled me, so piercing they seemed to see through my wooden bowl. For a moment, I could have sworn he knew the truth—that I *was* Shiori.

But then he looked away, and the moment was gone.

Disappointment stung my chest. He didn't know. How could he? I looked and acted nothing like that carefree princess he had met once, so many long years ago.

He let go of the brush and hung his head. "I shouldn't have said that. It isn't fair to you. Just know that I care about you, Lina. I couldn't be there for Shiori, but I will be there—for you. Whether you need me or not."

I swallowed, staring at our hands. I should have shaken my head and told him I didn't want him to be there for me.

But I did no such thing. Even though my burdens were mine, and mine alone, there was a simple comfort in having Takkan with me.

I twined my fingers with his, and narrowed the space between us—as much as I dared.

I wished we'd never have to let go.

CHAPTER THIRTY

Eager to work again, I returned to the kitchen, ignoring Rai's and Kenton's shrimp-eyed stares. By noon, they'd forgotten Zairena's rumors and I was kneading dough for noodles, with a soup already simmering on the stove.

All was well until Hasege barged inside, brandishing his sword.

Unlike Zairena, he had never made an appearance in the kitchen before, and I braced myself, certain she had sent him to make my life miserable. More rumors that I was a sorceress, a public shaming for the bowl on my head—whatever it was, I was ready.

Except Hasege was not here for me. Scorn flickered in his eyes when he took in my presence, but his hard gaze swept past me to the cooks. To Chiruan.

"Your time is up, old man. Come with me."

Confusion twisted the chef's broad face. "My lord, I know that dinner is running behind tonight, and that the chicken last night was overcooked, but—"

Steel sliced the air, and Hasege's sword landed at the edge of Chiruan's throat.

"I said, come with me."

Chiruan set aside his cleaver. "At least give me the dignity of telling me what I've done wrong."

"What you've done wrong?" Hasege repeated with a laugh. "All right, for the sake of everyone here. You, Chiruan, are guilty of murdering Oriyu, honored sentinel of Castle Bushian."

My hand jumped to my mouth. Chiruan, the assassin? That was impossible.

"S-s-sir, Chiruan has been Castle Bushian's chef for over thirty years," said Rai, as shocked as I was. "He—"

"He is A'landan," Hasege reminded us all.

"*Half*-A'landan," Chiruan spluttered. "This is nonsense. Oriyu died of Four Breaths. I have no—"

"This was found in your room." Hasege held up a tiny bottle shaped like a long gourd and splashed its contents into one of the pots simmering over the fire. Within moments, a sickeningly sweet smell pervaded the kitchen, and the pot's contents blackened as if someone had thrown soot inside.

Four Breaths.

"You were saying, old man?"

Chiruan coughed and turned his cheek. "That isn't mine." He faltered. "It isn't."

"It was found within a pouch of gold," Hasege said as one of the sentinels drew forth a sack of gold makans. "Far too much money for an honest, hardworking cook like you."

"I've never seen that before—"

"Another word, and your tongue will be forfeit. The same goes for anyone else who speaks in this man's defense." Hasege moved his blade from cook to cook before returning it to Chiruan's throat.

Everyone shrank back, curling up like millipedes as Hasege and his sentinels rummaged through the pantry. I cringed as glass bottles and jars shattered, Chiruan's carefully curated sauces and cooking wines carelessly tossed to the ground.

They found Chiruan's box.

"Open this," Hasege demanded of Rai and Kenton, pointing at the lock.

"Only Chiruan has the key."

"It's nothing," Chiruan said, pleading. "Just spices and recipes. It's been in my family for years—"

"Bring it to Lord Takkan for inspection," ordered Hasege, cutting the key off the chef's neck. "And take Chiruan to the dungeon."

As the sentinels obeyed, I started to protest. Hasege shoved me against the wall. "Stay out of the way, demon," he warned. "Unless you want to be next."

I reined in my spinning thoughts, certain that Chiruan had been framed. After a long, brittle silence, Hasege finally left, and I threw off my apron and dashed back to the castle.

Pao blocked me from entering Takkan's rooms. "His Lordship is busy. He's just returned from Iro Village, and he isn't to be distur—"

I reached over him and rapped my knuckles on the door. It was the height of impudence, but I didn't care.

As Pao started to yank me away, Takkan appeared at the door.

He was still wearing his cloak, its deep blue folds draped over his shoulders. Shadows clung to his frame, and his eyes, usually brimming with focus and intent, looked tired.

"Let her inside."

Pao sent me an exasperated look before he backed away. I would need a mountain of sweet bean cakes to claim his favor again.

Chiruan! I gestured wildly. *He's—*

"I know you are upset, Lina," said Takkan. His voice was tenser than I'd ever heard it. "But the evidence is clear as day. Chiruan has murdered a man, and committed high treason against the emperor, and against Kiata. I know he was a mentor to you, and I am grateful for his kindness, but this war has many loyalties divided. Sometimes the truth is the hardest poison to swallow."

Everything he said made sense. It was exactly what Andahai or Benkai would have done if someone they trusted had betrayed them. And yet, I couldn't believe it.

I was searching for a slip of paper to tell him so when I saw Chiruan's box.

It rested on Takkan's desk, freshly opened. I recognized its smooth red lacquer, the abalone-shelled etchings of young children at play, the splatters of oil and sauce that Chiruan meticulously wiped from the enamel each night. He hadn't gotten a chance this time.

The lid lay on the ground, its silk casing stripped. Takkan

picked it up and held it beside a lantern. "What do you read, Lina?"

Swallowing hard, I leaned toward the lid.

Painted on the inside of the lid were lists of ingredients and cooking times and temperatures. Variations too.

GOLD, one was titled. FOR SLEEP.

Below it: BLACK, FOR DEATH.

The blood drained from my face, my vision swimming in and out. I squeezed my eyes shut. So that was what Takkan meant by evidence.

"We will hold off on a trial until the recipe has been confirmed," said Takkan, closing the box. "But it doesn't look promising, Lina. A good man is dead. Let us take some comfort in knowing that his killer has been found, and pray that we find some answers."

My face stung with the ugliness of it all, but I nodded mutely.

No one had access to the box except Chiruan. Not Rai or Kenton, or any of the servants. I wished I could ask Chiruan why. Why Oriyu? Why had he betrayed Kiata in this way?

The sentinels would get an answer soon enough. Maybe the reason *was* as simple as money. I thought of the gold makans jangling in that hemp pouch—Chiruan's reward. Perhaps there was more: maybe a position in the palace if Yuji rose to the throne. I couldn't think of anything else.

Does it matter? I asked myself. *Does it matter why someone you trust betrays you?*

I was thinking of Raikama now, not Chiruan.

No, I answered. But I still wanted to know.

"Careful of your curiosity, little one," Raikama used to tease when I was small. "Stray too close to the fire, and you'll only burn."

Ironic that my stepmother should've given such a warning. I was already burning, and she—Raikama—was the one who had set the flames.

After Chiruan's arrest, everyone in the kitchen was like a ghost, half there and half not. Once I finished helping Rai and Kenton clean the sentinels' mess, I shut myself in my room. Much as I wanted to, I couldn't embroil myself in the fortress's affairs any longer. My time in Iro was approaching its end, and I still had one final task to complete before I left.

I covered the paper panels on my windows and doors, then spread the starstroke across my lap. The threads were exquisite, a lustrous braid of gold and violet and red, like the three magics that had forged it. Demonfire, the blood of stars, and Emuri'en's strands of fate. I needed to weave them together tight enough to rein in my stepmother's dragon magic.

Don't make the holes too loose, Kiki said as my fingers danced across the starstroke, making knot after knot.

Stop worrying. The holes were as wide as my smallest finger, tiny enough for Kiki to slip through, but not one of Raikama's snakes. I had already made sure of that.

I'm not the one with my brow furrowed. What's the matter, Shiori? Shouldn't you be glad you're almost done? You're going home soon.

Yes, it should have gladdened me that we were so close to the end of this horrible journey. But in all honesty, I would have preferred if it never ended.

I had not forgotten the price we would have to pay to break our curse. All winter, I had tried to block it out of my mind. But now that the net was nearly finished, it was never far from my thoughts.

One of my brothers would have to die.

Over and over, I tortured myself with the different possibilities. That I might never hear Andahai scold me again. Never hear Benkai's words of assurance. Never build kites with Wandei or laugh with Yotan, or argue with Reiji. Never trust my secrets to Hasho.

With every knot I tied, my heart hurt a little more. As my net swelled in size, the tiny pearl in my chest glimmered and throbbed, sometimes aching so acutely I had to stop and catch my breath.

Did Raikama's pearl ever hurt her? I wondered what it must have been like for her to leave her country for the palace. Alone and melancholy, burdened by secrets she could not share with anyone.

I gritted my teeth. Was I truly commiserating with my stepmother?

A little. She used to look so happy when I ran into her apartments, as if I were her only friend in the world. Why did that have to change? What had made her hate me?

Wits, Shiori, I muttered silently, picking up my net again. *Raikama is evil, that's all there is to it. There's nothing to understand.*

That was what I told myself night after night as I worked on the net, until I tied the ends of the very last strand of starstroke.

Until at last my net was completed.

It was splendorous, long and wide enough to reach the far corners of my room. The demonfire gave it a shimmering light, like sparks, and the blood of stars made it vibrant, as if I'd somehow captured all the colors of the universe. If I told someone I had crushed a thousand rubies to make it, they would believe me, for that was the only way to describe Emuri'en's strands of fate. With the three magics together, the net shone with a light that could have ensnared my gaze for all eternity.

Beautiful as it was, looking at it brought me no joy. I stuffed it into my satchel, not wanting to see it again until the wretched day that I'd have to use it against Raikama. I didn't even want to think about my stepmother until then.

But it seemed I had no choice in the matter. That night while I slept, a long-buried memory surfaced, uninvited:

"Why did you put the snake in Reiji's bed?" my stepmother asked. "It upset him."

"He deserved it. He broke my favorite doll."

"Just because Reiji was unkind doesn't mean you should be, too. Think of the snake—you might have hurt it."

"Or it might have bitten Reiji," I said wickedly.

"Shiori!"

"I don't like Reiji," I said stubbornly. "And I

don't care for snakes. They're the natural enemy of cranes."

Raikama laughed. "It is cranes that eat snakes, not the other way around. Snakes are my friends. They were my only friends, once."

"Even the vipers?" I asked. "Hasho said those are poisonous."

"Especially the vipers. They practically raised me."

She said it so seriously I couldn't tell whether she was joking. "Well then, you're the only snake I like, Stepmother."

Raikama tousled my hair. A glow beamed off her face, gold and radiant as the moon. I started to point, but Raikama's hand jumped away from my hair. In a heartbeat, the glow was gone, as if I'd imagined it.

Gone too was her humor, and her voice became serious. "One day, you won't say that. One day, you'll despise me."

"I couldn't hate you."

"You will," she said at length. "A viper is poisonous, whether it wants to be or not."

"But not all poison is bad. Sometimes it's a medicine in disguise."

Raikama blinked, taken aback. "What?"

"You told me that once, when someone tried to kill Father with a poisoned letter. Don't you remember? You made an antidote with venom from your snakes."

She studied me, a half smile forming on her lips. "You have a very good memory."

"You saved him. That's why I could never despise you." I paused, testing out a word on my tongue. I ventured, "Mother."

Her smile quickly dissolved. "I am not your mother, Shiori. You are not a child of mine. You will never be."

Before I could stop her, she touched my eyes, and I forgot the memory for many, many years.

In the morning, Kiki danced on my nose, waking me with the snow shaken off her wings. *Seryu wants you to meet him tonight by the river. He has news.*

CHAPTER THIRTY-ONE

The lonely moon hung round and bright as a dragon's eye. Freshly fallen snow chilled the air, leaving little time for second thoughts as I wound to the back of the fortress.

"A bit late to be heading out, Lina," Pao said, not letting me pass. "It's already dark."

In the past all I had to do was suggest Chiruan had sent me, and Pao would have let me go anywhere. But Chiruan was in the dungeon. I held up my torch and my pail, mouthing a slew of nonsense: *Mushrooms, ice, trout, river.*

"Not so fast, not so fast," Pao said, leaning forward. He grunted. "I don't know how Takkan does it. I can't understand a word you're saying."

That's the point. I shook my basket at him and motioned in the direction of the kitchen. *Need to go.*

Pao harrumphed. "All right, go, go. But don't linger—or I'll tell Lady Bushian."

Not needing to be warned twice, I scurried out.

Fireflies danced over the river, so many they looked like

the sparks of a bonfire. Kiki sat on my shoulder as I crouched by the bank, my body trembling from the cold.

In the water, the full moon wavered, its silvery light making the frost shimmer. *Seryu, I'm here.*

I poked the end of my torch to the frozen river, watching the surface crack and fracture into thousands of interconnecting lines. I waited. The ice parted, and as the currents rippled and swirled underneath, two ruby eyes, large as quail eggs, glinted from within the watery tempest.

"You look better fed than last time," greeted Seryu, taking on his human form in the water. As usual, iridescent gills sparkled on his cheekbones, and jade-green scales peeked out from his silk robes. But he looked different today. His hair was shorter, only to his chin, and for the first time, his eyes were devoid of all mischief.

"Better fed, and warmer. Then again, a paper busybody told me you've been staying in a castle, protected by Kiata's finest sentinels. You didn't tell me that one of them was your betrothed."

Irritation prickled Seryu's voice, which I didn't understand. *What difference does it make? For all he knows, I'm nobody.*

"You may have a bowl on your head. But even a fool like Bushi'an Takkan can see that you're hardly nobody."

I glowered at the dragon. *He isn't a fool. If I didn't know better, I would say you sound jealous.*

"Me? Jealous of a mortal?" Seryu scoffed. "Dragons don't bother with such petty emotions. Besides, I'm the grandson of the Dragon King. I have plenty of admirers of my own."

How? I inquired. *I thought you rarely surfaced.*

"You humans aren't the only ones capable of appreciating my grandeur," retorted Seryu. His expression shuttered into a scowl. "At home, my reputation alone attracts dozens, no, hundreds of admirers!"

He heaved a woeful sigh. "But you've always been one of my favorites, Shiori," he admitted, suddenly softening. "If you weren't so . . . so human, I'd—"

You'd what?

"Never mind."

The dragon was acting odd today. Prickly one moment, melancholy the next. I grimaced, fearing that meant I wouldn't like his news.

The net is finished, I told him, getting straight to business. It was cold by the river, and I didn't want to freeze. *Kiki said you had news.*

"Two dragon days is hardly long enough for me to regain my grandfather's favor," Seryu said irritably.

"What are you saying?"

"I don't have news, Shiori. I merely bear a message from my grandfather."

I turned to ice. *What is it?*

"He regrets he did not shatter your bones above the Taijin Sea," said Seryu thinly. "And he assures you that the only reason your brothers—who fly across the sea in search of your stepmother's name—have not yet been reduced to sea-foam is because of her pearl."

What is this about Raikama's pearl?

"He's ordered me to tell you that *if* you survive your encounter with the Nameless Queen, he demands her pearl. It belongs to the dragons."

Very well, I'll give it to him—if he tells me how to break my curse.

"The Dragon King does not bargain," said Seryu with a growl. "The next time you see me, you will have her pearl."

His image began to ripple and fade in the water.

Wait, Seryu!

Only his red eyes lingered now, duller than I'd ever seen them. "I can't help you break your curse. I have already tried. But you're clever. I'm sure you will figure it out."

I was tired of needing to be clever. Of needing to figure things out. I just wanted to go home and be with my family, to wake up and find this had all been some horribly vivid dream.

I crouched closer to the river as if to whisper. There was something heavy on my mind that I wanted to test out: *I've been wondering about my stepmother. What if . . . what if it isn't a curse? What if . . .* I touched my bowl, feeling foolish for the words I was about to say, but it was too late to turn back. *What if sometimes poison is medicine in disguise?*

His full face reappearing in the water, Seryu stared at me as if I had grown horns and whiskers. "You think she had good intentions for turning your brothers into cranes?"

I don't know what I think. I'm just trying to understand why. Why did she do it?

He sniffed. "Humans, always trying to find the reason behind this or that. What would it change?"

That I couldn't answer. How could I, without knowing what there was to understand?

"The pearl in her heart is not like any other dragon's. It is corrupted, and she too must be corrupt for possessing it. That's all you need to know."

Seryu was right: her reasons couldn't possibly justify her actions. What she had done to my brothers and me was unforgivable. Only a cruel heart could yield such a curse.

So why didn't I believe it?

"Don't make things complicated," Seryu said pointedly. "Save your brothers, then bring the pearl to my grandfather. Promise this to me, as one friend to another."

I gave a numb nod.

"Good." Relief rolled off his shoulders. "Now I must go."

I won't see you before then?

"I wish you could, Princess, but no. You won't miss me anyway, now that your affections have veered toward that unremarkably human lordling."

I blushed before I could stop myself.

"Ah, so Kiki wasn't spinning tales."

Takkan's a friend. And I wish you would stop using human *as an insult. I'm human, and so are my brothers.*

"I did say he was unremarkable." Before I could fire off another retort, Seryu dipped back into the water. When he resurfaced, his feathery green eyebrows were knitted. I wondered what was happening in his underwater kingdom, for his demeanor became suddenly stiff, as if he was being watched.

"I'll send word to your brothers that you've completed the net. Do your best to survive until I see you again."

The water stilled, and he vanished, leaving me to bear the weight of Raikama's curse alone.

By the time I returned to the castle, I was exhausted, half-frozen, and very much looking forward to collapsing by the hearth. But I forgot my fatigue when I saw Megari curled up against my door, violently ill.

"Lina," she rasped. "You're back. I couldn't sleep. My stomach."

Her face was wan, her eyes glassy and puffy, and her limbs so limp she could barely keep herself up.

"My stomach," she moaned, vomit on her lips. "Help me."

She shivered as she slumped over me, listless. Her pulse was ebbing fast.

Frantic with worry, I scooped her into my arms. *Stay strong, Megari,* I thought, carrying her. *You'll be all right.*

You're not taking her to the smirk-happy priestess, are you? Kiki exclaimed from inside my sleeve.

I was. Much as I hated to admit it, I needed Zairena's help. I prayed she was in her room tonight. I rapped my knuckles on her door, not relenting until she answered.

"Are you possessed? How dare you—" Zairena started, but then her eyes widened. "Megari!"

She immediately signaled for the guard at the end of the hall. "Bring Lady Megari to her chambers."

I started to follow, but Zairena waved me away. "Go back to sleep. You've done enough, and we don't need the entire fortress knowing Megari is ill."

But I ignored her, helping the guard put Megari back into her bed.

I stroked the girl's hair, wishing I could tell her a story. I settled for strumming softly on her moon lute. A tray of half-eaten tangerines and dried red dates rested on one of her tables. And a plate of old persimmon cake. Emuri'en's strands! I hoped she hadn't fallen ill from eating one of Chiruan's desserts.

It felt like hours before Zairena returned with tea. When she saw me, her lips parted to make a characteristically unpleasant remark. For once, she thought better of it and passed me the tea. Together we helped Megari drink, tilting her chin up to dribble the liquid through her pressed lips. After the pot was drained, Megari's breathing slowly eased and she drifted back to sleep.

"She'll be better in the morning," said Zairena.

Thank you, I gestured, truly grateful. Perhaps Zairena *was* a priestess after all. The tea smelled of ginger and orange and hawthorn berries—all ingredients for relieving stomach pains.

"Wait." Zairena's face was weary, her fingers stained with tea and herbs. "It was a good thing you brought her to me. Thank you, Lina."

I blinked, startled by the gesture of peace, reluctant as it was.

Who would have guessed? Kiki muttered once we were

alone. *It took Megari almost dying for that viper to withdraw her fangs. Do you believe her?*

I collapsed onto my bed, utterly spent. It didn't matter whether I believed her. By the end of the week, I'd be gone from here.

And if the gods willed it, my winter in Iro would be a memory left far in the past.

CHAPTER THIRTY-TWO

There were only two farewells that mattered, and I didn't know how to go about either one of them.

I started with Megari. She was back to her usual cheerful self, and when I visited, she was trying to decide what to wear to the Winter Festival.

Puddles of silk and satin surrounded her, dresses and sashes and slippers scattered about the floor. "Lina!" she cried, wading through the mess. She held up two ribbons. "Help me, I'm trying to decide on colors for my braids."

My gaze lingered on the scarlet ribbon, but I pointed at the blue. It was the color of the Bushian crest, and it matched the collar and cuffs of the dress Megari was wearing.

"I thought so too. Here, why don't you have this one, then?"

Megari wove the scarlet ribbon into my hair. "Red looks pretty on you. You should wear more of it."

It had been my favorite color once. Now I could hardly see

it without thinking of my brothers, the six crimson crowns they were cursed to wear.

"Are you excited about tonight?" she asked, dragging me to the window. "It's going to be spectacular. The best yet."

I'd never thought much of the Winter Festival before. In Gindara it was such a minor event that we tended to combine it with our New Year celebrations. But I could imagine why Megari loved it so. Even from the castle, I could see the hundreds of lanterns bobbing from Iro's rooftops.

"The ice sculptures are my favorite," Megari went on. "You can't see them from here, but they're beautiful. Last year, there were dragons and boats and entire gardens made of ice! They'll last until the New Year, if we're lucky. Then it'll finally be spring, and I can take you to see the rabbits on the mountain."

I swallowed, reaching into my satchel for my writing book to show her the farewell message I'd prepared.

Megari, I'm leav—

The pounding of drums made my hands jolt, and the page ripped as a horn blared from behind the fortress.

What's happening? I mimed.

Megari let out a disapproving sigh. "Everyone's off on the hunt." A beat later, horses galloped and the gates opened.

The hunt?

"It's tradition." Megari turned to her moon lute, making a face when she pulled a string that was grossly out of tune.

"How many arrows it takes to shoot their target predicts how many days of snow there will be next year. Silly, I know. Takkan hates it, but since Father's not here, he has to lead. He's the best marksman, after all. Even better than Hasege."

Something in my stomach began to curdle. I lurched for Megari's desk, my hand writing furiously.

"'What do they hunt?'" Megari read over my shoulder. "Usually an elk or a deer, but at breakfast, Hasege said he saw wild cranes circling the forest—"

I didn't wait for her to finish. Ink splattered my robes as I dropped the brush and ran for the door.

I wished I had wings. The snow was to my knees, and plowing down the hill into the forest was a battle in itself. As the wind howled, biting my ears, it seemed to taunt: *You won't reach your brothers in time.*

Arrows exploded into the clouds every few minutes, a shot of terror rippling down my spine as I watched my brothers circle the trees, their crimson crowns stark against the gray sky.

Fly away from here, Brothers! I screeched in my mind. *Flee!*

But they could not hear me.

Finally, I saw hoofprints in the snow, a trampled path leading through the forest. I followed it, my pulse thundering in my ears as I stepped into the tracks to hasten my pace. There they were—Takkan and his sentinels. Pao had his arrow pointed to the sky—at my brothers! I threw myself in front of his horse.

"Halt!" Takkan shouted as the horses reared, their hooves so close they flicked snow into my face.

"What the—" Hasege spluttered, recognizing me. "Are you mad, girl? How dare you interrupt the hunt!"

Takkan was already dismounting, but I couldn't wait for him. I jumped, seizing Pao's bow and flinging it into the snow.

Before anyone could stop me, I went from horse to horse, frantically emptying the sentinels' quivers. With an armful of arrows, I ran.

Brothers! Brothers!

They saw me. Hasho soared closer, the rest descending carefully into the forest. Kiki found them first, in a grove of snowcapped firs.

I was breathing hard, dizzied by white everywhere I looked. I didn't realize that I was freezing until Hasho brushed a wing against my cheek and I felt nothing. Gently my brothers cocooned me in their feathers, bringing warmth back to my blood.

I dropped the arrows and hugged each of them, even Reiji. Had it really been two months since I'd seen them? We had a thousand questions for each other, but I was most worried about their safety. Quickly I drew them all behind the trees so the hunters wouldn't see us.

Are you hurt? I asked.

Only Hasho, replied Kiki for the cranes. She darted to my youngest brother, who showed me the underside of his wing.

It was just a graze, but the sight still made me flinch. I

crouched to press snow to the wound, but Hasho shook me away, letting it shudder off his feathers. He was squawking furiously, and I turned to Kiki.

He says no need to coddle him, translated the paper bird. *He's more concerned about you. . . . Your brothers heard that an assassin was caught in Castle Bushian.*

I'm all right. I didn't want to talk about Chiruan's arrest. *The net is finished. Tell them I'm ready to leave.*

While Kiki spoke, Benkai's round eyes observed me. He made a low murmur.

He says you don't look ready, responded Kiki for my second brother. *Seryu told them you were taken into Castle Bushian by none other than your betrothed.* The paper bird cocked her head. *He asks if this is true.*

It's true.

Benkai's beak parted, as if to say, *Ah, that explains much.*

I didn't know why my face burned. Or why I thought it necessary to say to Kiki, *I thought they wouldn't be here until tomorrow.*

They're early. They have news for you. An excited whoop trumpeted out of Andahai's beak, and Kiki flapped her wings for him to quiet down. *They've discovered Raikama's true name.*

I held my breath. *What is it?*

They were looking in all the wrong places, Kiki went on as Wandei, my quietest brother, puffed up a little with pride. *A'landi, Samaran. Then Wandei remembered that your father went to the Tambu Isles fifteen years ago. He'd asked him* to bring back some teakwood—it doesn't rot like birch and willow do, and it's strongest for building—

Reiji cut in with an impatient cry, and Kiki shot up. *I'm just doing my job! I can't help it if he's digressing.*

Sending my brothers a glare, Kiki sat on Yotan's shoulder and relayed the rest of the story: *Emperor Hanriyu had been invited to go to Tambu, along with all the kings and emperors and princes of Lor'yan. Your brothers found records in a monastery in the South. They broke in so many times that the monks were readying a pot for bird stew.*

Kiki shuddered. *Bird stew? Now I'm extra glad to be made of paper.* She wrinkled her beak before continuing: *There was a girl in Tambu, said to be the most beautiful in the world, and your father was to judge the contest for her hand. In the end, she chose none of the suitors and instead came with your father to Kiata. Her name was Vanna.*

Vanna. I turned it over in my mind.

In Tambun, it means "golden." Kiki sniffed. *A bit on the nose, isn't it? Why not call her Snake Eyes, if they were going to be so obvious?*

Hush, Kiki. The tale fit. The name, too—though perhaps a bit too well, like Your Radiance.

It was the last piece of the puzzle. Once we confronted Raikama, we would be free. And yet my stomach twisted with dread. As if we were about to do something terribly, terribly wrong.

Hasho nipped at my skirts, his crane eyes remarkably clear.

He wants to know what's wrong, said Kiki.

I didn't respond.

They thought the news would make you happy. They know you're afraid of what's to come, but breaking the curse is the only way we can help your father regain control of Kiata. Even if it means one of them dying, it is a price they have all promised to pay.

It isn't only that, I confessed slowly. *I'm . . . I'm beginning to have doubts about Raikama. Why did she go through all this trouble to curse us if she wanted us dead? With her power, she could have easily killed us.*

Andahai huffed at me. *Now is not the time for philosophizing,* his look read. *We have her name; we have the net. Soon we'll be free of her, and Father will know her for the monster she really is.*

That was what we'd all wanted from the start, so why was I uncertain?

Do you remember when she first came? I asked. *She loved us like her own. Remember how she convinced Father to get you that horse you wanted, Andahai? And, Wandei, how she helped us build our best kite? We loved her.*

My brothers shifted uneasily, but Reiji kicked at the snow. His beak was the sharpest of all the cranes', and it twitched now with anger. I hardly needed Kiki's help to grasp what he was saying:

Of course we loved her—she put a spell on us. After all this time, you want to start believing that our stepmother is good? Kiata is falling apart, and I would bet my wings that Raikama has something to do with it.

To that, my brothers flapped their wings, making sounds of agreement.

Even so . . . My hands fell to my lap in defeat. Nothing I said would sway them. *Think about it. Please.*

Snow seeped through my robes, the cold burning my knees. As I started to get up, a heavy cloak wrapped over my shoulders.

"You're fast, Lina," said Takkan.

Admiral whinnied from behind me, tied to a tree. Takkan gestured at the cranes, bowing his head in apology. He approached them carefully, and I gave a nod to my brothers that he could be trusted. Still, Reiji snapped his beak at him— until Andahai pulled him back by the wing.

"It's only me," Takkan said quietly. "I sent the others home. The hunt is over."

He knelt to wrap Hasho's wing with the cloth of his family's banner. "We've never seen cranes at this time of year, or else we would not have . . ."

I placed a hand on his arm.

Benkai studied Takkan and me, his eyes discerning. I could read exactly what he was thinking: *Could this be—*

Takkan, your betrothed? Kiki cut in for my brother from inside my sleeve.

Ever in good spirits, Yotan tossed snow at me humorously. *Dare I guess, you actually like him?*

My paper bird was taking far too much pleasure in this. She relayed Hasho's teasing: *I seem to remember you telling Father only monsters lived up north.*

353

My hand was still on Takkan's arm, and I lifted it quickly, as if I had touched fire. My brothers laughed, squawking, and I wanted to pluck their feathers.

He's just a friend, I told them all with a flick of my wrist.

He'd have to be a good friend to ride off after a girl with a bowl on her head, says your brother Reiji.

Kiki snickered from within my sleeve, and I glared. *Yes, he's a good friend.*

Andahai stepped forward, the least amused of them all. I didn't need Kiki's help to understand what he was saying: *Quick then, tell him goodbye. Since you're here and you have the net, you might as well come back with us.*

A smile tilted Takkan's lips. "Six cranes," he observed. "Like the ones you folded." He took in how protectively my brothers surrounded me. "They know you."

I was glad I couldn't say anything in response. I swallowed hard, not ready to begin my farewell.

"What is it, Lina? You look sad."

I *was* sad. Sadder than I ever expected to be at the prospect of leaving this place. Leaving Takkan.

His cloak weighed heavily upon my shoulders, and I was starting to take it off when Takkan drew close. "Did my mother already tell you the news?"

I shook my head. I wasn't sure I could handle more news. *What has happened?*

His gaze focused intently on me. "Lord Yuji has murdered A'landi's khagan and stolen his enchanter. The Wolf is now his to command, and he's amassing an army to seize Gindara."

Shock made my chest go tight, and for a moment, I couldn't breathe. My brothers began squawking, their noises incomprehensible as they circled me, shouting over one another.

Takkan watched us curiously, his brow creasing. But he gave no indication of his thoughts.

"I must leave Castle Bushian tonight," he said.

My lips pursed tight. *Tonight?*

"Yes, during the festival. I'll draw less attention then. You look panicked, Lina. Don't worry, this isn't farewell."

It was for me. I was leaving now—with my brothers.

I stepped back, my heels sinking into the snow. I didn't know how to say goodbye. *I . . . I have to—*

Andahai let out a squawk and pushed me toward Takkan. *Go to the festival,* he was motioning. *Go, go.*

I looked at him in surprise. Of all my brothers, he was the one I least expected to sympathize.

They say Hasho needs time to rest, conveyed Kiki as Benkai gave me his blessing with a lifted wing. *And that it wouldn't hurt to stay in the fortress a few more hours. Besides, if Takkan's news about Lord Yuji is true, they need to strategize their return more carefully.*

Andahai stepped forward, and from inside my sleeve, Kiki communicated his instructions: *Meet us here again tonight after Bushi'an Takkan leaves.*

I promised. With a trembling heart, I hugged my brothers and turned to Takkan. He was watching, his head tilted at an inquisitive angle. But he said nothing, honorably keeping his promise not to ask about my past.

They're special to me, I explained with a wave to the cranes. I placed my hands over my chest as they flew away. *They're my brothers.*

As I rode back with Takkan to the castle, I wondered just how much he understood.

CHAPTER THIRTY-THREE

I donned my best robe, a scarlet one patterned with peonies and kingfishers, and put on my warmest gloves. Except for the bowl on my head, I almost looked like my old self.

I slung my satchel over my shoulder, further compromising the effect. Scratched and water-stained, it ruined any semblance of elegance I might have had. Something Zairena pointed out as soon as she encountered me on the castle stairs.

She wrinkled her nose. "Must you carry that bag at your hip everywhere you go?"

Normally I would have left it in my room to avoid interactions like this, but I was leaving after the festival. I wouldn't have time to return to the castle.

I shrugged, slipping my scarf inside as if that would explain away her questions.

Zairena clicked her tongue. Instead of her mourning robes, she wore a pale indigo gown, with pink inner robes elegantly matching her sash and cuffs. Fox furs wrapped her shoulders, and her ivory gloves peeked out of bell sleeves as she raised her lantern, tilting its flame close to my satchel.

"Here, carry this instead." Zairena offered me her silk purse. It was the same red as my robe, with swirls of gold embroidery woven into its lustrous fabric.

"Don't be such a mouse, Lina. At least try it."

Before I could stop her, she exchanged my satchel for her purse. "See what a difference such a little thing makes? You look almost pretty, even with that bowl on your head."

It was true. The silk purse shimmered against my sash, as if it belonged there.

Zairena leaned close to my ear. "I wouldn't be surprised if Takkan notices."

I whirled to face her.

"What?" She smirked. "I don't care that he's taken up with you. Perhaps that was our misunderstanding from the start. Now don't get my purse dirty; I want it back after the festival." She flashed her teeth, a smile that was not quite kind, but probably the best she could do.

The purse *was* beautiful, it just wasn't for me. I didn't need or want Zairena's help to feel pretty, and certainly not to catch Takkan's attention. I handed it back to her, shaking my head.

"Suit yourself," said Zairena, returning my satchel to my shoulder.

When she left, I glanced at Kiki on the rafters above. These days, she enjoyed fluttering from beam to beam rather than suffocating in my sleeves. *Aren't you coming?* I asked her.

To watch you moon over the lordling's singing?

I crossed my arms. *I thought you were looking forward to it.*

Music makes me sleepy, Kiki said, feigning a yawn. *I'd rather wait here than have to hide in your sleeve anyway. Just don't linger too long. Your brothers are waiting, don't forget.*

I blew Kiki a kiss, then hurried out, hopping into one of the wagons bound for Iro. As its wheels trundled down the hill, I watched the sky. Reds and pinks brushed the clouds—violet, too—like dawn and dusk blended together.

There would be no moon once the sun fell. Tonight Imurinya returned to heaven and became a specter of her past: the goddess of fate. I only prayed that she would look kindly on mine.

The festival performances had begun earlier in the day, and the seats in the front of the theater were all taken, so I sat among strangers on a wooden bench in the back. Snow flying in from the windows tickled my face. Chimes tinkled in the background, and drums from the festivities outside pounded.

It seemed that the entire town was here. There had to be a thousand people in the theater, all carrying unlit round lanterns that bobbed against their knees. Children bounced on their feet, eager for the next performance to begin.

The sun had mostly sunk, but one last glare from the west swept over the stage as Lady Bushian stood and welcomed the people of Iro to the festival.

"Tonight we celebrate the end of a long winter, and the light that comes after darkness. As a tribute from Castle Bushian, my children will perform Iro's most beloved tale to honor and thank all of you for a year of hard work, loyalty, and harmony."

She bowed, then welcomed Megari and Takkan to the stage.

Megari sat primly on the stool set out for her, and adjusted her lush blue skirts before picking up her moon lute. Her shoulders lifted, and with a downward sweep of her hand, she strummed an opening chord.

As Megari's eyes lit, absorbed by the music, Takkan stepped forward. "When Emuri'en fell from the heavens to earth," he began, "her thousand cranes prayed for her to be reborn. And so she was—as a human child named Imurinya."

Smiles spread across the theater as children and adults alike recognized the tale Takkan and Megari had chosen.

Takkan sang:

Imurinya was not like other children.
Her skin shone silver as the moon, and
her hair gleamed with starlight,
so bright none could see her sorrow.

She soon bloomed into a lady,
melancholy and alone
but for the rabbits on the mountain,
who did not fear her radiance.

Then kings and princes arrived,
begging for her hand.
Of each, she asked a simple gift:
a gift that would make her happy.

They brought rings of jade and crowns of pearl,
sumptuous silks and chests of gold.
What use have I for such riches? *thought Imurinya.*
I am but a maid from the mountain.

Her hope began to fade, until
the last suitor gathered his courage,
a humble hunter with a humble gift:
a wooden comb carved with a plum blossom.

All ridiculed him for daring such a simple piece.
But Imurinya silenced them with a gentle hand
and asked: "Why should a comb make me happy?"

The hunter replied, "The rabbits have told me
that past the light you shine,
your eyes are dark with sorrow.
I have no gold, and I have no kingdom,
but I would give this comb to hold up your hair
so that I may see your eyes and light them with joy."

And so Imurinya loved and wedded him.
But shortly after, tales of her light reached the heavens,
and the great gods recognized their sister Emuri'en
    reborn.

They sent cranes to fetch her
with a peach of immortality to restore her
    goddess-hood,

but Imurinya would not return without her mortal
    husband,
and he was not welcome among the gods.

Clever as she was, she split the fruit,
serving half in the hunter's soup and half in her own.
Together they flew midway to heaven,
claiming the moon as theirs.

Now once a year, on this winter night,
her thousand cranes return her to heaven
and she becomes Emuri'en once more,
goddess of fate and love.

Takkan's voice grew quiet, and the last strains of his song
were so soft that no one dared breathe. He lifted his lantern,
its rich blue paper painted with rabbits and cranes and a silver moon. His eyes searched the crowd until they caught my
gaze. He smiled, and inhaled a deep breath:

To honor her darkest moon,
we light our lanterns
so some of our light will touch the sky,
just as hers touches our earth.

At last Megari strummed a final chord.
As the silence lingered, I inhaled, feeling a gentle ache in
my chest. Imurinya's was a story of love and loss, so different

362

from my own, and yet I couldn't help but empathize. In her own way, she too was cursed, unable to go home.

She's more like Raikama than me, I thought. The contest for Imurinya's hand reminded me of my brother's tale of Vanna and her suitors. Raikama never liked hearing about the lady of the moon. I felt a twinge of sympathy for her. Could it be because Imurinya reminded her of herself?

I pushed aside the thought. Tonight was for celebrating new beginnings, not dwelling on the past.

Led by Takkan, everyone in the chamber raised their lanterns and lit them, until the light of Imurinya herself seemed to smile upon the theater. The attendants opened the doors so we could see that the lantern lighting had begun outside, too, casting a golden glow upon the river and on the slope of Rabbit Mountain.

And with the gentle snow gusting through the open doors, fresh and white against the theater's vermilion poles, I realized Takkan had been right all along.

Iro was the most beautiful place in the world.

When I found Takkan, he was putting on his armor while his sister stashed festival food in Admiral's saddlebags. Megari tugged at his sleeve when she saw me.

"There she is," she cried, nudging Takkan with a wide grin. "Now aren't you glad you stayed here instead of going off to search for her?"

For some reason, the look of chagrin Takkan shot his sister made my stomach flutter.

"Takkan was so thrilled you came," Megari pressed on, oblivious to her brother's growing mortification. "He wrote the song, did you know? Well, only the words. I wrote the music."

I touched my heart. *I loved it. So did everyone else.*

"I thought you'd like it." Megari smiled slyly. "The lantern walk has just begun—you two should go and see it. Don't wait for me—performing always leaves me famished."

She ran off before either of us could stop her.

"Now I suppose I know how my mother feels when I run off to battle," Takkan joked.

You're leaving already? I gestured toward Admiral.

"Soon," he replied, regret thickening his voice. He cleared his throat, lowering his lantern so it was level with mine. "I wasn't going to without saying goodbye."

That made me happier than I wished to admit.

We walked together, the laughter and drumming from the festival buzzing in my head as our steps synchronized. We passed a row of ice sculptures. They were as magnificent as Megari had said: tigers and butterflies, dragon boats and empresses wearing phoenix crowns, even a replica of the imperial palace. I couldn't choose a favorite.

For once the food didn't entice me. I was floating, just like the lanterns on the river. They all looked like little moons, round and full. Each had a red string tied to the top, something I had never noticed in all my years of celebrating midwinter in Gindara. I stopped and pointed.

"It's a local tradition," said Takkan helpfully. "If you tie a red string to your lantern and place it on the river, the sacred cranes will carry your strand of fate to the person you're meant to love."

A beautiful story, but quite implausible. If that were so, everyone in the kingdom would journey to Iro and set their lanterns on the Baiyun River.

Perhaps the point of such legends was simply to bring hope.

"The Winter Festival is Emuri'en's celebration," Takkan went on. "Not just to revere the moon; it used to be an evening for people to meet, and perhaps to fall in love."

I kept my eyes on the water, watching the icy surface glitter under the lantern light. Ignoring the slight quickening of my pulse.

"Did you ever get to see the full moon over Rabbit Mountain? We say that's when—"

Imurinya's watching, I mouthed. My shoulders sagged with regret. No, I had never seen it.

"She might not be watching tonight," Takkan said, lifting his lantern toward the mountain, "but I still say that's quite a sight."

I looked where he was pointing, and my breath caught. There was no moon, but the light traveling from the shimmering Baiyun River illuminated its two peaks, and the wind had carried off a few of the lanterns so they floated in the sky, like tiny suns against the mountain.

He knelt beside the river, and I did the same. "I must be

drunk on moonlight to tell you this . . . but after I left you at Sparrow Inn, I . . . I couldn't stop thinking about you. I didn't know anything about you, and yet I had never met anyone so determined—or brazen. Not even Megari." He laughed, then his expression turned serious once more. "Somehow, I knew I would see you again. It was as if I could feel our strands crossing. Yet when you came to Iro, you seemed different. Sadder, more withdrawn. I'd look for you in the kitchen as Pao and I walked around the castle. I wanted to make you smile."

I remembered. Every time I caught him walking the grounds, I'd slow down my work, heartened to see him getting stronger with each passing day.

"I quickly learned I couldn't compete with food."

My shoulders shook with laughter. *Few people can.*

"But you liked my stories. That, I learned." He touched his lantern to mine, so tenderly my stomach swooped. "Perhaps they served as my wooden comb. I would tell you stories from dawn to dusk if it meant filling your eyes with happiness."

I reached out, hooking my arm under his—I didn't know what possessed me to do it. Maybe it was the story, the beauty of the lanterns surrounding us, or even the cold numbing my senses, but mortification flooded in a moment too late. I tried to pull back, but Takkan didn't let go. He drew me closer, and my shoulder melted against his.

I thought he would kiss me. Great gods, I *wanted* him to kiss me.

But then the fireworks started, shooting up into the sky and shimmering among the stars. Against the dusk and the snow, we lowered our lanterns into the river, watching them glide down with a hundred others, a few carried off by the wind up to touch the lake of clouds. It was all so beautiful I dared not blink. I wanted to etch this moment in my memory.

"Will you be here when I return, Lina?"

Takkan's voice was so soft I almost didn't hear it.

A lump formed in my throat, warm and raw. I turned away from him, pretending to stare at our lanterns drifting along the water.

What makes you think I'm leaving?

He'd gotten good at reading my lips. "When I first offered to bring you here, you refused. I know that Iro was little more than a place to pass the winter for you, yet I can't help but hope you'll stay."

I stared down.

My silence was telling, and Takkan bent until our heads were level. His voice trembled when he spoke: "I would not have you be alone, Lina, not in your joys or your sorrows. I would wish your strand knotted to mine, always."

Now I looked up at him, glad he couldn't see the bewilderment in my eyes.

Had I unwittingly used my magic to spellbind him into such a declaration? He didn't even know who I was. Who I *really* was.

Instead of answering, I rested my head on his chest,

tucking my crown, bowl and all, under his chin. I could feel his breath catch, yet he didn't say anything. He wrapped one arm around my waist and held me.

Reason demanded that I leave right then, before the mountain air got to my head—before I cared too much for Takkan. But it was too late for that.

All I wanted was for this night to last forever. To find that our strands had been crossed and knotted all along. Ironic, wasn't it, that I—a girl who always wanted to make her own choices—now wished for nothing more than to surrender to fate? I chuckled quietly at myself.

By all accounts, I never would have chosen someone like Takkan. He was far too earnest, too good. Someone who always followed the rules, while I took pleasure in breaking them. Someone who preferred to stay at home, while I yearned to sail as far away as I could.

I would have mercilessly played pranks on him, I thought, smiling as I imagined the two of us as children.

None of my brothers would have given their protection to a thief who'd tried to rob them. None would have found the beauty in a simple mountain, and none would have been content to live their entire lives in the North, far from court and battle.

I turned to face him, brushing my fingers against his cheek. When I'd first met him, I'd thought his an ordinary face. Straight nose, brown eyes, a pointed peak in his hairline. Handsome enough. Yet every time I saw him, he grew on me a little more.

Now I saw in his eyes the richness of summer soil. His

nose looked endearingly ruddy from being in the cold, and his voice was like a favorite song I never tired of hearing. Funny how he'd stolen his way into my heart, when *I'd* been the thief the day we met.

I tried to warm his nose with my hand, but Takkan caught my fingers, bringing the tips of my gloves to his lips. He tilted my chin, his breath tickling my nose.

He was going to kiss me.

Finally.

I half closed my eyes in anticipation, my toes curling inside my boots. After months of telling myself Takkan meant nothing, I wanted to stay in his arms until the sun rose. I wanted to hear him say my name, my real name, and tell me again that he wanted me to stay in Iro.

Demons take me, I *wanted* to stay.

But I couldn't. Megari always said I was like a girl in one of his stories. With the bowl on my head, she probably thought me shrouded in mystery and enchantment. She wasn't wrong, but my magic had only brought misfortune and sorrow to the ones I loved. If I were a character in a tale, I would be no hero. I was the firebrand who had shaken everything from its place. One by one, I needed to fix my mistakes.

I still had many choices left to make. Staying here—no matter how much I wanted to—was the wrong one.

His lips were almost on mine, the tips of our noses touching, when, without warning, I twisted myself out of his embrace. If I stayed any longer, my heart might burst, and all the walls I'd built around it would crumble.

"Lina!"

I hurried away, not looking back.

Emuri'en, be kind, I prayed, with a glance at the moonless sky. *Let us survive the trials that await us. Don't knot our threads together, only to sever them.*

As I slipped out of the festival, the last thing I saw was our lanterns disappearing along the bend of the river.

I was searching for a horse to take me into the forest when Kiki slammed into my chest.

Shiori! she shrieked, flapping her wings violently in my face. *Look. Look!*

Not now. I batted her away, still distressed about how I had left Takkan.

My paper bird was wild, her wings flapping in my hair and in my ears. She bit my hair, dragging me toward the closest lantern. *Look!*

A trace of black ink glittered off the bottom of Kiki's wing as she danced about the flame.

What of it? I asked tiredly. *I'll help you wash it off tomorrow.*

Black, Shiori. It was gold earlier, from the dye on Zairena's thread. You washed it off with snow days ago, don't you remember?

Now Kiki had my attention. I examined her in the lantern light. Sure enough, her wing was black as ink.

Four Breaths.

I sat on the threads, Kiki said quickly. *The threads on her spinning wheel. And—*

She didn't need to say any more. Understanding dawned, and I reeled back the way I'd come.

Zairena. It was Zairena all along.

CHAPTER THIRTY-FOUR

I circled back to the festival, my head thundering as I wove through the crowd.

All this time, Zairena had been the assassin. I needed to find Takkan before he left. Every moment she was here, he was in danger.

There he is! cried Kiki, pointing a wing at a man walking up the narrow road back to the castle. In the dim lantern light, the figure looked like Takkan from behind. Same height, same stride, same armor. But as I got closer, I saw that his shoulders were squarer, and his movements heavier.

Hasege! I ran after him. The sentinels needed to know, too.

Zairena's the assassin, I tried to mouth, my hands whirling.

He didn't understand. His face was redder than usual. He looked drunk, his cinder-black eyes hollow.

I gave up trying to explain. *Where is Takkan?*

"Takkan?" he said with a grunt. He edged toward one of the horses. "He was just looking for you. Get on, I'll take you to the castle."

His willingness to help surprised me. I hung back, not trusting him. *He's in the castle?*

"What?" Hasege clicked his tongue. "You don't believe me, Lina? Look there: my aunt is heading back to bid Takkan farewell right now." He cocked his head at the wagon carrying Lady Bushian up the hill.

Shiori . . . Kiki wavered. *I don't trust him.*

I didn't either, but I needed to speak to someone—if not Takkan, then Lady Bushian—and it would take too long on foot. I jumped onto Hasege's horse.

The fortress lights burned like fiery brushstrokes against the night sky. As Hasege's horse galloped up the hill, apprehension thickened in my gut.

My window was lit. But I had left no candles burning.

The horse came to an abrupt halt against a tree. As snow tumbled from its branches over my cloak, I jumped off, more shaken by the light in my room than the shock of cold.

"Go on," said Hasege, dusting snow off himself. "He's waiting for you upstairs."

Shadows loomed across the castle halls, the corridors seeming to stretch longer than I ever remembered. I didn't believe Hasege about Takkan, not for an instant, but something *was* off. My footsteps thumped against the stairs as I climbed two, three at a time. I raced to my room.

My door was ajar.

With a hand on my dagger, I barreled inside, not knowing what I was expecting to find. My room was empty. Untouched but for the candles lit on my table.

I clutched my satchel, thanking the gods I'd brought it with me.

But as I started to leave, its straw exterior began to glimmer, as if I were blinking too fast. It had to be a trick of the light. The straw was slick with melted snow, and I wiped it with my hands, sure that was the end of it.

Then the satchel in my hands vanished completely. In its place, I held a silk bag.

Zairena's purse.

Demons of Tambu, Kiki swore.

It had been an illusion, washed away by the melted snow. Which meant that my actual satchel . . . the starstroke net . . .

I was already searching, overturning my bed and throwing my blankets on the floor. In my anguish, I didn't hear the voices echoing down the corridor outside my chamber—not until it was too late.

"Can't this wait until Takkan returns?" said Lady Bushian, her voice loud. "I don't understand what could possibly be so important that you drag me away from the festival during the lantern lighting."

"I've been trying to warn you, Aunt." Hasege's silhouette was stark against the paper walls, the dark shells of his armor pronounced in the candlelight. "But only Zairena would listen."

Zairena entered my chambers, standing primly by the doorframe as Hasege and Lady Bushian followed.

"Are you looking for this, Lina?" she asked, holding up my satchel.

Without thinking, I lunged for my bag. A stupid move. Hasege grabbed me, shackling my wrists with his iron grip.

Zairena smiled. My desperation only emphasized her point. "Stand back," she said, ushering Lady Bushian away from me. She raised the satchel. "This bag contains dangerous magic."

She loosened the buckles and opened the flap. I held my breath, certain that no one would see the starstroke net glittering inside. What I didn't expect was for the shadow of a wolf to spring out of the bag.

It loped across the walls and bared its fangs at Lady Bushian, who went so pale I thought she would faint. Hasege let go of me and brandished his sword, swinging at the wolf as it prowled toward my window. There, the creature writhed and twisted, until at last Zairena closed the satchel.

With a hiss, the wolf vanished.

My ears thundered. How . . . how had Zairena done that? She couldn't possibly have—

"Magic," Hasege seethed. "Now do you believe me, Aunt?"

Lady Bushian clutched her heart, gasping. "What . . . what in the great gods? How—"

"How?" Zairena folded her arms dramatically. "Lina is a priestess of demons, planted in Castle Bushian by Lord Yuji himself to do his bidding."

She's lying, I tried to communicate, desperately shaking my head.

But I could tell from Lady Bushian's eyes that Zairena had won. No matter what I said, her trick with the wolf shadow had convinced them of my guilt.

"Do not fear," said Zairena, comforting Takkan's mother with a touch on the sleeve. "Hasege and I always sensed there was an evil force within Lina. I've been preparing for this very moment."

Too late, I dove for the open door, but Hasege blocked me easily. He hooked his arm around my waist and restrained my arms, so roughly I cringed.

Kiki, I thought, thrusting my elbow out at Hasege and giving my bird the chance she needed to crawl out of my sleeve. *Find my brothers. Find Takkan.*

Then I leapt, smacking my bowl on Hasege's nose. It was just enough for Kiki to shoot away, unnoticed.

Hasege let out a cry. "Why, you—"

"Hold her still," Zairena interrupted, speaking over whatever foul name Hasege was about to call me. She reached into her hair for a gilded pin, its tip alarmingly curved, like a scythe. Her eyes gleamed.

"This was given to me by the priestesses of Nawaiyi, an ancient needle once used to exorcise demons. Our Lina pretends to be mute, but I wonder if it's only so she can hide her true self. Let's have a test, shall we?"

Without warning, Zairena stabbed the needle into my ankle. All at once, my senses shattered. Pain rankled deep into my bone.

I clamped down and bit hard on my lip. This was nothing, I reminded myself. After months of working with starstroke, this was nothing.

But Zairena was relentless. She struck again and again. Sometimes she waited cruelly between stabs, as if to give me a chance to breathe. But then the next would be even deeper, the rise of her arm barely enough time for me to gather my wits and hold in my scream.

My vision swam in and out of focus, and I dug my nails into Hasege's armor, about to faint.

"Enough, Zairena!" shouted Lady Bushian. "That's enough."

Tears streamed down my cheeks. I couldn't stand. I could barely feel my legs.

"There is no hope for her," declared Zairena with a shake of her head. "The demon will not leave."

"What does that mean?" Lady Bushian breathed.

Hasege's black eyes glittered. "It means she must die. She must be burned."

"Burned?" Lady Bushian repeated with horror.

"Yes," said Hasege. "We must do it as soon as the festival is over, or we risk bringing danger to Castle Bushian."

"It is the only way, Lady Bushian," Zairena agreed solemnly.

Lady Bushian regarded me. *It isn't me,* I mouthed desperately. *It's Zairena.*

But Zairena's trick with the wolf had poisoned Lady Bushian against me. For a long moment, she said nothing. And then: "What about Takkan? Perhaps we should wait for him—"

"There is no time. Lord Yuji's army approaches Gindara. He will soon call upon the demon within Lina to aid him in his treachery."

Lady Bushian's shoulders heaved. She wouldn't look at me as she nodded her assent.

"Don't tell Megari," she said as Hasege took me away. "It would break her heart to know how Lina betrayed us all."

Snow drifted through the window of my prison cell, melting into small puddles on the pebbled ground. It was the least of my troubles, but great gods! If this was really to be my last night on earth, I wished to spend it warm and dry.

For the thousandth time, I tried to kick down the door. But curse Zairena, the needle was no special relic meant to exorcise demons. It had been poisoned, and the numbness in my legs persisted long after her attack. I couldn't run away, even if I wanted to.

The minutes bled into hours. I grew tired of punching at the walls, and nursed my bleeding knuckles against my cheeks.

It had to be past midnight when I heard the footsteps. They were light and quick, a child's.

Megari. She'd brought a small basket filled with paper— the sort used at the temple for making wishes. No ink.

"The guards took the ink stick and brush," she said, fidgeting with the charm she had tied over the basket. It was one for strength and protection. "Paper isn't much of a consolation. But I thought . . . I thought you might want to fold your birds. I'll fold some too, and maybe together we'll have enough to ask the gods to set you free."

I wanted to hug her, and I clasped her hands. Her eyes were red and raw; she'd been crying for me.

"I've tried to talk some sense into Mama, but she won't listen. She says that you're a sorceress." Her voice trembled. "But once Takkan gets back from Gindara, I know she'll listen to him."

I bit my lip. Megari didn't know how little time I had. I was going to be burned at the stake tomorrow.

Zairena is not who she says she is, I tried to tell her. *She's the assassin. Not me, not Chiruan. She's the real priestess of the Holy Mountains.*

"Slow down, Lina. I can't understand you."

I reached for the paper, but the door to my cell clanged open, and Zairena entered, serenely balancing a tray with four covered bowls.

"You'd better leave, Megari," she said. "Lina needs to sleep before her ordeal tomorrow."

Megari whirled to face her. "What ordeal?"

"No more questions. Go, or I'll tell Hasege that Pao let you inside."

Zairena knelt before the bars of my cell. "What an irksome child," she said once the girl was out of earshot. "I thought she would be my greatest hindrance, but imagine my surprise that it was you, *Shiori.*"

At my name, the hairs on the back of my neck bristled. She knew.

Her eyes glinted wickedly, and she busied herself with the tray she had brought, arranging the four bowls.

"Yes, I know. We priestesses of the Holy Mountains are taught to sense magic, though you . . . you were astonishingly untalented. I thought of you merely as a pebble in my shoe, an oddity with that bowl on your head carrying about that dirty satchel. Hardly worthy of my attention." She paused deliberately. "Until you worked starstroke on my spinning wheel."

She lifted the lid on the first bowl, revealing a glimmering strand of starstroke.

"Brazen of you, spinning an entire mountain's worth on my wheel. Here I thought you were sneaking into my room to steal my thread." She laughed at herself. "I was going to kill you for that, the same way I killed nosy old Oriyu. But then I found this little sliver of magic in your room while you were taking care of dear Megari. Useful against dragons, I hear."

I reeled for my satchel, but Zairena swiftly evaded me. "You needn't worry, Shiori'anma. I'm not going to give the net to Lord Yuji, that dithering fool. Or to the Wolf." She patted the satchel. "Once he finds out I've engineered your death, we won't be allies any longer."

I clenched the iron bars, trying to rise to my feet, but my legs wouldn't cooperate.

"Are you wondering how I knew the princess would be weaving starstroke?" Zairena asked.

No, I wasn't. But Zairena was in a smug mood, and I had no choice but to listen.

"The Wolf told me he encountered your brothers in A'landi. They met him in the guise of his former master, a famous seer."

Something inside me shattered, and I felt suddenly ill. Great gods! It was the Wolf who had told my brothers to make the starstroke net. He'd given us the satchel so I would bring him the starstroke from Mount Rayuna. So I would weave a net . . . to steal a treasure far greater . . .

Raikama's pearl.

I went cold.

"I know," Zairena pretended to sympathize. "Enchanters are a greedy lot, aren't they? I *told* him to forget the Nameless Queen's pearl and just focus on your blood, but he wanted both."

My blood?

"You didn't know you were Kiata's bloodsake, did you? No one can blame you. I'd guess even the gods and dragons have forgotten what it is by now—and among us mortals it's belittled as legend. But your stepmother is clever, and that pearl of hers must have given her the power to see you for what you are. Wise of her to hide her talents from you. She must have thought you'd be safer not knowing. She was almost right. *Almost.*"

My thoughts were spinning; I struggled to understand.

Zairena smiled. "You see, the magic in your blood is native to Kiata. A rarity these days, and it is the only magic capable of freeing the demons held within the Holy Mountains. The Wolf has sought you out for this very reason, and I played along so he would share with me what he knew. You look confused. Rightly so; all you fools have twisted our stories and forgotten what we truly stand for."

Her voice grew thick with pride. "We priestesses are not allied with demonkind. We belong to the Holy Mountains.

Our task is to keep their evil trapped within the mountains. And so we have been waiting for you, Shiori'anma. You are the bloodsake, and therefore we cannot allow you to live."

The words thundered in my ears. I scrabbled back, as far away from the bars as I could, reaching behind me for a loose stone or brick—but there was nothing except Megari's paper and puddles of melted snow.

"Now, if you had told me you were the princess sooner," Zairena went on, "I would have given you an honorable death. Less humiliating than what Hasege has planned. But I couldn't use Four Breaths on you, not when Chiruan had already been caught. . . ." She paused. "Still, I have to say it's quite beautiful how it all worked out. The plan always was to collect your ashes."

I flinched, despising myself for it. My fingers dug into the moist dirt, and I flung a pitiful handful at Zairena. My attack barely touched her, and the dirt landed instead on her tray.

Hiding a smile, the priestess knelt again, wiping the tray clean with a towel, then lifting the lid on the second bowl. A dried persimmon.

"You may have guessed I have some talent for poisons. Take Megari's favorite food, for example. Don't look at me like that, Lina—it was just a bit of gloom water, nothing as grievous as Four Breaths. Besides, she was asking *so* many questions—I had no choice. I always gave her the antidote in time. It earned me Lady Bushian's trust. Yours, too."

Anger dazzled me, hot and white and blinding. If not for the iron bars separating us, I might have strangled Zairena right there and then.

"Oh, you'll really wish you could kill me by the time I'm finished." Zairena chuckled as she nibbled on the persimmon. "Poisoned persimmons, I'll have to keep that in my book. If only it had worked with Four Breaths." A sigh. "That *is* the tiresome thing about Four Breaths, the smell. Even Oriyu noticed the incense when he came into my room. I seem to have had the best luck hiding the odor in dyes. After all, one rarely sniffs a sash before wearing it, now does one, Princess?"

She opened the third bowl. A gold cord, like one used for tying a sash.

I shook my head. I didn't understand.

"This was on the sash you wore when you fell into that lake at Gindara," Zairena explained. "Lucky for you—it had enough Four Breaths to put you in a slumber for days. But none of us foresaw that the Nameless Queen would recognize it in time. She nearly killed me."

The world tilted, and I could hardly hear what Zairena was saying.

All this time, Raikama had been trying to protect me! My head was swimming, and yet I'd never seen so clearly before. The answer had always been there.

Raikama had blocked my magic to try and protect me, to hide me from everyone I knew, so the Wolf couldn't find me!

"After you disappeared," Zairena prattled on, "the Wolf sent me to Iro as punishment, to wait idly in case Takkan found you. Who would have guessed that he would? Clever, wearing that bowl on your head and pretending you could not speak. All this time, you were right under my nose."

I was hardly listening to her anymore. My hatred had reached a boiling point, and I threw myself at her.

It was a pitiful move. I couldn't get far with my muscles numbed, and I fell against the bars. Clinging to them, I swung at her, and water from my sleeves, soaked from the puddles in my cell, splashed into her face.

Zairena recoiled. Water dripped from her forehead, causing the powder to run down in white streams that clumped around her chin. Golden specks glittered on her skin—traces of Four Breaths.

As she wiped it with her sleeve, Zairena's face began to glimmer—the same way my satchel had.

First her mole disappeared. Then the rest of her features began to change. Her mouth stretched wider, her eyelids grew deep and hooded, and her face aged decades.

I let out a silent gasp, recognizing my maid from the palace. Guiya.

"Remember me, Your Highness?" she said, hunching her shoulders and pretending to tremble. She laughed. "The real Tesuwa Zairena perished with her parents. Am I a sorceress, you're wondering? No, no. My magic is insignificant, compared to the power you and your stepmother wield."

Water, I realized. It was why she always carried an umbrella, always shielded herself from the rain and snow. It washed away the illusion, revealing who she truly was!

With heightened drama, Guiya opened the last bowl on the tray. Inside were ashes.

I didn't understand.

"The remains of the bloodsake before you," she announced. "His ashes were consecrated on the Holy Mountains—the last of the dark magic left in Kiata. We priestesses hoarded them for decades—until we learned of you."

My stomach curdled as Guiya dusted ashes over her face, and her features shifted once more into Zairena's.

She covered the bowls and started to rise. "You really did have the luck of the dragons, Princess. But that luck has finally run its course. Tomorrow the Holy Mountains will be at peace once more, and we priestesses will sing for you. Tomorrow we will add your name to those who came before you. We will remember you for centuries to come, as we remember all those who have dishonored the gods.

"Tomorrow you will die."

CHAPTER THIRTY-FIVE

It was still night when they came for me. Stripes of dawn shone faintly through the iron bars, the moon a hopeless sliver.

Pao wouldn't meet my eyes as two other sentinels lifted me onto the wagon. I could tell Hasege's order to have me burned did not sit well with him. Maybe that was why he let me bring Megari's basket.

As the wagon lumbered down the hill past Iro, I tried to free my hands. The sentinels sitting beside me lurched, kept their daggers drawn threateningly until I gave up.

It was no use anyway. The ropes were bound tight.

I spent the rest of the ride trying, and mostly failing, to fold paper birds. My fingers were stiff from the cold, the ropes chafing my wrists. But it was better than sitting idle in the wagon. Better than thinking about the fate that awaited me.

Below, Hasege and his men were shoveling snow and gathering wood. All this time I'd been brave, but I faltered when I saw the stake. It lay on the cusp of the forest, enclosed by severed trees. I couldn't have imagined a more desolate place to die, atop a pile of straw and sticks in an unmarked field of snow.

"Lady Zairena suggested we perform the rite at least a mile from Iro," Pao said solemnly when he caught me looking off to the side. "So your spirit won't torment the city."

We were nearly there, and he reached into the pouch at his side, taking out a short string of paper birds. "From Megari," he said stiffly. "There were more, but Lady Bushian wouldn't allow it. . . ." He wavered. "Both bid you goodbye."

Sorrow welled in my throat as I nodded. Pao laid the string of birds across my lap, and I counted them as the wind nipped at their wings. Seven birds. A number for strength.

I searched the skies for signs of my brothers or Kiki. With every minute that she was gone, my heart sank. Fear was growing inside me, my entire body trembling no matter how I tried to steady it. This wouldn't be how my life ended— alone, surrounded by enemies.

My brothers would come for me. I knew they would.

The last of the paper Megari had given me was carried away by the wind, and I rested my tired hands over my lap, clutching my basket. Feeling was slowly returning to my legs, only to be numbed by cold. Maybe I would freeze before I was burned to death. There was some irony in that.

Guiya wore Zairena's face again, and she sat on a white mare by Hasege's side, her eyes dark and unreadable. My satchel's strap was deliberately crossed over her torso.

How I wished I could dunk her in the snow and expose her illusion. Anything to wipe the smirk off her face.

Hasege himself tied me to the stake. Ropes dug in at my waist and ankles, and as he pulled them so tight it hurt to breathe, I spat at him.

He glared. "What is this? More sorcery?" Before I could stop him, he flung Megari's string of birds into the snow. He tried to take my basket too, but I wouldn't let go. His eyes narrowed with cruelty. "Bring the torch."

As the sentinel carrying the torch approached, I shifted my balance, my feet tingling as they strained against the uneven wood. I tried to look unafraid, but it didn't work.

"Wait," cried Pao. All this time, his jaw had been clenched, words of protest clearly weighing on his mind. "My lord, I think you should reconsider."

"Again with the objections, Pao?" Hasege grunted. "If you haven't the stomach to slay a demon, then you can leave."

Hasege turned to the sentinels who had gathered for my sentencing. "This girl murdered Oriyu," he said. "Framed Chiruan for it. Even Lady Bushian has seen proof of her evil ways. If *she* is afraid of the girl, every one of us ought to fear her as well."

"We don't *know* that she killed Oriyu," argued Pao. "She could have been framed herself. We should wait until Lord Takkan returns."

"Wait?" Hasege growled. "Takkan is weak and too easily swayed by her dark magic. Waiting for him will bring ruin to Iro."

Hasege held a torch to my face. "Haven't you ever wondered why we cannot see her eyes? It's because she is a demon." He spun to face the men. "I know all of you are loyal to Takkan, but our duty as sentinels is to expel demons from Kiata. By shielding this monster, he betrays the gods themselves."

The men looked at each other. Their loyalty was to Takkan, but fealty to the gods mattered above all.

"She isn't a monster," argued Pao. "She's just a girl."

"She's a demon," Zairena shrilled. "This is hers, is it not?" She opened my satchel, and a swarm of shadowy beasts loped out. Foxes and wolves, bears and tigers—some so grotesquely shaped they resembled no creature that walked the earth.

The men gasped with horror.

"Now do you believe me?" Hasege boomed out as Zairena closed the satchel, shutting her false demons inside. "She must die."

As Hasege rallied the men, I stopped listening. The sun was rising, its light prickling my eyes, and I scanned the blank sky. Surely Kiki had found my brothers by now.

But every time I spied movement, it turned out to be a shifting cloud. Not a crane.

Not my brothers.

I swallowed my disappointment. So what if my brothers didn't come for me? Was I just going to stand here like meat on a skewer waiting to be burned, holding a basket of useless paper birds?

I dropped the basket and started working the ropes, wriggling and twisting. Hasege had bound me tight, and there was little give. I gnashed at my wrists, sawing the ropes with my teeth. The fibers were tough, and even if I had all day to work, I wouldn't be able to free my hands.

But better this than listen to Zairena pray aloud, murmuring pleas to the gods that my spirit find peace with Lord Sharima'en and not return to trouble Iro. I wished again I could throw a fistful of snow at her to wash away that wretched illusion. But the priestess was clever and kept a wary distance.

Shiori! Kiki called from far away. *Shiori!*

I looked up, my breath catching. Kiki was too far and too small for me to see, but six cranes pierced the clouds, their great wings bathed in crimson light as they glided through the dawn light toward me.

My brothers!

The branches under my feet crunched, and Zairena stopped midprayer to glance at me. Then she looked up at the sky, and a dark scowl came over her face.

"Shoot those birds," she commanded. "She is using her dark magic to make them help her. Shoot now!"

Kiki! I urged as the sentinels picked up their bows. *Tell them to get out of here!*

Reiji and Hasho ignored me. They dove, their wings knocking the torch out of Hasege's hands before they burst back into the sky. As the flame sizzled in the snow, Kiki bolted for one of my scattered papers to catch the embers.

What a mess you've gotten yourself into, Shiori, she said as she set the sparks to the ropes over my wrists.

The ropes burned slowly, loosening their hold on my wrists. I slid my hands free in amazement. *You're a genius, thank you!*

Wandei's idea. A bright one, that brother.

I was unknotting the ropes around my waist when a shadow swept over the pyre. Zairena.

Guiya's illusion was as perfect as it had been before: powdered face, youthful eyes—sharp and glittering—the mole on her right cheek. The priestess's fist was clenched, and she raised it high, throwing a handful of her cursed ashes upon the pyre below me.

Fire flared and surged from the ashes so powerfully I would have flown back were I not still tied to the stake. It was a sickeningly bright shade of red, but its heart was black like the smoke rolling into the sky. *Demonfire.*

It spread quickly—too quickly—twisting around the sticks under my feet, climbing up the mound of wood, and surrounding me with walls of flame. Panic rioted in my chest, and I undid the last knot at my waist and moved down to my ankles. The heat was growing in intensity, the smoke so thick my lungs hurt as they struggled for each new breath.

But the fire did not touch me. As I crouched to free my legs, the flames flickered away from my face, as if there were an imaginary shield protecting me.

A bead of light glimmered in my chest, faint but pulsing. I clutched at my heart. Could it be that Seryu's pearl was warding off the demonfire?

I tested it, leaning toward the flames. The demonfire jumped back, and the pearl glowed bright, brighter than it ever had before. But amid the chaos of my brothers fighting Hasege's men, no one was watching me. No one except Guiya.

Hastily I yanked off the rope around my ankles, freeing

myself from the stake. The flames parted for me as I fell forward and stumbled away from the pyre.

Hurry, Shiori! Kiki cried. *Guiya, she's—*

Kiki didn't have to finish her sentence. It was impossible to miss Guiya's looming figure. Her eyes fixated on the light flashing in my chest, she pried open my satchel and reached inside.

No! I was two, three steps at most from the snow. I leapt—

The net flew from Guiya's hands and swallowed me quickly, its magic clinging to the prize it sought. Out of my chest tumbled the fragment of Seryu's pearl, falling neatly into Guiya's waiting hands.

Once again, the demonfire roared high, the force of its heat throwing me back, deep into the pyre. The smoke formed into claws, pinning me down when I tried to charge through the flames.

A smirk tugged at Guiya's lips, and her eyes glittered with triumph. "So long, Your Highness," she said, trying to peel the net off of me, but I wouldn't let it go.

She laughed and threw her hood over her head. "I'll get it once I return for your ashes, then. Don't fear. You are not the first that we have burned in the name of the mountains. It won't hurt—that is the priestesses' gift to you."

Before any of the men realized she was working sorcery, Guiya mounted the closest horse and rode toward the edge of the forest. There, behind the headless trees Hasege and his soldiers had chopped to fuel the pyre, she watched me burn.

Tears scalded my cheeks, and I could smell my hair beginning to singe, an awful acrid smell. The sole reason I wasn't in ashes already was because of the starstroke net, my only shield, but it would be moments before the demonfire worked its way through the holes in the net and seared my skin.

My brothers, who had been distracting the sentinels until now, swooped in to help me. Arrows hurtled through the sky, nicking their wings as they circled over me. Feathers exploded and hailed down on my pyre, but my brothers didn't retreat. They dove to pluck me out of the fire, Andahai and Benkai lifting me while Hasho beat out the flames in my robes with his wings.

From the fire emerged claws of smoke, coiling around Andahai's and Benkai's necks. Squawking with alarm, they dropped me—and I fell back against the stake. As they scrambled to pick me up again, my other brothers flung snow into the fire, attempting to put it out. The flames only grew taller.

Tell them to get out of here! I yelled to Kiki. *Go! This is demonfire. They cannot help me.*

Meanwhile, the sentinels had advanced, drawing their swords and swinging at my brothers. Benkai and Andahai gave up, their anguished cries deafening in my ears. But Hasho stayed, his feathers broken and wings scraped by arrows. He was so close I could see there were tears in his eyes.

Go, I pleaded, turning away to hide my own tears.

At my feet, the paper birds were burning, their basket already in ashes. The charm Megari had tied to the basket was nearly gone too, along with its words of strength and protection. As I lurched to save it, the last birds withered in the bright red flames, and with them my last hopes.

You should go, too, I thought to Kiki. *Go. While you still can.*

When you die, I die, my bird replied. *If you're not afraid, I won't be either. I'll stay with you to the end, Shiori.*

I hugged her, tucking her under my bowl. I didn't need a thousand birds, not when I had Kiki.

The wood sizzled, my balance wobbling as the fire grew in strength and size. Smoke filled my lungs, the heat overwhelming me. I squeezed my eyes shut, willing myself to be calm.

I thought of stealing honeyed sweet potatoes from the Summer Festival, of brewing fish soup with floating radishes for Takkan, of grilling cakes with Mama. Maybe she'd be there in heaven to make them with me, and I could finally get the recipe straight and hear her sing again.

Kiki twitched. *Shiori,* she breathed. *Look. Look!*

I forced my eyes open, but the smoke was too thick. . . . I saw a flicker of blue, and a glint of steel. But that was all.

Then I heard him.

"Lina!" Takkan shouted. His blade flashed high, and I could see his figure, blurred through the flames, coming for me. A hundred steps from the stake, Hasege intercepted him. Their swords engaged, locked in a deadly duel.

At my side, Pao was shoveling snow into the fire. One by one, the other sentinels began to help, but the flames showed no sign of weakening.

I lifted my head skyward, trying not to cough from the smoke. The demonfire lashed at my back, seeping into my skin. Guiya hadn't lied; it didn't hurt. My skin didn't even char or blacken—instead the fire went straight for my blood. I could feel my heart flare. . . .

We built kites every summer, the seven of us, I murmured to myself. I wished I could build another kite—with my brothers, with Takkan. I wished I could read the letters he'd sent me.

"Lina!" Takkan shouted again. Fear for my life gave him a sudden strength, and he overpowered his cousin, striking him in the back of his neck. As Hasege collapsed, Takkan charged toward the fire.

Die, Shiori, the flames hissed in Guiya's voice. *Or he will too.*

The priestess skirted the edge of the forest, overlooking the fire. She had a bow raised, the arrow aimed straight at Takkan's heart.

Fire roared all around me, consuming my senses. "Takkan!" I screamed. "Watch out!"

The shock that rippled across his face was the last thing I saw before the bowl on my head shattered. And the fire swallowed me whole.

CHAPTER THIRTY-SIX

I woke covered in embers, my clothing scorched and blackened. The starstroke net glittered on my lap, illuminating plumes of smoke. The air was so thick and the world so dark that I wondered whether I was still on earth at all—until I started to pick out shapes in the ashes. There was the string of paper birds Megari had made for me, and what remained of her protection charm. I rolled over for the charm, then coughed, unable to prevent my lungs from gasping.

Praise the gods, Kiki cried with relief as she wove through the smoke and landed on my stomach. *It was so dark I thought we'd died!*

I sat up, my entire body trembling as I kicked off the starstroke net. The two broken halves of my walnut bowl lay beside me, and my fingers leapt to the top of my head. For the first time in months, I touched hair—thick and coarse sheets of hair—instead of the bowl.

My hands, still shaking, moved to my throat next. Demons take me, I had spoken! I sprang to my feet, fear leaping in my chest.

Your brothers are alive, said Kiki, reading my thoughts. *But they're still cranes. You must have broken only your part of the curse.*

She was right. I picked up a piece of the wooden bowl. I'd become so used to its weight on my head that I felt strangely light without it.

It wasn't meant to be a curse, I whispered silently as the bowl crumbled into dust in my hands. *It was a shield. One to hide my magic from the world, and . . . to protect me from it at the same time.*

Kiki landed on my arm. *Protect you from your own magic?*

I nodded. *My own and others'. The bowl broke to save me from Guiya's demonfire. Otherwise, I would be a pile of ashes by now.*

If it wasn't a curse, then all this time, you could have spoken? Your brothers wouldn't have died?

Of that, I wasn't sure. *She needed me afraid so I wouldn't go home to Father or tell anyone who I was. She needed me to hate her so she could hide me from the Wolf.*

I swallowed hard, finding my voice at last. "Where's Takkan?"

As soon as I asked, I saw him lying against the gray piles of brushwood. There was no arrow in his armor.

He was uninjured.

I removed his gauntlets and wrapped my fingers around

his. His hands were cold, and as I warmed them, I brushed his hair from his eyes and placed a soft kiss on his forehead.

"Takkan."

His eyes opened, and a relief that mirrored my own flooded his face. He pulled me close, draping his cloak over my tattered robes. His heart beat against my ear, wild and anxious.

"I thought I was too late," he said hoarsely. "I thought I'd lost you."

"I could say the same." I spoke haltingly, almost clumsily. My voice was rough from the smoke and from months without use, and my words sounded better in my mind than they did aloud. Funny how naturally I used to chatter on, my tongue moving faster than my thoughts. Now I was thinking hard, and I still sounded like a dolt.

I swallowed. "You almost got yourself killed, rushing into the fire like that."

"I would do it again without hesitation," Takkan replied. "To hear your voice. To finally see your eyes."

He traced my cheek with his fingers, the same way I had traced his at the Winter Festival, and I stopped caring about how clumsy I sounded. I was alive, my part of the curse broken.

As I held his hand, pressing his fingers against my cheek, Kiki peeked nosily out of my hair.

"Is that a paper bird?" Takkan asked, blinking.

I nodded. "Her name is Kiki. I made her . . . with magic."

Takkan didn't look surprised. "And these—" He picked up the string of paper cranes strewn among the ashes. Their wings had scorch marks, and some had been so badly burned that they'd lost their beaks. "Can they fly, too?"

"No. Kiki's special."

"Like you?"

I didn't get a chance to reply. The sentinels were drawing near, their heads lowered in apology. I couldn't tell whether it was for me or for Takkan, whom they had all but betrayed—except for Pao.

I held out the charm Megari had given me. The ink had melted, and the fabric was charred, but I passed it to Pao. "Tell Megari I'm sorry I couldn't say goodbye. I'll miss her."

He gave a solemn nod.

"Sorceress!" a voice spat from behind.

Hasege. He'd awoken and shoved aside the sentinels to charge at me. Takkan leapt to tackle him, but Hasege's dagger flew out, the blade hurtling for my heart.

"Lina, watch out!" Takkan yelled.

The cloak I wore flared to life, its fabric sweeping over me like a shield. It spun Hasege's dagger away, and the weapon fell into the snow with a thump.

"See, magic!" Hasege shouted. "What are you doing, tying me up! Have you lost your senses, Takkan? She's a sorceress—"

"And that is the only reason I am not executing you here and now, Hasege," said Takkan coldly. "Only because of Lina's magic did she survive your treachery. You are exiled from Iro. From this day forward, you are no longer a sentinel, and no longer of the Bushian clan."

He slammed Hasege's head into the snow, muffling his

protests. He and the other sentinels began tying up Hasege's limbs and readying to take him away.

Ignorant brute, Kiki murmured from my sleeve. *I'd pay good gold to see his face when you tell him who you really are.*

Shiori'anma, most beloved daughter of the emperor. Princess of Kiata. It had been so long since I felt like my old self that I had forgotten the rest of my titles.

I'm not telling anyone who I really am, I thought to her, dusting the ashes from my arms. I spied my satchel buried in the snow, and I knelt to pick it up.

What?

I'm not staying.

Takkan was with the sentinels, loading Hasege onto the wagon to be brought back to the castle dungeon. I could hear him shouting orders, occasionally stealing glances at me. He probably thought I was going back with him, too.

I wasn't. I needed a horse to catch up with Guiya. The closest one was Admiral, and as I began to mount him, Takkan arrived at my side.

I could tell he had a thousand questions for me, but instead he held Admiral's reins, keeping the horse steady.

I ignored his help, pulling on the straps of the saddle to hoist myself up onto the seat. Admiral grumbled, but he didn't resist. He no longer feared me.

"Don't forget these," Takkan said, handing me the cranes his sister had folded.

I thanked him wordlessly, slipping the paper birds into my satchel.

Once I was saddled and strapped, I parted my lips to bid

Takkan farewell, but he jumped onto Admiral's back behind me.

"What are you doing?" I protested.

"What does it look like? I'm coming with you."

"I don't—"

"You can't expect to steal my horse and take off without me." He kicked Admiral into motion. Takkan's voice hummed against my ear. "Besides, I have a story I think you may like."

A story?

Kiki landed on my shoulder. I half expected her to scoff and complain that Takkan would only slow us down. But she didn't.

"All right," I agreed, ignoring the flutter in my stomach as Takkan reached for the reins. "Tell me on the way."

We followed Kiki deep into the Zhensa Forest. Snow was drifting down from the pine trees. It was difficult to talk while the wind blustered, but I could feel the questions weighing on Takkan's mind.

By the afternoon Admiral needed a rest, so we settled by the south bend of the Baiyun, where the river grew wide.

Don't take too long, Kiki said, flittering around our heads. *I'll search the skies for your brothers. They should have caught up with Guiya by now.* She lingered to make one last quip: *This is a rest stop, not an opportunity to flirt with Takkan now that you can speak.*

Takkan led Admiral to the river, letting him drink to his heart's content. I needed a rest too, though I refused to admit it aloud. For someone who'd nearly been burned to death at the stake, I was doing surprisingly well. But when I caught a whiff of the smoke that clung to my clothes and hair, my shoulders shook.

"It'll get better," Takkan said softly, observing me. "It'll take time, but rest will help. Water will, too. You must be thirsty."

I *was* parched. I hadn't realized until he mentioned it.

I drank greedily, handful after handful. Nothing had ever tasted so wonderful in my entire life, and I soon had a stream running down my robe.

"Slow down," Takkan said, laughing as he shook his head. "The river flows all the way to Gindara. There's plenty more, even for a thirsty thief like you."

I wiped my mouth with my sleeve. "Don't you have questions for me? Like why I had a bowl on my head, and why I couldn't speak?"

"What is there to know?" he responded. "All that matters is that you're alive. I thought I'd lost you, Lina."

I melted to hear his voice so achingly tender. I hadn't thought I'd ever be capable of melting, not before this moment.

I blamed the shortness of my breath on drinking too quickly, but that didn't explain why my knees buckled or why Admiral snorted behind us, merrily slurping the river water. The snow was melting from the trees and dripping onto our shoulders. The world around us seemed to fade away; all I saw in this instant was Takkan.

I folded into Takkan's arms as he held me close. I couldn't deny that he meant something to me. When I'd been on the stake, mere breaths from dying, I had wished for a moment like this—him holding me, me listening to my heart skip as his pounded steadily against my ear.

But now I untangled myself and gently pushed him away. I could speak, which should have made it easier to lie, but I found I couldn't. Not to Takkan.

"You should go on to Gindara," I said, unable to look him in the eye. "I need to catch up with the cranes. And with . . . Zairena."

"Zairena?"

"She isn't who she says she is. She's a priestess of the Holy Mountains, one who used magic to take on the appearance of Lady Tesuwa's daughter."

"Then she'll be dangerous. All the more reason for me to come with you."

"I don't need your help."

"I'm not leaving you." His jaw tightened with resolve. "Don't you remember what I told you? I would not have you be alone."

It was what he'd said to me at the Winter Festival. *I would not have you be alone, Lina, not in your joys or your sorrows. I would wish your strand knotted to mine, always.*

"What about the emperor's war?" A hard lump formed in my throat, and I reached for another sip of water. "You've . . . you've been called to fight."

"I'm bound to you first. I always have been."

"Bound to me?" I repeated. "All I did was make some

403

crooked stitches over your wound, Takkan. You don't have to act like you're indebted to me for life."

"I am not the sort of man who reneges on my pledges."

"Then I release you from it."

"I don't think you have the authority." Takkan's mouth tilted, and his gaze pierced mine. "Not when it's been in place for eleven years."

The words were a thunderclap to my ears. "You . . . you know?"

"Don't you want to hear my story now?" he said. Only the slightest tremble in his voice betrayed his nerves. "It's about a princess with six brothers, one who never read her letters from the simple, unworthy boy who only wished to know her."

"Oh gods," I whispered, overcome. Emotions clotted in my throat—an unwieldy mix of rapture and embarrassment. I wanted both to hug him and hide from him at once. All I could do was bury my face in my hands. "I . . . I never called you that, did I?"

"You made your distaste for the North quite well known, Shiori," said Takkan good-naturedly. He paused meaningfully on my name. "I wasn't surprised that your disdain extended to me."

Shiori. I liked how he said my name. As if the syllables were the first notes to a song he loved to sing. A small smile touched my face. "How long have you known?"

"I wasn't sure until today—when I saw you," Takkan admitted. "But I thought it. I *wondered* it many a time. First, when I met you in Tianyi Village, the way your shoulders danced and your feet tapped when you were cooking—as if you were listening to a secret song. I remembered seeing Princess Shiori do that at the Summer Festival when she was eating something she loved.

"There were little things, too, like the way you hide food in your sleeves or how a dimple appears in your left cheek when you smile."

I blinked. "You noticed all that?"

"I wanted to notice more. But you never wrote me back, Shiori," he said, pretending to chide me. "Or else I might have discovered it was you on that first day in Sparrow Inn."

My cheeks burned. "I kept your letters. Every single one— they're buried under the trove of talismans I collected and wished upon that I wouldn't have to marry you."

It was true, and I was mortified I had just admitted it. "If only you had told me they were stories . . . I might have run to meet you. I was worried you'd be boring."

Takkan chuckled. "Now I hope you don't fall asleep reading them. There's still time to run away, after all."

I didn't laugh. I reached for his hands, placing my palms atop his, and finally uttered the words I'd wanted to say for months now: "I'm sorry I missed our ceremony."

"I'm sorry I was angry with you. I regretted it as soon as my father and I left, but I was too proud to come back." Takkan twined his fingers with mine and squeezed my hands gently. "I don't want to be released from my pledge, Shiori. But if you do, I would never keep you against your will. I would come with you to ask our fathers to set us free."

I believed him—I would believe anything Takkan told me.

"I'm happy he chose you," I said, swallowing. "It would be a lie to say I don't care for you."

"But?"

"But we can't pretend nothing's happened. Even if we defeat the Wolf, we can't just pick up where we left off five months ago. I'm a sorceress. My father can't simply pardon me because I'm his daughter."

"Why not? Perhaps it's time that magic returned to Kiata."

"You wouldn't say that if you knew." My voice filled with anguish. "My magic is dangerous."

"But you aren't," said Takkan.

I withdrew my hand from his and pressed it to the nearest tree. The elm's branches were gray with winter, and I buried the apprehension rising inside me, replacing it with memories of warmth and spring. "Bloom," I whispered, and the branches glowed silver and gold until leaves budded on their spindly arms, bright as beads of jade.

Takkan drew a stunned breath. "That doesn't look dangerous at all. That's amazing."

"No, it's not amazing," I said as I released the tree. Its branches went bare and gray again, and I gritted my teeth. How to show him?

I reached into my satchel, meaning to show him the starstroke net, but instead I felt the seven paper birds Megari had folded.

I whistled softly to the birds. "Awaken."

Paper wings rustled against the bag. Then up they flew, disappearing before I could call them back.

"I can lend bits of my soul away," I explained. "Kiki's the only one that's lasted. It's why my stepmother cursed my brothers and me. It's why the Wolf wants me—"

"Slow down, Shiori. Slow down. I'm not understanding."

Of course he wasn't. My emotions were out of control. It had been so long since I could speak, since I could use my magic, the rush of it coming back was too much all at once.

I let out a shaky breath. My tongue felt heavier than it ever had before, and the words came to me slowly:

"You know the stories, Takkan. About the demons trapped in the Holy Mountains? The gods sealed them inside, binding them with divine chains so they might never wreak their evil upon Kiata again." I chewed on my lip. "Well, it turns out that my magic can break those chains. That's why the Wolf wants me. He must have orchestrated everything, even Lord Yuji's betrayal. Even the Four Breaths in the letter you found . . . that was meant for me. All this time, the pain and trouble you, my father, everyone went through . . . was because of me."

Takkan hadn't moved. His expression hadn't changed at all. His brow was clear, his lips an inscrutable line, his eyes ever steady. Then he spoke: "For the last five months, I thought you were dead. There wasn't a day that I didn't pray for you, that I didn't kick myself for leaving Gindara without seeing your face. If you think that there is anything you could say to dissuade me from coming with you, then you are sorely mistaken."

"But the demons—"

"Would have to rip me from your side," Takkan said firmly. "I'm afraid you are stuck with me, Shiori, even if you don't ever wish to marry me. I pledge to protect you."

I stared at Takkan, unsure whether I wanted to kiss him or knock some sense into him. Yes, he'd seen into my thoughts. He must have gotten good at that, these past few months.

"Now, where do we go from here?"

"To my brothers," I whispered.

"The cranes. Six cranes."

I nodded.

"Then let's go."

"Wait," I said. Even now, seeing him with his hat slightly askew and ready to fall off his windswept hair, I was imbued with an involuntary rush of warmth. "Are you going to kiss me or not?"

The surprise on Takkan's face was worth a thousand stories. "You know, you're even bolder when you can speak, Princess Shiori."

"I have many months to make up for."

Takkan laughed, but he touched his nose to mine, drawing so tantalizingly close that our breaths mingled in the cold air.

I closed my eyes.

But this was not our time.

A horse whinnied from behind the trees. Hasege's stallion shot out, its gray coat streaked with red. Guiya lay over the horse's neck, her snow-white robes spilling across the saddle. Her braid was undone, her hair matted with ashes from the Holy Mountains. She'd been attacked.

When she saw me, her eyes became white and wild. "Still alive, I see," she rasped. "You are ever the pest, Shiori'anma."

I was hardly listening. In Guiya's grasp, wings pinched together, was Kiki!

Run, Shiori! my bird shrieked, squirming and twisting. *Your brothers, they're—*

Guiya closed her fist, crushing Kiki. She tossed her into the snow and charged, sparks of magic dancing from her fingertips. The ashes in her hair spun into a powerful current, taking the shape of a sword. Pointed at my heart.

"For the mountains!" she yelled.

Takkan reached for his bow, and I for the dagger in Admiral's saddlebag.

But before any of us could land a blow, arrows wailed from unseen assailants. Takkan and I pulled each other behind trees for cover, but we weren't the targets.

The arrows struck Guiya in the back, one mercilessly impaling her neck. Dark blood oozed from her lips. With a strangled cry, she slipped off her horse and sank into the snow. Dead.

I ran to Kiki, scooping her up and smoothing out the folds of her crinkled body. She burst up, fluttering her crumpled wings. *Run!* she shrieked. *They're here!*

Jumping out of the trees, Lord Yuji's soldiers descended upon us with menacing cries. In their clutches were six cages—my brothers!

CHAPTER THIRTY-SEVEN

My brothers' beaks were tied shut, their wings jostled against the bamboo bars. Their eyes were mournful, more human than I'd ever seen them as cranes. It pained me to look.

A dozen swords were pointed at Takkan and me. There had to be over a hundred soldiers. Each wore a wolf's mask, and armor painted shell white, blending in with the snow that wreathed the moss-covered trees.

"You're a difficult one to find, Princess Shiori," Lord Yuji said, sweeping a bow. "Iro was quite possibly the last place I expected you to be. Fate does have a way of making things interesting, doesn't it?"

"Release them," I said quietly. The sun was sinking, and shadows touched my brothers' wings.

"His Majesty was most concerned when the imperial children disappeared," Lord Yuji went on, as if he hadn't heard me. He wore an easy smile—one I had come to hate. "When I return to Gindara, I must inform him that they've been found."

Anger stirred in my chest, magic heating my blood. The rocks and pebbles at my feet lifted off the ground, swirling around the hem of my skirts.

Yuji pretended not to notice. "I have little interest in harming your father, if you must know, Princess. As we speak, my army lays siege to Gindara. I have confidence he will surrender the palace to me—in exchange for the lives of your six brothers." He acknowledged Takkan with a lift of his chin. "Young Bushian is surely an unexpected bonus. His father will pay handsomely for the life of his only son."

I'd waited long enough. Kiki dove to stab Yuji's eyes, and I launched a barrage of stones at his army while Takkan fired arrows at the treacherous lord. I might as well have thrown flowers at the soldiers. An invisible shield protected Yuji and his men. Every arrow, every stone bounced off. Kiki flew back into my hair, frightened.

"I heard you were a sorceress," said Yuji with a low chuckle. "Is this the best you can do?"

Takkan lowered his bow and closed the distance between us, his shoulder touching mine. "Look, Shiori," he said under his breath. "Around his neck."

I narrowed my eyes at the amulet hanging at Yuji's chest. It was bronze, far more plain and dull than the wealthy warlord's usual adornment, but there was a wolf's head carved into the surface. The amulet seemed to tremble against his fine robes, as if the magic it held was too great to keep inside.

"Show yourself, Wolf," I shouted.

Smoke curled from the amulet, at first just a tendril, and then many dark ribbons seeping out. It smelled bitter,

411

like overbrewed tea, and its thick, velvety haze clouded my vision.

"Shiori!" Takkan shouted, reaching into the smoke to pull me out.

We clung to each other, Kiki nestled in my hair. I could feel enchantment at work, enchantment far stronger than my own. I couldn't stop my satchel from lifting itself off my shoulders. I scrabbled for its strap, but it hurtled away, flying off to Lord Yuji's side.

There, the smoke gathered and started to condense, finally solidifying into the shape of the Wolf.

My brothers screeched, their wings flapping wildly. They had met him before.

"I believe this is mine," snarled the Wolf, my satchel firmly in his grasp. His fingertips aglow, he opened it, and the light poured forth. "Ah, a starstroke net. A piece of legend. It's just as impressive as I'd hoped."

For an enchanter, *he* did not look terribly impressive. A curtain of flat, ashen hair framed his narrow face, and his chin sported a long beard. His eyes blazed yellow—but not the luminous yellow my stepmother's took when she used her power. His were murky and liquid, like those of the wolf I had encountered that afternoon in Iro.

"It was you on the mountain," I whispered.

"I am honored that you recognize me, Princess." The Wolf closed the satchel. "Your stepmother did a fine job of hiding you from me—I didn't even know it was you in Iro. I trust you enjoyed those few extra months she bought you. They will cost her dearly."

"How?" I demanded. "You have no magic in Kiata."

"I didn't," he agreed. "But it seems that over the years, you Kiatans have forgotten that enchanters without magic take on their most vulnerable form. The form meant to remind them that great power comes at great cost. Do you care to guess what mine is?"

"A wolf," I said flatly. His presence was already growing tiresome.

He clapped. "Well done. A wolf I was, powerless, and almost as simpleminded as your dear brothers when they are cranes. Until I came upon this."

His large hands clasped the fragment of Seryu's pearl. "If only I had known you carried a piece of dragon pearl within you, Princess. I would have saved you the trouble of going to Mount Rayuna for me, and wasting all these months on the net."

I was seething with rage. It was bad enough that he had impersonated Master Tsring and given the satchel to my brothers—that all those months of hating Raikama and making the net had been part of some horrible trick to steal her pearl!

But to hear it from his complacent lips, as if he were *apologizing* to me.

The dagger at my hip shuddered, and I channeled my fury and hate into it until it flew from my side to the Wolf's heart.

The enchanter raised a hand, and the blade halted midflight.

"Careful, Shiori'anma." The Wolf chuckled. "Rage can be dangerous, coming from one such as you."

413

Slowly the dagger turned until it was pointed at Takkan.

In a blur of motion, Takkan swung it away and attacked the Wolf. He was so fast the enchanter wasn't expecting the strike, but before he could do any real damage, an invisible force lifted Takkan into the air. A shadow fell over him, and he became still as stone.

"Useless human." The Wolf scoffed. "He's brave, I'll give you that. Aren't you going to beg me to free him?"

My hands were balled into fists at my side—the only indication that I was furious. No, I was not going to beg. The Wolf wouldn't kill Takkan. Not yet.

He was an enchanter under oath to Yuji. And Yuji had expressly said he wanted Takkan alive. Even now, I could see the Wolf straining under his oath to the man. There was a gold cuff on his wrist, same as the one the wolf had worn.

"Enough with the theatrics," cut in Lord Yuji. "Hurry on with it and kill the girl. You say you need her blood; well, I've brought her to you."

"Indeed you have," said the Wolf, with a sweeping bow to Yuji. He released Takkan and reached for his sword. Its blade was already red—Guiya's blood, I supposed—and he shook it dry. He turned to me. "A pity, all good things must come to an end. But first things first."

"First things first," repeated Lord Yuji gleefully. "Any last words, Shiori'anma? It isn't like you to be quiet."

He was wrong. Months under my stepmother's curse had taught me to find strength in silence. Had taught me to listen, and observe. Anger bristled in me as I watched Takkan dangling midair, and hatred thickened my blood as my brothers struggled in their cages.

"Finish her off and take us to Gindara at once. Kiata's throne is waiting."

The Wolf bowed. "As you wish."

Then the enchanter raised his sword—and plunged it deep into Lord Yuji's abdomen.

"Thank you, *Master*," he said. "You have served your purpose."

Shock flew through the lord's eyes as his rich robes swelled with thick, dark blood. "You . . . you are bound to me!" he croaked. "Your oath . . ."

The Wolf smiled darkly at the warlord's horror. "I grow weary of this game, juggled from master to master." He yanked free the amulet hanging around Yuji's neck. "It is time to be my own master."

Then he pulled the blade out, and Lord Yuji crumpled to the ground.

With one shove, the Wolf threw his former master into the river. I watched, stunned, as the waters carried Yuji away.

The Wolf had just broken his oath. He had taken his last breath as an enchanter and would soon awaken as . . . a demon.

Why he would doom himself to such a fate, I had no time to understand.

The moon was rising, and shadows spilled across the forest. Already my brothers were beginning to transform. Their limbs grew sinewy and long, and their feathers smoothed into skin.

But this time, they were not the only ones changing.

Whorls of black smoke spun from the Wolf's amulet, swathing the golden cuff on his wrist. Like a rip of thunder, the cuff shattered. Then the true change began.

The Wolf's flesh began to splinter. As he cried out, his voice changed from man to beast—a scream to a warbling snarl. His human frame convulsed, shoulders stretching out and nails growing long, piercing through the smoke at odd intervals. Skin ripening with fur, bones and muscles resetting themselves into the form of a beast.

"Something isn't right," Takkan murmured. "If he's turning into a demon, the Holy Mountains should be claiming him. He shouldn't still be here."

I agreed silently, but it wasn't the Wolf's transformation that transfixed me. It was Seryu's pearl.

Shadows eclipsed the fragment, smothering its light. And it too was beginning to change; it was merging into the Wolf's amulet, possessed by its great and terrible power. It had to be the reason the Wolf could resist his summons to the Holy Mountains.

I needed to take it from him.

Around us, Lord Yuji's terrified soldiers ran for the trees. Takkan took his bow and shot into the billowing storm. His arrow pierced the Wolf's flesh, only to dissolve into dust.

"It's no use," I yelled, hooking him by the arm as he called for Admiral. While the horse galloped our way, I rushed to my brothers, picking up my fallen dagger to hack open their cages.

Hurry, hurry! Kiki cried. *We need to get out of here.*

416

My brothers were still changing. Sharp cries of agony racked their throats, their wings melting into arms and their feathers into cloth and skin. As their eyes sharpened with consciousness, Takkan and I pushed weapons into their hands. The darkness around the Wolf was growing, spiraling into the woods, killing everything it touched. Soldiers collapsed, their bodies turning to dust as the smoke spilled over them.

"Run!" I shouted. All six of my brothers, newly human, lurched at the sound of my cry. "Get out of here!"

I pushed Takkan to follow them, but he wouldn't leave. Not without me.

"How can I help?"

Only Takkan would ask that so calmly when we were a stone's throw away from a demon. "Follow my brothers! You'll die if you stay."

"What about you?"

"I need that pearl. It's fusing with his amulet—"

I didn't get to finish my sentence. Takkan spun for the Wolf, charging blindly.

Demons of Tambu! Kiki cursed. *The boy's even more reckless than you are.*

I was already racing after him, my alarm surging with every step.

"Takkan!"

He aimed his last arrow at the Wolf—at the white light flashing in his tenuous grasp—then released it.

The arrow disappeared into the smoke. The entire forest seemed to go still, a dark pall settling over the trees as the Wolf completed his transformation. The moment stretched on for an eternity before a shard of light rolled out of the shadows—Seryu's pearl.

Takkan stooped to pick it up just before the Wolf lunged toward him.

"Awaken!" I screamed, summoning the trees to shield us both. Branches stretched and wove into walls, blocking the Wolf's grasping claws.

The shield wouldn't last forever.

Hastily I grabbed Takkan by the hand, pulling him up. Together, we leapt onto Admiral's back and raced to join my brothers. "What were you thinking? You could have been killed."

"The odds of death were high," he replied, catching his breath. "But not assured."

I wanted to hug him. "You courageous fool."

"If that's what you call me now, rather than 'that barbarian lord of the third rank' "—he passed me Seryu's pearl with a grin—"then it was well worth it."

Along the edge of the forest, my brothers had rounded up extra horses for themselves and were shouting at us to hurry. Behind us the branched walls were beginning to crumble. Black smoke spilled over the Wolf, rising into the sky toward the mountains.

I let out a sigh of relief. Without Seryu's pearl, the Wolf could not resist his call to the Holy Mountains for long. We were safe.

Then invisible claws wrapped around my neck.

"Shiori!" Takkan shouted. He grabbed my hand as our horse reared and the Wolf started to drag me away.

Let go, purred the Wolf against my ear. *Let go, unless you want him to die. Unless you want all of them to die.*

Pain pricked my eyes. I saw my brothers charging toward the Wolf. "Don't fight!" I shouted as the darkness surrounding the demon swelled. "He will kill you."

"I won't let you go," Takkan said through his teeth. "Come on, Shiori."

"You have to." I drew as close to Takkan as I could, our lips so close I could feel his breath.

Our foreheads touched, and I pushed Seryu's pearl into Takkan's hand. It would protect him and my brothers. Kiata too, if I couldn't defeat the Wolf.

Then I let go.

Away from Takkan I flew, the Wolf's laughter booming in my ears, so deep even the trees shuddered.

Before I could blink, we shot up into the sky, leaving the forest far behind.

There was no turning back now: we were joining the demons inside the Holy Mountains.

CHAPTER THIRTY-EIGHT

Night fell. The sky turned to ink, blotting out the sun, and darkness cloaked the world below, too. I could not tell whether we flew over sea or forest or mountain.

It mattered little. I knew where we were going.

The gods had decreed that all demons were prisoners of the Holy Mountains, and now that the Wolf had transformed, he could not resist their pull.

Nor could I resist his.

We were flying so fast that I could hardly blink or breathe, but every chance I got, I wrestled the Wolf, grappling to free myself of his hold. Kiki speared his eyes with her beak while I attacked him with my dagger, but it was a losing battle. He was smoke; he had no flesh to wound, no bones to break.

There was only his amulet. No longer was it bronze, but black as obsidian, the face of a wolf still scored into its surface. Every time I tried to reach for the amulet, the smoke shifted to conceal it, until I was practically drowning in my own despair.

Finally Gindara glittered beneath me. I'd forgotten how close my home was to the Holy Mountains. Against the cloak of night, the city was alight with lanterns and torches. I could see the Sacred Lake, its waters reflecting the glow of the pale moon. Too quickly, we passed the palace and flew into the foothills, drawing ever nearer to the mountains.

A light shone from the valley and trees below. Like us, it was moving, winding through its woods like a snake.

"Your stepmother," rasped the Wolf. His claws curled over the satchel of starstroke, and he clutched it gleefully. "Her pearl is quite exceptional. I'll look forward to relieving her of it, once I'm done with you."

"You should have thought about that earlier," I shouted. "You killed your master, remember? You're a demon."

"You think I would break my oath so carelessly?" the Wolf jeered, clearly reveling in what he knew and I did not. "Only a bloodsake can breach the seal upon the Holy Mountains, which means that only you can free the thousands trapped within." He paused to let the words sink in as horror gathered on my face. "Yes, that's right. I've been waiting all this time for the birth of a new bloodsake. You, Shiori. Once your blood spills across the Holy Mountains, the demons will unleash their fury upon Kiata at last. With your stepmother's pearl in my grasp, I will be their king."

"No," I whispered. With all my strength, I launched myself at the Wolf and stabbed my dagger into his amulet, driving the blade deep.

For a moment, his red eyes widened. His claws curled around the amulet, and his hold on me faltered.

Then my dagger sizzled, melting clean away, and Takkan's knotted blue emblem flailed against the wind. I tried to catch its cords, but my fingers grasped only smoke.

The Wolf laughed and laughed.

Fear iced my heart. I had nothing left. No weapon, no dragon pearl, not even the starstroke net.

Nothing but the clothes on my back.

"Bloom!" I shouted. My sleeves came alive like extra arms, one flaring to cover the Wolf's eyes, another whipping the satchel out of his grasp.

As the net plummeted into the darkness below, I let out a small sigh of triumph. If I couldn't save myself, then at least I would keep Raikama's pearl safe from the Wolf.

I held in a scream as he dipped toward the mountains, making for the largest one in the center. We were hurtling so fast at its snowcapped peak that I barely caught sight of the seven paper birds flying up to Kiki and me. The same ones that Megari had folded and I had brought to life.

They carried a red thread, which they tied in a knot around my wrist.

Raikama summoned them to help us, Kiki translated for the birds. She cried, *Miracles of Ashmiyu'en! She's going to save us. She's—*

Kiki was wrong. No one could save me.

Smoke stung my nostrils, and I was thrown sideways. The Wolf flung aside the birds, his eyes bright and red. They burned into me as darkness consumed my world.

By my next breath, I was inside the Holy Mountains.

I landed with a thump against what felt like a bed of flowers. No, that couldn't be.

But flowers they were. Lotuses and moon orchids, peonies and even the young buds of chrysanthemums.

Pushing myself to my feet, I blinked, certain this was an illusion. Larks chirped, and cicadas were trilling their summer symphony. I walked as if I were underwater, my movements so heavy I had to drag one foot in front of the other.

It didn't take many steps before I recognized where I was.

Your stepmother's garden, Kiki breathed, coming out of my sleeve.

I scooped her to my shoulder. "You're here too? You should have stayed outside."

I've already told you. Where you go, I go. If you die, I die. It's in my best interest to help keep you alive. Now wits, Shiori.

Wits, I repeated, spinning to take in my surroundings. Yes, this was Raikama's garden, but the trees looked taller than they should be. And me . . . I looked down at my small feet in sandals I had long since thrown away.

I was a little girl of seven again, with silk orchids pinned into my braids and jade and coral necklaces dangling over my collars.

No, not an illusion. This was a memory.

The snakes arrived. There were hundreds, and they came from every direction. Slinking down from the wisteria trees, draping along the thick branches, and swimming through the pond.

Some had horns, and others had claws. Every single one of them had blood-red eyes.

These were not snakes. They were demons.

"We've been waiting a long time, Shiori," they whispered. "A taste is all we'll need. Just a taste."

I froze, as if petrified by their voices. The Wolf was the first demon I had seen in real life, but my brothers once delighted in terrifying me with tales of demons. The most powerful ones could steal your soul with a touch, and even the weakest demon could make you forget your name with as little as a glance.

Not to mention, they were monsters. Bloodthirsty, power-hungry monsters.

And I was the first human they'd seen in centuries.

The red thread tied to my wrist yanked me away from the pond, a sharp reminder to return to my senses. I leapt, gathering my magic to defend myself. The fabric of my sleeves flared like wings, lifting me high above the demons, and I sailed over the grass until I landed by the gate. It was open, and I made as if to run through.

But it was no gate. I slammed into a wall of rock.

The illusion holding together Raikama's garden stuttered, revealing granite walls and an empty cavern.

There was no way out.

Fear gripped me as demons snapped at my ankles, hissing and baring their fangs.

"You won't find an escape," they growled as the illusion of Raikama's garden flickered back into focus.

For an instant, I caught a glimpse of their true forms. Skin as red as cinnabar or as gray as death. I saw the extra eyes and heads, the horns and tails and jagged sets of claws. They were nightmares come alive, enough to make gooseflesh rise on my skin.

Except for the chains.

I hadn't understood why the demons came to me in disguise—pretending to be my stepmother's snakes or even imperial guards by the gate. Not until I saw that they were trapped in place. Bound to the walls of the mountains, chained by decree of the gods.

That's why the demons are luring you to them. They can't come to you! Kiki realized at the same time.

That was *their* problem, I thought. Mine was that I had no way out.

In this scenario, the demons would win. Easily.

I pounded my fists against the wall. "Stepmother!" I shouted. "Help me. Please."

Follow the thread, Shiori. It'll take you down to the base of the mountain. Above, the seven paper birds Raikama had sent fluttered. In their beaks was a long red thread, the same as the one they'd knotted to my wrist.

Hurry, said the voice. *The demons will try to trap you in your memories, but you must not get lost. Follow the thread. I'm waiting for you at the end.*

I touched the red knot on my wrist, drawing strength from

Raikama's words. The thread was leading me to the pond, where demon-eyed carp leered greedily.

"Here we go, Kiki."

I jumped.

Instead of landing with a splash, I fell through a ceiling and landed hard on a wooden floor. The planks were cold as ice, another illusion.

I was inside the palace, but not the palace I grew up in. Rooms appeared where they shouldn't have, and I wandered through a labyrinth of halls with endless turns and twists. If not for my thread, I would have been lost forever.

Demons lurked, haunting me with old memories. Smells of my mother's fish soup, or my favorite dishes from the kitchen, forgotten years ago. Careless plucks of zither songs I'd once been forced to learn, tutors and maids who had long since come and gone.

Some took on the shape of guards, ministers, even my brothers. "Princess!" they cried. "It's time for lunch. Won't you come!"

"Shiori, join us for a game of chess. Won't you, Sister?"

They must think you're an idiot to fall for those tricks, Kiki mumbled as I ran on. I agreed and ignored them all, focusing only on the red thread. I followed it, fleeing out of windows, jumping into mirrors, even bursting through wooden folding screens. Every room felt like a new level in an endless tower, and I had to reach the one at the very bottom.

Finally I was at the base of the mountain. I could tell because the string grew suddenly taut.

"Stop yawning!"

I whirled at the sound of Hasho's voice.

My youngest brother was dressed in his ceremonial robes. His hat was too big for him, presumably to hide his demon eyes. "You're late, Shiori," he chided. "What's that you have in your sleeve?"

I touched my sleeve. I was wearing my ceremonial robes as well, the same thick jacket I'd worn for my betrothal ceremony. Pink satin slippers and heavy silk robes embroidered with cranes and shimmering chrysanthemums. A gold sash was tied around my waist.

This memory was recent, so the details were crisper. I heard the low moan of the whispery wood under my sandals, the whistle of plum and cherry trees swaying in the summer wind, my sudden yearning to jump into the lake to escape the heat. It was so real I couldn't stop my heart from aching.

I started after my thread, refusing to fall for the demons' ploy.

Then Hasho spoke again. "Come, Sister," he said, gently this time. "You're already late."

His face was full, not gaunt and drawn as it was now after months spent as a crane. His dark eyes danced with life, and a dimple touched his left cheek as he laughed at me.

"Is it your betrothed you're worried about?" he said. "I saw him. He doesn't have any warts or boils. He's handsome, like Benkai. He smiles often too, though not as much as Yotan. You'll like him."

My brother started to nudge me toward the two grand doors ahead, but I darted away before he could get close. No matter how much he looked like Hasho, I knew he was not.

"Don't touch me."

His eyes lit like demonfire, and Kiki shrieked as demon-Hasho tried to capture me. I evaded him neatly and spun, following the thread toward the audience chamber.

I stopped at the entrance. The doors were closed, unlike all the others I had encountered in the mountain.

Through the space between them, I saw the thread carry on, streaming toward a light beyond the mountain's walls. I knew at once that this radiance came from Raikama's pearl.

She's there! Kiki exclaimed. *We're so close.*

I slid the doors open, half expecting a thousand more demons to rise from the shadows.

But there was only one.

The Wolf.

He sat on what appeared to be my father's grandest throne, polished with vermilion lacquer and canopied by a wooden screen of gilded cranes. Unlike the other demons, the Wolf did not hide his true form. He'd become taller, more muscular and lean. He bore the head of a wolf, with pointed ears and fangs that curved out of his jaw, and gray fur swept over his neck and limbs, but he carried himself like a man.

He was draped in an elaborate ensemble of silken robes, his jacket a horrific tapestry of dying gods and bleeding dragons and enchanters destroyed by the blood of stars. A golden headdress sat atop his head, more magnificent than any of my father's. It would have looked ridiculous, with the strings of pearls and clouds of diamonds—if not for the three ivory cranes hanging from each side of his crown.

Six in total. All bloodied.

I gritted my teeth, taking in the red thread that stretched across his lap. Its end trailed into a jagged fissure in the mountain—Raikama had to be just outside.

A smile spread over the Wolf's face as he saw the color drain from mine. He opened his claws, the thread running down his palm like a thin stream of blood. "A demon such as I can steal your soul with a touch, did you know? I'd mark you as mine, perhaps even doom you to life as a demon. But you are lucky, Shiori'anma. Your blood is too valuable for such a fate."

He ran the thread along the edge of one razor-sharp nail. "Instead, let us play a game, bloodsake," he murmured. "You get the thread before I kill you."

I was already running.

His claw came slashing down at my throat, but everything happened so quickly I didn't even have time to flinch.

I landed on my stomach, my fingers catching the thread. Paper scraps drifted, wings and beaks. Megari's birds! They had taken the impact of the Wolf's blow.

I didn't wait. I leapt for the fissure in the mountainside. Icy air rushed in, stinging my face. And light! Blinding, effervescent light.

"Kiki!" I cried suddenly, looking for my bird.

I'm here, I'm here. She was clinging to my sash.

Thank the great gods. I was worried that the Wolf had gotten her.

Cold hands grasped mine, pulling. Through the mountain's cracks, I could see my stepmother. Snakes surrounded her, hissing as she wrenched me from the mountain. Light poured from the pearl inside her heart, and I started to scramble out, my elbows digging into soft earth, then my knees.

I was nearly free when the Wolf seized my ankle. His touch sent a numbing chill rushing through me, and his voice was suddenly in my head. *A demon's touch has great power,* he purred. *I could take your soul, Shiori'anma, but lucky for you, your blood is more precious.*

His nail bit into my heel, rooting itself in deep, and a scream reeled out of my lungs.

Back into the mountain I sped, against my will, the metallic tang of my blood scenting the dank air.

"Shiori!" Raikama shouted. She caught me by the arms, the slender thread connecting our wrists flickering under the moonlight.

Behind me, the demons clamored for my blood. Soon our positions would be exchanged. I would be trapped forever in the mountain, and they would be free.

My mouth chalky with dirt and debris, I scraped toward Raikama, straining against the Wolf's pull. So help me, I was not going back into that mountain.

These last few months, I had never given up on my brothers. I couldn't give up now on myself.

I summoned every ember of strength I had. I'd always had a strong will, but a strong heart? I thought of the pain I had endured to work the nettles—the fiery thorns and sharp-edged leaves—the despair of those long months I'd toiled alone in Mrs. Dainan's inn, the agony of knowing that a simple sound from my lips would be all it took to kill my brothers.

All of it, I had overcome.

"And this too, I will overcome," I whispered into the mountain.

The walls trembled, rubble spilling from unseen heights. The stones were small at first, mere pebbles skipping down into the hollow.

Then they grew. Skips turned to thuds, and hulking shadows eclipsed the dappled light shining from Raikama's heart outside the mountain. Boulders dropped. They were relentless, falling at the speed of my racing pulse. Soon the demons were no longer moaning; they were shrieking.

Amid the uproar, I peered back at the Wolf. His eyes glinted, bright as the blood slicking my ankle.

"Let's play a game," I shouted, echoing his earlier words. "You let go before I kill you."

Even as I spoke, a hail of rocks crashed down, the sound echoing from the walls. They tumbled, brutally pounding against the Wolf. That hurt him, I could tell, so I ordered more to fall. Dust frosted the Wolf's fur, and the look he gave me was so scathing, so twisted with fury, that I thought the battle was won. Then the corners of his mouth lifted, and a wide smile spread across his face.

"So be it," he said, lifting his claw from my flesh. My blood soaked his nail, the same red as his eyes.

With a fierce cry, he turned into smoke and disappeared into the mountain.

I didn't even have a chance to breathe. Raikama pulled me through the fissure and out of the mountain, where I lay gasping in the cold air.

Her pearl shone inside her chest, a luminous beacon of

pure magic. She looked more fragile than I'd ever seen her before, her golden eyes tired, her shoulders shrunken, the scar on her face gleaming in the light of her pearl.

"We have to seal the mountain. Lend me your power, Shiori. I fear I don't have enough."

I took her hand, grasping it tight. Light from the pearl flashed, overwhelming us. My eyes watered, and I shut them, focusing on the mountain. Smoke billowed through the rip Raikama had created, and my stepmother pressed her back against the rock to keep the demons within.

In one final flare, a burst of light rippled across the face of the mountain itself. And then silence. I couldn't hear the demons crying anymore. No smoke rippled forth.

When it was over, Raikama sagged to the ground.

I dropped with her, and her snakes parted to make room for me. They were slithering over a satchel covered in snow. The same one I had dropped—the starstroke net.

"Stepmother?" I whispered.

I was still holding her hand. The last time I held it, I had been a little girl, and my tiny fist could barely wrap around two of her fingers. Now my hand was larger than hers, my scarred fingers longer than her smooth ones. But her skin was cold, as it always had been. When I was little, I loved trying to warm her fingers with my own. I had marveled that I couldn't.

"Thank you," I whispered, crawling to be closer to her. "You . . . you came for me."

She touched my ankle where the Wolf had clawed me, and

the wound closed slowly, leaving but a crooked pink scar. "Do you remember what you said when we first met?" she asked.

"No."

"I had taken my first steps onto Kiata's soil. I had been many weeks on the boat, and I was tired. I was nervous, too. But I wanted to make a good impression. Especially for you, Shiori. Your father had told me so much about you. He'd said your mother had died a year before, and you were inconsolable."

The memory, distant as a dream, came rushing back. I hadn't been able to stop staring at her—not for her beauty, but because her smile had seemed so tentative, so nervous when she met my brothers and me—and when it came time for me to greet her, I did something that horrified Father's ministers. I embraced her.

For a moment, she had glowed—just like Imurinya.

"Are you from the moon?" I whispered, remembering now. That was what I'd asked her.

"No. I come from no home," Raikama had replied, in stilted Kiatan.

"I didn't know your legends then," Raikama now explained, "so I didn't know what to say."

For years, I was certain she was from the moon. Then I forgot.

Now I knew it was her dragon pearl that made her glow. Now I knew why she never liked the legend of Imurinya. It reminded her too much of herself.

"Do you have a home now?"

"Yes," she said. "Home is where I don't need my light to feel warm. It's with you, your brothers, and your father."

She drew a ragged breath, trying to come up onto her elbows. But something hurt her, and she would not tell me what.

"Take us home, Shiori," she whispered. "Take us home."

CHAPTER THIRTY-NINE

Even with the guidance of Raikama's thread, the journey home took all night. I was not strong enough to carry my stepmother on my own, and being a paper bird, Kiki was of little help. Using my magic to aid us only tired me, so I slung my stepmother's arms around my shoulders and followed her ball of thread through the woods, one heavy step at a time.

"Come back for me in the morning," Raikama rasped when I stopped to catch my breath. "I won't go anywhere."

It was a lighthearted joke like the ones she used to tell when I was little, but I couldn't laugh. No. I wouldn't leave her.

Kiki led the way, flittering about the thread as she waited impatiently for us to catch up. She kept her distance from Raikama, but she was always watching her. My stepmother noticed.

"That's quite a bird you have," she said. "It comforted me to know you had her as company when I sent you away."

"She's my best friend," I replied. "We've been through much together."

A long pause. "I'm sorry I killed her once. I'm sorry for many things, Shiori."

"I know."

My stepmother was silent the rest of the walk, her eyes closed, her chest so still that I couldn't tell if she was breathing. Her beautiful face was like porcelain, leached of color. She did not bleed, but deep down I knew her life was ebbing away. The pearl in her heart shimmered fiercely, as if trying to put her back together again.

Maybe she's hibernating, Kiki said, noticing the worried crease in my brow. *Snakes do that during the winter, you know.*

"I hope so, Kiki" was all I could muster. "I hope so."

By the time the thread led us back to my stepmother's garden, it was nearly dawn. My brow was moist with sweat, my shoulders sore from bearing Raikama for hours. I set her gently underneath a tree and called for the guards.

No answer.

"Guards!"

Raikama touched my arm. "They're asleep, Shiori," she said feebly. "Your father, too."

I didn't understand. "I'll wake them."

"No," she said, not letting go. "They'll awaken when spring arrives. Lord Yuji's forces came to attack, so I put the whole city to sleep." She paused. "There are good men in Yuji's army. Loyal men, who had no choice but to follow their lord into battle. I would not have your country torn apart by needless bloodshed if I could stop it."

She squeezed my arm, the shadows under her eyes betraying what such a spell must have cost her. "The city will be frozen until spring. You and your brothers will be safe here."

"Let me help you."

"You already have," she replied. "By weaving the net."

I shook my head. I didn't understand. "The Wolf tricked me. I made it to break the curse—"

"And so you will break mine," said Raikama. "Take my pearl."

"But you'll die without it."

"Please. It's hurting me."

Still, I hesitated. The satchel suddenly felt heavy. I opened its flap, the light from the starstroke net immediately pouring out as I lifted it. But I could not bring myself to lay it over my stepmother.

Snakes slithered to Raikama's feet, rubbing against her affectionately. "Snakes have always been sensitive to magic," she said. "They're cousins of dragons, did you know?"

I nodded mutely.

"Do you remember the day you came into my garden to steal one of my snakes?"

Another nod. How could I forget?

"They sensed your magic even before I did. It was powerful—and dangerous; many would covet it. You were so curious about them, Shiori, and about me. At first I didn't mind, but as I grew to love you, you made me so happy that my light began to shine too brightly. I knew I couldn't keep my secrets from you forever."

I closed my eyes, remembering the rare occasions my stepmother would glow with that light so radiant and beautiful, I'd wonder anew if she was the lady of the moon herself. Sooner or later, I would have asked her if it was magic.

"That was why I closed my heart to you. I buried your memories and did all I could to keep you away from magic, even if that meant keeping you from me." Her breathing grew more uneven. "But then your powers surfaced anyway, and you met that dragon. I knew it'd only be a matter of time before someone else found out about your magic."

"You could have told me. You could have told Father."

"I wanted to," she admitted. "So many times I came close, but I was afraid of revealing my own secrets. Of losing you and your father—my family. Then I lost them anyway."

Her voice fell soft, each word straining from her lips as if it pained her. Just seeing her eyes, glassy with tears she struggled to hold back, I was ready to forgive her for everything.

But not yet.

"Why curse my brothers?" I needed to know.

She swallowed visibly, leaning her head back against the tree.

"That was not entirely my doing," she confessed at last. "In Tambu, my affinity with serpents gave me some power, but that was more of a curse. Best forgotten." She lowered her eyes, and I wondered what dark past she had left behind. "Here, my magic comes from my pearl. It is unlike any other, as you might have noticed. Dark and broken—like my heart, once." She inhaled deeply. "It augments my power and obeys my commands, but not always in the way I wish."

She raised her gaze to meet mine. "I meant to protect you from the Wolf, Shiori. I meant to hide who you were and send you away, at least until I found a way to deal with him. But when you told your brothers I was a demon, I panicked. I tried to make them forget, but I couldn't. All I knew was that I needed to protect them as well as you. Turning them into cranes was how the pearl chose to obey my wishes."

My voice was small. "Would they really have died if I had spoken?"

"Yes. The pearl does not lie."

Her certainty made my throat close up. "But why?"

Raikama wrung her hands. "Monster I may seem, but I am human like you, and I have made my share of mistakes. One of those was turning to the pearl, especially when I was afraid. . . ." She sighed, finally answering, "The pearl takes fate and twists it to its own purpose. Turning your brothers into cranes, whisking you far to the North and forcing you to make a starstroke net, crossing your strands with the Dragon King—all this it has done because it wishes to return to its owner." Her jaw tightened. "That owner has never been me."

"Its power has been a burden to you." I finally understood.

Raikama gave the slightest nod. "Free me of it, Shiori. Please."

I warred against myself over whether or not to honor my stepmother's request. In the end, I knew I could not disobey her. Not now.

Slowly, I lowered the net, spreading it across her body as if it were a blanket. Goose bumps had risen over her bare arms; her sleeves were torn and frayed. Funny—I had woven the net to this size intending to incapacitate her, not to keep her warm. But how glad I was for it now.

The starstroke glittered, its braid of three magics shimmering intensely around the broken pearl in my stepmother's chest. Raikama's hands clenched at her sides, her nails digging into the dirt. She was holding in a scream, I could tell, and she let out a sharp gasp as the net grew brighter, overpowering the light from her pearl.

It rolled out of her heart like a drop of night and floated above my open hands.

The dark magic swirling inside the pearl mesmerized me, just as it had when I first saw it. It landed on my palm, then its light dimmed until it was nearly dark.

Without the pearl, my stepmother sank against the tree, a peaceful smile spreading across her face. Her hair went entirely white, and scales mottled her skin until she bore a serpent's face—her nose pushed in and raised high, and her pupils thin as slits. Yet she seemed more comfortable in this body than she ever had wearing her mask of beauty and radiance.

I set the pearl on top of my satchel, not wanting to leave my stepmother's side.

"Will you tell me about the girl you used to be? Vanna?"

"Vanna?" Raikama repeated.

"Isn't that your name, Stepmother? Your true name."

"It is not." She paused, her expression suddenly far away. "It was my sister's."

"Your sister's?"

"Yes, I had a sister, long ago. One I hated more than anyone—and loved more than anyone. Everyone called me a monster, except my Vanna. She was as kind as she was beautiful. Golden, everyone called her, like the light inside her heart."

"The pearl." I understood.

Raikama nodded. "She was born with a dragon pearl in her heart. It was more of a curse than a blessing, for it attracted demons as well as princes and kings. I tried to protect her from them, but . . ."

Her voice faded, but there was no need to finish the story.

"I'm sorry," I whispered.

"It should have been me," Raikama said quietly. "I was a monster, Shiori, inside and out. I did terrible things, hoping I'd find a way to break the curse on my face and look like everyone else. In the end, the person I loved most paid the price. When Vanna died, her pearl buried itself in my heart to keep it from breaking, and it fulfilled my dearest wish—in the cruelest way. It gave me a new face—my *sister's* face."

Raikama touched the rough scales on her skin. "I wanted to die," she said hoarsely. "Seeing Vanna's face on my own every time I looked in the mirror . . . it was more painful than seeing my true face." Her fingers lingered on her scar. "I didn't think I could bear it, not until I met your father. He'd lost his wife, whom he loved more than life itself, and he was kind to me. We understood each other's sorrows, so I came with him here, to become a part of his family."

"Stepmother . . ."

She reached for my hand. Our wrists were still connected by the red thread, but its brilliance was fast fading—a sight that made it suddenly hurt to breathe.

"My greatest regret is that I failed to protect Vanna," she said. "I would give anything to change that moment in time, but not even the strongest magic on earth can alter the past. You were my second chance, Shiori. When I learned that danger might come to you, I swore I would do whatever it took to protect you. The way I couldn't protect Vanna."

"You have," I said. "You've saved us all."

She didn't reply, but she straightened against the tree, gathering what remained of her strength. Her scales snagged the glint of the rising sun, glimmering like opals.

"It is nearly dawn," she said. "Time to end your brothers' curse."

"But I . . ." I couldn't finish my words. *I don't know your name.*

"You've always known it," said my stepmother, as if reading my thoughts. "What is that song you used to sing in the kitchen?"

My jaw parted, and I stared. "But . . . but those were memories with my mother."

"No." Her voice was gentle. "Those memories were with me."

She began to sing, in a low, rueful voice I hadn't heard in years:

Channari was a girl who lived by the sea,
who kept the fire with a spoon and pot.

Stir, stir, a soup for lovely skin.
Simmer, simmer, a stew for thick black hair.
But what did she make for a happy smile?
Cakes, cakes, with coconut and sugarcane.

I staggered back, unable to believe it. Stolen mornings in the kitchen laughing with my mother as she taught me to make fish soup. All of them were with Raikama?

"You missed her so much you wouldn't eat," said my step-mother softly. "You'd cry, quietly, and refuse to speak." She paused. "For months, it went on like this, and your father didn't know what to do. I was new in the palace, and I had just lost someone dear to me. Making you happy made me happy."

"You used your magic on me."

"For a short while," she admitted. "I wanted to give you memories of your mother. Memories that would make you smile, even when you came to despise me."

Even when you came to despise me. The sadness in her voice made it impossible for me to be angry with her. I squeezed her hand tighter. She was the only mother I had known.

"What does Channari mean?" I asked when I finally found my voice again.

"It means 'moon-faced girl,'" Raikama said, touching her ridged skin. "Poetic, isn't it? And fitting. Vanna *was* the sun to my moon." She stared at the fading stars. "I'll see her soon."

"No," I urged. "Don't go."

Dawn blossomed across the sky, and my stepmother

averted her eyes from the sun. She let go of my hand. "Your brothers will soon be turning into cranes. Let us spare them another change. Let us end what I began."

I nodded numbly in agreement. Then, taking Raikama's pearl in one hand, I whispered, "Channari."

The pearl began to spin on my palm, its light enveloping my entire being. On its dark, gleaming surface, I could see my brothers. They were running through the forest, searching for me, shouting, "Shiori, Shiori!"

It was Hasho who spotted the sunrise first. The rays of dawn stretched through the trees for my brothers' limbs, and they braced themselves for the change.

But the ribbons of sunlight took on the shape of snakes. They shone, wrapping around my brothers' arms, whispering in Raikama's voice: "Your sister has set you free. Go well, sons of my husband."

The vision of my brothers faded, and the pearl came to a halt, lying heavy and silent on my palm.

"And now it is my time," Raikama said, letting go of my hand.

"No. Stepmother, you—"

"The magic I worked upon the mountains will not hold forever," she interrupted. "You must go somewhere the demons cannot follow, at least for a little while. There, you will do something for me."

For one last time her voice turned imposing, a reminder that she was my stepmother. But no longer the Nameless Queen.

"Anything."

"Return the pearl to its owner. This you must do before it breaks completely. The Dragon King will know of whom I speak."

"But he wants it for himself."

"Yes, and the net will protect you from his wrath, but only for so long. Do not let him trick you, Shiori. The pearl will be dangerous in the hands of anyone other than its owner. As you have seen it, with me." Raikama swallowed. "Promise me that you will only give it to the dragon with the strength to make it whole once more."

"I promise."

"Good." Her voice became distant, filled with regret. "It is something I should have done long, long ago."

Then, ever so tenderly, she cupped my cheek with her hand. "Tell your brothers I'm sorry. For my deceptions, and for what I've put them through."

She tipped her head against the tree. "Tell your father that I care for him very much. In my life before him, I knew little love, and my greatest joy was that he gave me a family to cherish as my own. Tell him I'm sorry."

She stroked a tear that trickled down my cheek as I shook my head, begging her not to go on. "And I apologize to you, Shiori. For all the pain I have caused you, but most of all, for saying that you would never be a child of mine. You are my daughter, not of my blood, but of my heart."

I couldn't hold the tears back anymore. "Stepmother, please . . ."

Her hands, now resting on her chest, lifted slightly. She wasn't finished speaking.

"Learn from my mistakes," she said, so softly I had to lean close to hear, "and learn from my joys. Surround yourself with those who'll love you always, through your mistakes and your faults. Make a family that will find you more beautiful every day, even when your hair is white with age. Be the light that makes someone's lantern shine." A long breath, her chest falling. "Will you do this, my daughter?"

I could barely nod, let alone speak. "Yes."

"Good." She leaned back, her hair completely white against the snow-laced tree. "Sing with me."

I tried to, but my tears got in my way. My mouth tasted of salt, and my voice was so hoarse it hurt. But as she sang, I joined in when I could.

Channari was a girl who lived by the sea,
who kept the fire with a spoon and pot . . .

Toward the end, her fingers went limp. The glow in her eyes faded, and our song melted into the wind, unfinished.

I held her and I wept.

CHAPTER FORTY

My brothers and I gave Raikama a small private ceremony in her garden. There was no procession, no official rites where she would be honored among our ancestors and given offerings of money and food. Even if the palace had been awake, I didn't think she would have wanted a grand funeral. The only thing she would have wished was for Father to be there.

When it was over, Takkan returned Seryu's pearl to me. I fashioned a tiny net to hold it in place, knotted it onto a cord, and wore it around my neck. Without a word, I disappeared into my room.

The room didn't feel like my own anymore. Nothing had changed: not the order of my books on the shelf or the array of hairpins and earrings on top of my lacquered jewelry boxes, not even the arrangement of my silk pillows.

Only *I* had changed. Unfathomably.

The first thing I did was rummage for a long-forgotten treasure. It was a box covered in red brocade, hidden deep in the back of a drawer under piles of talismans and charms, a decade's worth of wishes.

Takkan's letters.

I read them over and over, laughing and crying at his stories, which filled my heart and made it ache at the same time. Many of them were about him as a boy, trying to discipline his spirited sister but often ending up joining in on her adventures. They made me miss Megari, and Iro, and, most of all, Takkan.

I read until my eyes were so bleary the words became blurs of ink. But I couldn't sleep, not until I placed Raikama's pearl on my pillow and the starstroke net on the table beside my bed. That, somehow, was enough to assure me that the last half a year hadn't been a dream I could simply wake from. That my scars, inside and out, were real. That I had promises that needed keeping.

Finally I slept, succumbing to a dreamless void that my brothers later told me lasted three entire days. Snakes surrounded my bedside, and I took them in. I was no longer afraid of them. After all, they only mourned their mother, same as I.

I didn't know what my brothers did while I slept, but when I woke, there was a mound of swords outside the palace walls, seized from every soldier in Lord Yuji's army. Takkan and my brothers had collected them, and now the weapons sat in the courtyard outside the apartments my brothers and I shared, huddled in a tight circle, as if they'd been friends for years.

I hadn't seen Takkan since the Wolf had taken me to the

Holy Mountains. Yet sometimes when I was half-awake, I thought I heard his voice, telling me stories. Reading his letters aloud.

He noticed me before my brothers did, and shot to his feet.

Seeing him made a spark of warmth bloom inside me, but I couldn't smile for him. He probably thought this was the beginning of our future . . . only I wasn't here to stay.

I held up Raikama's pearl. Seryu's too, which I wore around my neck. "I'm going to the Taijin Sea. To Ai'long, the realm of dragons."

Waves rolled across the beach, the water sparkling like freshly fallen snow. Over and over in a perpetual rhythm, the waves crested and fell, washed up the shore and then ebbed away—as they had done long before I was born, and would continue to do long after I was gone.

Coming from behind, Takkan and my brothers narrowed the space between us, but I wasn't ready to begin our goodbyes. I wasn't ready to leave, when I had just come home.

"I still have a few minutes left," I murmured to them as I watched the sun. It had only risen halfway above the horizon, casting a burnished glow upon the Taijin Sea. Under its light, the water seemed more like gold than snow, with traces of violet from the dying night and beads of scarlet from the aging dawn. The sight, unnaturally beautiful, made my satchel feel heavier. Raikama's pearl was inside, in its nest of starstroke.

"Are you sure you don't want to wait for Father?" Hasho asked.

"It'll be better if I don't."

It would be weeks before Father and the rest of Gindara woke. Besides, I didn't know how to tell Father the truth. That I was the bloodsake of Kiata. That I was a rip in the seams that the gods had sewn to keep magic out of our country forever.

"Father will be in enough anguish as it is," I added. I swallowed hard, imagining his reaction to Raikama's death. "I'll be back soon enough."

As soon as the words left my lips, I wished I could take them back. I hadn't even told Seryu that I wasn't giving the pearl to his grandfather. The Dragon King wouldn't be pleased, that was for certain. Well, with or without Seryu's help, I'd keep my promise to Raikama. I'd find the pearl's true owner.

Kiki hovered above me as I slipped off my shoes, leaving them on the shore. *Do you think I'll be able to swim as well as I fly?* she asked. *Maybe Seryu can give me fins.*

I didn't reply. The sand under my feet was moist and cold, and I shivered as the sea washed up against my ankles.

There was one last thing to do before I went in. Hasho brought me a box made of teak, a wood native to Tambu, wrapped in one of Raikama's brocade gowns. Each of us seven had placed a little piece of ourselves into the box— Andahai a jewel from one of his crowns, Benkai an arrow, Reiji a chess piece, Wandei his favorite book, Yotan a paintbrush, Hasho a feather, and me, seven paper birds.

Raikama wouldn't be alone when she returned to the Tambu Isles.

Carefully I wrapped the box with a strand of the red thread my stepmother had always used to find her way home.

"Reunite her with her sister," I whispered to the box before setting it on a gentle current. In silence, I watched it float away until it disappeared beyond my sight.

One after another, my brothers embraced me. Hasho held on the longest, and he whispered, "Don't stay away too long, Sister. We'll miss you."

Last came Takkan.

There was sand all over his robes, and his hair kept whipping at his cheeks, but I'd never thought him more dignified—or dear to me—than at this moment. He bowed, keeping a respectful distance.

"My brothers aren't going to put you in the dungeon for giving me a hug," I teased.

"I know," he said quietly. "I only worry that I won't want to let you go."

I threw myself into his arms then, burying my head under his chin.

He stroked my hair. "I want to come with you."

"You can't." I looked up, knowing from his tightly pursed lips that he wished for a different answer. "I wish you could. Don't worry, I'll be in good hands."

"If the legends I've heard about dragons are true, I have reason to doubt that." Takkan met my eyes, his own unwavering. "But I know you can take care of yourself, Shiori. Better than anyone. I'll wait for you."

I took his hands. I wasn't sure when I'd see him again. It was said that time passed differently in the underwater kingdom than it did in this world. It could very well be years before I saw him again. Would things be the same between us when I returned?

If I returned?

I pushed the thought from my mind and mustered a smile. "Keep my brothers out of trouble."

"I seem to recall you were the troublemaker, Shiori. Not them."

My smile became real, and I started to turn for the sea, but Takkan wasn't finished. "Take this with you." He passed me his sketchbook. It was the same one he'd carried at Sparrow Inn, the pages stained with charcoal and what smelled like soup.

"More letters?"

"Better," he promised. "So you don't forget me."

I touched my forehead to his and pressed my lips to his cheek, not caring if my brothers saw. "Our fates are linked," I said tenderly. "How could I forget you?"

The tides gathered in strength. A green tail gleamed out of the sea-foam, and Seryu emerged in his human form.

I whispered a goodbye to Takkan and broke from his side. As I stepped into the water, my feet sinking into the sand, Kiki rushed after me. She fluttered in front of my nose. *Don't tell me you're not taking me with you, either!* she cried, sounding betrayed.

"Of course I am," I replied. "Where I go, you go, remember?"

Slightly mollified, Kiki hopped onto my shoulder. *Well, say so next time.*

My brothers were greeting the dragon. They acknowledged each other with nods, and Takkan, too, bowed his head.

I half expected Seryu to introduce himself the way he always did, listing his titles and making it known to all that he was the grandson of the Dragon King. But he merely glanced at Takkan, his feathery eyebrows twisting together in an unfathomable knot.

"Is there really a kingdom under the sea?" Yotan asked, wriggling his toes in the sand as the waves rushed his way.

"The most beautiful kingdom in the world," said Seryu. "It makes Gindara look like a decrepit old village."

"Careful, dragon," warned Benkai. "You forget you're on land. And speaking to Kiata's princes."

"Oh, I'm well aware of both," replied Seryu tersely. He answered no more questions. "Are you ready, Shiori?"

I hiked up my skirts and strode into the water. "Yes."

Kiki wrapped her wings beneath my collar. *Promise me, Shiori. If I get too soggy, you won't bring me back as a fish.*

I chuckled, pinching her beak. "I promise."

Seryu extended his hand, claws uncurling. "Hold your breath. Salt water stings the nose, or so I'm told."

I took one last glance at Takkan and my brothers. My heart was with them, no matter where I went. No matter how different things would be when I returned.

I held my breath. It would be the last one I'd take for a long while.

Then, hand in hand with a dragon, I leapt into the Taijin Sea.

～つ

Deep in the Holy Mountains, the Wolf prowled in search of a way out. The others had already tried, but they were chained.

He was no longer.

The demons were bickering that everything was in vain, but the Wolf was not listening. For on his claw was a precious smear of the girl's blood.

He scraped it against the mountain, painting its white veins red.

The mountain began to sing, the tiniest of cracks forming, and shadows loosening from within. Demons gathered, thirsting for vengeance, hungry for ruin.

He would feed them. Soon.

As an enchanter, he had hundreds of names, maybe even a thousand. But he was an enchanter no longer. He was a demon now, and he needed only one name.

Bandur.

ACKNOWLEDGMENTS

My gratitude goes to Gina, my agent, who has guided me through launching five books, and whose wisdom about publishing, writing, and life never ceases to amaze me. To Katherine, my editor, for thinking there was something special about *Six Crimson Cranes,* and whose brilliance made Shiori's story shine brighter than I could have possibly envisioned. To Alex and Lili, my publicists, for their dedication and cheerfulness, and for always going that extra mile to get the word out about my work.

To Gianna, Melanie, Alison, and the wonderful team at Knopf Books for Young Readers, for your support for *Six Crimson Cranes* from day one. Thank you for helping me create this beautiful book, inside and out. To Tran, for yet another sumptuous, stunning cover, and for making Shiori and Kiki come alive. It's been an honor to work with you on three books, and I hope we're just at the start of our collaboration.

To Alix, for the epic and gorgeous lettering that brings so much character to the story.

To Virginia, for Kiata's breathtaking map. I'm in love with the dragon, the flying cranes, the rabbit on the moon. Thank you for visualizing the ever-expanding world of Lor'yan in a way that is sure to spark readers' imaginations.

To Leslie and Doug, the most insightful critique partners a girl could ask for, who have seen me through countless drafts and shelved manuscripts, and always give the advice I need to hear.

To Amaris, Diana, and Eva, for being my oldest, dearest friends and for reading my book in spite of your busy lives. I can always count on you to give me your honest and constructive opinions—they are worth more than gold.

To Lauren and Bess, for reading the earliest draft of *Six Crimson Cranes*' first chapters, and for giving me the encouragement to move forward.

To Anissa, for being a champion of Shiori's story from the beginning and for countless conversations about art and anime—I'm so grateful we met at BookCon all those years ago!

To my in-laws, for visiting from across the world and helping me babysit while I wrote and wrote, and for cooking the most amazing roast pork. I'm also still thinking about those glass noodles with garlic shrimp.

To my parents, who let me read to my heart's content when I was a kid. Thank you for filling my head and heart with stories, and for encouraging me to make them grow in my own way. And, Mom, thank you for teaching me to make soup and bake cakes.

To Victoria, for always giving me her opinion on the romance (always "more!"), and for inspiring the strong young women that I write about and look up to.

Adrian, who tirelessly reads and edits every one of my books, who cooks for the kids and doesn't complain when I get up in the middle of the night to scribble a new idea, and who laughs with me when I text him for opinions, even though we're one room apart. Love you always.

To my daughters—there are two of you now! You bring joy to my toughest days and remind me why stories are worth sharing. This book is for you.

Lastly, as always, to my readers. Thank you for continuing this journey with me and for reading this far. I hope Shiori's story has brought some light into your life and found a place in your heart.